Very Public Data

by

Matthew Eberz

authorHOUSE®

AuthorHouse™
1663 Liberty Drive, Suite 200
Bloomington, IN 47403
www.authorhouse.com
Phone: 1-800-839-8640

This book is a work of fiction. People, places, events, and situations
are the product of the author's imagination. Any resemblance to actual
persons, living or dead, or historical events, is purely coincidental.

First published by AuthorHouse 5/7/2008

ISBN: 978-1-4343-6762-4 (sc)
ISBN: 978-1-4343-6763-1 (hc)

Library of Congress Control Number: 2008902375

Printed in the United States of America
Bloomington, Indiana

This book is printed on acid-free paper.

Dedication

This work is written in honor of those that have served their country and their fellow man. There are a number of Americans who served during World War II and whose body lies now in some unknown grave on an unknown battlefield. The names of a few of these soldiers have been used in this work as a tribute to their sacrifice so that they may be remembered.

Missing in Action WWII
David R Curry, Bucks County Pennsylvania, CPL
Phillip L. Brock, Cook County, IL, SGT
Martin O. Lindquist, Fulton County, GA, SGT
Ernest E. Wall, Clark County Washington, SSG
Richard B. Phillips, Anson County NC, SGT
Arthur Bickell, C, SSG
Fuentes, Manuel Jr., PA, 1LT
John W. Watson, PA SGT
Paul P. Trujillo, Wyoming SGT
John F. Buckley, CPL Dallas Texas

Robert G. Cole, Congressional Medal of Honor winner from the Battle of Carentan June 1944, and who was later killed in battle on September 18, 1944, during Operation Market Garden

Acknowledgements

The author wishes to acknowledge the efforts of certain people who have contributed to this work and to thank them for their efforts and valued consul.

Ruth Miller Eberz, Sandy Carlton and Farrel Zehr Editors
Sandy Carlton, Final Edit

Katherine Simon McAllister and Rebecca Kasten Eberz readers and story advisors

Sergeant Charles "Chuck" Finnigan, separated at Fort Sheridan, Illinois 1946, for his consol and friendship.

Special Dedication

It was cold that day in Pennsylvania in the winter of 1961; the snow was deep and the roads were icy and if not impassable they were most certainly dangerous, so much so that traffic was almost nonexistent. I was a nine year old boy out playing with my eleven year-old brother and his two friends. Dressed in my standard outfit for extreme cold, a flannel shirt, sweater, an overstuffed cotton coat with hood, a scarf wrapped around my neck and *two* pairs of pants, the corduroy ones on the outside. The gloves were cheap cloth and the boots were black rubber with those metal buckles that were so common in that era. It was heavy but it was warm. The four of us had walked to the end of the neighborhood, actually my brother and his friends walked I, uninvited, had tagged along behind. There were homes in various stages of construction and we soon found ourselves ice skating, or more accurately, boot skating, on the ice that now covered the unfinished water-filled basements. We should have known better; the water on the top of the ice warned us, but we didn't listen and as I slid across the far side the ice broke and I fell through. The weight of the many layers of clothes took me instantly down and I remember fighting to reach for the edge of the ice that once supported my play but I was too heavy, too weak, and the ice too slippery; I was unable to get out of the freezing water.

Its odd how when something like this happens and how you remember it, at least it is for me. As I think back on it I do not see it from my vantage point in the water, I can only see what happened as if I were standing behind the entire scene, watching. I remember now seeing my brother laying on the ice and his two friends holding his boots. I can clearly see him lying in the freezing water holding my hands, and I can see myself as he pulled me from the freezing water. After pulling me from what was certainly a freezing grave, and bypassing the many other homes along the way, I can see myself walking between my brother and his friends as my clothes froze on me. We walked, shivering the half mile trip back home, were our mother awaited with what we knew would be all the care we needed to both get warm again and to escape whatever punishment might be forthcoming for going where we knew we should not have gone.

I don't remember much more of that day other than my father making someone pump out every one of those basements. I don't remember the cold I felt, I don't remember what my parents said to me. I only remember "watching" my brother save my live.

There is a movie, *It's a Wonderful Life*, in which a boy named George Bailey saves his little brother who had fallen through the ice. The story tells the tale of a man who doubts the worth of his life until an angel comes to earth and shows George what the world would have been like without him. If that angel were to come to my brother he would be able to show him, my children, my grandchildren, a man pulled from a car wreck and an alert system for missing children all of which would not be here if he had not done what he did on that day. What we do does touch so many others and I can certainly tell you this without hesitation, it is a wonderful life.

This book is dedicated to a real life George Bailey, Paul Edmund Eberz, my big brother.

Chapter 1

Nightmares

Just as Sam turned to look back, he saw Ream take the gun from the soldier's holster who falls backwards from the force of the surprise attack. Ream immediately raised the gun, Sam turned to see where he was aiming. His eyes opened wide in the bright sunlight, as he saw Ream was aiming at a tall soldier standing at the gravesite. He tried to shout, to warn the man, but nothing came out of his mouth. He was frozen, unable to speak. In those next terrible few seconds Ream fired, and as Sam stood there unable to move, time seemed to slow down to super slow motion. He saw the weapon fire—the bullet leave the barrel and streak towards its victim; he tried to move but couldn't.

Sam could see the intended victim's back; a tall, athletic-looking man in military uniform standing in front of an open grave. He could also see the man was totally unaware of what was about to happen. As the bullet neared its target, a second smaller man, also in uniform, jumped into its path. Sam saw the bullet hit this man's left shoulder, the shattered bone fragments of his arm striking the shoulder of the man he was trying to protect. The force of the bullet pushed both the rescuer and the intended target to the groungd.

1

The gunman fired a second shot, and still Sam was incapable of moving, incapable of stopping the gunman from firing again. He watched as the gunman fired, this time hitting the would-be rescuer squarely in the back. The force of that second bullet pushed both victims to the ground. As the gunman tried to get off another shot, a young MP grabbed for the gun; it went off and the MP took a round in the arm. In an instant two police officers and four MPs were all over the gunman. He was finally subdued by a dozen hands pushing him hard into the ground.

Sam stood there at the center of this surreal spectacle. He could only watch as the gunman's intended target rose, noticed the blood coming from his shoulder and then grimaced in pain. The wounded soldier stood there for a moment like a man who had been awakened from a deep sleep by a loud noise and who was now struggling to grasp what had awakened him. Without moving or speaking, Sam observed the wounded soldier and then watched the MPs as they wrestled with the gunman. Sam then looked at the would be rescuer on the ground. He was not moving, his eyes open, blood trickling from his mouth, left shoulder soaked in blood and a pool of blood forming under his back.

Police, reporters, soldiers and civilians, who had been attending whatever event had been underway at the time of the shooting, were now all rushing about either in a panic to escape the shooting or a frenzy to report what had happened. Hundreds of people moved about in all sorts of manner, all except three— Sam, who was in some frozen, unmovable state, the mortally wounded soldier lying motionless on the ground, and finally the wounded man, the intended target, whose face Sam had not seen.

Sam looked to the intended target, the tall soldier who now looked up, saw Sam standing there, and knew just by the expression on Sam's confused face, that Sam had done nothing to stop what had just happened. That Sam had just stood there while the gunman fired and fired again; stood there while the deadly second shot ripped though the fallen man who now lay mortally wounded on the ground in front of him.

Sam recognized the man whose eyes were staring at him so intensely that he could feel his hatred for what Sam had failed to do. Sam could tell that this man was both unbelieving and unforgiving of Sam's actions, and Sam felt ashamed.

The wounded soldier who had been staring at Sam looked down at the mortally wounded man on the ground beneath him, then called him by name.

"Dana!" the soldier screamed. "Medic! Medic! Someone get a medic, now!"

Sam saw that everyone was now looking at him, but still he was powerless to move.

"Sam!" He heard someone call.

"Sam!" He heard it again, then felt someone shaking him.

"Sam, wake up. Wake up!"

Sam shot up in his bed and for a moment, he did not know where he was. He felt a hand gripping his arm, looked for its owner, and then stared at the woman for just a moment as he realized it was Mary. He was in bed, and it had happened again.

"Sam. Are you alright?" Mary's voice was now clam and quiet. She gently stroked his sweaty forehead.

Sam realized he was not in Chicago, not at the gravesite, not at the site where his dear friend Dana had given his life to save his. "Yeah!" He looked at her, then back forward, and he could see his reflection in the mirror on the opposite wall of the room. He was a sweaty mess; his t-shirt soaked through, his face contorted in confusion and frustration, his eyes swollen with sweat and tears. It was an all too familiar scene.

"Same dream?" Mary asked as she got out of the bed and walked to the bathroom.

"Yes." Sam sat up in the bed, pushing his back to the headboard to get some support. "I'm sorry." He looked around and listened for sounds outside of the bedroom. "At least I didn't wake the kids."

Mary came back into the room carrying a towel and a glass of water.

"Here," she said as she extended the glass to Sam. Sam took a small sip then chugged the rest. Mary sat on the end of the bed and then wiped the sweat from his face.

"Sam," she said quietly as she looked tenderly into his eyes. "You know Dana's death was not your fault. Ream did it, not you. No one could have imagined that would have happened." She paused, "This is not your fault."

Sam continued to stare at the empty glass and did not look up at Mary.

"Every time I have this dream it's the same. I am watching it all happen. I see Ream shoot and I see Dana throwing himself in front of the bullet as I look into the grave. I watch as Ream fires again. Then I see Dana fall to the ground, and then I see me. I see the man who Dana saved staring back at me, and it's me staring at me as if I were two different people, one the enraged victim and one the hapless bystander. He stares at me, and I see such hate and anger in his eyes, it burns me so that I have to look away."

Sam looked at Mary, then back at the glass. He took both his hands and brought them to his face covering his eyes as he wiped his forehead with his fingers. He stopped and held his hands over his face not speaking.

"You have eliminated all reminders of Dana from every aspect of your life. You even refuse to put out the pictures of him, even the one of the two of you at Fort Story that you love so much." Mary whispered to her hurting husband. "No one blames you, Sam."

Sam took his hands away from his face and turned to Mary.

"But I blame me." He slipped out of bed, went into the bathroom and closed the door behind him.

Monday, 0715 hours October 9, 1994, Dawsonville, thirty miles north of Atlanta, Georgia

Sitting just thirty miles north of Atlanta, Georgia, beyond the towns of Roswell and Alpharetta, and the community of Cumming, the town of Dawsonville was fighting a losing battle against the conversion from rural to urban living that the other three had already lost. The rolling hills and heavily wooded lands north of the Chattahoochee River once were home to many horse ranches. Both humble and wildly expensive ranches, with their hay fields, large barns, riding paddocks, and corrals, once spread their flowing green fields over hundreds of rolling stream-filled acres. As the city of Atlanta grew, the natural sprawl reached northward to the green, open spaces of the northern suburbs. The steady pace of development was kicked into high gear with the announcement that Atlanta would be the home of the 1996 Summer Olympic Games, and by 1992, the number of horse farms remaining in Alpharetta could be counted on a single hand. One by one, mile by mile, the developers gobbled up the ranches and replaced them with communities of crowded condos, town homes, and single-family communities. Houses replaced barns, schools replaced farms, and strip malls of dry cleaners, beauty shops, pizza parlors and video stores soon were as common as the beautiful ranches used to be.

The Dawsonville area remained one of the last outposts safe from the sprawl. Whether it was the distance from Atlanta or the presence of an occasional chicken farm that discouraged developers, the area seemed immune, if only temporarily, to the frenzy that was gobbling up land. It was here in 1990, that David Lytle, having moved to Georgia, ended his search for a home with enough land 'that he didn't know he had neighbors." After two months of searching, he found his place; a small two-bedroom home on eight acres of land just south of the Dawson Forest Wildlife Management Area. This was a state-protected area of nearly nine hundred acres. Best of all, there were twelve miles of hiking trails, which for David meant solitary running trails.

It was a magnificent fall morning. As David ran down the trail, just barely lit by the rising morning sun, he re-adjusted his baseball cap, a plain black one with the letters LNMB embroidered on the back bottom edge. He looked into the sun, felt its warmth on his face, and thought of his youth.

David was six feet tall, broad shoulders, smart, tough, and above all he was in-shape; or at least that's what he thought when, right out of high school, he joined the Army. He was an athlete, a basketball player, baseball shortstop, and in the best shape of his life, but he quickly found the Army definition of 'in-shape' was not the same as his. Their definition did not include the ability to play basketball, but it did include the ability to run.

Every morning at 0530 hours, in the pitch black before the beginning of the scorching summer's day at Fort Bragg, North Carolina, David and a hundred boys of Alpha Company, Fourth Platoon, 1st Training Brigade would begin their day with a brisk five mile run under the watchful eye of Staff Sergeant Stanley Bender, who David thought was just about the toughest, most accomplished NCO in the entire Army. David could handle all the pushups and sit-ups but he hated the running. Every day he managed to get through it by sheer will. Six weeks later, he graduated from Boot Camp and off he went to Airborne Training. Here they proceeded to run him to death with five-mile runs twice daily, every morning and evening. By the end of it, he hated running even more than before, if that was possible.

After Airborne training, he looked forward to joining a real outfit, to get away from the 'chicken-shit' running and get down to serious soldering. Unfortunately, for David, Staff Sergeant Stanley Bender had the same idea about leaving the training of recruits behind and when David reported to Fort Benning, he also reported to Bender's Infantry Platoon. As he had wanted, David was learning all about real infantry tactics and techniques, but Bender's passion for running the troops was damn near killing him. Soon he began to hate the idea of just waking up, as he knew running long miles in heavy boots awaited him.

Despite his absolute hatred of running, he volunteered for Special Forces training where he knew ten mile runs were the order of the day. But he wanted to be part of what he thought was the best unit in the world, and he was willing to do it just to be part of the team. He applied, was accepted, and got his orders to report in six months.

When the orders came into the company, Bender got them and sent for David. David received the word that Bender wanted to see him, reported immediately to Bender's office, and knocked on his door.

A strong, masculine voice from inside the room loudly called, "Enter," and David opened the door and stepped inside quickly.

Bender looked at David who was standing at attention in front of his desk. "The response to your request for Special Forces Training came today." Bender paused just a moment to let Lytle sweat about the answer. "You're in." Bender extended a handful of papers to David, "Your orders, Lytle."

Without thinking of the protocol, the excited young Specialist shouted, "Out frickin' standing!" Then realizing how he had spoken in front of the senior sergeant, he immediately apologized.

Bender smiled at David, "No need to apologize soldier; it *is* out frickin standing." He motioned for David to sit in the chair next to his desk. "Lytle, you're an outstanding soldier; smart, intuitive, and a born leader. That's why we endorsed your request for SF training." He leaned forward to David and softly spoke, "But you're not going to make it through."

David was taken back, "Like hell. I'll make it."

"No you won't." Bender shook his head from side to side as he stood. "You won't make the runs. They are ten miles and you can have two of them a day."

David was indignant with the sergeant, "I've never fallen out of a run and I never will." David stood and matched the sergeant's stance.

"No, you haven't. You make it on guts alone most of the time and that's what tough guys do." He stared at David with an intense, cold, piercing look, "But tough just isn't good enough for SF. If you are going to make it you need to change."

David didn't have a clue what Bender was talking about and stood there unable to answer.

The sergeant sat back down at his desk, picked up a pen as if to start to work, then looked up to David. "Specialist Lytle meet me at the track tonight at twenty-hundred hours." He looked back to his work and without looking up at David, "And wear PT clothes and sneakers—no combat boots. Understood?"

"Affirmative." There was no response from Bender; so after thirty seconds of standing there in silence, David left the office without another word.

All afternoon David sweated the idea of having to run around that damn track. How he hated the endless, meaningless, foot pounding trips around the endless oval. It wasn't bad enough he had to run five miles every morning, now Bender was going to make him run at night too. He didn't want to do it, but he knew Bender had the power, and if he wanted to go to SF training, he had to let Bender run him to death.

At exactly 1955 hours, Bender walked onto the track where David was waiting.

"Evening, Sergeant Bender," David greeted the NCO as warmly as he could, under the circumstances.

"Evening, Specialist Lytle. You ready to learn how to run tonight?"

"Affirmative," David responded with his typical proper military manner. Then almost as if he had no control over his mouth, he added, "And how many laps are you going to *learn* me tonight?"

"None." Bender said as he stretched.

"Say again." David asked.

"I said, 'None.'" Bender looked at the oval, "I hated that frickin track." Bender stopped his stretching. "Lytle, I am sure you would run any distance the SF boys tell you to. And unless your heart exploded, I suspect you will find a way to drag your ass across whatever finish line they draw."

David silently agreed.

"But that won't get you through. You can't fear getting up each morning knowing you are going to have to do something you absolutely hate. You can't be the soldier you need to be with that attitude. It wears you out." Bender pointed his finger at David in anticipation of David countering his argument. "I can read you like a field manual, Lytle. You excel in every training event we throw at you. You're involved, engaged, and the others see your attitude and they follow. The mornings are another matter. Every morning you show up, like a robot; no enthusiasm, nothing positive. When you run, I look at your face; it's like you are zoned out or in some evil trance. What are you thinking about when you run?"

"I'm thinking about just making the next lap; that's all."

"That's it?"

"Affirmative."

"You just stare at the back of the man in front of you."

"Affirmative."

"You absolutely hate it, don't you?"

"Affirmative."

"Understood." The running track was next to a large forested training area, and fifty yards from the far end of the track there was a dirt trail that led back into the woods. Bender pointed to the trail, "We'll start there."

The two men started jogging towards the trail then entered it. Soon Bender had a rhythm and he was more gliding than running, while Lytle was doing the airborne shuffle and already struggling.

"How far are we going?" David asked.

"I don't have any idea. Just depends on the evening, the mood and what your body is telling you."

"Well, my body is telling me it hates what I am doing to it."

"Then stop."

"Say again." David didn't know how to respond. He wasn't a quitter and wouldn't give Bender the satisfaction to see him fall out.

Bender stopped running and looked at Lytle. "You aren't getting it. This isn't punishment; it's an outlet—if you let it. You keep thinking of this as torture, and if you do, your attitude will suffer. When you are running, you're only thinking; when will it end? When I'm running I'm thinking of the upcoming day's activities, or this beautiful forest I'm running through, or if I'm really lucky it's about some lovely lady."

Bender motioned ahead and they started running again. Two minutes later Bender asked, "What are you thinking about?"

David had been constructing imaginary finish lines and then staring at them as he ran forward in an effort to keep up, but when the sergeant asked he replied, "The weather."

Two minutes later Bender asked again, "What are you thinking about now?"

This time David was actually thinking about the weather. Tomorrow was Saturday and he had a date with a young female specialist from the finance company. The newspaper said it was going to rain tomorrow and he was thinking about what they were going to do.

Every two minutes or so Bender would ask the same question, and David would tell him whatever he was thinking about at the time. Fifteen minutes into the run Bender stopped. "This is far enough for now. I'm going on. I'll pick you up on my return."

"I can keep up," David stubbornly replied.

"I suspect you can, but I don't want you to. I have some thinking to do." With that, Bender continued down the dirt trail and disappeared into the forest. David stood there expecting Bender to return in just a few minutes. When it got to ten, David sat down on the trail and just rested. His mind drifted from subject to subject and he didn't hear Bender call him when he finally arrived back twenty minutes later.

David was amazed how this big man had run and didn't look tired.

"How far do you run?" David finally asked.

"I don't have a distance. I do a time. Depending how I feel I start out with a number and run out half the time. If I am tired at that point, I turn towards home or if I feel great I just continue." He took a few more casual, effortless strides and continued, "I don't do it for the exercise David, I do it for the peace. There are no phones to answer, no idiot Second Lieutenants I have to baby-sit, no deadlines to meet, and no reports to write. I can be alone with whatever thoughts I have or whoever I wish I was with." Bender smiled a devilish smile, "Or one I had been with."

David knew exactly what he meant, and as he ran, his thoughts turned to tomorrow and to young Specialist Rebecca Kasten from the Finance Company, who had finally agreed to go out with him after he had asked her no less then eight times without success.

Before he knew it they were back at the beginning of the trail.

"Unless the company has some night training scheduled I run Fridays and Tuesdays. I'll see you next Tuesday, same time."

"Roger that," David replied as they both went there separate ways.

Tuesday came and David ran with Bender for eighteen minutes before he told David to wait. That Friday it was nineteen. After two months of running together David asked Bender, "Do you want to wait here? I can pick you up on my way back."

- - - - - - - - - - - - - - - < > - - - - - - - - - - - - - - - -

The rewards of his new method were clear; for the first time in his life, he liked running, and in fact now loved running. More than just being in better shape David looked forward to his twice-weekly run; this sixty minutes became a time of thinking, relaxing, and even dreaming.

With his newly developed skill, David excelled at Special Forces Training and after graduating tops in this class, he began a ten-year career in what the military called 'black ops.' Between missions, he would return to his running regiment. But now it wasn't for physical training, it was for his mental health. It enabled him to forget; to forget the mission, the politics that caused it, and the death that resulted from it. For ten years he fought undeclared wars in the jungles of unnamed countries, and assassinated 'enemies of the state' as ordered by higher command. Each time leaving without notice for days or weeks at a time and then returning to tell friends nothing except he was on an unannounced training mission.

The special ops life was difficult. The hard work, the constant training, and the nature of the duty, made it mentally trying on the individual, but it made it impossible for the development of any sort of stable love life. Despite the challenges of the life style, he was a soldier, one of the best. He was content with his life, until he left a squad of his men behind in a jungle, the name of which did not appear in any U.S. Army history book.

He had taken three teams by chopper into the jungle. Then, after a day of traversing the dense growth on foot, they set up on the edge of the forest less than fifty yards from the target. The target was a group of local drug leaders who were to meet in a jungle fortress for one day to discuss territory ownership and set prices for their illegal drugs. It would be a textbook operation. They came in by stealth, having been totally undetected and now waited motionless just yards from the target. When they were sure the targets had all arrived, Team Alpha, which had a position just inside the edge of the forest and just southwest of the target, would take out the exterior guards with silenced rifles. Team Charlie would enter the building and eliminate the occupants, while Team Bravo provided cover.

When Charlie completed the assault, they would return under the cover of Team Alpha and then Alpha and Charlie would retreat through the jungle under cover of Team Bravo if necessary. Team Bravo had taken a position on the southeast side in the edge of the forest and would provide cover on the flank. If Alpha and Charlie met resistance as they pulled back Bravo could cover. If Bravo met resistance when they pulled back, Alpha and Charlie would be in a position to support. There had been one concern about the plan. Upon departure, the covering force, Team Bravo, had to cross thirty yards of open terrain to return to the jungle and that concerned David and Team Bravo's leader Heit Lang. But G2 said the 'hostile' force numbered ten or less so the risk was acceptable.

The initial assault went by the book. Alpha took out the guards with silenced weapons; only four slightly audible pops ended the lives of the two guards at the front door and the two who were smoking at the rear entrance. Team Charlie entered the building and with deadly efficiency eliminated all eight drug bosses and their eight personal guards. Only one guard got off any rounds at all and they missed their target.

Team Charlie returned through Team Alpha's lines and set up their firing position to cover team Alpha's withdraw. Then teams Charlie and Alpha would cover for exposed Team Bravo.

Just as Alpha began its evac, it all went to hell. Alerted by the one guard's errant shots, a contingent of nearly one hundred of the local drug leader's militia came screaming up the hill from the north side and attacked with an undisciplined but violent assault. Teams Charlie and Bravo mowed the unexpected attackers down in an effective and deadly crossfire.

All was still within the parameters of the plan until Bravo attempted to evac back towards Alpha and Charlie. Alpha and Charlie kept the militia down in the north enabling Bravo to begin the evac, but twenty yards into the open zone, Bravo began to take fire from a new militia force behind them. Alpha and Charlie could not engage this new threat as Bravo team was between them and the militia. Bravo immediately took two dead and one wounded and had to return to their original position.

Teams Alpha and Charlie held the militia on the north but could not engage those to the east without hitting Team Bravo in the process. Team Bravo was trapped and despite inflicting heavy casualties on the enemy force, David knew the situation was untenable and when darkness came, they would be overrun. He called for immediate evac by chopper but command would not send the rescue team because they did not want U.S. forces seen in the area. All of David's men were in commando uniform and without any forms of ID; they were expendable and as far as any outside government would know they were mercenaries hired by a rival cartel.

Of the five men in Team Bravo, two were dead, two were wounded severely but still fighting, with Heit the only uninjured man. After another ten minutes of heavy fighting Heit had been hit in both legs and his escape was no longer possible. Teams Alpha and Charlie also had problems. Their ammo was nearly exhausted and they had three casualties, one severe.

Knowing the hopelessness of the situation Heit volunteered to stay behind and hold off the militia while David took the surviving members of the teams out through the jungle to the scheduled evac point. David said nothing on the long flight back. When the chopper finally landed he found, and then almost killed, the officer who had refused to order air evac. It was David's last mission, and five days later he was a civilian.

Now, ten years after having left his men behind, and twenty-one years after he ran down that dirt trail and found a new peace through running alone in nature, he was still running. He loved his morning runs, but they were less frequent now. His knees were no longer what they used to be, allowing him just three runs a week. He stood watching the sun rise higher in the sky, he felt the warmth of the sun on his face and he thought it felt good to be alive. He took off down the trail, finished his run, returned to his house, then did a hundred pushups, and worked fifteen minutes on the heavy bag that he had installed in the unused second bedroom.

He showered, shaved, dressed then went outside to the back porch with his coffee and notes. Once outside he put the cup and notes on the table and then, as he did every day for the last ten years, turned towards the south where he left his friends behind and quietly and privately saluted.

Monday, 0715 hours October 9, 1994, Stateville Correctional Center Joliet, Illinois

Ream had severe arthritis in his lower spine, and in that instant when he felt the sharp pain, he thought he was experiencing another all-to-familiar episode. Three years in a jail cell, an isolation cell to boot, had taken its toll on him. The day he entered the cell he was perfectly healthy; a strong, in-shape, strikingly rugged looking man who looked and acted more like a man in his late fifties then the seventy-five he was. He was also a meticulously manicured and well-dressed man who prided himself on taking care of his physical form. As such he had all the health money could buy, including a complete workout center in his home and a personal trainer to ensure he maximized his use of it.

Over the last three years he was allowed out of his cell just one-hour per day. The most exercise he could squeeze in was walking in a secured inside garden, which was the size of a basketball court. Today was a special day; he was going into Chicago and would be out of the cell all day. Standing in an unfamiliar corridor in the General Population area with prisoners he had never seen before, he awaited processing for his trip into the city.

When he felt a second more intense pain, he reached around his back and felt a warm liquid on his hand. He then felt something hard in his back. He reached around to feel the source of his pain. There was blood flowing from where it apparently had entered and he instantly knew he had been stabbed. His seventy-five year old body, already weakened by age and three years of prison-induced inactivity, quickly succumbed to the loss of blood and he slumped to the floor. Sitting in a pool of his own blood he could barely focus on the activity around him; he saw people moving but it made no sense to him. The pain he had so suddenly felt was gone, but then so was any feeling at all. He heard nothing. He couldn't hear the sounds of the prisoners around him as they jockeyed to get into a position where they could say they saw absolutely nothing. He didn't hear the sounds of the guards' shoes as they ran towards him. He couldn't hear the prison horn that now was blasting the alert. He did not hear or even see the guard, who had a grip on his shirt and was shaking him in a vain attempt to keep him conscience. But he could hear the sound of his own breathing and heartbeat, and he knew he was dead.

Just before the last of the earthly air he was to breathe escaped from his lungs, he managed to form two words, "Das Ende."

Chapter 2

Transition

Major Sam Call had failed to be promoted to the rank of Lieutenant Colonel and without that, he could not stay beyond twenty years of service. There were to be two subsequent opportunities for the Selection Board to reconsider and select Sam for promotion, but the very public activities by Sam during the Ream affair eliminated the chance of any favorable outcome on Sam's behalf. So on June 7, 1993, exactly twenty years after his first day of active duty, and without fanfare, parades or toasts from his assigned unit, Sam had quietly, and unceremoniously, retired from the United States Army.

Immediately after retiring from the military, Sam had joined David Lytle's investigation company as a 'High Tech' investigator. It made sense; David had been instrumental in helping him break the Ream case. They worked well together and a strong bond had been formed between them. Two men, for which honor meant everything, fought hard to make a long past wrong, right. It was a bond neither man could or would break. So when David heard Sam was leaving the Army he was quick to offer Sam a job as an investigator specializing in corporate investigations. Sam's first job was just an administrative gig, reviewing email logs and documents looking for evidence of insider trading.

Nothing too serious and definitely no chance of running into bad guys who didn't think twice about eliminating a nosey PI.

His second job was along the same line, then on his third he got some fieldwork; followed a target, photographed him and his lady friends. The target was a handsome, thirties something young man that women just seemed unable to resist. Unfortunately for him, his very wealthy sixty year-old wife didn't care for his running around. After two weeks of following the man and recording his six encounters with three different women, David and Sam provided the report to the client. On the last day, Sam had followed the target while David went to the client's home. Sam followed the target to his encounter then called David as the target started home. When the target arrived, he was met by his wife, David, and the client's lawyer, who had already prepared the divorce papers and had obtained a restraining order keeping the young man from coming near his soon to be former residence.

When the young man entered the house, his wife called for him to come into the den, which was right off the main entrance. As soon as he entered, he saw his wife, her lawyer and David, and then when Sam came in right behind him he knew what was up but pretended to be clueless.

"What's going on here, Ann?" The young man said in his best innocent voice as he looked at his wife then at the others in the room.

"I told you I would not be made a fool of. All this here for you and you couldn't keep it in your pants." She paused and stared at him. "And doing it with women from my country club—you bastard." She turned and looked at her lawyer who immediately gave him two sets of papers.

"These are the divorce papers." He held them out, waited for the young man to take them and when he did, the lawyer presented the second set. "And this is a restraining order preventing you from coming near this residence."

"And the club!" The wife added angrily.

The lawyer pointed to the door." You should leave now."

The man turned to his wife and, with all the emotion and conviction of an Oscar winning actor, pleaded with her. "I swear to you baby this is all a mistake. I never..."

David thrust a handful of graphic photos into the man's face and stopped his performance before it began. Realizing the numerous photos of him naked with several ladies of the country club were more evidence than he could charm away, he dropped the innocent act and took on the tough stud character.

"I need my things," the young man said arrogantly as he started for the staircase behind them.

"They are already packed and ready to be shipped You need not worry about that," the lawyer added.

The young man stepped around the lawyer to go upstairs but David moved in front of him. The young man put his left arm out and tried to push David, but David grabbed the young man's left hand, twisted it, and instantly the man was in intense pain and subdued. David then led him out of the house right past Sam with the lawyer following, carrying the papers that the young man had dropped when David grabbed him and placed him into submission. When David came back inside the house, the client thanked him and promised a bonus for providing the added pleasure of seeing the young man thrown out. The entire event took two minutes and Sam was impressed how well David orchestrated the entire affair.

So now, after one year of assignments, Sam was an experienced investigator of sorts; although he had not had any of the physical cases that David encountered, and for that he was thankful. He had just finished a job in Alabama, completed his report, sent it to David, and took a week off to be with the family. Now, after working all day at the house, he was to meet David and his operative Bob, at the Casa Nuova restaurant to go over his new assignment.

Chapter 3

IdentityPoint Inc.

Monday, 1830 hours, Alpharetta, GA

"How can I get a job there? I don't think they are going to want me working there; after all, I do have a rep now of a whistleblower, and I don't think they will be big on that. They will take one look at my resume and trash it," Sam said to Bob and then looked to David Lytle for concurrence.

"Well, if you go in as Sam Call they will." Bob replied as he picked up his coffee cup and tried to get the waiter's attention, but he just walked by. "I don't believe it. What is this about me and getting coffee in this place? It's like I'm not here. Why do we come to this place anyway?"

"Settle down, Bob. Like I've told you before, you are just so unremarkable looking, you just blend in. They don't ignore you on purpose." Sam smiled and gave a wink to David who was sitting on the other side of the booth. "Besides we love this place. Casa Nuova has the best food in all of Atlanta, and I'm in love with Maria."

"Hey don't let Antonio hear that." David made a grave face as he put his hand to his throat and simulated getting his throat cut.

With that the waiter walked by and Sam held up his hand to signal him. Ricardo was a nice looking man in his late thirties, who always wore black dress pants and a long sleeved black shirt. He was not overdressed, but well dressed for a waiter in a small casual Italian restaurant. His hair combed all the way back across his slightly balding head, and his black eyes and pronounced features told all the world of his Italian heritage; a heritage he wore proudly. Sam asked, "Ricardo, can we have some more coffee here?"

"Of course my friends," Ricardo said in his perfect English that was wrapped with just the right amount of real Italian accent. He had not lost the flair of the native language and he used it along with his charm and elegant style to enhance the food and service. Ricardo looked at the other two men in succession looking for their response; Bob anxiously nodded yes.

"I'll be right back," Ricardo quickly got two individual size pots and brought them to the table.

"Grazie," Sam said as Ricardo poured his coffee.

"Prego," Ricardo replied then left the men to their conversation.

Bob sat with a blank stare on his face, with his head down looking at his empty cup and the little pot that Ricardo had left for him, but had not poured as he had done for Sam and David.

"Hello, Bob. Earth to Bob, anyone there?" David said as he and Sam just looked at each other then back at Bob.

Bob stared at his empty cup, refilled it then took a sip. "At first it just pissed me off that they ignore me, but now I am beginning to think I am...," Bob paused for the right word."

"Invisible?" David smiled and put his hand on Bob's shoulder. "Now, Bob, don't get paranoid on me. It's just that you look so content and peaceful and you tend to blend into the background. How many times do I have to tell you that's why you are so good at what you do. Who wants an undercover man that everyone notices?"

"Yeah," Bob said unconvincingly.

"So?" Sam replied in an effort to get things back on track.

David looked back at Sam, "Well when is Mary coming?"

"I told her around twenty-hundred hours, but I'll call when we're done. Only takes five minutes for her to get here, and she's in the mood for cannelloni."

"Twenty-hundred hours? Aren't you two ever going to use real clock time?" Bob asked.

"Sorry, Bob, that's 8 PM for you civilians," Sam joked.

"Da. I know. It's that you're both just civilians now you know," Bob added as he poured, then drank his coffee.

David looked at Sam and then to Bob. "We will never be *just* civilians Bob." Then he looked at Sam and they quietly nodded to each other.

David took a sip of his coffee. "Well, let's finish up," David said. "So you were saying, Bob."

Bob just drank his coffee and ignored David.

"Oh yes. Where were we?" David asked the little group.

"How I was going to get a job at IdentityPoint." Sam responded looking at Bob and trying to get him to speak again. "You have a plan, Bob?"

Bob reluctantly continued, "Yeah, no problem. But not as Sam Call, as Sam Cohen."

"Sam Cohen! Who is Sam Cohen?" Sam asked.

"He's you," Bob said as he finished his coffee.

"Say again?" David asked.

"Look. Sam can't go in as himself, so he needs another identity. I did some checking and there are a hundred Sam Cohens in the system, twelve from Philly alone. All you need is a social security number and we can build you an identity." Bob looked to David for agreement, but David just looked back at him in silence.

"I met this former FBI guy, Michael Right, who is a consultant there, he used to be an undercover guy for the bureau, he gave me some great tips."

"Michael *Right*?" David said emphasizing his last name.

"Yeah, why?"

"Seems like an odd name, you know. Isn't that *right* Sam?" David joked.

"Yes, seems *right* to me. You sure that's his *right* name," Sam again played on the man's name.

"Yes, but he doesn't spell it the usual way, he spells it M-I-C-H-A-L-E." Bob said with a straight face.

David and Sam gave each other a look, but neither took the bait and they just looked at Bob.

"You were saying *Michale* gave you some good tips. Like?" Sam asked as he rotated the two fingers of his right hand in a circular motion as if to say 'let's go on'.

"Okay. First, try to keep the false ID as close to your real one as possible that way you are less likely to trip up on the details."

"Like?" Sam asked again.

"Like your first name. Use your real first name. If you are working your cover and you bump into someone you know from your real life or another cover they most likely will just call you by your first name. When's the last time someone walked up to you in passing and said, 'Oh, hi Sam Call.' They say, 'Hi, Sam,' don't they."

Both Sam and David nodded in agreement.

"As for the last name, use a common one, not Smith or Jones, but one that has a lot of names in the phone book and that have your first name too if possible. This adds 'family depth' to the identity."

"Sounds good so far," Sam added. "Go on."

"Adding address history is easy. Always use an apartment address and throw in some post office boxes. It's hard to trace a PO Box, and apartments turnover a lot so you won't screw up by taking a real address and then the bad guys look it up and find that Uncle Harry and Aunt Betty have lived there for forty years."

"Who's Uncle Harry?" David joked. "You have an Uncle Harry, Sam?"

"Very droll David, very droll," came Bob's reply.

"Anyway. Now you got a real name and real addresses. Oh, and pick addresses in towns you have actually been so if they question you, you can talk the talk."

"Your FBI friend seems to know his business," David added.

"Yep."

"So what's the kicker Bob?" Sam asked. "There has to be a kicker."

"Well, yeah. It's the Social Security Number. You need one that has been issued, but not in use."

"A dead man's social?" David asked.

Before Bob could answer, Sam jumped in. "No I wouldn't think so. That would show up on their systems wouldn't it? So would a phony number."

"Exactly! You're getting good at this." Bob always got a little excited when he could teach his experts something new. "You need either an un-issued number, which are just about impossible to get, or one from a dead kid."

"Excuse me!" came Sam's startled reply. "You want me to be a dead kid?"

"No man, listen. When a child is born the parents usually get a social for tax reasons, and as the kid grows up and gets a job he starts to use it on applications and for filing taxes." Bob stopped for a moment and reflected on what he was going to say, then continued. "But not all kids live to grow up. They die of an illness or get killed. Either way their death isn't reported to the social security administration."

"Why is that?" David asked.

"Because people only report deaths to them for death benefits, and since the kid didn't work, the parents don't file," Bob said, but didn't finish as David completed the thought.

"And the system still thinks they're alive."

"Yes," Bob concurred.

"So you have a number for me?" Sam asked.

"Yes. IdentityPoint has people look up a system that allows you to look up by SSN. So since I was born in the same year as Sam, I just took the first five numbers of my name and then started inquires with 0001 and continued until I got a no-record response. Now you have a social that won't conflict with someone else's record. I got lucky, only took me two days."

David looked at Sam and then made a gesture with his hands as if to say, 'Sounds good to me'.

"So, I made up a resume for Sam." With that Bob opened his small brief case and gave a file to Sam that contained his new resume, complete with life history."

Sam looked it over for a minute. "Impressive work, Bob." He looked at David and nodded then gave the folder to him. "But don't you think they will check it out?"

"Oddly enough IdentityPoint doesn't use their own systems to do background checks when they are hiring, they just run it through a Wants and Warrants system to check if you are a bad guy, and since you don't really exist you can't be wanted."

"Sweet," David said.

"Besides, since I am working in the Human Resources department, I can make sure I am the one that does your in-processing." Bob sat back in the booth with a new sense of importance having hit a home run on the resume and identity gig for Sam. "Well, I've got to run, bowling tonight, you know." With that Bob stood, nodded to both of the men and left.

"He does great work," Sam said to David as he looked at the resume again.

"Yeah. He is something, the best operative I've ever had."

Sam looked up at David. "You think he will ever get it that we tell all the waiters to ignore him?"

Both men just laughed.

"So are you ready to be a Project Manager at IdentityPoint?"

"Well, I did enough of it in the Army, so I think I can fake it for awhile. Especially since this project is just getting underway and I will be working alone just developing requirements," Sam said as he gathered up the resume, put it back in the folder, and placed it on the seat beside him.

"I think all you're going to get is about four weeks. Bob has gotten a ton of info by pretending to do H/R audits and getting to talk to just about anyone he needed. But the proof is in the data, and he can't get that. You are going to have to get into the systems and get what we need." David was serious now and talking very quietly. "Our client called in a favor from one of the company's technology VPs and said you were a friend of her husband so you are in. You start tomorrow."

"Not a problem, David, but don't forget Mary and I are off to the islands in two weeks. There can be no missing this one for me."

"I understand, not a problem, Sam." David said as he stood and shook Sam's hand goodbye.

David left and Sam waited for Mary. It was 1945 hours but he knew Mary would be ready and waiting. He called her on his cell phone, and she said she'd be there in ten minutes. Sam looked around the restaurant. It was Monday night, the slow night, which is exactly why Sam, David, and Bob met there on Mondays. Less people meant less chance of being overheard or recognized.

Co-located with a travel agency, a dry cleaner, and a frame shop that had since gone out of business, Casa Nuova was located in one of those thousands of characterless strip malls of four or five stores that have been built on just about every street corner in suburban America. From the outside it was nothing to brag about; a basic brick front, one-story building that offered no special amenities or other features that would entice a couple to want to try it out.

Sam and Mary had moved to Atlanta after Sam retired from the Army and joined David's investigation firm. They had been in their home for six months before they even tried Casa Nuova. They loved eating out when they could and when Sam was home in between assignments they liked to try something new. They got in the car on one Friday night, but before they got a mile down the road, the sky opened up and it started to rain in buckets. They had found Atlanta a nice place to live and the weather was certainly nice enough, but when the weather did go bad, the traffic came to a halt. So on this night when the rain came, the traffic predictably came to a crawl. Sitting at a traffic light and frustrated with the driving, Mary saw Casa Nuova and suggested they try it rather than sitting in traffic all night. One night, one meal, and it became their favorite place to go.

The little restaurant held about thirty tables and booths, and from Wednesday through Saturday it was packed. The walls were decorated with scenes of Italy and wine bottles to give it the charm of an Italian Ristorante. But the charm was not in the decor, it was in Maria. She was the owner, hostess, and make no mistake about it, the boss. When Sam first met her, he said to Mary that if you were to try to describe a perfect Italian restaurant operator it would be Maria. Standing just a little over five feet three, she towered over everyone with her charm and presence. She had curly black hair, a round face and eyes that lit up the room. With a smile and attitude that made you feel like she was your best friend, she met her 'regulars' at the door with a hug and kiss that made you feel good just being there; like you had come home from a long trip or you had just stepped into you favorite aunt's house at Christmas time. It didn't take long before Sam and Mary became regulars; on slow nights, Maria would sit with them and they would talk about families, travel, and life.

Sam saw Mary come in the door and he rose to greet her. She came to the back where they always sat, he kissed her hello, took her coat, and they both sat down.

"Good day?" Sam asked.

"Not bad. A glass a wine and good food will be just what I need." Mary said as she looked at Sam and then thought about how he looked. It had been over a year, but she still wasn't used to seeing him in civilian clothes and not in uniform.

Sam looked up and saw Maria coming out of the kitchen. They saw each other and he stood to greet her.

"Good Evening, Mr. Call." She reached up to hug Sam who was a foot taller. He kissed her on the check and gave her a big hug.

"Good to see you, Maria," Sam said as he stepped back so she could greet Mary.

She stepped forward, bent down and kissed the seated Mary. "Hello, Mary."

"So good to see you, Maria."

Sam sat back down, and patted the seat to invite Maria to sit.

She saw Sam's invitation. "Just for a moment," and she sat. They chatted for a few minutes and then after Maria asked Mary if she was hungry, she related the specials for the night, and then left them to decide on their dinner.

"I think that is my favorite part."

"What's that, Sam?"

"Just hearing her tell us the specials, the way she says it—it's just so…" Sam waited for the right word to come.

"So Italian?" Mary interjected.

"Yes." Sam laughed. "It always sounds so great no matter what they are serving. I guess that is why we have never eaten off the menu. I've always had one of the specials."

"So tell me, what's the new assignment?" Mary asked as she sipped the Chianti Classico Sam had ordered her in anticipation of her arrival.

"Well, Bob's been doing the investigation at IdentityPoint for a month, and he has some really damning stuff, but it's mostly 'cafeteria testimony', just word of mouth stuff someone told him over lunch.

For the most part it won't stand up in court unless you get some collaborating data."

"And that's your part?" Mary asked.

"Affirmative." Sam took of sip of the wine. "I love this stuff." He looked at the wine and then extended his glass to Mary as to make a silent toast. She picked up her glass, did the same, clicked the glasses, and took another sip.

"So what's the plan?" she asked as she looked around the restaurant.

"Well, our client says that their company has acquired over sixty companies during the past three years. Now when a big company buys a small company, the stock of the small company, especially a start-up company, goes way up. That's a huge win for the stockholders of the small company. Now it's illegal for the executives of the big company to own stock in the acquisitions – the whole insider-trading thing. Our client believes that her senior executives have been profiting from the purchases, but she doesn't know how."

"Interesting," Mary said as she took a bite of the garlic toast. "I love these things."

"Yeah, and they are so addictive."

"So why does she believe this is going on?" Mary asked, and then made a circular motion with her fingers to indicate to Sam to continue.

"Well, before a company buys another company there is normally a period called Due Diligence where the buying company checks out all the books of the company to be purchased. She was on the personnel committee and one of their committee duties is to inspect the ownership documents of the company principals. In a privately held company the stock ownership is not public, the company maintains that list."

"So what did she find?"

"In many cases she was having difficulty in getting the names of all the stock holders of the acquired companies, and she brought that up to the President who said he'd check that out."

"And he didn't," Mary volunteered.

"Well, she doesn't know for sure but what she does know is she is off the review committee. They hired a full time person to just do that, and apparently he is a friend of the Chairman of the Board."

"And that avoids any further possible discoveries."

"That's where I come in." Sam reached into the basket and took more bread.

"You are going to spoil your appetite if you keep eating the bread."

"No, I won't, I love the bread and I always eat everything Maria serves." Sam bit a piece of the garlic bread and smiled.

"I was just being nice, you keep eating all that bread and that ten pounds you've gained will be twenty real soon."

Sam's mouth dropped open. "That's cold, Woman."

"Not as cold as our bed will get if you become one of those post military career fat boys."

"Damn, Woman, how can you say that? I am not gaining weight. I am just letting my extra hard military body adjust to a more common civilian existence. After all, when I go undercover in my new investigator role, I have to look like the rest of the common folk; not like the rock hard, military stud I have been for twenty years." Sam sat up straight in the booth, brought both his arms into his chest, and flexed them like a weight lifter demonstrating his muscles.

"Stud?" Mary looked at Sam and cocked her head. "All I can say is, you get any bigger and you won't be getting under *cover* with me anytime soon."

Sam looked down at his stomach and sucked it in as Maria came over to the table.

"So, you two ready for dinner?" Maria asked as she smiled her infectious smile at both Sam and Mary.

"I sure am," Mary said.

"Not me."

Maria looked disappointedly at Sam as he put his head down like a scolded schoolboy. "Mary says I am getting fat, and I can't eat here anymore." Sam looked up at Maria and stuck his lower lip out.

"Oh no, Sam, you look fabulous." Maria looked at Mary then back at Sam. "I think you are a hunk."

Sam quickly jumped in, "See that Mary, I'm a hunk." He turned back to Maria. "So tell me the specials again."

"You are so bad, Call." Mary said as she shook her head and laughed.

Maria, in her Italian accented English, again highlighted the specials for the night

"They all sound so good. What are you going to have Sam?" Mary always waited so that if it was the same thing she wanted then she could get another choice and still get some of Sam's dinner. It was like a twofer, only better.

"I'm having the scallops and shrimp in the lobster sauce."

"Perfect!" Maria said and then turned back to Mary.

"I'll have the pork rolled in Prosciutto ham and provolone."

"Very well. Enjoy!" Maria then left them to tell Antonio and to make sure the dinner was made just perfect for her good friends.

"God, I love this place." Mary raised her glass." To Maria, this restaurant, and six weeks of no kids."

Sam raised his glass and gently clinked it to hers. "Oh yes. And thank God for your mother and her farm."

"It's a ranch, not a farm. You raise livestock on a ranch; you grow food on a farm."

"Ranch, farm, what's the difference? We get six weeks alone." Sam smiled.

"What's the difference? I would suggest you not ask the question to a Texas rancher."

1830 hours, Washington D.C.

Christopher Garrett drove into the parking garage, took a ticket from the self-service machine, and drove slowly up ramp after ramp, until he saw the all too familiar sign on the wall. A large number six was painted in white on a red background confirming he was in the correct place on the sixth floor. Each parking place was numbered and as always, he tried to get a parking spot as close as possible to space number sixty-six. That spot was perfectly situated as to provide him with a clear view up and down the ramp as well as the elevator door, which took the patrons down to the road level entrance or office building entrance on the first floor. There were no other building entrances so the garage filled from the ground floor up. There was no reason for anyone to be on the sixth floor unless the parking places on the floors below were full, or as in Garrett's case, they were meeting someone.

This garage was perfect for clandestine meetings. It was an old garage with only passable lighting, no security guards, an automated ticket dispensing system and an automated payment system for those with cash. The limited human staff along with the security cameras that were only installed at the elevators made this a perfect covert meeting spot. Garrett waited for his contact to arrive, and as he sat there in his car waiting, he thought about how this had all started.

His thoughts took him back to the time he had been in the FBI for just three years working background checks, minor fraud cases but nothing of any significance and certainly nothing that would make anyone in the chain-of-command notice him. He and his partner had just completed conducting what seemed to have been his hundredth clearance investigation where they had asked fifty questions that were intended to trip the interviewee into providing damaging information on the applicant. Just like the ninety-nine other sessions, their questions had failed to yield any negative information. They had just left the residence of the subject's mother when they received an all-points call for assistance. A major bank robber, who had held-up fifteen banks in three states and killed four people in the process, had been reported in a high-rise apartment complex just two miles down the road. When they arrived on scene, there were ten unmarked FBI cars with eighteen officers who had already made their plan of attack, and it didn't include him and his rookie partner. The two of them were dispatched to provide backup of two other senior agents, a male and female team, in the back alley of the facility. The senior agents' job was to catch the suspect if he exited the rear of the building, and Garrett and his partner were to sit in the car in case the senior team requested help.

They were in position only a few moments when the back door of the building burst open and the suspect, gun in hand, surprised the two agents who were just walking to their positions on either side of the door. In an instant, the suspect struck the female agent across the head with his pistol, and she went down hard on the concrete roadway. The male agent drew his service pistol, but the suspect shot him in the head before the agent even cleared his weapon from his holster. The suspect paused to look at the female agent, who was dazed and struggling to get to her feet. She was attempting to get her service pistol, but she was so dazed she couldn't even control her legs enough to stand.

As Garrett saw the suspect move on the female agent he and his partner exited their car, drew their weapons and moved quickly towards the suspect yelling, "FBI. Drop your weapon." The suspect had already seen the two approaching and rather than kill the female agent he grabbed her, pulled her to her feet and used her as a shield telling them both to drop their weapons or he would "blow her pretty blond hair all over the wall."

Garrett had his weapon pointed at the suspect in just the exact position he had learned at the FBI Academy. He tried to focus on the suspect, who was a big man well over 230 pounds, standing six feet two, and at least seventy pounds heavier and six inches taller than his captive who now had no hope of overpowering the larger suspect. From thirty yards away Garrett focused on the suspect's head, which was the only exposed portion of his body as the suspect had his left arm around the female agent's throat, pulling her into his chest and his right had his pistol at her temple. Sweat was pouring down the suspect's face from what must have been a dash down many flights of stairs and as the sweat got into his eyes, it was making his vision difficult. Garrett knew the other agents must have heard the shot; he also knew that all he had to do was to hold the suspect at bay for just a few more seconds and a horde of FBI Agents would surround the suspect.

All he needed was another thirty seconds and he would get past this crisis. The suspect must have realized this also and he again yelled for the two agents to drop their weapons. The rookie agent started to lower his pistol and in that instant the suspect moved his weapon away from the female hostage who dropped down slightly from the loosening of the large man's grip. The suspect fired quickly at the rookie agent striking him in his protective vest. The non-fatal injury spun him around and knocked him off his feet.

The suspect started to turn to the left to engage Garrett, but before he could squeeze off that next round, a bullet slammed into the suspect's head. It entered right above his nose and made a neat round entry wound; then penetrated through the brain getting wider as it smashed through the hard skull, crushing it, and creating sharp fragments that exploded through his brain ripping the brain tissue as it went. The now wider, mushroom shaped bullet exited the back of the suspect's head leaving a hole the size of a lemon, or perhaps the size of a small woman's fist, like the one whose life he had just held in his hands. The suspect's body fell straight back and his lifeless body made a sickening thud as it struck the concrete driveway.

Garrett moved quickly to the suspect's position, and as if he were reading directly from the FBI instruction manual that he had studied so well at the academy, he secured the suspect's weapon then holstered his own. When he turned to attend to the fallen female agent, he saw the other agents who had come around from the front of the building just in time to see his incredible shot.

For months he was the talk of the office, and to this day, he is still introduced as the man who threaded the needle from thirty yards in what had become office folklore. He had received a commendation for his actions. Right after that he moved into major casework where he felt the exhilaration of putting away the real bad guys on a very routine basis. Six-months later, he got an un-requested transfer to a special division investigating spy operations based in Germany where he spent the most frustrating eighteen months of his life. Every time he got close to capturing the suspect or putting an end to a spy network, they slipped across the border or the host country failed to prosecute.

His morale had sunk to a very low point before he met Luby. Garrett was frustrated with the process that let the bad guys get away and he was considering leaving the Bureau. He was at the Headquarters in D.C., in the very same parking garage he now stood, when Luby suddenly appeared at his car door. Luby was head of a special operations group. Garrett knew of him by reputation only, just about everyone did, and he was known for getting the job done. He was also known to be highly committed to the cause of the Bureau. Some thought he was beyond committed; fanatical was more the case. He was revered by the head brass and rank-and-file alike for his success but there was some scuttlebutt about his methods and especially how a number of his targets came to meet their end by sudden accident, or simply disappeared. In those cases, the official word was always death was most likely caused by rival groups. However, the word in the office was that he led a very special group that enjoyed a certain level of freedom of operations that no others enjoyed. Either way he knew this was a man who got things done. When Luby asked if he wanted to join his group, Garrett didn't have to think about it and accepted before Luby had even finished explaining the secret nature of the organization.

That was five years ago. As he stood there waiting he thought of how it had gone. How he had moved, and moved quickly, from operations by the book to this, success at any cost, including murder or 'removal from the grid' as Luby called it. It hadn't been a month after Garrett joined that group that he found that there was an even smaller sub group in the organization, NECO, whose members were certainly unknown to the FBI brass and even within Luby's own special operations group. Even within NECO itself, the participants were not known to each other unless they worked together on a job. In the five years since he had joined the team, he had worked with just eight others. Although he had been appointed by Luby to communicate with the Committee, he had never met them nor knew who they were. All he knew is that they gave Luby missions that NECO executed. Garrett didn't know who the committee members were, but he suspected they were all senior FBI men or members of the government. Otherwise the group could not have continued all these years, which apparently had been a considerable time period, possibly since the late 1950's or 1960s. He did know one thing about the Committee and Luby, they were all fanatical about protecting the United States.

As he stood by the door of his car with his keys in his hand waiting, he heard an engine come to life. He looked up and saw a familiar black Lexus as it moved slowly from the far end of the floor and stopped by his car. He walked out to the Lexus as the driver's window opened and revealed Luby behind the wheel.

"It's done, Sir," Garrett said to the man in the car.

"When?" came Luby's reply.

"Early this morning."

"Good. How much did this cost us?"

"Fifty thousand." He paused and then added, "Unless he gets fingered for it and then it goes up to a hundred, which he wants given to his wife or he talks."

"That's unacceptable. Have you arranged to take him off the grid?"

"Yes. A second man on the inside will take him out as soon as the hitter returns to the general population." He stared at Luby who looked back at him through his sunglass covered eyes.

"How much will that cost us?"

"Ten grand."

"And the original fifty?"

"It was placed in a post office box and his wife was sent the combination."

"Interesting. What was in the box?"

"Twenty grand, as you instructed."

"Where's the rest?

"I still have it."

"Does the committee know any of this?"

"Just that we paid fifty to the first hitter."

"Put the rest of the money in the same safe deposit box as last time. You still have the second key?"

"Yes," Garrett replied.

"So what's the status on the wife?"

"Lee called in earlier. She lives in Baltimore and drove down last night, picked up the money from the box here in D.C., and then drove without stopping straight to Atlantic City where she went directly to the Hilton Casino. He couldn't follow her, too many cameras."

"Make sure the lady is taken off the grid before she returns to Baltimore. I don't want any more loose ends. Got it?"

Garrett replied just one word, "Yeah." Luby had already started to raise the car door window and drive away leaving no time for discussion of any kind. Garrett was thinking about the mission as he watched the car go down the ramp. He knew the target and the hitter had to go; both were scum so what did it matter? He didn't like having to take the wife 'off the grid'; her only crime was to be the wife of a scumbag criminal. He snapped back to reality and then looked to make sure no one was around; he would hate to have to clean up another loose end.

Chapter 4

The Business of Data

Sam had reported to IdentityPoint on Tuesday morning and processed in through the Human Resource (H/R) department, which would make sense to any casual observer, as the chief of the department was the project sponsor. It would be normal for a new Project Manager to spend a few hours on the first day with the sponsor making sure the project manager understood the goals and objectives of the project. Sam knew exactly what his objectives were in regards to this H/R software project. The first objective was to make sure not too much happened for two to four weeks, so when he accomplished his second objective, getting fired by Ms. Sherron Watkins, she would be able to save face, continue with the project and none would be the wiser as to Sam's real purpose at IdentityPoint.

Sam and Ms. Watkins had spent several hours going over the key players, who to avoid and who could be counted on to assist him. Sam was going to need access to some data systems, and not all of them would be related to the new H/R system. Ms. Watkins gave him two lists; one of the people that could be trusted and could assist him in the data search, and a second list of those in the company he definitely could not trust. The first list was much shorter.

Sam had to be cautious of drawing attention to himself and most importantly not causing any fallout for Ms. Watkins even after he had departed. With or without finding the answers to her questions, it could never be known that he had come here at her invitation to investigate her own company; that certainly would be the end of her career as an executive at IdentityPoint and possibly at any other corporation.

After meeting with Ms. Watkins most of the morning, he spent the rest of the day familiarizing himself with his environment including his office, the computer he had been given, the facilities, and the people. He spent most of the afternoon at the cafeteria, walking the halls and visiting work places just so he could get a feel for the surroundings. He had finished the first day by making appointments with support personnel to turn on his system access and to arrange training for certain applications.

Wednesday 0910 hours, October 12

It was the morning of his second day on site, and Sam sat in his new office and waited for the instructor to show up. Finally, ten minutes after the class was supposed to start two engineers came in.

"Hey, you Sam Cohen?" The first man asked as he entered the room and stopped at the front of Sam's desk.

"Yes, hello. I'm Sam. You must be Guy Doud."

"No. I'm Thomas Fleming. He's Guy." The first man said as he pointed to the smaller of the two men, who was a head again smaller and a good fifty pounds lighter. He wore black rimmed glasses with small lenses that were popular in the 1970's. He had light brown hair that was cut in such a manner that it looked like it never had to be combed, as it was short and had no curl or wave nor any real length. He wore black khaki pants and a short-sleeved shirt that buttoned down the front with a pocket on his left side. Sam took one look at him and thought all he needed was a plastic pocket protector and he could have been the photo used to illustrate the word *geek* in the dictionary.

Fleming was altogether different from his cohort. He was larger, close to six feet tall, heavy, but not fat, and dressed very stylish in the latest men's fashion. His hair had obviously been done at a salon and was cut in such a way that it was slightly wild by design, sticking up across the top from a good application of styling gel. He also wore glasses, but they were ultra lightweight silver frames that Sam knew cost a small fortune. He extended his hand, greeted Sam as did Doud, and then they both sat down.

"Well, as you may know I am here to put together the requirements document and then develop the project plan for the Human Resource project." Sam opened his notebook and tried to be as professional as possible. He needed to show some progress in the development of this project to avoid any suspicion from those around him. Sam went over the goals of the project and how the system would work and then he got into the real reason for their visit. He needed training on the use of some of the company's personal data systems.

"Well, that could take some time; there are a bunch of them," Fleming said. He looked over at Doud for concurrence, which he got as if on cue. "Let me show you the main system for that type of inquiry, its called PeopleFinder." He stood as he spoke and walked around the desk behind Sam to where the workstation sat. Sam had already gotten up to make room for Fleming who sat down without a word, launched Explorer on his PC, and then as soon as it was on screen he entered the URL for the website and pressed the Enter key.

"All you have to do is enter your user name and password and hit return." He entered his and another screen quickly took its place. "Then you select the block 'Why you are asking for the report,' click any reason and then press Enter again."

Sam was watching what Fleming was doing and he had seen that the screen had a list of ten different reasons for the inquiry. "What about that previous screen? What do I select?"

"Just select this one." He pointed to the selection that read, 'Testing and System Verification' that was the last one on the list.

"Okay testing," Sam echoed.

"But it doesn't really matter which one you select this is a 'Self Verifying' system." Fleming said as he clicked the Return button and waited.

"Self verifying?" Sam asked.

Fleming looked up at Sam who was standing behind him and to his left as he worked. "Yeah. The application relies on the user to tell what he or she is using the system for. We don't check it. Whatever the user says is what is recorded."

Sam didn't quite understand the significance of the last statement, and Fleming could see it by the blank stare on Sam's face. "Look here." Fleming pointed to one of the other selections. "This one says, For Pre-employment Purposes. Say a company gets an account with us for the purpose of doing pre-employment background checks for prospective employees. They send IdentityPoint an application to get to our data and state that they need it for pre-employment checks. We give them an account. Then when they log on they tell us why they are looking at someone's record."

"For Pre-Employment," Sam responded.

"Yes," Fleming echoed.

Sam looked at Fleming, then the screen, and then back at Fleming. Sam started to ask, "What if the person is not doing it for pre-employment purposes, say it's for..." Sam hesitated in completing the sentence. He didn't want to provide the real reason he was asking the question and arouse suspicion in his motives. He was just going to respond, 'just fooling around,' when Fleming jumped in.

"He's spying on someone."

Relieved he had not had to suggest his real reason, or provide some sophomoric response, Sam quickly agreed. "Yes. How about that?"

Fleming looked to Doud and shrugged his shoulders. "We wouldn't know. He signed a paper saying it would always be for Pre-employment. So to us it's always for Pre-employment purposes." Fleming turned back to the system and continued. "Besides, no one ever checks anyway."

Fleming took the mouse and set up the screen to make it easier to train Sam. "You can see that there are numerous ways to seek information. You can enter the social security number, or the full name, or a combination of name and address, or name and birth date; it can be either full name or partial name." Fleming selected then de-selected the choices to show Sam how the system worked. "So who should we check?" Fleming looked over his shoulder at Sam. "You? You want to see your report?"

Sam almost panicked knowing that using Sam Cohen could possibly blow his whole cover. "No, no. Use a name you always use. That way you will be familiar with it, and can explain things easier."

Sam looked at the silent Doud for concurrence, who then made his first utterance. "Makes sense, Tom."

"Okay," Fleming said and almost without pausing entered the subject's name, letter-by-letter until the name 'Don Orrick' was on the screen.

"Why that name?" Sam said as he watched the screen for results.

"Well three reasons. He was a close friend of one of the guys here, and he knew Orrick's data. Second, he's dead so the data doesn't change, or at least it shouldn't. And third, and most important, oddly enough there is only one Don Orrick in the entire database and it makes the analysis easier."

Sam did not respond but watched as the screen filled with data, and then as Fleming scrolled though the pages.

"Damn. Look at all that data." Sam said as Fleming scrolled through page after page of data.

"Yep. Impressive isn't it," Fleming said with some pride of authorship. "Name, aliases, SSNs, addresses, Real Property records, deeds, a list of relatives, businesses he owned or was a part of, cars he owned, phone numbers he had, and even a list of neighbors in case you want to call them for additional info."

"Holy crap!" Sam forgot to control his emotions for a moment. "Sorry," Sam apologized to both Fleming and Doud.

"No, I think Holy Crap is in order," Fleming replied as he smiled and returned to scrolling the data. Nineteen pages of data on a man who has been dead for ten years. You should see an average report, it's huge!"

Doud looked at Sam and nodded in silent agreement.

"This report is clean. It only has data from this guy because his name is unique and no one has used his social but him. Some reports have all kinds of crap in them. Wait until you see a regular report, one that included like names or like addresses. Or a simple transposed social security number; then a link is formed to another person's data and bam, you got a ton of stuff."

Sam chatted with the two men for a few more minutes; then as they left, he thanked them for the lesson. Once they departed, Sam sat at the desk and pondered the power of the system he had just seen. The volume of data was impressive for sure but what surprised him the most was all the associated data that came with the report: the relatives, the neighbors, the company associations, even the cars of the companies. It was easy to see why the investigative world loved these systems.

Sam strummed his desk with his pencil and thought of another case; the case from Chicago, Dana, the POWs and Ream. He pondered how Ream had refused to speak of the graves, how many were German POWs who died in captivity, and how many were really American GIs and not the Germans the world had believed they were. It was unfinished business and as hard as Sam tried to keep it from his mind, it was always there, haunting him. He looked at the screen and the blinking cursor. It almost seemed to call to him to enter the name. He knew better. He knew he shouldn't mix the two cases, and he had no idea who was looking at his inquiries, whether or not they got audited for appropriateness or not. If they were and if he started to make inquiries, how would he justify them? He decided it was worth the risk. He placed his hands on the keyboard and typed in the last name, R – E – A – M. Then moved the cursor to first name field and entered M – I – C – H – A – E – L, then waited. In an instant, the screen filled with data.

"Damn that was easy," Sam said aloud.

Sam scrolled down from section to section then decided to print the report. He selected the 'Print the Report' option and the pages started to pop out of his little HP DeskJet printer. Sam took the first page off the printer as if it were a fragile document, ready to disintegrate with just the wrong touch. He held the document with two fingers then gently swung the page around so he could read it. He gasped as he saw the name, Michael Ream, almost as if it were not the name he had entered nor expected. As he looked over the first page of the report, the printer continued with its scheduled job and page after page was pushed into the output tray. Sam watched in amazement as the printing finally stopped.

"Thirty pages! Christ, what do they have in there?" Sam looked at the application, which was still on the screen and spoke to it like it could hear his words. He took the report and scanned the pages. It had his name, a space for aliases that was empty of any entries, current address, past addresses, possible relatives, which was empty, neighbors, automobiles, and finally real property. This was too much to digest here in the office and besides he had a training session scheduled at 1030 hours.

0910 hours, Stateville Correctional Center Joliet, Illinois

They had shut down the prison for hours looking for the weapon and the hitter, but he had disposed of the shiv thirty seconds after the hit and joined a dozen other inmates, who slipped into the library before the prison was locked down. They sat around for three hours while the guards looked, questioned, and then looked some more. Finally, they reopened the cafeteria and he joined the other hundred inmates in his group for a semi-cold and very late breakfast.

He was in the last year of an eight-year sentence for a second conviction for extortion and assault and battery. The parole board had given him the formality of appearing before the board, but he didn't even bother presenting himself. He was a pig; they knew it, and he did too. At forty-three, he had already done 20 years in jails. At 18, he got two years in county for a brutal assault on his high school girlfriend, who wouldn't perform certain demanded sexual acts for him as he desired. At 22, he was convicted of manslaughter and did eight years of a ten-year sentence in state prison.

He even did two years in Kentucky on a breaking and entering charge, a crime which he did not commit. He was at that time on the run from the Pennsylvania Police for murder and they had almost caught him twice already. When a young cop pulled him over for speeding in Kentucky, the cop thought he was another man, who he did resemble and who was wanted for simple assault. When faced with the alternative of spending a short tour in a minimum-security facility or admitting who he really was and facing a murder charge in Pennsylvania, he took the two years minimum security. By the time he got out, the Pennsylvania authorities had stopped looking for him. Including yesterday's stabbing victim, he had successfully killed seven people, two in prison, and he was feeling very superior.

As he passed through the chow line, he was given an extra bowl of cheese grits, for which he paid ten bucks a month to the cook. It was double the price for unauthorized seconds but they were worth it to him. He was northern born and the thought of eating grits was as foreign to him as life without boiled peanuts to a southerner. But he had stayed at a Bed and Breakfast once called the *Main Street Inn* in Highlands, North Carolina and the cook there made these cheese grits that were to die for. Ever since then he had them wherever and whenever he could.

He ate the first bowl, the one containing the potassium chloride, before he ate anything else. Then he started on his breakfast of eggs, bacon and toast, saving the second bowl of grits as a desert of sorts. He ate every bit of each bowl, even using the toast to clean out the last few morsels of the grits. Three minutes later, even before he had finished his eggs, the fat man's heart was already pounding from the effects of the drug. Two minutes after that as he was finishing his second bowl of grits, he was sweating like a horse and his heart rate was already over 150 beats per minute. Ten minutes later, as he was depositing his dishes at the clean-up area, he was feeling faint and his heart was around 220 beats per minute. He thought it was just indigestion. Five minutes after that, while he was jogging down the steps to his workplace in the prison laundry, his heart exploded.

An hour later, the prison administration staff was calling his wife in Baltimore to inform her that her overweight husband had just died of a heart attack.

There was no answer at her residence.

1030 hours, IdentityPoint

One of the specifications for the H/R system that Sam was supposed to be building for IdentityPoint was that the system had to recognize when a SSN was suspect. Sam had no expertise on the subject and after asking around found that the expert in the area was George Bailey. Bailey, 'the old timer' as he was called, had been with the company since it had broken off from the parent company and was part of the team that turned a money losing group into a billion dollar Public Records machine. Sam had called Bailey, explained what he was doing, what he needed. Bailey was more than helpful, and agreed to meet with him the same day. Being the ex-military man that he was, Sam was a stickler about being on time; so he had already reconnoitered Bailey's office location and knew exactly what time he had to leave his own office to be on time at Bailey's. With the precision of a Swiss watch, Sam arrived at Bailey's office, knocked on the doorframe of the open door, and waited to be acknowledged. An older man, perhaps in his late fifties, sitting behind a desk with pencil in hand working on some papers, looked up when he heard the knock.

"Hi. I'm Sam Cohen; I called about getting some tutoring on the Social Security Number system."

The man stood up from behind the desk and prepared to greet Sam. He was a thin man, not sickly at all, just thin and trim. His hair had thinned many years before, and he was bald in the front all the way to the middle of his head. He wore large round glasses with amber colored frames, and he was dressed in khaki pants and a long sleeved checked shirt that was buttoned all the way to the top. Sam thought that for a man nearly sixty he was looking fit.

"Hello there, I'm George Bailey," came a warm and friendly greeting.

"Good to meet you," Sam responded as he extended his hand in greeting. "Thanks for making the time for me."

With a beaming smile and bright eyes sparkled with enthusiasm, he seemed more like a young technology geek just getting in the business than a man on the near edge of retirement.

"Have a seat Sam, and I'll see what I can do for you."

Sam took a seat and looked around the room, which was very sparsely decorated. A picture of a lady that Sam assumed was the man's wife and a small poster on the wall were the only personal trappings in the room other than some stress relieving squeeze balls that seemed to be the advertising gimmick of the year. The poster was of the movie, 'It's a Wonderful Life'. Sam looked at the poster and thought of the character in the movie, then said aloud, "George Bailey," Sam pointed to the poster and to George.

He smiled, "Oh yes, it is a wonderful life young man."

Sam instantly felt at ease with this man of many years. His open, friendly manner immediately made a person feel comfortable and Sam could already see many similarities between Jimmy Stewart's character and this kindly man.

George pulled out a reference book and opened it in front of Sam. "This can be a little confusing. Just let me know when I don't make sense."

"Okay, will do," Sam said. He thought how most people would have said 'tell me if you don't understand' not throw it back on himself, as if it were his fault that he didn't explain it properly, not Sam's for failing to pay attention property. Sam thought it said a lot about this man.

George started in. "The SSN is composed of nine numbers. The first three are called the Area number; they start at 001 and go to 999. Now there are some exceptions for things that are called Railroad numbers and Pocket numbers but those are minor; what is important is that these Area numbers are assigned to states." He pointed to the page and the first set of numbers. "See here. The numbers 001 to 003 are assigned to New Hampshire."

Sam looked at the page and saw how the numbers had been assigned in groups to all the states in the union, including American possessions of Puerto Rico and Guam.

"Now the next two numbers are the Group numbers. Each Area number has a complete set of Group numbers from 01 to 99." George paused and looked at Sam. "Got that?"

Sam just nodded in concurrence.

"Now here is a weird part. For some reason the numbers are not issued in sequence, like 01, 02, and 03 and so on, and I really don't know why."

Sam looked at the book and the notes at the top of the page. "So they issue the numbers 01 to 09 first, but only the odd numbers?"

"Yes," George responded. "Then even numbers 10 through 98. Then they go back to even numbers 02 through 08, and finally 11 through 99. Weird, huh?"

"Very," Sam agreed.

Now the last part of the number, the sequence number 0001 through 9999." George paused. "There is one more thing."

"What's that?" Sam asked as he looked thought the reference book.

"The state issues from a few Area numbers at the same time." George looked at Sam as his student pondered that last bit information.

"It's really not hard," George added as he turned the book to the page on New Hampshire. "Look here." He pointed to the book. "See on the left side of this matrix New Hampshire has issued 001, 002 and

003 Area Codes. At the top of the page there are years." He pointed to a row of numbers running horizontally across the top of the page."

"Got it." Sam said.

"Now if we pick a year, say 1952, and if you look at the three Area numbers they all say 26. This means that they issued SSNs with Group numbers 26. Get it?"

"No problem," Sam said as he looked more intently at the book.

"Okay, hold on Sam. Now look at 1953." He pointed to the numbers in the columns for each Area Number. "The number for 002 and 003 were still 26. This means that they still were only issuing numbers from the Group series 26. But if you look at Area number 001 you can see the number 28."

"I see that," Sam said.

"This means that for Area number 001 they finished issuing Group number 26 and started issuing 28 in that year; you just don't know from this reference book exactly which sequence numbers were issued."

Sam studied the book and then said, "So it is likely that the number 001-26-9999, which is the last number in the series, was issued in 1953."

"Correct, Sam." George smiled like a teacher whose student just provided the right answer to a question, a question the student would have previously thought too hard for him to know.

Sam thought a second and added, "So looking at Massachusetts, for Area number 010, that the Group number 32 was issued in 1957, 1958, and 1959. And since they show the number 34 in the column for 1960, this means they issued 001-32 in the years 1957 through 1959 and the next number, 34, began in 1959 and continued in 1960, we just don't know the sequence number. Right?" Sam pointed to the numbers and waited for the response.

"That it does Sam."

"So if I were to see the number say, 010-32-1000, and the date of birth of the person was, say 1962, and since 32 stopped being issued in 1959 it would be a bogus number," Sam asked.

"Well close, Sam. It is a good number, but what it indicates is fraud since the issue date of the number is before the person's birth date."

"Of course," Sam said as he nodded his head.

"But the reverse is not true." George was quick to add.

"How's that George?"

"Because a person can get a new SSN, say if his original one was compromised, or in the case of an immigrant."

"Understood," Sam was quick to respond.

"Since they only issue from the open set of numbers, whatever they are, a 50 year-old can have a 20-year old Social, but a 20-year old cannot have a 50 year-old social."

Sam looked at the book and then at George. "So what was so confusing about that?" They both laughed. "I owe you a cup of coffee, George." Sam stood, extended his hand to George who stood, and shook his hand.

"Come on, I'll buy you a cup in the cafeteria."

"You know the coffee is free there Sam." George said as they stated out of the office.

"All the better," Sam laughed.

1030 hours, Atlantic City, New Jersey.

She spent two days and three nights gambling, never leaving the hotel casino. As far as gambling went, she had done fairly well playing Blackjack and the slots. She was up almost $1,200 when she hit a bad streak at the Blackjack table. The loss was acceptable and she knew her husband would expect most of the money to be available when he got out of prison. If it wasn't, she knew there would be consequences. She had checked out of the hotel and had been driving back to Baltimore for the last hour. She needed to use the rest room, and she had needed it for the last twenty minutes. She finally spied a rest area and pulled in. There wasn't another car in the parking lot.

- - - - - - - - - - - - - < > - - - - - - - - - - - - - - - -

The car he had been following pulled into the rest area; he slowed his car, so that the driver would not see him enter the rest area behind her. He had been hanging around the Atlanta City hotel when he got a call and a job from his government contact; it was a simple job with a big payoff. All he knew was her car license number and that she had cash. His job was to make sure she didn't get to Baltimore, and as payment everything she carried was his. He watched her park the car and walk quickly into the rest room. He then parked his car and, after looking around to make sure he was alone, followed the path she took to the rest room.

- - - - - - - - - - - - - < > - - - - - - - - - - - - - - - -

She had just finished washing her hands, checking her make-up in the restroom mirror and had taken two steps out of the ladies room door in route to her car when she was grabbed from behind. There was a hand over her mouth and her instinctive reaction to scream resulted in no sounds at all. She felt the sharp pain as her assailant shoved an eight-inch kitchen knife into her side then twisted it. Her eyes rolled in her head as the knife was withdrawn, and her life began to run out through the jagged wound. She dropped her purse. She fell to the ground in total disbelief of what was happening. Pushing herself up on her elbows, she saw a man running away from her with her purse, and reached out her hand in an unanswered plea for help. Unable to speak, she crawled ten feet towards the street in search of help, and then collapsed on the filthy pavement.

1345 hours, IdentityPoint

Sitting at his terminal in his temporary office at IdentityPoint, Sam was, for all those who happened by, diligently working on the H/R system which he was supposedly hired to create. His industrious efforts at the keyboard however were his continued investigations into any company or anyone whose name appeared even vaguely connected to the acquisitions reports Bob had provided.

Having substituted four cups of coffee for a skipped breakfast, Sam was in dire need of settling the coffee monster in his stomach, which was now not only making audible sounds but was giving him minor discomfort. Many of the employees left the building for lunch, either to escape the 'hospital food' as so many called it, or they were seeking out a variety from the numerous restaurants and other fast food places that the city had to offer. But not Sam, he loved institutional type food, and given the choice between a Caesar salad at good restaurant, a sandwich at Subway, a hamburger at McDonalds, or a tray full of meat and potatoes from the mess hall, he'd take the mess hall chow in a New York minute every time.

He signed off from his computer and headed for the cafeteria. Two minutes later, he was in line with tray in hand looking down the lunch line in the first serving area with the selection of entrees and vegetables. There were two other meal sections further down the line, a short order grill where one could get hotdogs, hamburgers and other fast food type meals, and beyond that was a large salad bar. But Sam didn't need to explore what specials had been put out today, as he was already eyeing the meatloaf.

Sam paid the cashier, and not looking for anyone in particular, but rather just an empty table, he proceeded into the dining area.

"Sam," came a familiar voice from in front of him. Sam looked towards the sound of the greeting and saw George Bailey facing him and sitting at a four-person table. Also at the table was a man with his back to Sam whom he did not recognize.

"Hi there George," Sam said as he walked up to the table.

"Why don't you join us?" George motioned to Sam to take the open seat to his left. "Looks like you got a lunch and dinner. A little hungry are you?"

As he sat down, Sam looked at his tray of meatloaf, mashed potatoes, green beans, macaroni and cheese, apple pie and a large ice tea. "I skipped breakfast."

"You'd think after twenty years of army mess hall food you'd be out there trying out all the new stuff." George paused for a second then continued on. "Like maybe sushi, or Salad bars."

"I guess I am just used to this stuff."

"You military?" The other man at the table spoke up.

"Retired."

"Sam, I'd like you to meet Mr. Harvey Nichols, he's the COO here."

Sam stuck his hand out to the man, "Pleased to meet you."

"It's my pleasure, especially to meet another comrade in arms." The man smiled at Sam and then at George with one of those over done looks like the politician would have when he was working the crowd. "So what service?"

"Army sir," Sam replied as he took a bite of meatloaf. He closed his eyes and smacked his lips like he had just tasted an exquisite steak or desert. "Damn I love this chow."

"Where did you serve?" Nichols continued.

"All over. Did my time at Benning, Bragg, couple tours in Europe, time in Virginia, Chicago, D.C., various other place; typical stuff." Sam took another bite, "You said comrade in arms. You military also?"

"Army, Special Forces all the way." Nichols smiled again and not so quietly banged the table with his hand in a show of some bravado of sorts. "You serve in Nam?"

"No sir, I was in college at the time. Didn't come on active duty until seventy-four."

"Too bad, it was a great time for us. What was your rank?"

"Major," Sam said as he thought about Nichols's last comment. He had served with hundreds of soldiers who had fought there and those few that would ever speak of it never referred to it as a 'great time.'

"Well Major, I made Colonel, and damn proud of it." Nichols looked smugly at Sam and then at George as if to get some concurrence from both that he was a man to be both respected and admired. "I served in '68 and '69. Writing about my experience too, I've called it, "The Kill Zone."

"I must get a copy." Sam did not like where this conversation was headed. He had served in his share of engagements in the undeclared operations over the past twenty years, but he didn't like talking about them or Viet Nam, and he was uncomfortable with those that did.

"Not out yet, still with the publisher." Nichols quickly moved past the subject of the book. "I enjoy talking with fellow soldiers. The civilians here just don't understand who we are and what we do."

"I can understand that," Sam offered. "So you are the Chief Operating Officer; an exciting job I'll bet. Must keep you very busy"

"Yes, I have to direct operations, control the budget, and generally run the show, but it's nothing like combat." Nichols leaned forward to Sam. "It doesn't have the finality to it, there's something about making life and death decisions. I can't expect them to understand that, it's something only a soldier can understand. Not knowing if you are going to live through the day makes it more intense, more real, more invigorating. Don't you agree, Major?"

"Well, I think that any day no one is shooting at me is a good day. And please call me Sam," Sam said and looked to George for assistance with his attempt to lower the testosterone level of the conversation.

"A man like you can appreciate what I mean. I can honestly say they were the best years of my life. I served with the best, real men, real soldiers, like my Sergeant Robert Cole."

Sam was trying not to be impolite to the second ranking officer of the company, but he was hungry so he continued to eat while Nichols rattled on. But when he heard the name, he stopped and looked up. "Did you say Robert Cole?"

"Yes I did. Did you know him?"

"I met him at a ceremony at the Infantry school. One hell of a soldier," Sam said.

"Yes sir. I served with him during Tet, my special ops team was attached to his unit when it was hit by the VC. Yes sir I can tell you it was hell." Nichols related how the firebase had been attacked, had rebuked numerous assaults, and how his team had gone out beyond the wire to interrupt the enemy and disrupt their operations by taking out selected targets by 'silent means.' He made a jab in the air as if he had a knife in his hand and he was thrusting it into someone.

Sam glanced over to George who had the look of someone who had heard this before, too many times before.

"Yes sir. We sure were a team Cole and I. Me in the bush and him in the firebase." Sam's attempt to ignore the topic had no effect on Nichols who continued to relate the events of his glory days. We crawled around that jungle for a week. It was a week of glory. Surely killed our share of gooks I can tell you that. You know Cole won the Silver Star for what we did there." Nichols made a fist and punched into the air like a fighter shadowboxing, "Damn I miss it."

Sam made an effort at a smile of agreement but made no comment.

"Well major it was a pleasure to meet you." Nichols rose from his chair, and extended his hand to Sam. Sam rose and shook his hand.

"Pleasure to have met you sir," Sam respectfully said.

Nichols brought his hand almost to his forehead and gave Sam a modified salute, turned and left. Sam sat down but stared at Nichols as he exited the cafeteria, then looked at George.

"What the hell was that all about?" Sam said as quietly as possible as so not to arose those sitting at a nearby table.

"That was *Colonel* Nichols."

Sam shook his head, "And you had to invite me to sit down, *why?*" Sam shook his finger at George. "And what was he doing in here anyway?"

"He likes to come down and mix with *troops* every once in a while. I've heard the same stuff, his 'week of glory,' God knows how many times."

"A week of glory," Sam quietly repeated as he stared in the direction of Nichols's departure.

"What's up, Sam?" George asked as Sam continued to stare into the empty hallway long after Nichols had left.

"Sorry, George, nothing." Sam went back to his meal.

Chapter 5

Thursday, October 13

Thursday, October 13, 0730 hours, IdentityPoint

"How's the French Toast?" Bob said to Tammy as he walked up to her table in the IdentityPoint cafeteria.

She looked up from her plate and the morning edition of the Atlanta Journal Constitution she had been reading to see Bob standing there smiling like a young smitten schoolboy. "Very good, Bob." Bob just stood there unable to find any words to say; as Tammy continued to look up waiting for Bob to reply. It wasn't that Bob couldn't hold down a conversation; it was that he was very self-conscious about being small, and that made it difficult for him to talk to women.

After a few moments of silence Tammy finally took the lead, "Are you going to sit down?" Bob looked around at the rest of the tables in the room, most of which were empty. He made a jerky motion as if nodding to Tammy that he was going to sit somewhere and acknowledging her question at the same time.

"I meant, do you wish to sit here?" She motioned to the chair directly across from her.

Although Bob tried to be cool and not seem too anxious, he almost dropped his tray trying to sit down. He fumbled to pull the chair out and sit. He went to put the tray on the table, but it was still six inches

51

off the surface when he let go. When it hit with a whack, the glass of orange juice spilled a little on the tray. He finally successfully sat down, and he looked around to see a few people who were at the nearby tables were looking at this awkward scene.

Bob sat for a second, sighed a little breath and looked sheepishly at Tammy.

"Well, that went well. Much better than I thought it would," Bob said.

Tammy giggled a little girl laugh, and Bob smiled and instantly felt more relaxed.

They chatted together for nearly thirty minutes about the news, the weather, Bob's job at IdentityPoint and hers, then what they liked to do away from work, which is when Tammy talked about her little four-year-old daughter. Bob loved that she felt comfortable to share with him stories of her daughter and he could see that her daughter was her whole life. Tammy didn't speak of her ex-husband and Bob was glad she didn't.

When the topic of conversation rolled around to work and what they had to do today, Bob told her that he was trying to help Sam Cohen, who was in desperate need of someone that knew a lot about the company data systems.

"Well, the best person to talk with is the architect of all these systems, but he has left the company." She stopped and had a sip of her cold coffee; which she dared not leave to refill for fear Bob would take it as a sign that she wanted the conversation to end, and he would run away. "It's very sad."

"How's that?"

She looked at Bob then slightly to her left and right as if she did not want anyone to hear her speaking. "They say he left on his own but it's not true. They let him go because an FBI man died and they said he was at fault."

Bob perked up at that, "Why was that?"

She leaned forward so as to ensure only Bob could hear. "They say he designed some system to protect them, the FBI people, it had to do with identities or something. He was a wiz at that stuff you know. Anyway, I heard it had to do with one name he failed to put on a watch list system and the FBI man was killed."

"Killed? How?" Bob was now in his detective mode, confident, thinking and anxious to know more.

"That's all I know. You might ask George Bailey. They used to work together on the identity systems," Tammy said as she noticed the time on the clock on the wall. "Look at the time, I really have to go."

"Oh, so sorry, I did not mean to pry."

Tammy stood up and picked up her tray. "What? Oh, no. That's not it at all, I am late for work."

"Bob looked at his watch. "Oh, okay. Thanks."

Tammy started to move away, stepped around the side of the table toward the tray turn in area and towards Bob. "It would be alright if you wanted to ask me."

"Ask you? About what? About the Architect?" Bob looked confused.

Tammy smiled, "Not the Architect. About asking me out."

Bob smiled and said nervously, "Sure, yes. That would be good."

"Yes, you know you can ask, or are you asking me?"

Bob was now totally befuddled and unprepared to handle the opportunity. He thought of asking her to dinner or a movie next weekend but "Yes. Yes," was all that came out.

"Good." Tammy smiled at how nervous Bob was. "So you are asking me out for?" She paused for Bob to fill in the day, which he did not so she added, "For the concert next Thursday in the park downtown?"

"Yes, I am. The concert," Bob echoed.

"Well, that would be perfect," Tammy said. "I already have a sitter for the night."

"Good. That's good," Bob struggled to find any words at all.

"We can leave right from work," Tammy added.

"Yes, right from work," Bob repeated.

"If the weather is good, would you mind if I drove?" Tammy asked as she started to go. "I love the wind in my face."

"You drive. Yes, that would be fine," Bob said as he stood there with a boyish grin on his face.

She smiled back, then walked away, turned in her tray and continued out of the cafeteria towards her work section. Bob stood and watched the entire thirty seconds it took for the operation. "Next Thursday. After work. She drives. Likes the wind in her face." He repeated the facts back to himself aloud. He thought for a second, "A date and a convertible. Cool."

Bob put away his tray and was totally oblivious to the people around him as he went to his place of work. By the time he got there he had come back to reality and was focusing on the mission. He called Sam and told him about the Architect, how he had real knowledge of all the identity systems and that his partner was George Bailey.

0745 hours, IdentityPoint

Sam had come in a little past 0730 hours and stopped in the cafeteria for some coffee. He saw Bob talking to a woman at one of the tables, but thought better about stopping by to say hello since it is an undercover operation. No sense in advertising that he knew Bob outside of the job. In this business and in these situations there was always a fine line between being too friendly with someone and being obvious in avoiding them.

He had gotten a large coffee to go and went to his office where he fired up his computer and opened the PeopleFinder application. He had been thinking all night about the Ream case and the report he had run on Ream. It got him thinking that maybe the report contained some connection between Ream and the missing POWs. He still believed that their identities could be found even though he had worked countless hours along with agents of the Federal government and the city government of Chicago in an attempt to discover who was really buried in the German POW graves at Fort Sheridan, Illinois. It was certainly a long shot that the identities could be found, but no more of a long shot to prove that Michael Ream was actually one of the German POWs, and that he had killed the first person to have discovered the plot back in 1945, all of which Sam had accomplished.

When Sam challenged Ream, the United States Army and the City of Chicago to open one of the POW graves, the city was shocked that it not only contained one dead body dressed in rotted POW clothing, but also the body of Sergeant Jonathan Simon, who had first found the plot fifty years before. The discovery not only surprised those at the cemetery who had no idea what was going to be in the coffin, it caused the always calm, if not stoic Michael Ream, aka Kurt Rossinger, to attempt to kill Sam. Ream's shots missed Sam but killed his best friend Dana. This attack convinced all those doubting agencies that even though it could not be completely proven, everything Sam had been saying was true, including that Ream was Rossinger.

A committee was created and Sam was able to put his theories and evidence before them. Sam believed that American GIs who were being processed out of the Army at Fort Sheridan's Out Processing Center in 1944 and 1945, and because they had no family to miss them, were murdered in order for some German POWs who were being held at the POW camp, to assume the murdered American soldiers' identities. Even with Ream refusing to refute any charges relating to those events, his actions at the cemetery were enough to convince most everyone to believe Ream was an escaped POW. However, it was harder to prove than anyone had expected.

Sam opened his briefcase and removed a folder labeled POWs, placed it on the desk and turned the pages until he found the list that he wanted. He read the top of the page.

```
The United States Attorney's Office, United
States Army, and City of Chicago Special
Joint Review Team, Investigating the Events
of 1944 and 1945, Relevant to the Reported
Deaths of German POWs, United States Army
Sergeant Jonathan Simon and Associated Deaths
of that Period.
```

Sam chuckled aloud when he read the name of the group, which he always did when he looked at the report. He remembered that when he was asked to participate in the joint team he had been so excited about the opportunity to bring the POW issues and the deaths of Simon and his friend Sergeant Ventrilli to a close. However, it wasn't long before he knew they weren't going anywhere fast as they spent the first month developing the task force name and fighting over jurisdiction.

The City of Chicago wanted jurisdiction over the Ventrilli case, because the body was found in the city. The United States Army wanted jurisdiction over the murder of Sgt Simon, since it took place on an Army installation and Army personnel were involved. The United

States Attorney's Office wanted jurisdiction over everything, but finally agreed to let the Army prosecute those involved in the Simon case if the Joint Team found that the parties were United States Army personnel. They also granted the City of Chicago jurisdiction on the Murder of SSG Ventrilli, but only if the team found that the parties involved in the murder were not Active Duty soldiers.

Sam once again shook his head at the name and then read through the list of the team's findings for their two-year investigation.

Point One.   There are nine graves at the National Cemetery at Fort Sheridan that previously had been thought to contain the bodies of German POWs who had died in captivity at Fort Sheridan from 1944 to 1945.

Point Two. Based on the evidence available, the first death of a German POW, Heinz Braune, was an accident and Heinz Braune is buried in that grave.

Point Three. The eighth grave, that was listed as containing the body of the German POW, Heinreich Bauer, when opened was found to contain two bodies, one later identified through photographic evidence and materials on the body as SSG Jonathan Simon, a member of the United States Army and who had been reported as discharged from the Army in September 1945. The second body has not been positively identified.

Point Four. During the period 1944 through 1946, there were over 25,000 German POWs who were detained at the POW camp of Fort Sheridan. These men were contracted out as general laborers, for which the U.S. Treasury gained funds from their labor, and a review of the available financial documentation for that period does show a shortfall in what revenue was reported and what could have been and most likely was earned.

Point Five: Four American Soldiers, Captain John Beakes (Post Commander, Ft. Sheridan, 1944-1946), Captain (Dr.) Baker (Medical Officer in Charge of United States Army Out Processing station Ft Sheridan (1943-1946), Lt Robert Dale (Administration Officer 1942-1946), and SSG Borders (POW Camp Chief Guard 1944-1946) who all had been in key leadership positions over the POWs and/or the Out Processing Center at Fort Sheridan at the time of the POW deaths, all appeared to have come into substantial amounts of money that were in excess of their military salary, were partners in a joint business venture after the war, and all died shortly thereafter. Due to these circumstances the causes of their deaths are now listed as suspicious.

Point Six. Of the nine POWs reported to be buried in the National Cemetery at Fort Sheridan, only the identity of POW One (1) Heinz Braune could be verified. The identity of Braune was confirmed based on the individual statements of actual witnesses to his death, which had been printed in the official post publication of Fort Sheridan, **The Tower**. Having located direct relatives of POW Kurt Meyer, POW Three (3), and Egon Kranz, POW Five (5), living in Germany, DNA tests were conducted. Based on those tests it has been determined that the bodies buried in those graves are not those of Meyer or Kranz. DNA testing has not been conducted on the six remaining bodies as their direct relatives could not be found and have been presumed to have died during the war or shortly thereafter. The home of record for those six (6) POWs were in cities previously in East Germany and no records have yet been made available to this task force.

Point Seven: The discharge orders for SGT Jonathan Simon, dated September 1945, were shown to have been altered after the original list had been printed in such a manner as to add his name to the list of those United States Army soldiers being discharged from the Out Processing Center of Fort Sheridan.

Sam turned the page and read their initial conclusions.

Tentative Findings:

Finding One. Based on the evidence thus far, it is the opinion of the Special Joint Review Team, that SGT Jonathan Simon was murdered on or about 7 September 1945.

Finding Two. The man currently known as Michael Ream, since convicted of the murder of LTC Dana Jackson and the attempted murder of Major Sam Call, is not the former U.S. Army soldier Michael Ream. This determination was made through medical records that identified the mother of the actual Michael Ream, native of Dyersville Iowa, had type A blood. The man convicted under the name of Michael Ream has Type B blood and cannot be the Michael Ream he claims to be. Based on the circumstantial evidence available to this Special Joint Review Team is it our Tentative Finding that the man now known as Michael Ream is actually Kurt Roessger, soldier of the German Army, who was reported to have died on 12 October 1945.

Finding Three. Based on the statements gathered previously by Major Sam Call and the late LTC Dana Jackson, and the inconsistencies of the statements and reported events surrounding the death of SSG Frank Ventrilli in 1945, it is the tentative finding of this Special Joint Review Team that the death of SSG Ventrilli was not accidental as previously reported.

Sam then skipped to the team's section concerning the current status.

Point One. From 1944 through 1946 Fort Sheridan out processed thousands of American soldiers who had completed their tour of duty and were being returned to the civilian community. It has been theorized that conspirators isolated potential American soldiers, those who had no family and therefore whose failure to return to their previous life would have most likely gone unnoticed, that these American soldiers were murdered and their bodies buried as German POWs who were reported to have died by accident.

Point Two. In order to prove this theory (Point One above) it would be necessary to prove through medical evidence that the bodies in the graves marked as POWs are actually those of American soldiers. Through the Special Joint Review Team's analysis there are over 150,000 candidate soldiers who have been identified to have out processed from the facility during that time. Using the POW's date of the death as a limiting factor the list lowers to 50,000 possible candidates.

Point Three. Although POW Three (3) and POW Five (5) have been proven not to be the German POWs it is unlikely that the same can be proved or disproved for the occupants of the graves referred to as POW grave Two (2), POW Four (4), POW Six (6), POW Seven (7) and POW Eight (8) as no comparison DNA candidates can be found.

Point Four. In the effort to identify the actual occupants of those graves the task force has been using a process of eliminating the possible candidate set by establishing the candidate's identity was true and accurate and therefore could not be the German POW. This has been done first through a records search, then individual interviews with relatives and/or friends of the candidate. Thus far the Special Joint Review Team has reviewed 846 candidates of the original 50,000 possible names. Of those 846, 227 were found alive and their identities proven to be accurate, 126 were found deceased and their identities proven to be accurate, 312 cases have some records available and are still pending, which leaves 181 candidates without sufficient records or leads to determine their identities. Due to various factors, including the death of most of the possible candidates, lack of records from the period 1944-1946, and lack of investigative manpower, it is unlikely that the identities of the actual occupants of the graves will be solved by this method of testing.

It was the hope of this Special Joint Review Team that one of the suspected German POWs could be found and could provide information on the murders of Sergeants Simon and Ventrilli, as well as confirmation as to the involvement of American Military in the possible conspiracy surrounding POW labor and the deaths of American soldiers. This could only occur if the Special Joint Review Team were to isolate a name of the American soldier killed in this conspiracy and thus lead to the man currently using that identity. Based on the daunting limiting factors faced by the Special Joint Review Team it is unlikely that the names will be uncovered.

Sam always felt a sense of failure when he read the report. They had come so far in the investigation, but it was obvious that there was just no way to sift through the information and reduce the possible candidate set to a reasonable number. He had not given up, but being a realist he knew that he was unlikely to uncover anything further on his own. That did not stop the dreams or the guilt over the loss of Dana.

So this morning, after a sleepless night of dreams of PeopleFinder Reports and dead GIs, Sam took his report on Ream and started entering the names and addresses of people he had found on the report in hopes of finding a link. For that last two hours, he had entered names, addresses, company names and generated literally hundreds of pages of data, none of which seemed to bring him any closer to solving the POW case.

As Sam sat at his desk, bleary eyed from watching the screen, and with the constant noise of the printer churning out reports, there was a knock at his door that he at first did not hear.

"Hello," came a voice at the door.

Sam looked up and seeing it was George Bailey, smiled. "Hi George. You looking for someone to buy you a cup of coffee again?" Sam said as he motioned for George to come on in.

"Actually Bob over in H/R said you might need to talk to me about our Architect."

"Oh yes, Bob mentioned that to me just a little bit ago. Said you worked with this Architect fellow and since he was the guy who built most of the identity systems and you worked with him that you would be the best guy to talk to about how to interface to them."

"Yep, just what Bob thought."

"Well sit down, George." Sam motioned for him to sit in the chair directly in front of his desk.

George looked down at the chair. "Should I put it down right on top of these here, Sam?" George was pointing to a stack of reports that Sam had been busy printing all morning.

"Sorry, George." Sam got up and moved the stack to the floor, next to wall and away from the desk.

"Doing lots of PeopleTracker stuff, huh Sam?"

"Yeah, easy to get the reports, but I am not sure what I got." Sam was then quick to change the subject. "But that's for another day perhaps. As we spoke before George, I need to interface the new H/R system to some of the current systems to get information to confirm what I already have, and I was wondering if you could help me with that."

"Sure thing Sam."

Sam explained what he needed and George carefully explained how he could format his inquiry in XML, and then pass it to their middleware that they had developed in-house. It was smart enough to ask the right database for the information, and then send it back with the corresponding XML tags for easy system reading. The whole process took over thirty minutes and Sam took very detailed notes.

"Well thanks, George. I really appreciate it," Sam said as he closed his notebook.

"You're welcome, Sam." George looked at Sam then looked at the stack of reports on the floor behind Sam's desk and then the one sitting in the printer that George saw Sam trying to ignore the entire time he had been in the room. "So why don't you tell me what you really need, Sam?"

Sam was somewhat stunned by the comment. He looked up at George, and trying not to stumble into anything, did not ask the obvious response of what do you mean? Instead, he tried to deflect it totally away from work. "Well, George, a Corona Light with a lime would suit me quite fine right now," Sam smiled and reshuffled his notebook and papers.

With George's bright and cheering demeanor, it was hard for him to look serious, but he was, and Sam could see it. "Sam, I don't mean to pry, but the number of reports you have and the training I gave you on Socials was way more in depth than I think you needed for the program. I think there is more here, Sam, but I could be wrong."

Sam sat back in his chair and knew trying to look innocent was not going to work. George was way too intelligent and technically savvy for him to bullshit, so he decided that the truth was the most likely choice; especially since he wasn't getting anywhere on the case anyway. "Well, George, I'm trying to find a connection between a German POW, who has been masquerading as an American soldier and citizen for the last fifty years, to eight missing American Soldiers, but I don't know who they are or if they are still even alive."

George stood there without showing any emotion as if thinking, but Sam could not tell what. Then without commenting on the apparent ridiculousness of the story he said, "Have you tried asking for a batch job?"

"A batch job?" Sam said awkwardly, having expected just about any comment except that.

"You know, to look for a common set of data. Maybe a relationship to a name and a date range perhaps."

Sam nodded his head as if to agree, but all the while he was wondering if George was playing with him, or if he just didn't get it, or worse he did get it and he was just joking around before he went off and told someone about what he thought. "Well, George, I guess that would be a good idea. I'll have to think on that." Then he slowly added, "Thanks."

There was a long pause where neither man spoke, until finally Sam offered, "Don't you think the reason I gave you was a bit out there? Over the top? Fabricated perhaps?"

George smiled again, "Why would an intelligent man such as you make up such a preposterous lie? If you wanted me to believe a lie, you would have made it believable." George paused for a moment, "Don't you agree?"

Sam nodded, "Yes I do." Not sure where this was going, Sam had to be cautious what he said next. He had been sent here to find the fraud at IdentityPoint, and he was being paid to do it. Now his personal obsession and the running of these reports may have compromised that. He wondered what he was going to tell David when this all blew up in his face and he was escorted out of the building.

Finally, George broke the silence.

"I didn't mean to make you uncomfortable, Major, and I'm glad you told me the truth."

Sam caught the reference as soon as it was said, but he thought he'd play along anyway. "Major?"

"Please correct me if I am wrong, but I believe it is Major Sam Call, late of the United States Army, and late of Chicago." George said without any air of arrogance or sense of victory in that he had gotten Sam, but rather just as if he was introducing oneself.

"Well," Sam paused. "I guess *late* of IdentityPoint would now be in order." Sam stood and prepared to try to gather his briefcase and exit on his own before security escorted him out or worse yet the police were called. Then concern struck him as he thought. What if they had been called already? "Unless there is something else, George, I will excuse myself and depart."

George hadn't moved nor made any attempt to leave or call security or anyone else for that matter. "I read about Chicago."

Sam stopped packing and looked at George and then realized George had not made any move to leave nor had his attitude changed. "I see. And what are you thinking, George, if I may ask."

"I am thinking that what went on in Chicago took a lot of guts to do. From what I read, you took nothing from it, financially I mean. By your presence here, under an assumed name, I would guess it is not because you wanted to enter the exciting world of computer software project management." George smiled a little and waited for Sam.

"You would guess correctly." Sam sat back down waiting for the other shoe to drop and see what George was going to do with this.

"So what are you doing here? If you don't mind me asking."

"Mind you asking? No, I think you certainly have a right to know that." Sam reached down, got his briefcase and opened it. "How did you know?"

"About you? Your identity?"

"Yes. Had you seen me on TV and recognized me?" Sam stopped from getting his folder as he waited for the response.

"No, Sam. I guess you forgot what I do for a living. I work in identity fraud. I build, or used to build, identity systems. I am kind of an expert in that field." George smiled with a grin of pride, not arrogance, just a look that said he was good at his job and proud of it.

"So," Sam was still curious as to how he knew.

George picked up on it. "Oh, how I knew? I ran a report on you, got your SSN and then ran you through our system and you got a very low score."

"Low score?"

"Yes. You see, I, or I should say, me and a friend of mine built these identity systems for this company. In doing so, we learned a few things about identities, record depth, address association, number of records, number of sources the records come from, and this list goes on. The point is, I can run a name through the system and it gives a grade based on how well it reacts to the system rules."

"And mine was bad?" Sam just stared at George like he was the young schoolboy who just had his failing test grade announced to the class.

"Bad? You were a near zero." George laughed a little, not so much as to embarrass Sam but because the identity was just so thin. "The only thing you did have going was that your social was a good choice. Oh and using the name, Sam Cohen from Philadelphia was a good choice, there are nine of them, and that tends to hide false identities well."

"I thought there were twelve?"

"No, just nine."

Sam looked at him and without speaking gave him the look that said, 'Well, tell me why?'

"It had been issued and it wasn't in use by someone else. But you are no spring chicken there Sam, and your identity," George did the quote thing with his fingers, "was really thin. Not enough data to indicate you were in the mainstream, as they say."

"I see."

"Odd isn't it."

"How's that, George?"

"Well a company like IdentityPoint that deals with identities and identity theft doesn't use its own systems to check on people before they let them work here. If they did, they would have stopped you at the door."

Sam thought how fortunate he was that Bob was the gatekeeper for reviewing resumes of new personnel, and if his resume was crap, at least Bob had been the one reviewing the crap. "So what am I doing here, you asked. That's an interesting question. The answer would be either about the job you saw me playing with." Sam pointed to the reports stacked in the corner, "Or the actual job I was supposed to do."

"Oh. I hope I didn't catch you with your hand in the cookie jar, so to speak," George said as he stood and picked up a report, turned to Sam. "Do you mind?"

"Help yourself." Sam watched for a moment as George looked at the report. After a minute or so, Sam added. "When I saw the power of the reports, I thought I might be able to find a link in them from Ream to the POWs."

"Ream is the German guy from Chicago?" George asked as he picked up another report.

"Yes. After everything went down and Ream was jailed we had hoped that he would give us the names of the actual Americans in the graves. They even offered to reduce the charges against him if he cooperated."

"Reduce the charges? For murdering your friend? I'll bet that was hard to take."

"Yes, it was. But it didn't come to pass as Ream never said a word, about anything. Hell, his attorney asked to be relieved from the case because Ream wouldn't even talk to him."

"And he got convicted." George looked at Sam and temporarily stopped reading.

"Affirmative, he got twenty to life."

"Good. I would suspect he will die in prison."

Sam thought about his age. "Correct. At his age twenty years would be life."

"So you are trying to find what, Sam?" George brought one of the reports back to his seat and sat down.

"Well, I was hoping that Ream's path crossed those of the other POWs and his PeopleTracker report would provide a lead to who they were. Let me get you something." Sam again reached into his briefcase, pulled out the memo from Special Joint Review Team, and gave it to George to read. George read the whole memo, and from the amount of time he took, Sam thought he read it twice.

Finally, George spoke, "I can see your challenge."

Sam nodded his response.

"Well, I was thinking. Ream's early post-war years were in Milwaukee with a company named PEI. Why not run a search on people who worked for or with PEI, in that time frame, and maybe shared an address with Ream."

"You can do that, George?" Sam asked excitedly.

"I can't, but a friend of mind Kris Knowles, in the Public Records section, can. He is a great guy, smart, knows batch ops like no one else, and he's a friend. I would try to do some data mining, but IdentityPoint stopped all work on the people warehouse concept when we lost our Architect."

"Yes, I heard about that," Sam said with a tone of sympathy knowing both the story and that George was his friend.

"Yeah, but I can call Kris, and he can write some processes that will select Ream's info, then do subsequent searches on the addresses, and then perhaps correlate them to date ranges. I can talk to him if you like?"

"What about me and my not being who I say I am, and all that?"

"Well, Sam, to tell you the truth, I am not a big fan of IdentityPoint these days, and as long as you aren't doing anything criminal or for personal profit, I would say it's none of my business." George stood, put the papers down and then stood by the door as if to leave.

"Well, I certainly appreciate that George, but I think I better tell you all of it before you jump in."

"Fair enough," George sat back down.

Sam told him about the fraud case he had been hired to investigate, and that the person who hired him thought that some of the senior people were manipulating funds through acquisitions.

"Yes, my friend the Architect thought something along those lines too."

"Really."

"He told me he was on the acquisition committee for a while, you know, doing the technology evaluations of a company before you buy them to make sure they were worth the money; then they stopped using him or anyone in the company as far as I know."

"I see. So how many companies has IdentityPoint acquired?" Sam asked.

George thought for a moment. "Well that last time I knew for sure was six months ago and I think I remember the number to be around 72 or 73."

"Are you serious? Seventy-three?"

"Oh yes. There're a lot of small niche players in this business. Records collectors of all kinds; death records, birth, marriage, divorce, court, purchases, insurance, bad debts, pilot licenses, boat license, boat registration, gun registration, liens and judgments, education, postal, and the list goes on."

"I didn't realize you bought from so many different types of providers."

"Someone opens a small company collecting some obscure type of record, makes their presence known in the Public Records world and IdentityPoint buys them."

"Must be nice for the stockholders of the little companies, return on investment and all. But I think that is a whole other story," Sam said, "Now back to my real task."

"Yes. I'm not sure what I can do for you there, but if you think you can get data from the systems within the corporate structure, then my Architect friend is the man to talk to." George opened his wallet, took out a business card, turned it over, and wrote a phone number. "Here's his number, and I put my home number too." George picked up the report on Ream and stood up to leave. "I'll work on this, and when the results come back from Knowles, I'll let you know. It shouldn't take long."

Sam read the name on the card. "This is a great card, George."

"Well, one has to have a sense of humor you know, Sam."

"Indeed they do, and thank you George. I don't know what to say about all this." Sam extended his hand to George.

"My honor, Sam." He shook his hand and turned to the door, opened it and then turned back to Sam. "You know, Sam, I wasn't always old, in 1965, I was 22, not too long out of high school and learning all kinds of new things in a place called Da Nang—Sempre Fi, Sam, Sempre Fi."

Sam smiled and gave a slight salute as George walked away.

1745 hours, IdentityPoint, Office of the Chairman

She gently hung up the phone, took a Kleenex from the box and wiped her hands. Then she picked up a bottle of hand cream from the corner of her desk, pumped some into one hand, then rubbed it into her hands as if it could cleanse her. She felt dirty and she rubbed her hands as if the cleaning of them could wash away her guilt and worse her own disgust in herself.

She was Executive Secretary to the Chairman of the Board of IdentityPoint, and she had been that for the last seven years. Extremely competent, efficient, and dedicated, she would often be at work twelve hours a day, never leaving before her boss. When he was away from the office on business trips, she never left the office until he was in his hotel room and she was sure he needed nothing more from her. That would often have her at the office at nine or ten o'clock waiting for his call; a call for a change in itinerary, or information he required for the next day or whatever he needed – it was her task to arrange it.

Thomas Leslie Thompson was an egocentric, narcissist, who wanted everything done for him. He was impossible to please but she did everything he asked. She would do anything for him—and had. Having worked for Thompson, then president of the company, just over two months, she was totally captivated by his charm and good looks, mesmerized by the power of his office and the powerful people she met each day through him. One evening they were working late together, Thompson had a speech to give the next day. He had her listen to him rehearse the speech then type the changes he wanted. He did not have to force her to stay, she wanted to. Listening to the speech time after time was not a chore for her, but rather like he was giving a private rendering just for her, for her approval.

At eight o'clock Thompson apologized for the lateness and having her miss dinner. He insisted she accompany him to dinner. Being a man of strong will she could not refuse; she didn't want to. They dined, and drank wine, and she ended up in bed with him. They were both married, but somehow it did not seem wrong to her. Thompson was not only a company president building a successful business, a business that had been named one of the top five businesses in the state and one of the top 100 in the nation, he was also committed to improving the lives of children, women and those in need of help. Through the efforts of many volunteer groups within the company, the awards for his charity work started to eclipse his business awards. He was more than just a man to her and she would be with him for whatever he needed.

They met once a week for two months. He was charming and sophisticated, and it was as if she were the most important element of his life. She organized his day, screened his visitors, cleared all his correspondence, and got him whatever he needed. For her, her time was immaterial, only his was important.

Sometime during the third month, the dinners stopped. They went right to the hotel where they had champagne, chatted, and then had sex. The next month the champagne stopped flowing as did the talking but the sex remained. He told her where and when and she obliged; whatever he wanted. There was no give and take in the relationship; she was serving him, both at the office and in the bedroom. It was not at all about her, and she knew that, but somehow she was unable to break free from him.

The months slipped by, and their meetings became less frequent and less dignified. If he called at all, it was late at night or when he had been drinking and hadn't scored with some other woman he had his eye on. Rather then have nothing, he would call her and she would oblige. Then after a year, he stopped calling for her altogether. They never spoke of those times – ever, and that had been six years ago.

She looked up from her desk, looked at the closed door of the Chairman's office, and thought to herself how she had gone from an eager and exuberant aide, to the object of his affection, to his lover, to his slut, to what she was now, his pimp and some sort of bizarre life housekeeper. Now she made the arrangements for the hotels, the dinners, even calling the other women to ensure they are on schedule for their rendezvous with Thompson. Like tonight, she had told Jennifer, Thompson's new assistant, to meet him at the Cabernet restaurant. She told her it was to discuss changes in the Lobbyist's schedule but she knew it was for Thompson to seduce her; Abranoff had called the day before and cancelled the meeting. She had also made the reservation at the Georgian Terrace Hotel and ordered champagne for the room.

The worse part for her though was not the sending of young assistants to Thompson, or not having him herself anymore, if was the lying to Thompson's wife that made her feel the most disgusted with herself. She had just hung up the phone having told Thompson's wife that his business trip to Florida had to be extended another night.

She rubbed her hands harder; the hand cream was not working.

1745 hours, Northbound out of Atlanta

The traffic northbound on Georgia 400 was as aggravating as ever, but he didn't mind it tonight; he was on his way to Cabernet and he always had a good time there. Cabernet was just off the exit at Windward Parkway, which was the 'Corporate Corner' of North Atlanta. For years Buckhead had been *the* place for corporate headquarters and the associated nightlife of the corporate executive. Four years ago there began a movement of numerous corporate headquarters out of the city to the Windward Parkway area. It was not just coincidence that a half-dozen exclusive golf clubs had opened in the area, and expensive multi-million dollar executive communities had been built. Presidents and CEOs now found themselves not having to fight the traffic into and out of the city. At the same time they were able to enjoy all the trappings of the country club life at the expense of the stockholders, and Thompson was no exception. Despite his multi-million dollar salary, the company still paid for his membership in two of the area's most exclusive country clubs.

He wanted to move his headquarters from downtown into this area, but he hadn't been able to sell it to the board members yet. He had four of the board members in his pocket and he knew it was only a matter of time before he had the fifth and controlling voting member on his payroll. It would come soon and the board would officially recognize the 'need' to move the headquarters and approve the expense. Until then Thompson would have to endure the commute.

He was almost there, and he was looking forward to it with all the anticipation of a teenager on a date. Cabernet was one of the exclusive spots for dinner with the business crowd, and many deals were made there over scotch and expensive wines. But Thompson wasn't looking for business; he was looking for high-powered action of another type—high-powered women. The restaurant was a drawing point for the business crowd; expensive prices limited the clientele to the CEO level, and the limited seating allowed for exclusive conversation. But it wasn't the restaurant Thompson was headed for, it was the bar.

The presence of the high-end business crowd brought equally high-end women to the bar. It brought in high ranking woman from the big companies who executed their version of drinking with the powerbrokers, but it also brought in those women, not of the corporate world, who were also looking for powerful men—and by powerful they meant rich. On any given night there could be seen more than one beautiful, overly exposed, and attainable woman at the bar who was seeking 'corporate connections.' Thompson enjoyed the thrill of taking a beautiful woman to bed, but he couldn't do it on his own; he needed all the trappings of his money, power and thousand-dollar suits.

Thompson drove his silver 1994 S65 AMG Mercedes into the parking lot. The valet who parked the cars kept a special parking place right by the entrance for Thompson's cars. Thompson loved his car, but he loved that it cost $185,000. Even more than that, he loved that people knew it—and if they didn't, he told them. It was the sleekest car in the lot. Every time he came to the restaurant the valet got a dozen comments on the car. He always made sure to tell them it was Thompson's car—Thompson paid the valet extra when that resulted in him being complimented on his car. Image wasn't just important to him, it was everything; how he was thought of by the members of the corporate world, how he was acclaimed as a corporate power broker, how he was talked about by the public as a benevolent advocate of public rights, and how he was sought after by women.

Thompson sat in his Mercedes for a moment pretending to gather up things, but in actuality, he was waiting until those patrons walking by got close enough to see him get out of the car.

The car door opened, "Good evening, Mr. Thompson." The valet understood the game Thompson played, and he had waited for Thompson to open his door before he made the grand exaggerated and louder than required welcoming jester.

"Good Evening," Thompson said with an air of detachment and sophistication. He didn't make eye contact with the valet nor did he call him by name even though the valet wore a nametag and had worked there ever since Thompson had started coming to Cabernet.

"I have your spot for you tonight, Sir," the valet said as he held the door. "Have a good evening."

Thompson did not reply, he just smiled as if saying 'of course you do', and then walked into the restaurant.

A pretty twenty-something hostess greeted him as he entered. "Good evening, Mr. Thompson, the restaurant or bar this evening?" When he came in alone, she knew it was the bar, it always was, but she also knew not to insult Thompson by insinuating anything.

"I'll sit at the bar this evening," Thompson replied as he looked around the restaurant for any faces which may put a damper on his evening plans. After a quick visual of the area, he nodded to the hostess who led him to a seat at the bar. It was a grand bar; dark woods throughout and expensive seating and fixtures made it more like an exclusive club than a bar. Thompson sat in his regular seat, and quickly surveyed the landscape that unfortunately did not provide a target for his thirst.

- - - - - - - - - - - - - - - < > - - - - - - - - - - - - - - - -

Harry was well acquainted with Thompson, and had served him for over two years. Over many months, they had worked out an unspoken system whereby Thompson would indicate the woman of his interest and he would then provide her with a drink 'courtesy of the gentleman at the bar.' He always made sure that the lady knew that the 1989

Château Clinet Bordeaux he was serving her cost two hundred dollars a bottle; his tip depended on it.

Bartending is what Harry did six nights a week; most people wouldn't want his job; hell, he knew most couldn't do his job. It wasn't mixing the drinks that was hard, a manual and enough practice and anyone could tend bar. What most couldn't handle were the hours. Harry started his day at 5 PM and ended it at 2 AM six nights a week. He usually got up between noon and 1 PM, ate his breakfast and then did his thing from 5 PM until 2 AM when he did what he enjoyed the most—watching people. From there he usually went straight home where he spent most of his time alone until 5 or 6 AM when he went to asleep.

He was 46 years old and had been a bartender for almost 25 of those years. He started serving bar, actually just popping the tops off of beer bottles, at a run-down Atlanta local bar. He was just hanging around at the bar after he had been fired from his retail job. It wasn't that he was bad at his sales job, took money from the cash register, or rude to the customers, it was just that he was always late for work. He was supposed to open the shop at 7:30 AM and if he was lucky he opened by 8 AM one day in five.

Harry loved the night; even as child he had a difficult time being 'up for school.' As a small child, when his parents put him to bed he would lay there reading until way after they went to bed. When he was a teenager he would stay up watching TV until 2 or 4 AM then drag himself out of bed for school; he was tired all the time. Sometime during his junior year, he wasn't sure just when, his body's clock just made a change and he was finally able to find some sort of normalcy. When he finished school he came right home, went to bed and sleep until midnight. Then he would be up the rest of the day. At first his parents objected, thought he was into drugs or worse, but when he started getting better grades in school, and actually being friendlier to them they just accepted that he was different.

After High School he tried college for a year, which was perfect for his life style; he had no problem with late afternoon classes and studying at night. The whole sleeping in late thing was like the college had developed the schedule with him in mind. He finished his first year with a B average but college just wasn't for him so he didn't return the following fall.

He made numerous attempts to find what he wanted to do, all of which either ended in him being fired for lateness or him quitting. As luck would have it, he had been in the bar for the last three nights running and the bar was really packed. The regular bartender who had the same problem Harry had, only in reverse, was unable to keep the whole nighttime thing going and after being harassed every night by the owner for being late, one day he just stopped coming in at all—he never called, never even came in for his last check. That night, when the clients were backed up at the bar, and the owner was swamped with making drinks, Harry volunteered to serve the beer. He liked it. The hours suited him just fine and he got to watch people and that was just about his favorite thing.

After three days of 'just showing up and volunteering' he decided he wanted to ask for a full-time job there but he knew he had to know how to mix drinks. Not only had he no experience with mixing drinks, he didn't drink himself—nothing, not even beer. He got a book on mixing drinks but he had a tough time remembering the proportions and using real booze to train himself was an expensive way to go. Since he didn't like to drink, tasting them to see if he made them right wasn't going to work. He had just about given up on the idea of being a real bartender when he had an idea. He filled all the liquor bottles with water and added food coloring making each type of alcohol its own color. He then carefully measured the ingredients for the ten most common drinks and when they were done each glass had a potion with it own distinct color. With those perfect samples sitting on the counter in front of him he started throwing together test drink after test drink and if the color of the drink matched his standard he knew he had it, if not, a quick dump into the sink and he's try again. After three days and hundreds of practice drinks he could make each of his ten standard drinks in no time, without measuring, without consulting the manual and every time the color was perfect.

On the fourth night he went to the bar and asked for the full-time bartending job. When the owner asked if he had any experience bartending other than serving beer, he just walked behind the bar, and made his ten standard drinks faster than the owner had even seen them done before. He hired Harry on the spot.

He stayed there for five years and probably would have stayed forever if the owner hadn't sold out to a developer who was buying up the entire block to build condos. Over the years he had been recruited several times to go to other bars but he had never wanted to make the change. After the bar closed he took a job at an upscale bar that catered to the hip, young crowd, where he stayed for seven years. It was a good place to work for a long time; a lot of people to serve and to watch and Harry perfected about a hundred drinks there. But over the last couple of years the bar started catering to a rougher crowd and drug sales went from discreet dealings between two college students to open use in the rest rooms. There was a drug bust just about every month, then every month, then every week. When a disgruntled dealer become incensed over the apparent infringement of his territory by another dealer and shot that wayward man in the bar, Harry finally had enough. He took a week off, interviewed at a new, and yet to open, upscale restaurant – bar called Cabernet and was hired on the spot.

That was six years ago. He hadn't missed a day in six years, never took time off. He ran the bar, managed the inventory, ordered all the supplies and product, made contacts with the wine suppliers and within six months of opening he had Cabernet known by every serious and well to do patron as having the best wine cellar in all of Alpharetta. When it came to managing the bar the manager didn't have to do a thing except to accept praise from the owner over how well the bar was run—which he accepted.

The patrons came and stayed, either impressed with Harry's ability in the drink-making department, which most bartenders shared his skills, or more so in his knowledge of wines, where few rivaled his expertise. There were also those patrons that came there not for his skills behind the bar but for his discretion. This area of town was big on high-powered people meeting for all kinds of reasons; from those brokering mega financial deals, to those making clandestine plans to steal connected and successful executives away from other firms, to those trying to satisfy their basic needs, like finding a woman; one that he could play with and the wife would not be the wiser. Of the three the latter was the most interesting for Harry to watch and there were numerous men who used Cabernet as their hunting ground. There was one executive in particular who hunted often and only for the best game, Thomas Leslie Thompson, Chairman of the Board of IdentityPoint.

Harry enjoyed the game Thompson played more than any of the others that played, or tried to play the game, at Cabernet. Thompson never relied on his own charm to capture the woman; he wasn't interested in those women who were looking for charm and wit. He wanted those that were impressed by cash. If she hadn't the opportunity to make the connection of money to him from his car, or from his thousand-dollar suit, he made sure the word 'wealthy' was said loud and clear by the wine he bought her.

When a beautiful, unescorted woman would come to the bar, Harry would look to Thompson. If Thompson gave the nod, then he would go into his act. He enjoyed it. He liked to watch the game unfold, how she reacted to Thompson's offer of the expensive drink and how long it took for her to sink her teeth into him. In his experience, it was not the man who controlled these games, it was the woman, at least it was in his bar. She knew exactly what she wanted and what she was willing to give to get it; she controlled who played in the game.

On the other hand, Thompson, and those like him, believed they were in control of the game through money and power. But Harry knew different, especially in Thompson's case. Thompson loved to play the part of the sophisticate, but he knew the real Mr. Thompson, the one who acted the connoisseur, but who actually couldn't tell the difference between the 1989 Château Clinet at two hundred a bottle and the Ruffino Bordeaux at twenty, that he would occasionally serve him all night, but charged him for the Clinet, and then pocketed the difference.

Harry cleaned a glass at the bar, reached up and put it into the rack above the mahogany bar. It was fairly slow tonight and he thought it might get a little boring. He glanced over to the hostess station, there was a man standing there in a very expensive suit and he could see that the hostess was waiting and that the man was not in any hurry to proceed. She was waiting, waiting for the man who was standing there quietly announcing to everyone in the room that he was there. Such ego Harry thought. It was going to be an interesting night after all, Thompson was here.

- - - - - - - - - - - - - - < > - - - - - - - - - - - - - - -

Thompson wasn't sure if he loved the sex or the conquest more, but it didn't matter as he always got them both. Tonight would be a different kind of conquest, the kind he loved best—the young assistant. Since taking over as Chairman of the Board, he had both an Executive Secretary and an Executive Assistant.

Jennifer was the fourth Executive Assistant he had in the last four years, and she had been in the job for two months. At just twenty-four, she was an honor graduate from Princeton, intelligent, and totally focused on a career in business. Her credentials were impeccable, which is why she got on the interview list with Thompson. She was very good looking with a nice slim figure and beautiful long hair, which she always wore up unlike the young woman she was, but more like an older matron. Her brains and education got her to IdentityPoint, but her looks are what Thompson hired.

Among her duties included researching all the people with whom Thompson was to meet, pre-meet with all journalists who wished to interview Thompson, and to make sure the only journalists to meet with Thompson were 'Thompson-friendly.' She had to research, write, review and assist Thompson in rehearsing all his speeches. It was a busy and exacting job, essentially because of Thompson. Image was everything to him, and any misstep, miscalculation, or mistake that reflected poorly on him would end in the termination or, at the least, a very public ass chewing of some staff member. So far, Jennifer had excelled in all regards. On most trips she accompanied Thompson, taking care of all arrangements including travel, cars, hotels, and meeting coordination. She checked him into the hotel and checked him out. She did everything except speak for him, all Thompson had to do was show up, and even that was via an arranged limo.

Thompson had taken her on three trips already and had started to set up his play for her. On business trips he had dinner with her alone on several occasions, confided in her with untruths to instill confidence and trust, spoke of his loneliness, and lack of love in his life. He was set for tonight, he would use all his charm on her, and if that did not work, he would use the threat of her never working in the industry again. It didn't matter to him what worked as long as he got her in bed. But Thompson was equally as careful as he was sexually devious. He had already given a memo to his corporate General Counsel about how Jennifer had come on to him, and how he rejected her, but felt he did not need to fire her, as long as she learned from the experience. He had set up the lie to answer in advance any later claims by Jennifer that Thompson had initiated the relationship.

When she arrived Thompson was sitting at the bar sipping his wine. She thought she was going to have an early night, but Thompson's secretary called and told her to meet Thompson at *Cabernet* and to bring the Backstop file. They were going to meet their lobbyist and discuss the plan on how best to approach the Senate on introducing legislation in favor of the use of more personal data in IdentityPoint reports. Jennifer saw him at the end of the bar and waved as she walked over.

"Good evening, Mr. Thompson."

"Hello Jennifer. I am sorry to drag you out for this, but it's important." He motioned for her to sit, which she did. "I just got off the phone with our lobbyist, and he is going to be an hour late. So what do you say we just have a drink and relax while we wait?"

She didn't think it was necessary for her to wait, but before she had time to say a word, the bartender approached.

"Two glasses of the 1989 Château Clinet Bordeaux please." Thompson smiled at Jennifer with confidence as he ordered.

The bartender leaned forward and said in a low voice, a voice low enough to be considered whispering but loud enough to be heard by the young lady, "Sir, I am sorry to say that the vintage has become so very rare that the price has risen to two hundred and fifty a bottle."

In his most suave manner Thompson said, "That's just fine, the young lady has worked hard and deserves it."

Jennifer was taken back so much that she didn't mention leaving. In a minute, the bartender brought the wine and they toasted to success. An hour later, the bartender told Thompson he had a call and Thompson excused himself to take the pre-arranged, imaginary call. When Thompson returned, he told Jennifer that the lobbyist's plane had been delayed and since Thompson had arranged dinner for himself and the lobbyist, he insisted Jennifer should join him, so as to not waste the evening. An hour and fifteen minutes later, after a Chardonnay at their seating, a Pinot Grigio with the salad, a Chianti with the Beef Wellington, and two glasses of Champagne with dessert Jennifer was hardly feeling a thing.

After dinner, Thompson told Jennifer he was driving her home, but first he wanted to check the suite at the Georgian Terrace Hotel where the lobbyist would stay when his plane finally arrived. He did not need to get the key from the front desk. He always used the same suite, and was there so often he had his own key. They bypassed the inquisitive eyes at the desk and went upstairs to the room. Once inside Thompson poured two glasses of Champagne.

Thompson returned to Jennifer who was both woozy from the alcohol and dazzled by the evening. He sat back down next to her, graciously thanked her for all help, and told her how he could not do all that he does without her, then he tenderly kissed her. Five minutes later, he took her into the bedroom suite, closed the door behind them, and then undressed her. Fifteen minutes later, they were both asleep.

Chapter 6
Friday, October 14

The Architect

1145 hours, Alpharetta

Sam slowly strolled up the walkway to the front door, and as he did he looked at the house and gardens that surrounded the house. Sam looked back at the walkway, a fifty-foot flagstone path set in small pebbles and nestled in a green, low ground cover that grew between the flagstones. Little blue flowers filled the green ground cover, which had almost grown over the large flagstone pavers. Sam scanned both sides of the home and saw gardens of all sorts of flowering bushes of numerous varieties lined the bark-filled gardens. However, the bushes looked like they had not been trimmed for some time; grass and weeds had begun to grow in the gardens, and it was all too obvious that these once beautiful gardens had been left to go to seed. He could see that the property had seen better days. It wasn't as though the house was falling down, the house itself was in great shape. The paint was nearly fresh. There were no signs of wear and tear, no weathered look about the building itself, but it was as if the occupants had stopped maintaining the outside some time ago.

Sam walked up the three wooden steps to the front porch, pushed the doorbell button, and waited. After a minute or so, the door opened.

"Can I help you?" It was a low, monotone voice that barely spoke loud enough for Sam to hear.

"Yes. I'm Sam Call. I spoke to you on the phone yesterday about IdentityPoint." The man didn't readily respond so Sam added, "George Bailey said I should call."

"Yes, I remember. Come in." He opened the door and let Sam come inside, then closed the door after him. Without further conversation he walked, or more accurately shuffled like an old man, into the hallway, then through the kitchen, and outside to the back porch. "Mind if we talk here?" He pointed to the wicker chairs that sat around a glass top table. Without waiting for a response he sat down in the chair that faced the afternoon sun and closed his eyes as he felt the warm sun on his face. Sam sat down across from him and while waiting for him to speak, he looked around quickly at the back yard. It was in the same, soon to be overgrown condition, as the front. The fishpond was green with algae, weeds were rapidly overcoming the gardens, and just like the front, it was obvious that not too long in the past this had been a well-maintained and lovely spot.

"My wife and I used to spend our time in the gardens." The Architect had noticed Sam looking around.

All Sam could think to say was a neutral, "I see."

"Not much point in it anymore." The Architect mumbled, looked about at the once beautiful gardens and became even more sullen. He closed his eyes once more, as if he were looking back and able to see what they had been like before. "So," he said as he opened his eyes and looked at Sam, "What is it that you need to know? George said it was important."

"Yes, it is."

Sam had not finished when the Architect interjected. "I wouldn't be seeing you at all if George had not called you know." His voice was not hostile just very matter of fact and totally devoid of emotion.

"I appreciate you taking the time to see me," Sam said.

"Mr. Call, time is what I have."

Sam looked at the man that sat across from him. He was in his fifties, seemed to be in good shape physically, certainly not overweight; he looked like he was athletic, or at least had been. His grey hair was long, not by design, but more like he was just two months late getting it cut. He had at least a three-day beard and together with his uncut hair, his faded blue jeans, and the somewhat tattered old blue flannel work shirt, he looked like he was in his late sixties not the fifties Sam knew he was.

"You see I joined the company when it first split off from its parent company, but it was a whole different environment then." He opened his eyes, sat normally in his chair, and looked towards Sam. "Sure we were busy as hell and we were doing a lot of things, building a lot of new systems while trying to fix all the crap systems we inherited. It was fast and furious and there was a lot of tension and confrontation, but not a bad type of confrontation."

"How's that?"

"Well it was just a lot of talented and dedicated people each trying to do their job and fighting for the resources they needed to get it done. There were arguments, but for the most part it wasn't personal. In those first three years, we were really cranking, and Thompson, the President, was on fire. This guy told the tale and we took it all, hook, line, and sinker. He was preaching how we were going to grow like gangbusters, and all the while we were going to be 'the consumer's trusted business partner' in the public records world."

Sam could see the Architect's demeanor change somewhat from the quiet, monotone voice to now one that was more angry and intense.

"And Thompson wasn't?" Sam asked as he began to squirm a little from the heat of the sun on the back of his neck.

"Not at the end. Hell, I don't know if he ever believed it or that it was just a line he told us all. He was good at it." He looked away from Sam then around the yard as if someone was there and he was looking for them.

Sam tried to re-engage the Architect, "So how did it work? Thompson's show, so to speak."

The Architect sat back in the chair again, closed his eyes as if he could read the words of a prepared speech by closing them, and he started to speak. "Well, it started when we first became IdentityPoint. They would have us all go to the cafeteria and he would come and give us speeches about how we were going to provide the world all the data they needed to make the world a safer place. We would build these systems that would enable businesses to find the bad guys, to prevent sex offenders from being hired by youth groups, enabling old people to check on fraud artists before they invested. It all sounded so good."

"But it wasn't?" Sam asked, then moved his chair a little to get the sun off his neck. The Architect either failed to notice Sam's movement or simply ignored it as he continued.

"Well, it seemed like it was for a long time. I mean I believed him, I even wrote down his quotes and hung them in my office, hell I bought the whole story."

"When then did it go bad?"

"Good question." He opened his eyes again and looked at the pond for a moment. Then the Architect stood up without speaking and left the porch.

Not knowing where he went, Sam remained in his chair for an uncomfortable two minutes before the Architect returned with two open bottles of beer. He put one down in front of Sam, and then sat back down. Without mentioning the beer, he took a sip and stared out at the pond. "I think it was when we bought CAS. It was a huge acquisition, and it changed the entire company culture." He took a quick sip and continued. "I still don't know why we bought them; we had EFA, and they did the same thing."

Sam took a sip of his beer then again attempted to re-engage the Architect. "It would seem that the company was growing and perhaps they were just interested in capturing more of the market."

"As good a guess as any." The Architect looked confused, as if he had just heard it for the first time. "The odd thing is you know there was no Due Diligence done by the technology team, or any team come to think of it, before the purchase was announced. I mean we had already purchased about a dozen small companies over the past couple years, and I was on the team that evaluated the acquisition's technology, but I didn't do an evaluation of this one until after it was announced we bought them."

"After! Isn't that a bit odd?"

"Extremely so."

"Why do you suppose that was the case?"

"I just don't know. Why is that?" The Architect paused for a bit then continued, "But that's not why you are here. What was it you wanted to know, Sam?" He put his hand up in a 'stop' fashion. "And George filled me in on both of your *missions*—as George called them."

Sam smiled and felt more comfortable after the military comment, "I know that you were an Architect at IdentityPoint and that you created a lot of their corporate systems. George tells me that you may know how to access the financial data, specifically that data involving acquisitions."

"Well, my work in that area was mostly integration efforts. My specialty was identity systems."

"I am looking for a way to search the corporate files, principally the financial systems to see if it can lead us to understanding all the cash flow in regards to acquisitions."

"In terms of what costs the company incurred, or who got the money from the buyout? That's the kind of money that makes investors rich."

"Yes, we are interested in who got money for stock ownership in those companies IdentityPoint acquired."

"I thought that might be the case. But I am sorry to say that the records only go to the first level of ownership; that is, if the stock was owned by a fund the record just lists the fund."

"And an investment company?" Sam asked already knowing the bad news.

"Same goes for that, I'm sorry to say." Then he looked away again as if in a trance or deep in thoughts of another more important time.

The silence was awkward and Sam picked up his beer, but only to hold it. "So did that cause problems for you?"

He sighed and then turned slowly back to Sam. "There are so many things wrong in that place, the public records side that is. Their systems were not secure and there was no way to guarantee they were being used properly. When the company added new sensitive data, like Social Security Numbers, drivers' licenses, and then expanded those markets, they had no way of auditing whose data was being accessed. Plus they had thousands of special government accounts that had no audit trail at all. They could search for any thing on anybody, and the system would have no record of what was searched or who did the searching."

"That seems like a serious problem." Sam acknowledged wanting to hear more, but he let the Architect go at his own pace. Sam saw that the Architect was in bad shape. His mind apparently wandering and it seemed difficult for him to keep focused, or at least it was difficult for Sam to keep him engaged in the conversation. Sam guessed that the loss of the Architect's career and his wife was just more than he could handle.

At times the Architect just seemed to stare into nothingness, and Sam made no effort to disturb him. Finally the Architect spoke. "I loved that place. Loved working there, loved what we were doing. But the higher I got in the organization, the more I knew, the worse it got." He took a long sip of beer.

"You tried to work around it, but one day you couldn't anymore?" Sam said to him.

"Yes, yes, exactly." The Architect spoke more freely now that he had someone listening who seemed to agree with him. "I was building a new system for the government. It needed to alert them if there was any inquiry on any of their people, but I knew of the non-reporting accounts and the audit log problems."

"But they didn't fix the problems or tell the new government client. Did they?"

The Architect looked down at his feet appearing ashamed. "No." He stood up and walked over to the rail. "I kept asking when we were going to fix the problems; undercover agents were at risk you know. You see I built a system that gave agents new identities, new names, socials, address history, the whole bit. It was beautiful."

That was the first time Sam saw the Architect smile. It was obvious that the Architect was very proud of the system he had built. "Then something happened, didn't it?" Sam knew already that something had gone wrong.

"Yes." The Architect's newly displayed expressions of pride and happiness disappeared as quickly as they had appeared, and he again looked despondent. "But not by those systems. It was me. I screwed up. I developed all these false identities and put the names in the watch system in case any of the bad guys did a search on any of the names the FBI would be alerted. But I screwed up, I didn't do it right and one FBI agent who was undercover with one of my identities was murdered.

"Damn," was all Sam could say.

The Architect was instantly animated, like a lawyer arguing a case before the jury. He looked at Sam then out into the yard as if he were addressing the jury. "When the FBI reported the murder to us we went though the systems to ensure none had made any checks through PeopleFinder or other systems and failed to report it to my system." The Architect paused and looked again at the 'jury' as if to ask for forgiveness. "We found a request in the PeopleFinder log for the identity and traced it back to an account that had been owned by a PI, but who had been dead for six months." His fists slammed down on the railing, and then he pulled them back to his face and covered his tears.

"When we found it I just knew it couldn't have been my system that failed, and I was sure it was the problem of those non-reporting systems I had fought over for a year." The Architect turned to Sam, there were tears in his eyes. "But it wasn't. It was me, my watch list. I personally created the names, the identities, and put them in the system. *Me!*" The Architect shouted. "Somehow, in managing the system, I removed one name from the system. I guess during upgrades or editing." The Architect put his hand to his head as if to help himself concentrate. "I, I just don't know. Either way the name was not in the system. The agent was undercover in a company using their legal import business to smuggle in drugs. They must have gotten suspicious of the agent, ran a report on him, and when the inquiry was done on the agent, the FBI was not alerted."

He turned and looked away from Sam and looked out at the pond. After a minute or two he recovered enough to speak calmly once more. "They immediately took me off the project." He turned back towards Sam and walked back to the table. "They kept me on for six more months doing menial jobs, and then let me go. They gave me a severance and had me sign a bunch of papers that I later figured out meant that if I said anything to anyone about anything I would be sued and prosecuted for revealing national security secrets."

"Christ, they really screwed you."

"No, I deserved it. My project, my screw up." He sat back down in his chair. "That was two years ago. I couldn't believe it was over. I kept thinking that they would realize they had made a mistake, and they would call me back. But after six months of staring out the window and waiting for a call that was not going to come, I finally realized it was over and I was never going back." The Architect downed the last of the beer, but held onto the bottle like it was still full. "I tried to get some work, but I couldn't get a job in the industry. After six more months, I just gave up looking entirely. Started just hanging around the house, not working, getting more and more angry. Finally the wife couldn't take it anymore and left."

He took a sip from the empty bottle, looked at it, and placed it down gently on the table. "She loved me, I know, but everyone thought I was to blame, and I couldn't get past it." He paused for a moment, got very quiet then muttered, "God, I loved her."

There was a long, embarrassing pause in which neither man spoke. The Architect pretended to look out at some unseen bird or other creature in the trees, but Sam could see he was just wiping the tears from his eyes and trying to gain his composure. Then he stood and went into the kitchen without a word.

Sam could hear him sobbing.

A few minutes later, when Sam no longer heard the sobbing, he went into the kitchen where the Architect was standing looking out the window. Sam walked up to the Architect who did not turn around to face him.

"Thank you again for taking the time," Sam paused and the added, "I'm sorry for your loss." He was at a loss as to what to say or how to comfort this tormented man, so he just turned and let himself out.

1145 hours, IdentityPoint

Bob casually looked around the room just to make sure no one had wandered in while he was removing the folders from the file cabinet. Everyone had gone to lunch and it was his day to man the phones, so he took the opportunity to do some research on the case. Over the last few days he had carefully looked through the cabinets for the files on acquisitions and any associated files that might support his analysis. There were a lot of files in a lot of file cabinets. His searching through them would have caused some curiosity, if not discomfort among the office staff, unless he had a reason that was known by the entire staff, one that was public enough that everyone knew about it and routine enough that it would not raise any eyebrows. Watkins had told her assistant Tom that she wanted a review of the files for EEO compliance. It was a review of a random sample of cases of complaints made by the employees. The task was a laborious review of the processes done, the forms completed, and the follow-up taken by the staff. It was Watkins's own system for ensuring the process was followed. It involved getting the case file, reviewing each employee's personnel file, checking the federal and state files for any follow-up actions required, and a host of other steps. It was a boring task that always netted the stuckee with lots of unpaid overtime hours, a desk full of folders, and eyestrain. Watkins gave the task to Tom knowing he would give it to the junior man, which to the delight of the rest of the staff, he did. It was a perfect cover for Bob to do his research.

In the fledging Public Records industry there were new niche companies springing up almost weekly. Just about every type of record was available in some form by some small provider. Court records, marriage license records, divorce, boat ownership, pilot license, liens, rental properties, gun sales, criminal records, along with a host of others were being harvested from every state and any business that had a means to capture names, social security numbers, addresses, birth dates, or physical data.

There were so many opportunities for business that no one had captured the market nor could, it was too broad. With the opportunity came huge hurdles to overcome, data format being the most difficult. Even in the court system, which had been automated in most states for many years, few courts stored the data in the same formats. Even within the same state court system, there may be fifteen different data format systems in a pool of just forty courts all of which made getting all the data, from all the courts, and loading them into one system with the same format, a daunting task.

There were too many sources of records and even in the more mature areas of the business, like court records, there were few standard automated record keeping systems. This nonstandard world meant that, in the best case, collection of the records for resale was done by developing a one method for collecting the records then augmenting it for each office or county. In the worse cases, it involved copying the records from the courthouse by hand and then manually entering them into a data system. Developing automated systems, to convert the raw data tapes into a standard data format for resale, was an expensive process that also required knowledge of data and the ability to reuse systems already proven able to make the transposition of data. The state of the industry made the arena ripe for venture capitalists that not only could provide cash to finance the growth period of the new venture but also could provide both human and systems expertise.

For the past five days Bob had been reviewing the acquisition records, researching the stockowners of the acquired companies in hope of finding some thread that would lead back to Thompson. Bob had been able to make a complete list of all acquisitions for the past three years along with a list of all stockholders who owned stock at the time of acquisition. He had entered the names into his spreadsheet and had sorted the list by name and by address but had found no obvious connections. The only names that repeated were investment companies, which was not all that uncommon. He hadn't found a single name that appeared to be suspect.

Chapter 7

Sunday, October 16

Intervention

1100 hours, Alpharetta

Sam drove his car into the driveway and parked outside of the closed garage doors. He walked around the car and opened the door for Mary who stepped out and, after Sam closed the door, walked with him to the front door.

"Do you really think this is a good idea?" Mary asked as they walked up the overgrown flagstone sidewalk.

"He sounded like he welcomed the visit when I called this morning. I am telling you, he will really like that we stopped by."

Mary slowed her pace as to not get to the door too quickly, "I appreciate you think this guy is on the edge, but do you think it's your responsibility to bring him back?"

"Mary," Sam stopped walking and looked at her. "I like the guy. Like I said, we met on Friday, and we had a big chat. Then yesterday I stopped by, and he seemed to respond well to my visit. I think he is okay, a little lost but okay nonetheless. Besides, he is lost without his lady—just like I would be without you."

"Oh, Sam, that is sweet." She kissed him on the cheek very tenderly, "You still know how to thrill a girl. Let's go meet your Architect."

They walked up the steps and rang the bell. Within a few seconds, the owner of the house was at the door and welcoming them inside.

"I thought that with the day being so pretty, we could sit out back on the porch," the Architect said, as he led them through the kitchen to the connecting porch. They sat at the same table where he and Sam had sat on their first visit. Everything looked the same except there were no beer bottles lying around and it was obvious that he showered and shaved in anticipation of Sam and Mary's visit.

"It is a beautiful day; a bit warm for October. Can I get you something to drink?"

"That would be nice," Mary responded.

"What can I get you?"

Without thinking of what Sam had said about the Architect's drinking she automatically said, "Just whatever you are drinking will be fine."

The Architect looked at Sam for his selection. "The same for me."

He went inside and Sam looked at Mary with a 'why didn't you say something else look' but neither spoke. A short time later, he returned with three glasses of ice tea.

They chatted for over an hour with each becoming more comfortable by the minute. They spoke of the house, the weather, Sam and Mary's children and even some politics, but nothing about the Architect's wife or IdentityPoint. Sam excused himself to use the bathroom; Mary looked out at the gardens in silence while the Architect sat back in his chair, head down and his eyes closed, almost as if he we're asleep.

He opened his eyes and without looking at Mary he said, "You know, I don't know when it happened." The Architect was speaking softly as if in a confessional.

"What's that?"

"When I became what I am now." He looked at her and had such a sorrowful look anyone could feel his pain. "When I lost my job, I was sure that it was a mistake; I just waited for them to call me back. My wife was so understanding, and she was there for me. I waited for a month and no call, then two. Soon, I didn't even recognize the days passing by. Days became weeks and weeks become months. I was doing nothing, and I let everything go. My wife went off to work and I stayed here reading the paper and waiting. The months became a year before I even noticed it, and by then I rarely dressed or showered—what was the point?"

Mary reached over and touched his left hand that was resting on the table, and he covered it with his right hand. "I had fallen into a deep black abyss of self-loathing, and there was no way out. It was like there was no time at all, I didn't know what day it was most of the time. I even remember having once to look at the newspaper to tell what month it was. I got up in the morning and then it was just evening and I went to bed. My wife would come home from work, make some dinner and try to get me to get back in the game, as she called it, but I just couldn't seem to hear her. Then one day, it was a Saturday I remember that, she came to me, right out here." He pointed to the chair to his right, "And she told me that she loved me, but there was no getting through to me. She kissed my forehead." He slowly reached up with his hand and touched the spot, "And then said to me, 'I love you too much to watch you waste away.'" She gave me an envelope, told me that she would be with a friend and for me to call when I was ready to want her again."

Mary could see tears in his eyes, and when she looked up she saw Sam standing in the doorway, watching and obviously allowing the man to talk to Mary alone.

"She's not gone for good, you know," Mary said quietly and tenderly to him.

He looked up at her, "Yes, she is, she couldn't be with me." He stopped and then took both his hands and brought them to his chest, opened fingers and shaking hands, but not touching himself. "Like this."

"I know why she left, and it's not because she didn't love you, and not because you lost your job. She left you because she loves you so much that she doesn't want you to have pain. To know she sees you like this, being less of the man than she knows you are."

His distorted face changed from a painful expression to one more of calmness. "Do you really think so?"

"I know so."

"How? How do you know?"

"Because I love my Sam the same way, and nothing would give me more pain than for him to think he disappoints me, that I no longer thought he was all the man I wanted, married and loved—which he is. When he first left the Army it was, shall we say, interesting, but it didn't take Sam long to realize a man doesn't have to wear a uniform to have honor. He changed careers, but it didn't change him."

He reached over the table, retook her hands, and mouthed the words 'Thank you' and Mary smiled and nodded back to him.

There was a sound in the kitchen as Sam very loudly put a mug down on the counter, and then came back outside. "I hope you don't mind, but I helped myself to a drink while I was in there. I was just so damn thirsty,"

"Not at all," the Architect casually wiped his eyes trying not to let Sam see him.

"Well Mary, we really need to get going. The kids are expecting our call," Sam looked over at the Architect. "They're on vacation in Texas you know."

They all stood, walked to the front door and exchanged pleasantries. Sam shook his hand, and Mary gently kissed him on the cheek. They walked to the car as the Architect closed the front door. Sam opened the car door for Mary and as she stepped to enter the car, he took her and kissed her very hard. He released her, looked at her tenderly, but said nothing, and then walked to his side of the car and got in.

Chapter 8

Monday, October 17

AliceK

0915 hours, IdentityPoint

Sam sat at the computer terminal in his small office at IdentityPoint having stopped at the cafeteria on the way in. He had planned to limit the stop to coffee, but the croissant with egg, cheese and sausage smelled just too good to pass up. He took a sip of coffee, sat back in the chair, and then took a bite of the croissant while the computer was booting up.

"You keep eating those things and you'll never fit back in your uniform," came a voice from the door.

Sam was startled by the voice and almost spilled his coffee as he swung around to see George in the doorway.

"I think I've noticed a couple of pounds on you in just the week you've been here."

"Have you been talking to my wife?" Sam smiled as he stood to greet George and then motion for him to take a seat.

"So how was your weekend, George?" Sam asked as he took a bite. "This is the low cal version. Substitute eggs, imitation cheese and soy sausage. Yummy!"

"I can see that." George nodded and patted his own flat stomach.

"At ease, soldier." Sam jokingly said to George who was now swelling his stomach out.

"That's 'At ease, Marine' to you soldier boy," George responded.

Sam nodded to acknowledge. "And don't be calling me 'soldier boy'. Army puke will do nicely, thank you very much."

George nodded back, "Army puke it is."

"I brought you the results of the batch run, it came in overnight. I didn't want to send it through email, so I put it on a disk."

"Understood," Sam said as he reached out to take the disk from George.

"I took the liberty of uploading the data for you into spreadsheet format," George said as he released the disk to Sam who took it and immediately put it into the computer. Sam opened Excel and then opened the file on the disk that was simply labeled, 'batch.xls'. Immediately the screen filled with the spreadsheet's rows and columns, and Sam watched as the cells filled with data."

"I labeled the columns for you. The name field is a full name, not separated into first and last names. The data just wasn't that clean. But the address fields converted cleanly, and there is a social for just about every name once you sorted and joined the data correctly." George had stood up and moved behind Sam's chair in order to point to the fields on the computer screen. Sam could see that the list had been sorted by names and then by addresses, and that there were many records for the same name. He could also see that, although not every record was complete with a date of birth or social security number, the way George had loaded the data, then sorted it, the data could be traced to enable a complete history on the person.

"Some records had everything," George started. "But some just had a name and an address, others had a name and social, and still others had the name and birth date. But when you match them together its child's play to make a complete record."

They looked at the list as Sam scrolled up and down the screen. "There are some 582 records which I think includes 165 names all of which have an address related link to PEI of Milwaukee during the period 1952 to 1965."

Sam scrolled down the screen and stopped when he saw the entry, Michael Ream, Lake Road, Lake Forrest, Illinois. "That's him."

"I know."

"Only one record? In that entire period only one?" Sam looked up at George.

"The batch process gets every record, then sorts them, and eliminates exact duplicates, so there may have been many records on him, but if they had the same information they would have been tossed."

"Not bad, George. You know if you keep at this you might become a reasonably decent data analyst."

George turned to leave, "Not me, Sam. I hate computers."

"Thanks, George," Sam said as he peered over his computer terminal at the departing man.

Without turning around George just waved and then continued on.

Sam continued to review the list. After five minutes he scrolled back to the top of the list and then opened up the PeopleFinder application, entered the first name and a few seconds later the screen filled with data. Sam reviewed the report on the screen then printed the important pages, stapled them together, put them in a folder, and then entered the second name.

0946 hours

In the computer room of IdentityPoint, hundreds of computers holding databases for data systems, filled with billions of records, hummed as they executed millions of transactions per day. Application servers received requests from Internet-based users, which in turn sent the requests to a host of middleware servers, which in turn sent request to hundreds of database servers, which in turn sent responses back to application servers, fax servers, email servers, and pagers servers, as well as audit systems and billing systems.

Throughout the process the automated systems received input from other systems and executed tasks as programmed. The middleware systems, which were just as the name implied, in the middle between the applications and the databases, received requests for information, recorded it, passed requests for the data to hundreds of databases, monitored the job, recorded the transaction to the Billing Log, and if the requestor was not one of those government agencies that had made special arrangements so as not to leave an audit trail of what they requested, the system would then record what was requested in the audit log. The Middleware would send a copy of the original request transaction to the Watch Servers systems. This part of the process took about three hundredths of a second to complete.

Next in the process was the data retrieval and print generation process. The SQL, or request methods of IdentityPoint were poorly designed, and although the request was executed in a fraction of a second, the fulfillment of the request could take minutes to produce. Hundreds of systems would be queried, mass amounts of data retrieved, and the applications would sort the data using various rules. Finally, the data would be joined together into a history and a report would be generated and passed to the requesting computer screen.

Meanwhile the Watch Servers, which had received the copy of the transaction, went about their tasks of checking the requested name against the watch lists from various agencies.

Every watch system scanned every transaction, and if the name matched a watch list entry, the system would send a transaction to a phone interface, pager interface, fax interface, or email interface. That interface in turn would format a message and inform the watch list owner that someone had just looked at one of their 'records of interest.' In this case of personnel reports, the watch system would generate a notice to the watch list owner that someone was looking at a 'watch record' even before the requestor received the report on their computer screen.

0946 hours,

Sam looked at the fifteenth name on the list, then entered it into the PeopleTracker system, pressed the Enter button, and then waited for the system's response.

0946.02 hours

The watch system known only as AliceK executed a compare on a transaction, and for the first time in over two years, the system had a match. As programmed, the system created a message and dispatched it to a phone server that completed a call notifying the watch list owner.

0946.22 hours, Washington, D.C.

Garrett was in one of the many FBI conference rooms listening to an update on one of the investigations underway by his group when the cell phone, which he had placed in the vibrate mode before entered the room, was now vibrating and alerting him to a call. He pulled his phone out of his pocket, lifted the phone cover and saw 'You have a text message' notification. He pulled up the message and read it.

Message from AliceK
Subject Name: David R Curry
User ID. DPC093802

He closed the phone and immediately left the room.

0947:30 hours

Sam received the report on the screen, and he began to look through it, page by page before printing it for a more thorough review later on.

0952 hours, Washington, D.C.

Garrett was back at his computer terminal with secure access to IdentityPoint. He selected a URL from his favorites list and within a few seconds, he was logging into IdentityPoint's security system. He entered the user ID, DPC093802, and pressed enter and almost instantly the screen filled with a form and then the form filled in.

```
User: DPC093802
Name: Sam Cohen
Company: IdentityPoint
Status: Contractor
```

He noted the data in a notebook he carried then logged off the system. He hoped that this was just a mistake, a typo by the user, or perhaps just random testing on IdentityPoint's part.

1145 hours, Chicago, IL.

At 0930 hours that morning David had solved the case; at 0945 hours he had briefed a very happy client and was already back at his hotel by 1130 hours. "That was a productive day!" He thought, "Now for a workout in the hotel gym, a long shower, followed by a world famous Chicago Style deep dish pizza and a couple of beers courtesy of the client. I'll get a flight back for midday tomorrow and veg out in the morning. Any why not? I've earned it." He had spent two weeks investigating the client's warehouse business, which had been losing inventory without any signs of a break in. Electronics were in high demand and thieves could get a good price on them even if they were hot.

David had been watching the operation as part of a repair crew. The owner had arranged for a friend of his to have David pretend to be an employee of his company that had been hired to service the big floor heater units they used in the warehouse during the winter. There was nothing wrong with them, but pretending to be fixing the units gave David a cover that enabled him to be on site without raising suspicion.

David had received a list of every person who had access to the warehouse and checked them all out but nothing stood out. He also checked the inventory and that all seemed to match. They didn't appear to take them in transit as the shippers documents showed they sent 'X' numbers of boxes or crates and the receiving section signed for the same number. It didn't appear that it was anyone in receiving as there were five different people who had received goods that later came up missing. Unless they all were in on it, but David figured that wasn't the case.

He had checked the security systems and determined they were tight, even for a low-end warehouse. The watchmen were on duty 24-hours a day and the security system recorded every time a bay door opened; so if there were any thefts at night, or during the off shifts, they would have had to unload the crates and carry the goods out by hand through the entrance door. That was just a regular thirty-six inch door and they never would have been able to get all the goods out without spending most of the night hand carrying the goods while avoiding the security guard and cameras.

An Accounting audit proved the goods had been received as ordered, but when the sales records were compared to the inventory there was a very large shortage. The owner and David were both sure it was an inside job, but after a week of watching the warehouse operations, he was stumped and figured that whoever was behind it had stopped. He had concluded that the recent audits must have been reporting previous thefts, and he had planned to let the client know he was probably not going to find anything.

David cleaned up his work area and completed his false repairs, which at least did include changing all the air filters in the system. He took all the boxes to the industrial trash compactor, and just as he was about to throw his trash onto the conveyor belt that took the trash up into the compactor, he saw a piece of a box that had apparently got caught on a sharp edge of the chute and got ripped off. Lying between the belt and the sidewall was a box label that said '2 of 4' on a large professionally printed shipping label that read *Chciago* Liquidation Distributors Elk Grove Village IL. It struck him; because he had gone for coffee a few minutes before and while he was walking across the warehouse floor he had to wait for a forklift that was carrying a large crate to pass in front of him. Seeing David, the driver stopped, but David motioned for him to continue and the forklift eased passed him. As it did, David saw the name of the company was misspelled on the shipping label, and Sam snickered at the misspelling of the name of the company, which was Chicago and misspelled Chciago.

David became curious and walked through the warehouse, where he found the rest of the shipment, three unopened boxes, still sitting on pallets. He pushed them, and when they hardly moved under his effort he knew they were definitely full. David then walked back to the loading docks, went outside through the large open bay door, stepped to the right and leaned on the outside wall. He took a sip of coffee and then slid his body down to the concrete deck. He sat there drinking his coffee as he watched the activity on the dock. The truck came in and the driver went inside, got a clerk from receiving, and when they returned they went back to the truck. After the clerk verified the number of crates, the forklift driver then took the pallets into a holding area and placed them into various locations for distribution crews to break them down and stock the shelves.

David watched and saw the receiving crews open boxes and then put the contents onto conveyor belts or just transport the inventory directly to the bins. They did not work an entire shipment, they just took whatever crate or box was there, so once the shipment had been accounted for at the dock, it was then quickly dispersed to shelves for resale. David researched the transit documents and got the shipper information of the shipment that David suspected had just been pilfered.

The next day David waited for that shipper's truck to arrive. When it did David watched closely as the same process he had watched for days was repeated. The driver came, he found a receiver to account for the shipment, but David noticed it was not the same man who received the shipment the day before. The two validated the contents, signed off on the documents, and the forklift operator moved the pallets. The forklift operator carefully entered the truck, retrieved his load, and then drove to a section of the warehouse, which was marked "D" on a large sign that hung from an overhead beam. He dropped the pallet carefully and if the pallet wasn't just in the correct spot the forklift driver used the fork extensions too shift the heavy pallet into the correct position. Then he returned to the truck for another pallet and repeated the process for three more pallets; each time he dropped them carefully in section D and shifted them with the fork extensions.

When the driver brought the last pallet, he didn't stop at Section D but went all the way to the end of the offloading area and dropped the pallet. Then David saw what he needed to see; the driver pushed the pallet to a corner of the room by hand.

David made a call on his cell phone to the client. While he waited for the client to arrive, David took a disposable camera out of his overalls and shot some pictures of the pallet and then more pictures as the young forklift operator took out a utility knife, cut each vertical corner of the box, and it collapsed on itself. He then took more pictures as the driver took the cardboard to the trash compactor and dropped it in. The driver returned to the now empty pallet, put it on the forklift, drove to the other end of the warehouse, and put it with the other empty pallets. In one minute the entire shipment was gone and evidence destroyed.

When the owner arrived, David pointed the thief out, gave him the camera, explained how the inventory was stolen by the driver before the shipment arrived, got uninvolved agents to verify the deliveries, and then how the forklift operator destroyed the evidence. The client was not only pleased that David had discovered how the thefts were done and who had done it, but it was a double treat to the client as the forklift operator was his wife's nephew who he despised. David heard that and knew it was bonus time.

Now it was 1145 hours and he was sitting in the hotel having stopped in the lobby gift shop/mini mart for a bottle of water and a power bar, but decided to 'go wild' and got a Coke and Milky Way instead. When he settled into the room on the tenth floor, he put the Coke and candy on a small table next to a lounge chair that had a great view of the city, and then went to the bathroom and washed his face. He walked back towards the window and picked up the complimentary *Tribune* the hotel had provided, but he had not yet read. He sat down and relaxed and ate his candy as he read the first page. He turned the second page, took a sip of his Coke, read the headline, and nearly spit the Coke all over himself.

Only Link to POW Identities Murdered in Prison

"Holy shit!" David gasped at the headline as he drew the paper nearer to him, as if it were to change the meaning. He read on.

Michael Ream, the man who reportedly had masqueraded as an American citizen for forty years and who had been convicted of the murder of one military officer and the attempted murder of another, and who may have actually been Kurt Roessger an escaped German POW, was found dead in the Illinois State Prison at Springfield. Ream, or Roessger, was the key subject in the three year investigation into the deaths of SSG Frank Ventrilli, who was first reported killed in a hit and run in 1945, and SGT Jonathan Simon who disappeared in 1945 and then was later identified as the second body in the now infamous grave opening at Fort Sheridan three years ago.

Ream was convicted of second degree murder and attempted murder, but has never made any statements concerning the murder nor the accusation that he was Kurt Roessger. Ream was coming to Chicago to speak with the Joint Review Team investigating the claims that American soldiers had been killed in 1945 and German POWs took their places and entered American society through their stolen identities.

Mr. Curling, District Attorney for Chicago and the ranking City of Chicago member of the committee, released a statement that, "The committee has come to the conclusion that Sergeant Simon was murdered in 1945, and the Sergeant Ventrilli was also the victim of a homicide, and that there are discrepancies of a serious nature in the records regarding the POW contracts of 1944 and 1945, along with the verification that two of the bodies buried in the POW graves were not who they were reported to be. However, to this point we have been unable to discover the actual identities of those unknowns who rest in these graves. The death of Mr. Ream is a severe blow to that investigation."

The announcement of Ream's death had been delayed for seven days while prison authorities conducted their investigation. There are no suspects in Ream's death at this time.

"Damn." David picked up the hotel phone, dialed "9" for an outside line then called a familiar number. "Bob, I'm packing right now, call the airline and get me a flight back right away, then call me back. Call Sam and set up dinner for tonight like usual, same time and place."

"What's going on?" Bob asked.

David stopped his packing and quietly said, "Ream's been murdered."

There was a pause as neither man spoke. "I'll get the flight data and call you right back."

"Roger," David responded in his military manner. "Oh, and Bob."

"Yes."

"Don't tell Sam anything about this unless he hears it himself from the media."

"No problem."

David thanked Bob, hung up, then called the desk and told them he was checking out. Bob called back in three minutes with the information on Delta flight 1175 leaving O'Hare at 1:10 pm local and arriving in Atlanta at 4:24 pm local time. Two minutes later David was in the elevator in route to O'Hare airport.

1432 hours, IdentityPoint

Bob had made two trips to Sam's office to let him know about the meeting, but Sam had not been there. He didn't want to leave a message on the company phone in the chance that it could be overheard by someone when Sam was playing it back. On his way back to his work area, he saw Sam coming down the steps from the second floor to the lobby. "Hey, Sam," Bob gave Sam a slight wave to get his attention.

Sam walked over to Bob who had stooped by a display cabinet that contained some memorabilia of the company that highlighted events in the company history.

Sam looked at Bob then past him at an odd display in the cabinet. "That's got to be the most bizarre item ever displayed in a corporate showcase.

"What?"

"That." Sam pointed to a pair of socks that were in the cabinet and displayed like you would see in a department store.

"Sam, I got a call from David."

"I mean why socks? I know the little card there states it represents the Chairman's individuality through his not wearing of socks." Sam looked at Bob. "Weird."

Bob looked at the socks and then at Sam.

"This place must be full of kiss-ass executives if they had to stoop to this level to honor the Chairman."

Bob was uncomfortable to start with, having to tell Sam about the meeting and doing it without being obvious that there was something wrong. Now he was even more uncomfortable with Sam talking about the Chairman's socks in the middle of the lobby. "I think it was actually suggested by Watkins."

"Watkins? You're kidding. I wouldn't have thought her the kiss-ass type." Sam shook his head.

"As I understand it was a shot, not a compliment. She knew he was too vain not to think her suggestion of displaying his socks as a symbol of his independence was too much for him to resist when it really was an outright shot at his immense ego."

"Damn, I like this woman more every day," Sam said. "What did he want?"

Bob looked at the socks then back at Sam. "I don't know what the Chairman wanted."

"What did *David* want, he called. Remember."

"Yes, yes. He finished his case in Chicago and is back in town and wants to meet tonight, same time same place."

"No problem. Mary and I had planned to have dinner there tonight anyway. She is meeting me there when she gets back this evening. She has been shopping all day for the trip to Biras Creek."

"Oh yeah, you are going on vacation. An island in the British Virgin Islands no less. That's going to cost." Bob quietly said.

"Already has."

"I tried to tell you earlier about the meeting tonight, but you weren't in your office."

"I had a meeting with the Benefits department all afternoon." Sam looked around to make sure no one could overhear him. "You know the VP up there is a total drunk. The guy has all the signs: the redness, the lack of concentration, and the odor."

"You know, Sam, you shouldn't jump to conclusions about people." Bob paused to let it sit for a moment. "It could be that he is just stupid and stinks."

Sam looked coldly at Bob. "There are some things that people do well and some they don't do well. Bob, telling jokes goes in the category of things you don't do well."

Bob looked at Sam and grunted.

"See you tonight," Sam said as he smiled and went down the hallway to his office.

1455 hours

Having returned to his office, Sam had finished his notes on the work session and took the opportunity to enter some more names from the PEI list into PeopleFinder. When the system provided a report, he saved it for a later review. Sam then entered the twentieth name.

1455.30 hours, IdentityPoint Data Center

The Watch Server compared the new transaction with its list and then for the second time in one day sent a message to the Phone Notification Server.

1456.05 hours, Washington, D.C.

Garrett opened the cover of his ringing cell phone. 'You have a text message' was again on the phone screen. He pulled up the text message and read it.

Message from AliceK
Subject Name: Phillip L. Brock
User ID. DPC093802

"Oh, Christ, no."

Garrett saved the message then entered a number and made a call.

"Sir, I've had a call from *Alice Kay* today, make that two calls." Garrett listened without emotion.

"Yes, Sir. I will get back to you."

Garrett sat back in his chair. His head was pounding and he reached up with both his hands and wiped his face. He ran his fingers through his hair then held on to his head as he leaned back in the chair and looked up at the ceiling. He stared at the stark white ceiling, his eyes moving from place to place, as if the answers were written on it and all he had to do was read them. There was nothing written there; he had no answers, just more questions. He thought to himself, "Would this be another 'loose end' he would have to fix?" He began to feel sick to his stomach.

1655 hours, Alpharetta

Sam had left the job at 1600 hours and stopped by just to see how he was getting along. He needed the Architect's help to get to the data at IdentityPoint, to unlock the databases, and to make sense of the systems he had written for IdentityPoint to record, analyze, and even manipulate the acquisition data. But somewhere between George Bailey making the introduction, and Sam meeting a sorrowful, defeated man, and with his understanding of this man's turmoil, Sam became more concerned with the man than the cause.

They had spent almost an hour drinking ice tea and chatting about their wives, life, and the all-important baseball pennant race. To Sam's absolute joy he discovered that the Architect was a Phillies fan, not the huge fan that Sam was, not the fan who could remember each and every member of the 1965-era team they both grew up with, not the fan that knew that Tony Taylor played second base for the Phils for fifteen years, and not the fan that knew that Steve Carlton won half of all the games the Phils won in that dismal year of 1972. But he was a fan who knew Tug McGraw was on the mound for every World Series victory in their 1983 World Championship, and he was a fan that knew that Mike Schmidt was the MVP for 1980, and for Sam that was enough to build a friendship on.

"Well, it's been good but I need to get going. Mary is expecting me for dinner." Sam said as he got up from the porch chair and extended his hand to the Architect.

"Yes, of course. Thanks for stopping by, Sam." He shook Sam's hand and escorted him to the front door. "Sam, George told me you needed my help with your case, but you haven't asked me. I'm more than ready to help out. I know what it's about."

Sam smiled slightly, not one of humor but one of gratitude towards a kind gesture, "Perhaps. Yes, perhaps, when I return from my vacation, we can talk more about it."

"Yes, Sam, that would be good. Enjoy your vacation," he said as Sam started down the walkway to his car. "And watch out for those coral reefs, they can be killers."

1820 hours, Alpharetta

He had no sooner walked in the door when Maria saw him, smiled so sweetly, and came right over to welcome him. "Good Evening, Sam," giving him a big kiss on his cheek. "It is so good to see you."

Sam gave her a big hug and the much shorter women almost disappeared as the much taller man gave her his usual bear hug greeting. "And it is so good to see you too."

"Meeting the boys again this evening?" She asked as she squeezed his hand.

"Yes, I am, then Mary is coming at nineteen-thirty hours, I mean seven thirty."

"No problem, after all the times you have been here, I'm getting used to the military time. Come, I have a quiet table for you." She led him to the back of the small restaurant to the last booth on the far wall. It was next to a wine rack that filled the rest of the wall so the only other people that could be near to them were in a booth directly in front of them. This allowed them to talk fairly freely and it provided the added benefit for Sam to see Mary when she arrived as he always met Mary for dinner after these meetings.

"And how is the lovely Mary this evening, I'm looking forward to seeing her tonight," Maria asked as she handed Sam the menu for this evening.

"Oh, she's not coming tonight." Sam paused, "I had to punish her." Sam didn't look up at Maria but took the menu.

"What did you say?" Maria hit Sam on the shoulder.

"Oh yes, Maria, Mary teased me today, so I sent her to her room for the night. She was a bad girl."

Maria frowned and then realized Sam was teasing her again and smiled, "You two love birds are so cute. Would you like a glass of wine this evening?"

"Of course. What about that Ruffino Classico Ducal Chianti you gave us the last time we were in? It was fabulous."

"Perfect!" Maria said as she walked away. Sam watched as she went to tell the staff to bring the wine. She was an incredibly happy person, Sam thought, and wished he could capture that happiness for himself. Most every night he and Mary came, they sat in the back of the restaurant and he would always sit so he could see the door. It was his

111

mother that taught him to do that. "When he is with a lady at dinner, a gentleman never sits with his back to the door," she would say. She said it was so the lady was never surprised by someone entering. It was the man's job to watch for things. His mother was from an older time, a dangerous time when gangsters were free to shoot people in restaurants while innocent people dined around them. Those days were long gone by. He wasn't really sure why he still followed that rule, but it was one of those things he just always did. Admittedly, it may be considered a little quirky, but on the bright side he always saw what was happening in the restaurant, and in Casa Nouva his principal observation was Maria. He was always amazed at Maria's energy, even when the place was packed and remained so for hours; she was always the picture of energy and gracious friendliness.

The practice of sitting looking forward again paid off as Sam saw Bob and David coming in the front door, he waved to them to join him at the table. When they arrived Sam stood, greeted both and shook their hands. Sam sat down and slid over but they both got in the other side of the booth.

"So, welcome back, David. How's it going Bob?"

"Thanks," David said quietly as if he had something to say, which he had.

"I can see something's up. What is it?" Sam was quick to pick up on it.

"I take you haven't read the Trib or heard what has happened in Chicago," David asked.

"No. I don't think I have." Sam looked at Bob for concurrence or perhaps he had heard. Bob made no response, just bit his lower lip and said nothing.

"Ream's dead," David said quietly and with a tone of someone who knew a reaction would follow.

"What!" Sam said it loud enough that the staff and the few early diners in the restaurant could hear him. He quickly realized his level and leaned over to David and asked quietly. "How? What happened?"

"They found him dead last week. He had been stabbed to death. There're no suspects."

"Holy Shit!" Sam said, and looked at Bob who Sam immediately thought did not look surprised at the news. "You knew, Bob?"

"First I heard of it was David's call." Bob said looking at David then back to Sam as if to get concurrence from David on what he said was true.

Sam looked down at the table and just thought for a few moments. "I wonder why now?"

"How's that?" Bob asked.

"I was wondering why someone killed him now, not last year or the year before. Just seems odd to me. I've got to call Curling in Chicago," Sam said as he looked up and saw Roberto coming to the table with his wine.

"Gooda Evening Gentleman," Roberto said with his Italian accent. "I hope you are all well this evening."

Sam extended his hand to him and they shook hands as they did every time Sam was there. "Couldn't be better Roberto, and you?"

"I am good, Sam, graci."

"Beni," Sam replied with his own slight accent.

Roberto took David's and Bob's drink order, and then asked if the two were staying for dinner. He knew the routine that the three of them would meet for drinks and talk, and then Mary and Sam would have dinner later; tonight was no exception. David ordered a Moretti, an Italian beer, and Bob a sweet tea. Roberto went through the specials anyway and then departed to get the drinks.

"I read the account in the Trib at the hotel. The article said that Ream was going to Chicago, and that he was going to appear before that team you worked with."

"The United States Attorney's Office, United States Army, and City of Chicago Special Joint Review Team, Investigating the Events of 1944 and 1945, Relevant to the Reported Deaths of German POWs, United States Army Sergeant Jonathan Simon, and Associated Deaths of that Period." Sam was staring off into nowhere and said the name as if he had been reading it from a card. He had read it and said it so many times, he knew it as well as he knew his own name.

David looked at Bob and shrugged a little as if to say 'Wow', then looked back at Sam without emotion. There was a pause while no one spoke, until David broke the silence. I think it is more than coincidental that he was taken out now, just before he was to see The

United States Attorney's Office, United States Army, City of Chicago, Special something team."

"Special Joint Review Team, Investigating the Events of 1944 and 1945, Relevant to the Reported Deaths of German POWs, United States Army Sergeant Jonathan Simon, and Associated Deaths of that Period." Sam smiled at them both, "Say it a thousand times, and it's like reciting your bank account number."

"I don't know my bank account number Sam," David kidded as he drank some of his beer that Roberto had just brought.

"You are such an asshole David," Sam joked.

"No, I really don't know my bank account number," David said again as if it were an important point.

Bob raised his glass, "To assholes."

They all smiled and toasted.

David then spent five minutes reporting on his success in Chicago and capturing the warehouse bandit, and Bob provided an update on his end of the IdentityPoint investigation, which was not going all that well.

Roberto returned to the table as Bob was finishing, "You gentlemen care for another drink?" He looked at Sam and David and they both acknowledged, and Bob raised his ice tea glass indicating he also wanted a refill, but Roberto did not seem to notice.

"Excuse me," Bob said as Roberto walked away. "Did you see that? I don't think he took my order. We need to find a new place, the service here is terrible."

"Calm down, Bob, I'm sure it was unintentional." David looked at Sam with a sly look and continued, "I'm sure he just didn't see you."

"I do have to say," Sam added. "It does seem like they act like you aren't here sometimes. Odd."

"Exactly! Exactly what I am saying, and we need to go somewhere else." Bob was excited and animated, but not so that the other guests around him heard his ranting, or at least they did not pay any heed to it. "This is definitely the last time."

"Let's get back on point shall we?" David said as he grabbed a piece of garlic bread from the basket on the table.

Bob gathered himself and continued. "Generally speaking IdentityPoint's General Counsel is supposed to manage all the documents that are required for submission to the SEC after an acquisition. Now since most of what the SEC is concerned with is insider trading they look at the owners of the acquired companies. With the exception of a couple, most of the acquisitions they have made have been small."

"How small?" David asked.

"Mostly between ten and thirty million dollars. I have been looking at the ownership records at the time of acquisition, and almost every one included investment companies as major stock holders." Bob drained the last of his tea and looked around the room for the waiter but was unsuccessful in getting his attention. "Now as you know, when a little company gets bought by a big company, if the stock of the little company is publicly traded, then the stock goes up, and it's easy to see how much money they made per share. However, when it's privately owned the stock price is internally set."

Sam looked at David, and they stared back at each other without getting the significance of what Bob was saying.

"You don't get it, do you?" Bob looked at both men. "Look, if IdentityPoint pays one hundred dollars a share for a company that is publicly trading for fifty dollars there will be questions asked. But since the private company numbers are *private*, they set the price, so whatever IdentityPoint pays…"

David finished the sentence, "to the private company remains private."

Sam looked at both David and Bob as he was the only one still not getting it.

"So," Bob continued. "Those people who watch such things, namely the SEC, would start to look at the major stock holders of the company for signs of insider trading." Bob raised his glass in another unsuccessful attempt to get a refill.

While Bob unsuccessfully attempted to get Roberto's attention Sam continued. "Since the stock and its price are private, there is no public stock price to raise an alarm; so if the owners made a huge windfall that would be up to the board of both companies, and not the SEC."

David signaled to Roberto who immediately came over to the table. "Could you get some ice tea for the gentleman?"

"Certainly, Sir."

Bob just sneered at Roberto, then returned his attention to Sam. "I think if our client is correct, and there is fraud, then its there."

"Where?" David asked.

"I looked at all the acquired companies, first checking all those that just had principals listed." He made a quick look to David and Sam to make sure they were following; then based on their looks, he decided to go into more depth. "You know those companies where the stock holders were all company officers. I did a reasonable search on the names to see if they were related to any of the IdentityPoint executives, but came up with nothing."

"So why am I thinking you found something in the other case," David asked as he thanked Roberto for the ice tea that he had just brought and then gave it to Bob.

Bob put his drink on the table and continued. "Our client has kept data from every one of the acquisitions, and from looking at that data, I can tell you that…." Bob fumbled with his words as he worked in the tight booth to get a paper from his pants pocket. "Of seventy-six acquisitions, thirty-five involved investment companies. Of that, twenty-two investment companies were involved once and six other investment companies were involved in thirteen acquisitions."

"I guess I don't see much there," David said as he looked to Sam who nodded in concurrence.

"Work with me on this," Bob said as he took more tea. "I looked at those that had two or more acquisitions, and I stumbled onto something interesting. Four years ago Louwaert Investments was involved in three acquisitions, and nothing since. Then Sunset Investment was involved in three, then nothing. Same thing for J&D investment." Bob paused to let it sink in with Sam and David, but also to be a little dramatic. "The thing is, when I looked up Sunset Investments in D&B, it's listed as Louwaert Investments doing business as Sunset Investments."

"So Sunset and Louwaert are the same company," David said.

"Yes, and so is J&D Investments, and so is Ricky Tech Funds, which was involved in an acquisition this year," Bob smiled as if he scored.

"Interesting," Sam said.

David nodded, "Affirmative."

"So one company has been involved in," Sam stopped as he counted, "in ten acquisitions. That seems like either they are really in tune in the Public Records world, or they got help." Sam checked his watch. It was getting late and Mary was due shortly. He had suggested they skip dinner tonight, but Mary wanted to come and see Maria before they went off on vacation.

"Well, that is a mouthful, Bob." David turned to Sam. "What do you have Sam?"

Sam shook his head. "Not much besides I almost blew my cover." Sam went on and described how he had been running reports on the POW case and how George picked up on it, but fortunately it turned out that George was not all that fond of IdentityPoint for what they had done to the Architect. Sam told them about his visits to the Architect's home and how far the man had sunk since he had left IdentityPoint.

"I went there to get info on the systems so I could look at the financials on line or go deeper into the personnel records, but he was so bad off we just talked. When I get back from vacation, I may try again."

"What about the POW reports?" David looked at Sam. "Its okay man, you didn't screw the pooch. Maybe you'll get lucky."

"Well, George had a friend in the Records Group run a batch report for me, and it isolated names of those who had an association with PEI during the years Ream had it. I've run a few reports, but I haven't done much with it. It's a start."

"Okay, I'm going to check with the client, then take a trip to see our boys in Florida. What's their name?"

"Louwaert." Bob passed David a small sheet of paper with the name and address of the Florida-based companies.

"Right. I'll leave tomorrow. Sam, you are leaving Wednesday. Correct?"

"Affirmative. Wanted to stay a week but it's really expensive. We got a deal on flights, and we're only staying four days so it won't be that bad. Be back Sunday night," Sam said as he munched on the garlic bread.

"Well, then I will see you Bob on Thursday night then." David looked to Bob for confirmation, but got none. "Hello Bob." David looked at Sam then back at Bob. "Earth to Bob, come in Bob."

"Could we do it Friday? I have a thing to do on Thursday."

"A thing?"

'Yeah."

"You mean like something more important than meeting with your boss on a crucial case?" David tried to look stern, but Sam knew he wasn't serious.

"Ah, yeah." Bob replied again without changing expression.

Sam looked at David. "More important than you, David? More important than work, David? You know what that means?" Sam smiled and then looked at Bob. "A woman. Bob has a woman."

"You have a woman, Bob? That can't be right, you never have a woman." David now was in full tease mode. David turned to Sam. "He never has a woman. He's gay you know."

"I suspected that," Sam replied, then put his hand to his mouth to hold back the laughter.

"I am not gay," Bob snarled then looked around to make sure no one heard him. He leaned forward and spoke softly, as if he were transferring state secrets. "It's just a concert."

"And who is this woman?" David asked as he picked up his beer.

"Her name is Tammy. She works in H/R with him," Sam responded before Bob could.

"How did you know that? I never said a word."

"You didn't have to Bob. I saw you the other day in the cafeteria with her, and anytime she is in the room you zone out," Sam said.

"I guess its love," David said to Sam as Bob sat unable to respond.

"To love." Sam raised his glass and David followed. They waited for Bob who finally raised his.

"It's just a concert."

1935 hours, Washington, D.C.

Garrett was upset to start with, but now he was more so. He had run Sam Cohen in the PeopleFinder and got almost nothing. There was far too little to confirm his identity or to track him down with an on-site. His last listed address was a post office box, and the one before that was an apartment in another city. The only thing he got was a social and running it through the PeopleFinder system showed him as the only user, which was a positive sign, but his mild concern had gone to extreme anxiousness when he couldn't verify the SSN as his. The system was down between the FBI and the Social Security

Administration, and he had been waiting for hours for it to come back up. It was the only way to verify numbers. Even the FBI didn't have the complete list, and it took a special account just to see the data he was about to see. He could have called and asked a clerk, but that would have raised a flag so he decided to wait for the system to come back on line

The SSN was the most controlled piece of data in the federal system and only the Social Security Administration had the complete file of which ones had been issued and to exactly whom they were issued. There were many manuals on how to validate Social Security Numbers, what sequence was issued when, but only the SSA knew if the entire sequence was issued and who got a specific number. Most of the intelligence agencies wanted the file, but they never got it. The best they ever did was to get a few non-issued numbers for their use, but that took an act of Congress, a secret one, but an act of Congress nonetheless.

What Garrett needed was to see if the number associated with Sam Cohen was Cohen's, or if it was stolen or had never been issued. It was the never issued ones that were the prime target for those trying to make a new identity. In the days before computers totally automated the issue process, blocks of social security numbers were provided to the issuing offices, which in turn issued them as needed. However, in some cases, there were errors and either the number got skipped or that particular issuing station didn't need the last few numbers in the sequence before the state changed to a new Group Code. In those cases, the numbers just remain un-issued. These un-issued numbers had no major significance to the law enforcement community until the late 1980's when automation kicked in and companies like IdentityPoint started running reports that inadvertently exposed federal and local agents who were undercover and using false social security numbers.

To get around the systems that had been developed to find fraud, the FBI and other agencies first started to use real SSNs, ones that had been issued to children who had later died. Because the children never grew up, never entered the workplace, and never acquired licenses, no records ever populated the Public Record systems. These types of IDs didn't set off the false SSN alarms but they were so 'thin' in record count and history that they rang false when run against new identity software.

When the FBI wanted to go into deep cover they used SSNs that had never been issued but had been "farmed" by the agency, by planting data into systems to make it look like a legitimate person. The FBI had gotten fifty such numbers ten years ago, and his group had been responsible for the 'farming' of the identities. They assigned names to SSNs and had been building histories for these 'people' by renting post office boxes, subscribing to magazines, starting business, and even renting apartments that no one used for years just to build credit histories and make the people look real. It was from that list of fifty that NECO had taken ten for their own internal use.

Garrett read reports while he waited, but the words stopped making sense and he really hadn't retained anything he had read for the last hour. He tried the login again and it finally worked. He entered the social security number into *SSA Secure* and instantly got back the response. He picked up his phone and dialed.

"This is Garrett. You still in Birmingham?"

"Yes," came the response from the man on the other end of the call.

"I want you in Atlanta tomorrow morning. Go to a company called IdentityPoint. There is a man there going by the name of Sam Cohen. I would think he is in his early to mid forties. I want you to ID him, get me a digital on him, and send it to me before the morning is over."

"Roger," was the only response and Garrett ended the call.

1955 hours, Chicago, IL

"A call for you Mr. Curling, it's a Sam Call. You want to take it? I told him I didn't know if you had left yet."

"Yes, I'll take the call." He hit the button over the blinking light on the phone and picked up the receiver. "Sam, old friend, I guess you heard."

"I just did. What the hell happened?"

"I don't know. He was being transported to Chicago. They put him in a holding cell and thirty minutes later he was dead. Someone had apparently pulled him to the bars and shoved a shiv into his back. He bled out all over the holding cell."

"Damn. Any leads?" Sam asked.

"Nothing. Locked down the facility for a week, but they didn't get any leads. All they can figure is he must have been associated with the skin heads, him being a Nazi and all, and that pissed off the brothers. At least that's the present thought." Curling took a sip of his water and sat back in the chair."

"Why was he going to the committee? Something new?"

"Nope, they were ending things and just wanted to see if he was going to give them anything. You know bureaucrats; they have to justify their existence, especially after all this time and so little to show for it."

There was a long pause when nothing was said. "I wanted him to suffer for a long time." Sam's voice was reflective, almost sorrowful.

"I understand, buddy. I don't know what I can say."

"There is nothing to be said. The son-of-a-bitch got the easy way out."

"Well, I haven't forgotten what you did for me; you were top drawer during the entire affair. You did me good with the press for sure, you know that, and if there is anything you need Sam, you know you can count on me."

"I appreciate that. If anything comes up call me."

"You know I will. Bye, Sam." Curling hung up the phone then swung around and looked out of his twentieth-story window at the Chicago skyline. He enjoyed his position of power.

Chapter 9

Tuesday October 18

0850 hours, IdentityPoint

He was a loyal 'company man' who had been with the group for years doing whatever the boss wanted. He never questioned the mission and executed every one with all the zeal and energy of a man possessed with a desire to rise to the top. He had worked hard, and he now believed he was the 'favorite son' of Luby. After all, he was included in the 'big meetings' and when Luby went somewhere outside of D.C., he was with him. After years of faithful service that included everything from carrying bags, to getting Luby women, to breaking into political offices, and even murder, he was sure he had done everything possible to ensure he was the heir apparent to Luby's throne. Although he now actually now worked for Garrett, which made him second in line for the job, he knew Garrett only got the job because of that one lucky shot. When the time came, he knew he would be the man, not Garrett. There was nothing he would not do for Luby.

It was a two-hour drive from Birmingham but David Lee had left as soon as he got the call from Garrett. He went straight to the target and checked out the parking area and its security in hopes of finding a place where he could observe those entering without causing suspicion.

The IdentityPoint campus consisted of a large two story brick and glass building that ran very long and narrow, spread over many acres of land. Fortunately for him the entire campus had just three fixed security cameras on the roof of the main building, leaving numerous gaps in the coverage of the parking areas. Security guards were only inside the building, and that made observation by him a piece of cake. He had already picked out a spot in the parking lot on an upper row, next to some trees, that offered an unobstructed view of the front door and was not in the camera view. He knew he could come early in the morning, remain in the car in plain view, and not be seen on the security systems.

It was now almost 9 AM, and he had watched hundreds of people enter the building. The odds were his mark had already arrived. He left his car and walked to the CVS pharmacy, which was just around the corner. Using the pay phone that hung in the open on the wall ten feet from the pharmacy's front door, he dialed the main number for IdentityPoint. When the automated system started, he waited for the option that allowed him to enter a name. He entered C-O-H-E-N, and the automated voice replied with "Sam Cohen, extension 3514."

He hung up the receiver, picked it up again and put in some change, and then deliberately dialed the wrong number, three-five-four-one instead of one-four. When the person answered, "Hello, Michael Babyak here," he told him he had the wrong number, apologized and hung up. He repeated the process and this time correctly dialed the number. The phone rang and the voice on the other end answered, "Hello."

"Good morning Mr. Babyak, Jim Robinson here from Sun Corporation."

"Sorry, this isn't Mr. Babyak," came the reply.

"Oh, sorry there, is this his secretary? Please put me through to Mr. Babyak."

Sam chuckled, "No, this is Mr. Cohen." Sam had already entered "Babyak" into the company directory and retrieved his number. "Mr. Babyak is three-five-*four-one* this is three-five-*one-four*."

He quickly responded, "I am so sorry for the inconvenience. Thank you so much," and then hung up. Now he knew Cohen was at his desk. He would wait two minutes and then execute his plan, and do it without his mark becoming suspicious at a hang up call. He walked back to the parking lot and then looked for a car that had been hit recently, not smashed, just a small dent. Next he went to the main entrance and spoke to the security guard at the desk.

"Excuse me. I seemed to have backed into a car in the parking lot. A man out there told me he thought the car belonged to Sam Cohen. Could you have him come out for me?"

"Certainly," The security guard picked up the phone, dialed and repeated the message to Sam. "He'll be right out."

A minute later Sam came into the front lobby and went to main desk. Lee had been standing out of the way by the display area with his cell phone and by the time Sam had gotten to the desk he had clicked three pictures of him. He saw the guard point at him and Sam moved towards him.

"I am so sorry, Sir, but I believe I may have slightly dinged your car out in the parking lot. Do you own a dark colored Lexus GS?"

"Why no, I don't. I have a silver Saturn."

"Oh, I'm sorry, the man next to the car I hit said he thought it belonged to one of the new contractors. I guess he was mistaken."

"No problem at all," Sam replied.

"I'll just ask the security guard to check it out for me. Thanks again." Lee walked over to the security guard as Sam went down the corridor and back to his office.

The security guard looked up from the desk as Lee approached. "Did you get what you needed?"

"Most certainly and thank you." He exited quickly and was on the phone before he got to his car. "This is Lee, Sir, I have the photo. I'm sending it by phone mail now." He paused to listen. "Yes sir I'm sure I got Cohen."

0915 hours, Washington, D.C.

Garrett waited for the phone's ring to alert him to the incoming email, and when it did he immediately opened it.

"Shit," was his only response.

He dreaded his next call. He knew what the result was going to be.

"Sir, I got confirmation on the user we spoke of yesterday. His name is listed as Sam Cohen; he's a contractor at IdentityPoint. I checked his file and it was too thin so I checked with SSA, and the social isn't his."

There was a paused while he listened to the man on the other end.

"Yes, Sir, I am sure. I checked with SSA and his number was issued to a Susan Melon, born Warminster, Pennsylvania 1952. I also confirmed with our connection at IRS that SSN was used on Income Tax returns of a Roger Melon from 1952 to 1964 and not since 64. This of course would indicate the death of a child in 1964." He paused again and waited, but he knew what the question would be.

"Yes, Sir, I have already sent a man. I now have a picture of him." He paused for a moment to gather his own composure. "Sir, Sam Cohen is Major Sam Call, the same one from Chicago." Garrett listened and then acknowledged the instructions. "I'll make the call, Sir.

Garrett put the phone down and looked out the window. He could see his own reflection in the glass and wondered when he got so old. It seemed as though he had aged ten years in the last two. His hair was a lot more grey and thinner. He had gained ten pounds, but he looked and felt a lot heavier. The weekly basketball games at the gym had ended over a year ago; he hadn't spent any serious time working out in six months, other than a twenty-minute session on the stationary bike. He had no personal life, hadn't seen a new movie in a year, hadn't played golf in two, and any idea of a serious love life ended when Carrie walked out on him. She left a note telling him that there was no sense in having a relationship with a man that was always out of town and could not be depended upon to show up even when he was in town.

He remembered the day he found the note on the mantle. He read it, cursed her, and then went to her closet, saw it was empty and confirmed she was gone. He sat down on the couch, mad as hell, then looked at the date of the note. She had written it two days before, and between his long hours and late nights—more like early mornings—he didn't even notice she had left. For the first time in a long time, he wasn't thinking of bad guys, covert operations, or the Bureau. A deep feeling of loneliness came over him.

Looking out the window of his private office, he could see the Washington Monument directly in front of him and the Capitol to the west and, although he could not see it from his office, he knew the White House was just six blocks to the west. He would often sit in this chair and stare in amazement at the D.C. skyline, especially at night when the lights of the city seemed to add a radiance, a magical quality, an almost reverence to the city. This was the city where everyday men shaped world events, where Presidents made decisions and the course of human events was actually altered. This was a city that had been designed by Pierre-Charles L'Enfant's in 1791 with streets laid out specifically so that no matter how statesmen approached they would see the Capitol directly in front of them and be intimidated. This was a city designed around power, that exercised power, that lived, breathed and ate power. He had been a part of *Washingtonople,* as L'Enfant's had first called it, 'part of this process, of the power,' and he loved it. He had never questioned that his use, and sometime abuse, of power was always for the good of the country.

For the first time he questioned what he was doing. He had been the man who took the killer down with one shot from thirty yards. He had been the talk of the Bureau. Now six years later, he was virtually alone, cut off from his friends and the rest of the bureau in a world of black ops, the mission, and serving his country. The rationale for which was now not so black and white anymore to him.

He thought about not calling, not setting in motion what he knew would end in a man's death. He could walk away and there would be nothing Mr. Luby could do about it. He would request a transfer, maybe as an inter agency liaison, that would give him free time for sure; perhaps he could get his life back. Luby had given him the order to contact John S. Wood, who was a very specialized individual whose services NECO had obtained two years earlier from a minor-league mob boss they had busted during a routine undercover mission. They failed to get the real boss and, just to save face, they had settled for putting Rizzo away. To keep himself from doing major time, Rizzo had offered up some interesting bargaining chips, one of which was Wood.

John S. Wood was a contract killer but not just any killer. He specialized in 'accidental deaths', and he was extremely good at his job. He had taken out ten targets that Garrett knew of and the local police had never suspected they weren't accidents. He was virtually untraceable with no record; he was thorough and up to this point had made no mistakes. What had made him untraceable was that he only dealt with one man and only through a cell phone, which he only had on between 09:45 and 10:00 each morning; after one call, that phone was disposed of. In fact neither Garrett nor any other member of NECO or the FBI that he was aware of had ever seen him. He was perfect for NECO's work.

Garrett looked at his watch and saw it was 0930. He looked out the window and he could see his own faint reflection in the glass. He looked at himself intensely, as if he were confronting someone he did not like, then said, "I'm not going to call." He continued to just sit there and stare out of the window for twenty minutes. He then swung his chair around and unlocked a drawer in the file cabinet, took out a brown envelope marked 'Evidence do not open', ripped open the top, and took out a piece of paper on which was written ten numbers; one phone number that when dialed would surely add up to death. He dialed the numbers, and then using a voice he had practiced for many hours and which he had used on four occasions, he spoke. "I have a job for you."

1010 hours, Surfside, Florida

Every morning he took a long walk at the same time, so that the cell phone would be on between 9:45 and 10 am. If anyone was trying to locate him through his use of cell towers his constant moving would make that impossible. Yesterday he was all the way down at the North Shore Nature Center, and the day before that, he had driven across Biscayne Bay to North Bayshore Drive. No one knew him or knew where he was, and he was going to keep it that way. As he continued to approach the shop, he worked through his next steps.

He had been sitting on a bench looking out at the ocean just outside of the Coronado Hotel in Surfside Florida. It was just before 10 AM and he had almost turned his phone off as he was anxious to get to his favorite place, *The Greek Place*, where he had taken a fancy to the gyros and a certain young woman who worked there. He would be there in no time, and he was excited he was so close.

Just as he was about to turn the phone off, it rang. He thought about not answering, just turning it off, perhaps never turning it on again, but he took the call and wrote down all the information in a small notebook he carried with him. He told the client he would be on the case immediately, gave the caller a new contact number and said everything else would be as usual, including the time limit and the money. Wood stood up, wiped the phone clean, and then threw it in the first trash can he saw on the way to his morning visit to Sophie.

After his gyros he would return to the hotel, log onto the Internet, and plan his trip to Atlanta. On his return trip he would take a flight that stopped anywhere that gave him a two hour or more layover, during which he would leave the airport, go to a phone store buy a new disposable cell phone, open a post office box at small shipping store, and with that he would be ready for the next job.

But before he left for the new job, he would see Sophie. Approaching the store door, he saw Sophie through the glass. She was standing behind the counter with her mother on the right side of her, towards the back of the restaurant, and away from him. Her father was at the carving station, which was next to the large plate glass window at the entrance of the restaurant and immediately in front of him, which made him very uncomfortable. He could see Sophie was directing her parents as always, keeping the shop going while mom and dad fought over everything. Wood entered the shop and greeted everyone.

"Hello." He nodded to the mother, and then to the father, who responded back with a nod along with a glare as well.

Sophie's father was a traditional Greek, and he wanted a Greek man for his daughter. He could see Wood was interested in his daughter, a blind man could see that, and he was not pleased. After Wood's last visit he had told his wife and his daughter, "He comes to the shop every day, the same time, orders the same thing, then sits on the stool and watches Sophie in the mirror. I ask you, is this normal?"

The mother would argue with him about it being Sophie's decision, "And after all," she would say, "she's almost thirty," and then follow that up with how she had refused all the boys they had set her up with anyway.

To which the father would always respond, "He's not even Greek," and that would end the conversation.

Wood turned his attention to Sophie. "Hello, Sophie, how are you today?"

She was twenty-nine years old, just under five and a half feet tall, brown hair, beautiful smooth, silky skin, and brown eyes. She was not thin, but in no way heavy. She never would be considered a beauty and certainly not one that stood out in a crowd. However if Wood had been asked to describe her it would be different all together. He had in fact described her to several imaginary friends with whom he walked on his morning trips to nowhere while he waited for calls that he often wished would not come.

Just this morning he had described her to one such friend as a charming, young, yet mature woman, who attracted the attention of those entering the *Greek Place*. She had beautiful light-brown skin that seemed almost porcelain-like in its smoothness, and her silky brown hair swung casually and always invitingly back and forth as she moved. She always wore a long full-length apron that wrapped around the front and despite that anyone could see she had a beautiful ample figure that she took effort to hide with her common looking, all-covering apron. Beyond her obvious physical beauty, which would be enough for any man, her eyes were her most intoxicating feature. They seem to sparkle whenever she looked at him.

On the other hand he was just under six feet tall, almost forty, slim, not very muscular, yet strong for his size. He was fairly common looking, brown hair that he maintained in a business cut, no glasses, no facial hair, and he dressed casual business. He did it to maintain his cover, to look like every other typical business man on the street. There was nothing about him that made him exceptional to women, except his bright 'Paul Newman-like' blue eyes. He had started wearing brown colored non-prescription contacts when he was working just to eliminate any chance of someone noticing them. With that change he was now totally anonymous, and in his line of work, anonymity is what he strived for.

Sitting on the stool slowly eating his gyros, he watched Sophie as she worked, and she watched him. The last time he was there he had intended to ask her out, but he wanted to ask her when she wasn't busy, and more importantly, when her father wasn't around. He sat there almost an hour nibbling his meal and sipping his drink trying to find the right moment. By the time the right moment came, he felt like an idiot having hung around and acted like a love-struck school boy. In the end he left without speaking to her.

He spent most of the remainder of the day counseling himself on being indecisive. He found an irony in his condition that he was a cold-blooded contract killer by trade but didn't have the nerve to talk to this woman. After several rounds of self-loathing, he convinced himself the next time he was in the shop he was going to ask her – no pretense, just ask. But today he was leaving, and he did not know for how long. He took a long look in the mirror and told himself, "When I return I am asking her for sure. I am not wasting another day."

He returned to his room, made his reservation, packed, and sat down for a moment in a nice comfortable chair by the window. He was a methodical and patient man who was paid highly for his services because he didn't make mistakes. He was a specialist among professional killers. What made him unique was his victims always died of accidental deaths.

He sat in the overstuffed chair and looked out the window watching the ocean. His thoughts of all his marks and how he had worked so hard to find just the right method of death that would fit each mark. The mark was to be killed but those wanting him dead needed more that just a simple killing. They needed it to look, feel, and taste like an accidental death; for if it did not, they knew the mark's death would point right back to them.

Unlike others in the field, he had not grown up in a tough, crime filled neighborhood learning to kill just to defend himself or as a job for the local gang. He was a middleclass kid from unremarkable parents who lived their lives, and died without fanfare. He did a short tour in the military, learned some skills, and then one day he was in a bar and out of work. Sitting at the bar drinking a beer by himself, he overheard two men talking about their partner and how they wanted him dead. He stayed at the bar and when the two men left he followed the talkative one home and got his address. It didn't take long to find out his name, company and phone number. He remembered how it went down.

He stood in the phone booth for ten minutes going over how he was going to do it, what words to say, how much to ask for, payment process, everything except should he do it. For some reason the thoughts of right and wrong and whether he should do it never came to mind.

He dialed the number and a man's voice answered. "Hello."

"Mr. Wray? Mr. Robert Wray?" he asked.

"Yes. May I help you?"

"No, actually I can help you."

"How's that?" came the reply.

"You remember Tuesday night, say around 8 pm, at *Jeff's Bar and Grill.*"

There was a pause as the party at the other end was both trying to figure out who this was and what he was calling for.

"Let me refresh your memory. You and your friend were in the booth right next to the bar. You were talking quiet, but not so quiet that I couldn't hear you wishing a certain someone was no longer in the picture."

"What?" came from the voice on the other end. "I don't know what you are talking about."

"Okay. So you never said anything and I never heard anything." He paused. "But if you did say something, and I had heard it, I could make that problem go away for ten K."

There had been no reply, but he knew the man at the other end of the call was listening and interested. Then without waiting for the other end to engage he continued.

"So let's just say I did hear it and I did make the trouble go away; seven days later I would expect to see ten thousand in cash delivered to post office box 2033. All I need for you to confirm your order is for you to say his name. This is a one-time offer, friend; when I hang up I will not be calling back. You have one minute to decide."

There was a long pause while the man at the other end thought. It was almost the full minute and he was about to hang up when two words were spoken on the other end of the call.

"Joseph Watson." Just two words spoken and two men's fate were cast; one was to die and the other was to become a professional killer.

"Done. Look for it to happen within seven days, and you will never see me nor hear from me again. Ever! When I do the job, if you think about not paying me just remember, I know you and you don't know me." He didn't give the other man any chance to speak, just hung up the pay phone and walked away.

The next day he started to follow the mark, who was a partner in a construction company that was building a thirty-story office building. He watched him every day and every night looking for when he would be alone, more importantly when he could shoot the mark and be in a position to get away. He wasn't all that crazy about shooting the man, but using a knife was too personal and required him to get too close to the mark. He had never killed anyone and using a knife, other than in a fit a rage, took careful execution. He had to get close enough to the victim and stab him in the right killing spot. If he erred in either, the mark might survive the knifing, or worse, see him coming and turn the knife on him. He decided on using a pistol, a 45-caliber to make sure the victim went down.

He had been in the army, been trained in weapons, but he was almost useless with a rifle or a pistol. He had done basic training, gone to the rifle range, the pistol range, and had even been awarded the Marksman badge. That meant nothing. The rifle range had targets at 25, 50, 100, 200 and 300 meters, and the shooter had to engage them in different modes. Each army rifle and pistol range had some variations, but generally the soldier seeking qualification got fifty rounds of ammunitions and had to engage the targets as they popped up at different times. To be awarded an Expert badge, the soldier had to score from a perfect 50 to a near perfect 45. To achieve Sharpshooter, the soldier had to score between 25 and 43. The Marksman badge went to everyone else who scored over eight hits.

Woods, who had scored just ten hits, thought back to his basic training days and remembered when he saw the scores posted on the barracks bulletin board, how his bunkmate remarked.

"Now you're qualified to kill a president from 300 yards."

"What?" Woods said, being surprised at both the subject matter and the implication.

"You are now just as qualified as Lee Harvey Oswald was when he shot Kennedy."

"What are you talking about?" Woods was uncomfortable with the subject matter and even talking about his miserable score. "I barely qualified. Hell, I was lucky to hit the close targets; I couldn't hit anything over 100 yards, let alone a man in a moving car. I just got Marksman, I'm no shooter."

As his bunkmate returned to his bunk, he turned back to Woods, "Exactly my point."

In the four years he was in the army Woods went to many rifle ranges, shot thousands of rounds of ammunition at hundreds of black silhouetted targets, but never learned to get any better with either a rifle or a pistol. One thing he did learn was that, if you wanted to ensure a man went down when you shot him, you shot him with a 45 caliber.

He followed his mark and very quickly he established that the mark had a routine, not the entire day just enough of one to get him killed, and he wouldn't have to shoot him, which he wasn't all that sure he could do. He did two things the same every day. He ate lunch every day at the same diner at the same time and at the end of every day he inspected the new work at the site, and right now that took place on the top floors.

Wood started following him on Tuesday and continued until Friday when he made his plan deciding an accident was far safer for him then a loud gunshot and a faked robbery at the diner. On Saturday he drove a hundred miles and bought some work clothes and a construction helmet that looked like the ones used on the site. After four runs through the washer, the clothes had a respectable worn look. He also took the safety helmet and dropped it on the cement driveway ten times or so to give it that 'thrown around' look.

On Tuesday, around three o'clock, he walked to the construction site and waited for his chance to gain access to the building. It was a lot easier than he had thought. A small group of workers came back from what must have been a break, and he simply joined the group when they entered the first floor, which was almost fully completed. He went to the bathroom and waited in a stall. Just before five he left the stall, and then took the elevator to the 29th floor. Most everyone else was going home and going down, and the few who did see him, saw a man in workers clothes, a helmet and sunglasses and nothing more.

At 5 PM, he inspected the 29th floor and saw there was no one on the floor. Unlike the first floor this one was just coming together with the outside skin of the building just being installed. Three walls were complete, but the fourth just had the concrete support pillars and the safety wire that strung between poles to keep the construction workers from stepping off the edge. At 5:15 PM he put on plastic gloves, unclipped the safety wire, and went back to his waiting point, which was a stack of wall materials next to the elevator.

At 5:44 PM he heard the elevator motor engage. At 5:45 the door opened and his mark exited the elevator alone. The mark went to the right, away from him and inspected the new skin that had been installed making some notes in a small notebook as he went. When he came back towards the elevator, he saw the safety wire was down.

"What the hell!" The mark said aloud as he wrote in his notebook "Someone could get killed, damn fools."

Wood almost said, "You!" Instead he took two steps forward, slammed a metal pipe against the man that struck him squarely in the neck, and the mark went down immediately without a sound. There was no blood, and no sign of a struggle, just the mark laying there moaning. Wood picked him up and half-carried and half-escorted the almost unconscious man to the edge of the building, then pushed him off. Three seconds later the semi-conscience man slammed into a pile of pipe.

The falling man's living, but unconscious body of skin, bone, and blood was no match for the pile of hardened steel pipes. When he hit he was almost horizontal. His face hit first and was met by a three-inch diameter, eight foot long galvanized pipe that lay on the top of the pallet. His nose was driven into his brain, his jaw was shattered and all his front teeth were driven into the back of his mouth. His forehead was crushed and the force of the landing was so severe that what was left of his face was wrapped around the pipe.

When his chest, full of life giving air, smashed into the tightly packed pallet of pipe, the pressure of the air in his lung and the sudden compression caused his chest to explode sending blood and pieces of flesh down between the packed pipes. His hips struck the end of the pallet, but his legs continued downward slamming into the side of the pallet. The open ends of the pipes together with the force of the impact impaled the man's legs and removed flesh from both legs much like a baker, using a cookie cutter, removed shapes from a flat sheet of dough.

His heart was ripped apart by the bone of his rip cage collapsing and nearly every drop of the eight pints of blood left his body. His brain felt the pain of the initial blow of the attacker and sensed the fall. Then, upon impact, every neuron fired, sending notification of their injuries or in reaction to its loss of contact to another, now severed nerve. His brain began to interpret the data; then there was a massive short circuit and every system in his body shut down. The entire process took two hundreds of a second.

Wood took the elevator down, and by the time he got there the few remaining people on site had gathered by the dead man. No one was paying attention to him, as he casually walked off the work site.

The next morning the newspaper had a report about a local businessman who had fallen to his death while inspecting a safety cable, which he had found undone, and had entered into his notebook just prior to the tragic fall.

Three weeks later Wood cautiously went to his post office box and retrieved an envelope addressed to Occupant P.O. Box 2033, which to his pleasure contained ten one-thousand dollar bills; it had been postmark the day after the 'accident.'

Wood had been a failure at just about every job he had—including the army. But his successful first murder for hire excited him. He was happy about the money, which he desperately needed, but more so he loved the feeling of how well he had done the job. It was the first time he took pride in what he had done.

He was pumped. He did some research on the top reasons for accidents and found interesting information that the major causes of accidents were: machinery, medical and surgical complications, poisoning, accidental shootings with firearms, suffocation, fires, drowning, falls, and finally traffic accident. He found that by far the most accidental deaths were in traffic accidents but he realized that it would be difficult to orchestrate a fatal accident, so he dropped that as a creditable alternative.

Continuing with his research he found that most firearms accidents involved boys ages fourteen to twenty-five. If one was looking for 'common accidents,' ones that would not raise suspicion, then it needed to be consistent with what the person normally would do. Getting killed by a farm machine but not working on a farm would be obvious, as would drowning by a person who never went to the water.

He thought of the man that he help 'fall' to his death and smiled as he read the statistics on construction worker deaths resulting from falls from buildings; he knew he had found his method of operation, but now he needed a source of business.

Wood was reading the paper when and saw a local crime figure named Rizzo was being indicted in an insurance scam. The entire case was based on the word of an equally dirty businessman, by the name of Charlie Ervin Jr., who got caught, then bought his way out of jail by flipping this minor league crime boss. Wood knew he couldn't hang around in bars waiting for another client, so he needed a contact with connections to the type of people who needed his services. He also knew that this crime boss could be just that man.

Over the next week he studied this potential new mark, following him, reading about him, studying his home and business life. The mark, being out on bail and keeping a low profile, made the job more difficult in some ways, but it made it easier in others, as the mark limited his activities to a few routine tasks. The mark lived in a rural area, just outside the city where he had a large home on four acres of land in a neighborhood of equally spacious homes. There was nothing in the mark's schedule that was routine. He didn't go to the store at the same time, go out to a coffee shop in the morning, or have an interest other than his business that had been closed to him by way of a court order until the matter under indictment had been settled. The only thing he did routinely other than work, was his hobby, which was making furniture in his fully outfitted home shop. He had his two-car garage converted into a wood shop, a shop of which any professional would have been envious.

Wood had decided 'Death by Machinery' to be his mark's fate. Now he had to plan how to tell the crime boss before he committed the crime; otherwise when he was successful, the authorities would call it an accident and he could not claim credit for it.

He knew that the police were most likely watching the crime boss; phone calls and direct mail were out of the question, but the task of informing him turned out to be easier than he thought. He knew that Rizzo always stopped at the local coffee shop. The place had easy access, lots of people and regularity. So he chose that as the spot for the meeting. Wood dressed up to look like a computer geek: wrinkled kaki pants and white shirt, complete with pens in the shirt pocket, and black eye glasses to add to the studious look. He went into the shop before Rizzo arrived, ordered a large coffee, and bought a newspaper. Then he went outside and sat at a table reading his paper and drinking his coffee.

Rizzo was a small-time gangster who enjoyed the status of being a crime boss even more than the money it made him, and he loved to play the part to the crowd. Every morning like clockwork he would come to the coffee shop by limo and, just for the show of it, he would remain sitting in the back seat of the limo until the body guard, who had been instructed to take his time, opened the car door for him. Then with equal regularity, he would chat with a few of the customers and relish in "Good Morning, *Mr.* Rizzo" and the occasional "Good Morning, *Boss* Rizzo" that he would get from his loyal cronies in the shop. He would get a coffee to go and a newspaper, get back into the limo, and then off to whatever trifle his brother, who was the real boss, allowed him to do that day.

When Rizzo exited the shop and was walking to his limo, Wood got up from his seat and walked right into Rizzo knocking the newspaper from Rizzo's hand and spilling a half a cup of coffee on the bodyguard. The bodyguard, being the low grade protection that he was—and perfectly suited for the low grade crime boss—was more concerned about his coat than his charge and tended first to his own coffee soaked coat. Wood however, apologized profusely for his clumsiness, reached to the ground and retrieved a paper. After the driver opened the passenger's door, the crime boss stepped in without a word. The body guard, finally realizing he needed to engage in some manner, pushed Wood back away from the limo, gave him a dirty look and then, after ensuring himself that the people watching from the coffee shop saw him act his part, he walked around the car, and got in as the driver hit the gas and the car sped off.

Inside the limo Rizzo opened the newspaper and an envelope with his name written on it fell out. He picked it up, and after examining it by holding it up to the sunlight coming through the window, he opened it. The one page note contained just nine words; Ervin will die in an accident within three days.

The next day Wood gained entry into Ervin's workshop and waited in the small bathroom in the far corner. If Ervin came in and went to the bathroom first the plan was a bust, but he had to risk it. An hour went by and Ervin finally came into the workshop and continued with his project of hand sanding a board that had been laying on a large worktable in the center of the room. When he finished that, he went over to a wall that had every imaginable tool hanging on neatly arranged hooks. He took a pair of safety glasses from their place and put them on. He then walked over to the table saw, and after selecting a board from the stack on the far wall that was neatly arranged by size, he measured it, marked it and then turned on the table saw.

He placed the board on the cutting surface, adjusted the guide fence, and started to run the board through the carbon tipped, highly sharpened blade. As the board neared the end of its path through the saw, he eased up on it. Then he felt something that was not right, but before he could react in any way, before he could realize why there was a hand now holding his left arm, and that the pressure on his back was another man, his assailant had pushed his left hand through the saw blade. In an instant the sharp blade had done its job. He stood there for a moment in utter shock as he realized his hand, cut clean though, now lay bloody on top of the board he had so carefully cut the moment before. He stared at the stump of his left arm that a moment before carefully measured and fed the board through the machine and now spewed blood everywhere. The cleanly cut arteries were pumping blood out like small engines, and he stood a full thirty-seconds in horror before he could react. He then thrashed about in confusion and looked about for both someone to assist him and for the perpetrator, who had already departed the building.

He fumbled around for another minute trying to hold the bloody stump, and to stop it from bleeding, but it was no use. The application of a tourniquet was more than he could muster with just one good hand and having lost all sense of control. There was no phone in the shop, and he needed to return to the house and call for help. However, he had wasted precious time. His blood was escaping quickly and now so was his consciousness. He held his bleeding stump with his good hand and stumbled to the house. When he removed his hand from the stump to open the door, a mass of blood blasted out and the sight of his blood splattering on the door sent him into further panic. He was barely conscious by the time he got to the phone. He picked up the phone with his remaining hand and then had to drop it to dial 911. He bent down to pick up the phone to speak to the operator, but by now he could only utter a faint request for assistance.

That night, the late news reported the story of a gruesome death involving a local businessman who cut his hand off and bled to death after an accident in his home wood shop. While the cameraman zoomed in on the blood covered table saw, the news reporter described in morbid detail how the business man had obviously been working alone in his shop when the tragic accident occurred.

A week later, using a photocopy of his original note and handwriting a phone number on it, he got another message to the crime boss. The next day the crime boss called him on his throwaway cell phone.

"Is this the man who dropped me a note?"

"Yes. I take it you now believe that newspapers can provide more than just current events," he said to make sure Rizzo knew he was the one who put the original note in a newspaper.

"Yes, that would appear to be true for some select people. So what do you what?"

"Nothing from you. You know the business I am in, and I believe you may know of people who may need my specialized services on occasion."

"That is possible."

"All I want is a reliable source of business. A partner who calls me when there is work to be done."

"What's in it for me?"

"Well, I am sure you don't need a piece of my business; that type of investment of your capital isn't worth the risk for you shall we say." He said trying not to speak directly about murder, money, or accidents just in case there was an unwanted listening ear.

"I'm listening," came an interested yet cautious reply.

"I would think that being able to provide such a service would bring you many other benefits in your field of work." He knew he had him, now all he had to do was to get through the call without panicking and it would be done. "Here's how it will work. One, I will give you a phone number which is good for only one call. It will be available only on weekdays between 945 and 10 AM; there is no answering machine or message capability. When you call, give me the name of the business you want handled, and I will give the price of the service. Two, I will take up to two weeks to complete the business arrangement. If it goes beyond that, I have decided that the contract cannot be completed in the manner required; I will not be calling to report it. Three, when you call, I will give you a new number for the next call. No one else can call but you. If someone else calls me on the number I gave you our arrangement is over. In the future I will also give you a post office box where the fee can be sent."

Nothing came from the other end of the phone for some time and he considered ending the call there, but then he heard what he wanted.

"Give me the next number." With that his business was built. Two months later he got his first call, and now six years later he was sitting in Miami looking out the window working on his eleventh case. He looked out the hotel window and said a single word "Sweet" as he thought of his success. That quickly moved to concern as he thought of his new mark.

1920 hours, Alpharetta

Sam entered the door of his house and went straight to the kitchen for a cold beer. He had been outside cutting the grass and trimming bushes, and doing all those things that men have to do when they became property owners. Normally he and Mary worked the yard together on a weekend, but they were leaving the next day and Mary said she had to pack for the trip, so he had been out there for the last two hours sweating his ass off in the hot Atlanta heat.

"Yo. Mary where are you?" Sam called loudly enough for her to hear him even if she was upstairs. "You still upstairs packing?" There was no response. "Women! My God, I have never understood why it has to take them so long to do anything when it comes to dressing or packing." He said loud enough for only himself to hear. He took another swig of beer and went to the base of the stairs that led to the second floor.

"What could possibly take so long?" Sam paused and waited for Mary's response, which did not come. "We are going to the beach; a secluded resort, all they have there is water and a restaurant." Sam called up to Mary and again got no response.

"Hello up there." He called again and still no response. He walked up the steps to their second floor bedroom where Mary was standing there looking at the bed, where he could see that she had clothes organized over every surface of the bed. Sam looked at a suitcase and saw if was nearly empty.

"My God, woman, what's going on? What's the problem? You need a suit and something for dinner. We already decided we are not going touring, sightseeing, or jaunting around the islands, you just need a swim suit and a dress."

Mary turned from looking at the bed to looking at Sam, and the look was one that Sam was not fond of. Her head was half cocked and she had her right eye slightly closed, which she did when she was really pissed, and without any words he knew he was in serious shit.

"*Just* a swim suit and *just* a dress? Where do you think we are going soldier boy, the local swim club. No, we are going to a secluded, exclusive, first-class resort for a once-in-a-lifetime vacation, didn't you read the brochure?"

"Sure I read it, and I have my suit for the beach, shorts to walk around in, and I have my nice black slacks and my dress red short sleeved shirt and the black one too. I also got my black loafers. I'm set." Sam smiled as if he had scored the winning basket.

"Now you may want to look like the local, but I need an outfit to fly there, then one for the beach that afternoon, then there is dinner, and I'll need a dress, a dressy one, then maybe something just for the evening to walk the beach in."

"Exactly, a swim suit, shorts, and a dress. You're done." Sam smiled but Mary did not.

"What about the next day?"

"What about it? Sam responded with a shrug of his shoulders. "It's the same all over again; a swimsuit, shorts, and a dress."

"Exactly." Mary put her hands on her hips.

"So what's the problem?"

Mary looked back at him with a cold stare. You aren't expecting me to wear the *same* swimsuit, the *same* shorts and *same* dress everyday. Are you?"

Sam looked at the bed and then back at Mary. "Hun, you must have a dozen outfits and they all look fabulous on you."

"Are you toying with me, Sam, trying to make me feel bad about myself? Because if you are, you know what will happen. I will make your life sheer hell.

Sam was now totally befuddled. He had no idea how he got where he was, but he knew he was really on the edge and better leave her to whatever mood she was in. So he thought the faster he left the better for everyone.

"Well dear, I will just leave this to you," and Sam started to leave the room.

Mary swung around and appeared to be as angry as she had ever been. "That's it!" she said loudly. "That's all you have to say. I am dying here trying to make sure you are not embarrassed by being seen with a woman with no taste, no sense of style. My God man, all you can say is, I will leave this to you?" She shook her finger and her head at the same time. "That's it, I'm not going. You go yourself." She stomped past Sam and slammed the bedroom door behind her. He could hear her stomping down the stairs.

Sam stood there for a moment in utter confusion. He wasn't sure what he had done, but when it became clear, and he was sure Mary would make it clear, it was going to have been something stupid and insensitive. He waited a couple of minutes, finished his beer, and went to find Mary and face the music. He walked down the stairs, but didn't see her in the living room, so he quietly called for her, but there was no response. He called her again, and still nothing. He went to the kitchen and there she was, standing by the counter with her back to him.

"Listen Hun, I am so sorry. I don't know why you stay with an idiot like me. You know, I think Rich's is open late tonight why don't we go and see what they got. What do you say?" Sam waited for her to turn around and just prayed she wasn't crying. He could never handle her crying.

She turned around and looked at him. She had a beer in her hand and smiled. "You are so easy, Call."

He stared at her. "What, about packing? You been up there three hours and you're not packed."

Mary laughed again. "I finished packing in ten minutes, who do you think I am Grace Kelly? I got two swimsuits, two sun dresses and assorted shoes and sandals, mostly sandals. And if someone doesn't like that I am wearing the same outfits, they can kiss my Texas raised ass." She paused, took a sip of beer and spoke again. "I just didn't want to work outside today." She looked out the window. "Damn, it's hot out there." As she walked past him she smiled and handed him a fresh cold beer that she had put on the counter for him, and then went on into to living room.

"Damn, she's good." Sam said to himself, low enough so she would not hear him. "What about all the clothes on the bed upstairs?" He yelled.

Mary poked her head around the corner, "They're for Laura and Kate. I was sorting them out." She smiled, pulled back, and then poked her head in again. "And you are right. I am good." Then she quickly exited back to the upstairs.

"You will pay for this woman, I guarantee you." Sam was in hot pursuit. "And I don't like that, 'They can kiss my Texas butt' thing either. That's my job."

1930 hours

No one paid any attention to the Ford Taurus that had driven down the street, then stopped at the curb. The dark blue sedan was unremarkable, which is why the driver selected the car. No one noticed the driver taking pictures of the house where the man was cutting his grass and no one noticed when the car departed the neighborhood.

Chapter 10

Wednesday, October 19

07:30 hours, IdentityPoint

The digital photos clearly showed he had his man; at least it was the same one in the photo he had seen on the Internet. He compared the downloaded digital photo to the Internet article he had printed off before he had left Miami.

"You've gained a little weight since you left the Army there, Major." Wood said to himself as he sat in his rental car in the parking lot of the *Meal House*. It was an old southern restaurant that specialized in country style home cooking like the meatloaf and mashed potatoes he had last night after conducting his initial stakeout of the Major's home. He had chosen to wait here, since it was right on the corner of Highway 9 and Campground Road. When Call went to work he could clearly see him come to the intersection where he would have to wait at a particularly long lasting traffic light. He also selected the location since it was very crowded with early morning drivers who came and went fairly quickly.

He had grabbed a large cup of coffee and a breakfast sandwich from a fast food place along the way and now was consuming both while waiting for Call. He had expected him to depart around 8:15 AM or so in order to get to IdentityPoint by 9 AM, which he had been told was his usual arrival time. As he sat there drinking and watching, he almost missed him. Call's car, along with a woman, was at the traffic light. He looked at his watch, saw it was just 7:31 AM and wonder why he was leaving so early. Perhaps he needed to drop off the woman, he thought as he pulled out of the parking lot to follow.

The target vehicle traveled south down Highway 9, then entered the main highway, Georgia 400, and Wood followed. It was not hard to stay with the target. The traffic ran quickly for one exit then slowed to thirty-five miles-per-hour. By the time they got to the next exit, traffic was at a crawl. Even through the slow traffic he was beneficial to his task of following his target, he began to feel anxious about the ridiculous traffic. After twenty minutes of crawling along at fifteen miles-per-hour, the traffic suddenly sped up to normal speed. Wood looked around him to see the cause of the delays, but there appeared to be no cause whatsoever. He just shook his head and concentrated on staying a few cars behind his target.

Wood became a little concerned when the target did not get off at the exit that would have taken him to IdentityPoint; instead he continued due south past the 285 connector highway, which encircled the city of Atlanta, then, went straight into the city on Route 85. He continued through the city past the stadium and then continued on 85 out of the city. The target put on his turn signal and started to exit to the right and Wood looked up at the sign above the road and saw it was the exit to the Hartsfield Airport.

"This is excellent," he thought. "He's taking his wife to the airport and that significantly simplifies the job." He was already thinking of how he was going to take him out. He imagined a scenario where he would arrange for Call to get an invitation from some pretty woman, go to a bar, get drunk and be seen. He could envision a fatal fall down the steps or perhaps the 'drunk' falling in the shower, both of which were so much easier to arrange than anything to do with a car accident. Just too many variables, not to mention the victim might live through the crash.

All it would take would be a 'chance meeting' from a pretty girl; he could buy one of them easy enough, and then Wood would be waiting for him when he returned home. He liked the idea of a seedy death for this guy. The wife would want to avoid any investigation.

Sex and booze related deaths, especially when it involved seemingly normal people, always made the widow want to avoid any embarrassing investigations.

Wood watched as the target car pulled into the airport car lot, but it was not the drop off lane, it was the long term parking area. He followed. The lot was full. His target drove around the lot then returned to the front, closer to the entrance of the departure terminal. After unloading his passenger and three suitcases, he left her and the suitcases and returned to the rear of the parking area where he parked. Wood had to scramble to find a spot, park and still be able to catch the target who was now jogging back to meet his passenger. Wood followed them into the airport. They went directly to the ticket counter, checked their bags, and it was now clear to him they were both leaving.

"Damn." He said out loud and looked up to the departure board but there were way too many departures to know which flight was Call's. He took another look at his mark as he went through the security gate.

"Fuck it," Wood said aloud and turned and started back out the same way he came, unconcerned with the hundreds of passengers moving to and from the ticket counter and baggage claim. He was oblivious to the security guards, the cameras watching, the children crying, and the single man with no luggage who was twenty feet behind him.

11:30 hours, Port Richey, Florida

David stretched out his hand to greet the older of the two men that had come out of the house. "Hi. I'm David; I called your office this morning.

"Hello. I'm Jim Louwaert."

"Dave Louwaert," the second man said as he reached to greet David.

"I understand from our secretary you are interested in the house."

"Well, not exactly. I couldn't afford something like this. My God, it's the size of a hotel," David said smiling as he spread his arms out to point out its size. "It must be thirty thousand square feet."

"Just a might over forty-five actually," Jim said. "The guest house is four thousand by itself," pointing to the stand-alone home that stood next to the massive stone home.

"That's a lot of house," David joked.

"Sure is."

"So are you interested in something like this? You know we didn't build the entire structure. We've only done the finished wood work; ceiling, cabinets, wood floors, and such."

"Yes, your secretary gave me a mini dump on what you did here. I'm looking for work along that line." David was trying to engage them in friendly conversation, so he could ask about the investment companies. They offered to take him in for a tour and David accepted. The minute they entered the house David was in awe. He had planned to fake being impressed, but the instant he saw the work, faking was not necessary.

The house had three distinct sections; the formal wing, the entertainment wing, and the bedroom wing, which was not to be confused with the guesthouse. The formal wing had a massive master bedroom and bathroom, along with his and her changing rooms, his and her offices, a formal library, formal dinning room, kitchen, lounging area, and reception. The bedroom wing had fourteen bedrooms, each with its own bathroom.

The really interesting area was the entertainment wing that was built in such a way as to give the floor the appearance of being a road, which led to the outside; an outside that was really one huge room with a ceiling painted with clouds. The 'outside' area had two, two-story stores on both sides of the 'road' and two more at the end of the road. There was even a working town square-like fountain in the middle of the road. Two of the stores were already completed, a candy store and a cigar store. To cap off this indoor town there was an indoor theater that actually had a full stage and could seat sixty people.

Jim and Dave had been responsible for all the major wood work, including the four incredibly detailed ceilings done in maple, oak, cherry and teak. They had built his and her offices, both one hundred percent wood; walls, floor and ceiling, his in oak and hers in cherry.

Each time David saw a new room he was more impressed and complimented the men on their work. With each room and each compliment the men became more at ease with David. After fifteen minutes of touring and complimenting, David sat down on the teak steps that led from the formal area into the teak lounge and the two men followed; one sitting on the steps with him and the other on a low wall that separated the lounging room from the rest of the open expanse of the formal wing.

"So tell me what we can do for you, David," Dave asked.

"Well, boys, I'm not sure I am in your league. I am in an investment group and we have purchased a small hotel around Boca Ciega Bay. We are looking to refit every room into luxury mini-condos. We would then sell the suites to individuals, then rent them out for them when they are out of town." David had picked Boca Ciega Bay, because it was close enough that they could do the work but far away enough that they would not be familiar will all the hotels in the area.

"Sounds interesting. How would that work?" Jim asked.

"Well, we sell the suites for 500 K each and rent them out according to the owner's schedule. We handle the booking, cleaning when the suite is being rented, as well as the insurance and such; they get forty percent of the rental and we get sixty percent."

"Sounds like a sweet deal," Dave Louwaert said as he looked at his brother.

David sensed it was now time to get into the investment company and see what he could get from them. From his experience, he knew that the honest ones were willing to talk openly about financial arrangements among fellow investors. It was the dishonest ones that held back.

"To tell you the truth, gentlemen," David started, "we haven't yet closed on the deal; I am waiting for the full conversion costs before I ink the deal. The group is used to a thirty percent return and this one really will depend heavily on the initial outlay."

"Thirty to forty!" Dave said as he shook his head and looked at Jim for what must have been permission to continue. "We're only getting fifteen percent."

"But we aren't doing anything, Dave, and there is no risk at all. And its fifteen percent of each deal not *fifteen* percent on our investment."

"Well, I guess that sounds okay," David interjected hoping to get more detail. "Our group has six members. Each put in two million cash, and we buy and sell real estate. This one is a little different for us in that we are going to own it, actually will hold it for a while, then sell it to a management company after we sell all the units."

"Sounds good," Jim said as he stood and stretched.

"Yes, you have to stay with what you know. We tried to invest in a computer company once. Didn't go so well, only thing we ever lost money on." David tried to look humble.

"That's what *our* company specializes in. Buying and selling start-up data companies."

"Really?" David said manner of fact way. "I would have thought with your talents, you would have stayed in the building or real estate areas." David swung his arms around and smiled once again reinforcing their excellent work.

"Well, we started a little company years ago, Louwaert Investments. We tried to back a couple of niche building companies, but it didn't go so well. Then we got lucky; we met a guy who was an expert in data companies. He told us how the industry was going to explode and that real win was going to be in backing little startups that were gathering data, a lot of them right here in Florida."

Jim's brother, Dave jumped in and continued. "He had money and contacts, but he needed an established company to make the investments, so we tried it. Going pretty well too. We have our entire investment back plus and we get twenty percent of all deals and he runs the entire operation."

Jim came back, "The guy is a wiz. He creates the "Doing Business As" companies to separate us from the competition." Jim did the quote thing around the doing business as. "All I do is sign some documents, and we make another hundred grand."

"Sounds like this guy has it all together." David added, then continued talking awhile, but he knew if their company was involved in anything illegal, they weren't. These guys were just two really fine carpenters that thought they got lucky in an investment group.

- - - - - - - - - - - - - - < > - - - - - - - - - - - - - - -

Garrett had just finished a late lunch at the corner deli when his cell phone rang.

"Garrett here."

"This is Lee. We staked out Call, followed him and we were able to finally ID our mystery hitter just like we thought we could."

"So why do I think there's bad news to go along with this?"

"Well, we followed Call and his wife to the airport; they left on an American Airlines flight to San Juan."

"How did you find the hitter?"

"Apparently he didn't know Call was leaving. When he realized it, he made a mini-scene and started looking at the departure boards and then I knew it was him."

"And our friend, where is he now? I presume he didn't follow."

"Nope, he went back to his hotel. That's where I am now."

"You have anything else?"

"We got his name, or at least the name he is using. Wood, John Wood of Florida."

"How?"

"We got it from Hertz. Flashed the badge and they showed me the screen."

"You stay put. I'll check out where Call is going and get back to you."

12:45 hours, Outside of F.B.I Headquarters

After using the F.B.I's systems to get what he needed, he left the building and looked for a not so busy section of the sidewalk to call Lee back. Finding a not-so-busy section was not-so-easy, and he had to walk two blocks over to the National Museum of American Art to find an area big enough where the people walking by weren't so close that they could hear every word. He took out his cell phone and called.

"Lee, it's Garrett."

"Yes."

"The San Juan flight was a connecting flight to Tortola in the British Virgin Islands. I don't know where he's going from there, but he's not trying to hide, so I'll know shortly."

"What about Wood, or whoever he is?"

"Actually it appears he may be John S. Wood. The ID looks real."

"No shit. He used his real ID. What an idiot."

There was a pause by Garrett and he almost didn't say it, but he did. "Idiot? We've been looking for this guy for four years and nothing. If he'd used a fake identity more than twice you think we wouldn't have known?" He took a breath, Lee said nothing. "This guy is clean, no record, no warrants, no bad debts, he's a perfect citizen. If he hadn't yelled in frustration at the airport, we still wouldn't know who he is."

Lee had not responded to his mild lecture, but Garrett knew he was still there.

"Stay with him. When I find where Call is going, you will convince Wood to follow and continue with the mission. I will arrange transport from this end and have it on standby. I'll call you when I have everything worked out. Don't call me unless he tries to leave. Got it?"

"Yeah," came a frustrated and slightly angry reply.

6 PM, Holiday Inn Express, Atlanta GA

Wood had returned to his hotel after his target had unexpectedly left. He was mentally exhausted; he got into the room flopped down on the bed and slept until nearly 6 PM. When he awoke he was still groggy so he went into the bathroom and washed his face with cold water. It didn't work. He took a shower, and when he was done, he stood in front of the mirror and looked at a man he didn't know. "You were sloppy today. You didn't research your man, you didn't prepare, and when he split you reacted in public and that could have been fatal." He stared at himself in the mirror, and then pulled his hair back from his forehead as if he were looking at a suddenly developed receding hairline; he hadn't. "You've never been caught, never even been a suspect." He put his finger on the mirror as if he were another person. "And you look like shit. How is Sophie going to want this?"

He walked out the bathroom, then returned to where he had just left. "You're through. This was your last job. You are going to eat a nice dinner, stay the night, and then fly home to Sophie." He walked back out and turned his head back to the mirror. "You know, you are very smart." Then he pumped his arms up like a strong man, "And good looking to boot."

Chapter 11

Thursday, October 20

0815 hours, Hartsfield International Airport

Wood checked out and then drove back to the airport through the same horrendous traffic he had fought the evening before while tailing his now departed target. Frustrated by the traffic, Wood pulled into the Hertz rental car return, dropped off the car, and hurriedly got onto the shuttle to the airport. He wasn't late for the flight; he just had to get away from all the traffic and the hustle and bustle. The bus pulled up to the Delta ticket counter and four business men dashed out; Wood retrieved his bag and stepped out of the bus and walked into the terminal. He stopped just beyond the entrance and looked for the proper check-in counter.

"Mr. John Wood." He thought he heard his name being called, but he knew that was not possible. No one knew him here.

But then he heard it again, "Mr. John S. Wood."

He turned around and there was a man, a well built, strong looking man in a grey suit. He quickly looked him and up and down, and in that instant knew he had never seen him before.

"Mr. Wood, you have a call," and the man extended his hand to him. Wood looked at the man's hand and saw he was holding a cell phone, which he wanted him to take. He picked up the phone and looked at it for a second not knowing who this man was, how he knew his name, or even why he was now taking the phone from this strange man. He should have just walked away, but at this point, he was more curious than cautious.

"Yes."

"Where are you going, Mr. Wood?" he recognized the voice as his client Rizzo.

"What? How do you know my name?" He had forgotten where he was and he said it loud enough for those around him to hear. But everyone around him was so involved in getting to and from their flight and did not care what he was saying or to whom.

Garrett, continuing to use Rizzo's voice, "Your target has gone to the British Virgin Islands. I am hoping that the flight that you are presently headed to is one to the islands, Mr. Wood. His choice of vacation seems to be perfect for your needs."

"Listen you," Wood stumbled for the right words, realizing that Rizzo knew who he was and that was a very bad development. "I'm done. I'm leaving." He held the phone close to him, cupping his hands around the phone trying to keep what he was saying between himself and the man on the phone. "Your friend has left and with that, I am done. This thing isn't going to happen, so forget about it." In an attempt to gain control over the situation he added, "You violated the contract; we're done. And don't ever call me again." He listened for a moment waiting for the reply, and then was more shocked at what he heard than even receiving a call from Rizzo.

"You listen, Wood," Garrett said in his real voice. "Who the fuck do you think you are, and who do you think you're talking to? Some no good defunct crime boss who doesn't have the power to make his bimbo wife stop fucking his driver? Wake up, Wood. We took you over four years ago when we took Rizzo down. He was more than willing to offer you up as well as everyone else he controlled just to stay out of prison." Garrett paused for a moment to make sure he still had Wood on the line. When he heard the airport sounds, he started again. This time he was pissed and he made Wood know it. "You think NECO doesn't know with whom it's dealing?"

"What happened to Rizzo? Who are you?" Wood was so taken back by the change in developments he could hardly speak. The man on the other end of the call did not answer and Wood could only muster, "I'm listening."

"You will finish the job, Mr. Wood. You will go to the islands, and complete the contract. Do you understand?"

Garrett waited for the response but nothing came.

"I said do you understand?"

"Yes," came a submissive response

"Good. You will go with Mr. Lee. He will take you to Dekalb Airport where a private jet is waiting for you. You cannot go to an island resort alone Mr. Wood, so there will be a young lady joining you at the airport who will accompany you on your trip. She is a friend of the agency, Mr. Wood. She is paid by the day and she is very social. Do you understand?"

"Yes."

"She will know you as Mr. James Rowe, and beyond that, all she knows is that you are a high roller who needs a woman for a business trip in the islands. Mr. Lee has your identity and your schedule. Go with him now *Mr. James Rowe.*" Without waiting for a response Garrett ended the call.

He stood there with the phone in his hand and then silently gave it to Lee.

"Come with me, *Mr. Rowe.*" Lee then spoke into what appeared to be thin air. "Bring the car around now." And then led him to the entrance where a non-descript dark car with darkened windows stopped, and they both entered.

17:10 hours, IdentityPoint

Bob had watched the clock for the last three hours waiting for the time to go. With each passing minute he became less focused on his job, which was difficult since he had been faking the research for weeks. He and the client had already planned that his poor performance on the research would be the cause for his firing. That would provide the client with the ability to remove Bob without bringing any suspicion onto herself. After all she had hired him and if he had free access to all the corporate files for months and then suddenly just left, it would spawn questions about what he had been doing.

Tammy finally came over to his desk. "You ready to go?"

"Sure." Bob instantly blurted out. He stood and was ready to leave almost instantly, having shut down his computer at 5 PM on the dot in anticipation of the event.

They left through the main entrance and Tammy led them towards the end of the first row of the parking lot.

"Okay." She stopped in front of a row of motorcycles and then removed one of two helmets that were attached to the back brace of one of the motorcycles and gave it to Bob.

"You have a cycle?" He looked at the big black motorcycle with its chrome roll bar on the front, chrome exhaust pipes, black leather seats and all black paint job. "We're riding on a bike?"

"This is not a cycle, and it is certainly not a bike. It is a Harley, the finest machine ever built, and American built baby." Tammy smiled at Bob with a pride of ownership and secured her helmet.

"When you said you liked the wind in your hair, I thought you meant you had a convertible." Bob was trying hard not to whine and seem less than excited, but it was difficult.

Bob, with the helmet awkwardly clutched in both hands, stood there motionless, staring at the Harley.

"I'm sorry, Bob, I thought you knew I drove a Harley." She sat there in the front seat waiting for Bob, who just stood there. "Perhaps you would feel better driving."

Bob looked at her, smiled slightly. "I could do that."

Tammy shifted her position to the second seat and signaled Bob to get on.

"I can't drive a cycle." He shook his head, looked back towards where he had parked his car, then back to the Harley, then shaking his head again Bob with a very nervous voice said, "No, no, no."

"It's a *Harley* Bob, a *Harley,* not a cycle."

"Yes, of course, and I can't drive a Harley either." Bob stood there hoping she would suggest he drive his car.

"Well then, you better get on." She shifted herself back to the front seat; hit the starter button and the engine roared to life with the deep throaty sound only a Harley can make.

Bob reluctantly put on his helmet and very cautiously got in his seat.

"Hold on," Tammy said as she started to drive out the driveway to the main road. She eased the massive machine onto the highway and turned up the throttle and the Harley streaked down the road.

"Oh. God!" Bob held on tight.

Chapter 12

Friday, October 21

Death by Accident

0725 hours, British Virgin Islands

It was the morning of their second day, and Sam was sitting on the porch of the cottage as the sun was just rising from the sea. He was warm in spite of having nothing on but a light robe. The sun had just started its journey, only halfway out of the sea, and Sam could already feel its rays begin to warm him further. He had awakened just before sunrise, made a pot of coffee in the little four cup coffeemaker on the bar, and now he was sitting sipping hot coffee and watching the day begin. The seagulls were already flying, looking for their morning meal, and their soft calls could be heard over the gentle sound of the small waves ending their long journey to shore. It was a rocky and shell strewn shore that was not well suited for strolling but was perfect for ensuring quiet solitude. This was the south east side of the island and what little shoreline there was quickly ended as it joined the rocky cliff that jutted into the sea just to the north side of the cottages. One could walk from the cottages up the steep westward side of the hill, but the step path abruptly ended at the sheer cliff that then plummeted straight down 100 feet to the ocean below. Sam looked north and thought how magnificent the sunrise would be from there and decided that before they left he and Mary would see the sun rise from on top of the cliff.

There was one strip of fifteen guest duplex cottages, on the ocean side of the island; each very much like the other, providing an exclusive getaway for thirty couples. Each unit had one entrance at opposite ends of the duplex. With all the tall, wild tropical plants and trees that surrounded the cottages they seemed more secluded than they actually were. All the cottages lay just thirty feet from the ocean, how they were nestled between the rocky ocean and the sandy hills behind them made the occupants feel like they were each alone on a tropical island.

There was just one cart path that ran along the length of the cottages that provided the guests with their access to the resort office and restaurant. From the cart path the guests walked across a sandy path past the rear of the cottage to its only door, a sliding double-door entry from the wood deck into the living room.

Inside the cottage there were only three rooms; a living room, bathroom, and a small bedroom. The living room had two wicker chairs and a couch on the rear wall that faced the glass doors and the ocean. There was a small nook that contained a mini refrigerator, sink, and coffee maker. Two quick steps and you were in the bedroom that had just enough room for a queen size bed and two bed side tables; one at the window side and one at the bathroom side of the room. There was so little space in the room that end tables barely cleared the side walls when placed next to the bed. The one closet had a single clothes hanging bar and four small shelves that were to serve as the dresser, bureau, and luggage storage area. One large sliding window ran the length of the bedroom, and in Sam's case was currently opened allowing the sounds and smells of the ocean to fill the room. The bathroom was simple, yet modern, and completely tiled in an ocean motif of seashells and exotic fish. There was a commode and a sink area that was just barely large enough to allow two people to prepare for the day. A screened door provided access to an outside shower that was attached to the cottage and had three other walls surrounding it, guaranteeing its visual privacy. There was no roof on the shower and it provided the first time user with an odd feeling of showering outdoors in a somewhat public view.

Sam sat there in the recliner thinking of the cottage; three rooms, one window, one door, and that was it—it was perfect!

"Hey, Stud. You alone?" There was a voice behind him. It was a female voice, but it wasn't a voice you heard at the office or on the street. It was deeper than a normal woman's voice and the owner was obviously trying to imitate the sexy voice of Lauren Bacall; a voice that could melt a man with a single phrase, and she was doing a good job of it.

Sam turned around and there stood a woman dressed in robe. She had pulled her long hair so that it hung over one shoulder and she was leaning against the side of the glass door. Her robe was only loosely tied, and Sam could see the outline of her figure in the rising sunlight and he was becoming aroused. "Good morning, Ma'am," Sam said as he attempted to swing around in his chair to get a better view.

"See anything you like?" came the question from the Bacall-like beauty.

"Oh yes. But we need to be careful. My wife is asleep in the bedroom." Sam stood and walked over to the woman who stood sultry against the door, her head down slightly and looking up at him through her carefully arranged hair.

Sam stood in front of her, staring at her eyes and he unconsciously reached out with his right hand and gently slipped his arm around her waist. She responded by straightening up her body and in doing so her robe, that had only been barely tied, now hung free. Her breasts were totally free of the confines of the robe and Sam moved his left hand to caress them. He buried his face into her neck and kissed her gently as she arched her body into him making him even more excited. As he pulled her close, she looked up and out at the sea.

"Oh wow, Sam, the sunrise is spectacular," and she pulled away from him and stepped further onto the porch to get a better view.

"Excuse me," Sam said as he remained in the same position at the door.

"Come join me, this is beautiful," came her non-passionate response.

"Hello. What happened to the sultry wench? I was doing something here, and I was *rising* to the occasion.

Mary looked back at Sam who now had turned towards her, and she laughed as she saw the evidence of his excitement.

"Not funny, Lady. You started it, now I think you need to do something about it. After all you just don't use me as your sex toy whenever you want." Sam attempted to look like a hurt young man as he crossed his arms and tried to look sullen.

"I don't know about that, Big Boy. When we came home from dinner last night, I think I recall you pulling my dress over my head before we were two feet into the cottage, then carrying me into the bedroom and screwing my brains out last night. Remember? Or is your mind clouded by the bottle of Pinot Noir you consumed at dinner? Or perhaps you forget yesterday when we first arrived and we started to get changed for the beach, and I wanted to shower and you came out there and did me in the shower."

"And the bed," Sam impishly added.

"So if I want you, Babe, to drop and please me, I think I have earned it."

"That's what I am trying to do, Babe, I'm here for you baby," Sam said as he tried to swagger out to her in a sexy movement. But as he just got to her his foot hit the chair and caught the full pounding on his big toe. "Oh shit, that hurt." Sam backed up and grabbed his toe and tried to massage the pain. In doing so his robe came completely undone and he was there for the entire world to see.

Mary looked at him, stared at his crotch and looked back at Sam's face.

"Smooth. I don't know how a girl can resist you, Sam. Sit down and I'll get my coffee."

Sam quickly reached down and picked up his coffee and reached out to her. "Put a head on mine."

Mary took the cup and filled it, got one for herself, then came back out. Sam was already lying down in the lounge chair, having retied his robe and was watching the sun that was now fully risen out of the sea. Mary gave Sam the cup and sat down.

"God, it's magnificent."

"It sure is, Mary, almost as magnificent as you."

Sam turned to Mary, she turned to him and he gently kissed her.

"I love you, Mary," Sam said softly.

"One thing I know Sam, is I know you love me." She kissed him back. "And I love you."

They sat back in their chairs and watched the sun rising in the east as they drank their coffee. Ten minutes later Sam got refills and they sat and watched the world go by without a word. Finally Mary asked the time. Sam looked up at the sun, made a movement with both his hands and looked at the shadow on the ground. "It's zero seven fifteen hours."

Mary looked at him. "What was that?"

"What?" Sam looked around as if looking for the mysterious source of Mary's confusion.

"The hand and shadow thing."

"I was telling time by the shadow of the sun."

"Of course you were."

"Are you doubting me, Mary? After all I am a soldier, a trained killer, a man who can be dropped into the jungle and live off the land for a week. A man who can navigate across mountain ranges with only the sky to guide me, accomplish my objective, and safely return."

"Sam, you get lost driving with a map in your hand."

"You are cold, Woman." Sam raised his eyebrows and pulled away in a faint air of offense.

Mary smiled at her poor excuse for an actor. "So what time is it really?"

Sam repeated the hands and the shadow movement just as before. "Its 0715 hours."

"Sam!"

"Trust me; I really know the shadow thing." Sam paused for a moment, "And I can see the reflection of the clock in the glass door behind you.

"Call, you are such a shit sometimes," Mary said as she started to get up.

"I know it." Sam smiled and looked at the sea gulls flying by.

"I am going to get ready for breakfast." With that Mary went into the cottage and Sam dutifully followed. They both went to the bathroom first and brushed their teeth. Sam shaved and Mary washed her face in the other sink. When Sam finished he splashed water on his face to clean up, and then Mary ran her hand over his face.

"Smooth," was all she said, and she kissed him very gently.

It was 0735 hours. Breakfast was scheduled from 0830 hours and went to 1000 hours and Sam and Mary liked to be there when it first opened. They didn't arrive until 0920 hours.

- - - - - - - - - - - - - < > - - - - - - - - - - - - - - -

Sam and Mary finished their breakfast and looked out over the anchorage at the yacht club across the bay and the dozens of sailboats at anchor waiting for students and guests.

"This place is unbelievable, Sam. The view alone is worth the money; I've never seen anything like this. The blue ocean is spectacular, and so clear; I can see fish all the way down there at our dock." Mary pointed over the wall down to the dock which served the resort. There were no windows on this side of the restaurant, they were on the ocean side where the breeze came every night, but on the west side, the side that opened into the bay was totally open to the view. The three sounding walls supported the roof on this round, stone building that sat on a small hill at the southern tip of the island of Virgin Gorda.

"Where?" Sam responded as he turned in his chair and looked over the wall that was just the height of their table and that also served as the outside wall of the restaurant. Every ten feet down the length of the wall a metal came out the center of the wall and supported the roof which provided shelter from what little rain there was, and more importantly, shelter from the sun that was ever shining eleven months of the year.

"Right by the end of the dock."

"Oh yes, there must be thousands of them. It looks like an aquarium."

"I am so glad we came, Sam. I think you needed to get away from all of what was going on. I know I needed it."

"I needed to get away from all that Ream crap," Sam said as he read the last page of the four page, photo copied document, that passed for the morning newspaper. "You finished?" He handed Mary his 'British' newspaper and motioned for Mary to swap him for the 'American News' she had.

"When we left the Army and went to Atlanta, Ream was in jail, obviously not going to talk and that was it."

Mary looked around to make sure no one could overhear their conversation. "Christ, Sam, what a circus it was. Chicago's DA was fighting with the state over jurisdiction and the state was fighting with the federal government. "

"And don't forget the Germans, they tried to be part of the action too; they wanted to make sure none of their soldiers got unfairly blamed for what went on at Fort Sheridan." Sam paused for a moment, looking out at the bay. "I just don't know, Babe, but one thing I know for sure, it wasn't worth Dana."

Mary could see moisture in Sam's eyes and she knew how he struggled with the death of his friend. She reached over to Sam, took his hand in hers and gently caressed his hand between hers. "I can tell you without question that Dana would argue otherwise." She held him for a few moments, then released his hands and took a sip of coffee. "Well, thank God, it's at least over."

Sam looked past her as she said it and looked out at the ocean as if seeking the answer in the hills of the islands surrounding them. After a few moments and without looking at her Sam quietly asked, "Is it?" Sam slowly turned and looked at his wife who was now looking back at him. "Why was he killed *now*? After all this time, why now? And why was he going to the commission to speak when he hadn't said one word in four years?" Neither said anything for a while after that; they both just sat quietly with their thoughts.

Finally Mary broke the silence, "Well, I think a day at the beach is what the doctor ordered."

Sam smiled, reached across the table took her hand and kissed it. Mary always had a way of making Sam feel better about everything and this morning was no exception.

When the waiter returned they informed him that they would be spending the day on Prickly Pear Island and asked for a picnic lunch. The waiter gave them a choice of sandwiches, then told them it would be ready in thirty minutes. They finished breakfast, thanked their waiter and then strolled back to their cottage. Ten minutes later they had changed into their suits, packed their backpack with books, suntan oil, and various sundry items and were on their way to the resort's boat dock on the north end of the island by way of the bikes that were provided to each guest.

- - - - - - - - - - - - - - < > - - - - - - - - - - - - - - -

He sat at his table alone and when the waiter came he informed him that 'the lady' was sleeping in and would not be joining him this morning. He took coffee from the waiter and then filled his plate from the breakfast buffet of fruits, cereals, eggs and sausage, then read the home-made newspaper while he ate. He had taken a table directly behind a couple and worked hard to overhear their conversations. When he heard them ask the waiter for a picnic lunch, he had heard all he needed. He took a couple a quick bites of his breakfast and returned to his bungalow to change. He quietly entered, changed into his beach clothes, and retrieved all the items he required for his day at the beach, including a pistol with silencer that had been provided to him by his client.

John S. Wood never used a gun in his work; not to kill the victim or even for self-defense. He was an expert in executing 'death by accident' and he accomplished this through thorough planning. By carefully observing the target, he could find some aspect of the target's daily routine or behavior that through some manipulation of events, he could hasten an 'accident that was waiting to happen.' He looked at the pistol and uncomfortably put it into his backpack. From the sitting area he glanced into the sleeping area; there was no door between the two rooms, and he looked at the woman sleeping in his bed. She lay on top of the bed with the covers under her and was in the same position as when she fell into bed the night before.

They had eaten dinner together during which she had consumed the entire contents of a very heavy chardonnay less the one glass he had. Back at the room she had ordered two more bottles and gotten fairly drunk; not stumbling down or loud drunk, just emotionally free. She was a woman who was paid for her services, and he was sure that with her body the men who paid for her service got their money's worth. He was not inclined to pay for sex nor to associate with a woman who made her living that way. But she was a stunning woman and after two and half bottles of wine she was no longer the aloof provider of sexual services, the one faking interest and eventually faking orgasm for some overweight, oversexed, and under-satisfied man. She was the one wanting to share love-making, or at least share the passion of the moment.

She had shed the red dress from dinner, the one that provided a tantalizing view of her full and intoxicating breasts and now was wearing a tiny silk teddy that left nothing to the imagination. The moment he came in the door she greeted him with a kiss and a glass of wine and they both sat on the moon-lit balcony for a few minutes. He wasn't sure if it had been his focus on the mission or his thought that she was perhaps more than 'eye candy' provided by the client and perhaps an agent sent to ensure he executed his mission that kept him from taking her. He sat there in the moonlight, drinking and thinking of her incredible body and struggled with thoughts of sleeping with her and how it could distract him from his mission. The internal struggle was for naught as when she had excused herself to go to the bathroom she had passed out on the bed.

He stood in the doorway and looked at her, thought just for a moment of spending the day in bed with her, blowing off the mission, and then escaping back to his life and to Sophie. Then he knew with some certainty that unless he finished the mission NECO, whoever they were, would not let him live. He wasn't sure they would anyway.

1020 hours, Biras Creek Resort

Mary and Sam rode their bikes down the dirt and gravel trail to the boat dock where the resort provided Boston Whalers; a two-person eight-foot aluminum boat outfitted with a small outboard motor. The little craft was capable of taking guests throughout the protected bay but was totally unsuitable for use outside the bay. After a five-minute peddle, they parked their bikes at a bike stand by the dock. There was no need to lock them as all the bikes on the island belonged to the resort and there was no place to take it if someone where to steal one.

They walked up the dock to a small wooden building that served as a maintenance area for the boats as well as providing an issue facility for snorkels, masks, and fins for the guests as well as managing the small boat fleet. A dock extended the full length of the front of the building and then thirty feet in front of both sides, forming a 'U' shaped harbor for the tiny fleet. The boats were already prepared for the guest's use with oars, two life jackets, and a fuel can. One employee serviced the entire facility, issuing the guests snorkeling equipment, signing out the boats, and providing any needed instruction on the boat's operation.

Next to the boat facility a small cabana offered drinks and snacks throughout the day.

"Let's go, Mary." Sam held out his hand to help her into the boat. She had already passed him the picnic basket, and Sam had stowed it along with the snorkeling gear and had shaken the gas can to ensure it was full. He was ready to go, but she stopped.

"I forgot my Dr. Pepper. I'll get some at the cabana bar."

"Hon, this is the British Virgin Islands, not Texas, and I don't think they'll have Dr. Pepper. Besides, the resort provided drinks in the picnic lunch." He extended his hand again, but she didn't take it.

"Be right back." Mary started towards the bar.

"They won't have any."

"Bet on it?" Mary asked, but Sam did not respond and she continued on.

"That stuff will be the death of you!" He shouted to her as she walked down the dock.

Two minutes later Mary returned carrying two cans of Dr. Pepper. She was smiling and strutting with an exaggerate swagger.

"Don't say a word." Sam extended his hand once again. Mary took it and got in, sat, and then put the soda in the cooler, looked at him and smiled that 'you're wrong again smile' that unfortunately for Sam came more often than he would have liked.

The young man who worked the facility walked by. "Need any help getting started?"

"No thanks, done this many times." Sam waved a thank you as the man walked on.

He pulled on the starter cord, but the engine did not turn over. He pulled several more times with the same result. Mary sat quietly watching without comment or reaction.

"Damn thing won't start. We'll have to get another boat." Sam stood and stepped out of the boat onto the dock. "I'll get the attendant."

Mary quickly slipped from her seat to the seat Sam had. There was a red cord that hung around the throttle handle; a bracelet-like cord that had another cord extending from it and at the end of that cord there was a metal bar-like key. Mary put the bracelet around her wrist, plugged the metal bar into the throttle handle pulled the starter cord and the engine roared to life. She took her hand off the throttle, the metal bar slipped out of the handle and the engine immediately stopped. She returned the bracket to the handle then retook her original seat with Sam watching all the while from the dock.

Sam returned to the boat, repeated what Mary had done and then guided the boat out of the little harbor.

"Why didn't you say anything?" Sam finally asked after he cleared the dock.

"You told me not to speak," Mary said from her seat facing Sam.

There was a long silence while Sam sulked.

"Zero for two, Sam, old boy. Not off to such a good start," Mary said from under her hat and sun glasses.

"I'm a strong finisher," Sam returned.

Mary smiled, "I'm counting on it." She sat in the front of the boat facing Sam as he piloted the little ten foot craft westward away from the resort's dock into North Sound. It was just past 10:30 and the sun was bright and warm and its radiant heat shown on Mary's face as Sam piloted the boat westward around the sailboats that were at anchor at the *Bitter End Yacht Club*, which lay between the resort and their destination, a small uninhabited island just a mile offshore called Prickly Pear Island. The island was very flat, no fresh water and totally unsuitable for housing. That, coupled with the British Government's desire to maintain the topical nature of the Island group, Prickly Pear was declared as a Natural Preserve thus keeping all development off the island.

The waters there were crystal clear, ideal for snorkeling, and the area was known for the beautiful tropical fish that lived among the conch shells and grasses. There were two other smaller islands nearby; Necker Island to the north and Eustasia Island just off the southeastern most point of Prickly Pear. Between Eustasia and Prickly Pear was the only southern entrance and the water between the two was extremely shallow. The stone and shell bottom was so shallow even the little boats that drew only a couple feet of water occasionally hit bottom. This condition kept all the larger boats away and the only boats that could get there were these small two-man metal bottomed skiffs like the one that Mary and Sam were in.

Even rubber boats that drew just a few inches of water stayed away due to the sharp reef that guarded the entrance. On the northern side, the water was deep but there was a reef that ran all the way from Prickly Pear to Necker then south to Eustasia. The reef was a mile out in the ocean and the waves constantly crashed onto the reef making it a graveyard for any boat that approached it from its northern ocean side. Although the leeward side of the reef did not have the waves crashing upon it, it was equally as dangerous as the suction of the retreating water could draw a man into the reef and to serious injury or death.

The combination of the shallow entrance to the south and the reef in the north made a huge, but relatively shallow bowl that did not provide any areas for deep dives. Because of the shallows, scuba drivers went elsewhere in search of caves and interesting sea creatures that lived in deeper water. That left this area for the novice snorkeler, and occasional lovers who wanted to use the beach for other than sunning themselves.

Having crossed over the shallow southern entrance and then passing a small point, Sam could see a long C-Shaped beach that provided easy access just about five-hundred yards away; so he turned his little craft southwest and headed into the cove. As he did another boat came around the same point. He saw that it had the same markings as his boat and knew that the boat and its single occupant were also from the Biras Creek resort. The other boat did not make the change in course, and Sam watched as it continued on his original course. Sam cruised his little boat parallel to the shore until he came to a spot that looked inviting; then he turned his boat directly into it and readied himself to land the boat.

"Okay, Mary, get ready the boat will bump a little bit as I land this thing." Sam told Mary as he slowed the little boat down in anticipation of reaching the shore.

"Aye eye, Sir!" Mary said jokingly and saluted. Your crew stands ready, Sir!"

When the bow of the little boat hit the shore Mary threw the anchor out and it landed on the beach with a thud.

"Boat secured, Sir!"

Sam turned off the motor and turned back to Mary as she laughed and saluted her captain.

"Better be careful mate or this captain will extract some extra services from the crew. It has been a long voyage and your Captain is looking forward to some pleasures from the local natives." Sam stood, puffed up his chest, and surveyed the beach like a sailor looking over the bow at an unexplored island.

"Well, Captain, I believe this is an uninhabited island; so I don't think you are going to get lucky with the local native girls." Mary said as she stepped off the boat and started to unload the picnic basket, beach towels, and her backpack.

Stepping out of the back of the boat into just a foot of water, Sam pushed the boat further onto shore to make it easier to offload. "No problem, I have been trained to adapt to all situations, and after all what do you think the crew is for?" With that, Sam ran through the water after Mary. She didn't make much of an effort to get away; he grabbed her, swung her around, bent her over and kissed her hard. Then he picked her up carrying her in his arms in front of him, while Mary playfully fought back.

"Oh, my Sir, please don't have your way with me, I'm an innocent young maiden." She joked with him and gently pounded on his chest like a woman being carried off against her will. She was ready for what was next. He would lay her down gently on the beach, and they would make love right there on the beach. And why not, the day was beautiful and there was no one on the entire island except them.

Sam carried her back towards the boat, but just as he got near the area where Mary had already dropped the towels, he turned and walked quickly into the water, took two more steps then threw Mary into the water. The unexpected action caught her by surprise. She yelled and then went all the way under getting a mouthful of seawater. She popped back up from the dunking with water streaming off her clothes as she spit out the strong tasting salt water.

"Now that should be a lesson to the disobedient crew," Sam said as he stood there with his hands on his hips looking all the part of a seafaring captain.

"You're going to pay for this, Call," Mary said as she slogged back towards Sam and pretended to be pissed. As she slogged past Sam, not paying any attention to him she suddenly yelled, "Mutiny!" and then tackled him, knocking him down and under the water he went. She ran to the beach and lay down upon the large beach towel waiting for him.

Sam ran up to her and stopped beside her. Standing there he looked down at her as she lay there wet and inviting.

"Okay now you are going to see exactly what Burt Lancaster wanted to do on the beach with Debra Kerr in *Here To Eternity*", and he dropped to his knees beside her just like in the movie.

"Oh, Sam, you are so dramatic." And with that she pulled him to her and they finally did exactly what she wanted to do the moment she saw the island.

- - - - - - - - - - - - - - - < > - - - - - - - - - - - - - - - -

The operator of the other boat had continued northward towards the reef until he was sure he was out of sight, then turned due west and headed for the shore of Prickly Pear Island. He had his plan. It was not what he wanted, and he did not get to practice his plan and that disturbed him. It was simple enough; he would wait until he could get the man alone and then threaten harm to his wife if he didn't follow his instructions. They would then take a short trip out to the reef where he would smash his head with a piece of metal pipe that he had secured from the boat dock for that purpose. Then pushing him overboard he would drown while at the same time the sharp reef would tear his flesh to pieces and thus destroy any sign of his blows.

The plan had three keys elements: First, he had to catch the mark away from his wife otherwise she would be aware of the kidnapping. He didn't believe this would be a problem as people, at times, commonly swam alone, took naps, or walked on the beach, and he felt sure he could work this. Second, he had to secure their boat, again without disturbing the mark's wife, so that he could set it adrift near the reef. Finally, he wanted to be gone from the resort before the body was discovered. He and his 'companion' were due to depart by helicopter at ten the next morning for San Juan, then back to the States by private plane. If all worked well, he would take care of the mark around 1 PM, and if no one else came by the island, the wife would be there all night with no way to get off the island. At the worst, she would get back around dark and it would take until at least the next day to find the body in the dark—and he wanted it found.

As he neared the shore just north of the small peninsula where his mark had settled, he killed the engine and the little craft floated to the shore. He exited the boat, secured the anchor on shore and made a quick recon to ensure no one else was near. Walking south about a hundred yards along the beach, he came to a vantage point where he could see his mark.

"Perfect!" He muttered aloud as he saw the mark and his wife on the beach; they seemed to be asleep resting under some tropical vegetation that stood around eight feet tall with branches that grew out like an umbrella. Two plants growing side by side provided excellent shade to beach goers wanting to lay on the beach and still escape the direct rays of the sun. He could see that his mark had taken advantage of the tropical 'beach umbrella.'

He looked around to finalize his plan. The mark was forty yards away, but his boat was just ten; so getting the boat would be easy, as long as he could get his mark alone. So to improve his chances of getting his mark alone, he quietly walked to the boat, took the anchor that was lying on the beach and pulled the boat even closer to his position. Sitting on the sandy knoll, protected from detection by the vegetation, he waited. Less than thirty minutes later it all came together; he watched as the mark awoke but did not wake his wife. He stood and apparently seeing his boat was further away from where he had left it he came to investigate.

Just as his mark got to the boat, Wood came out from his hiding place.

"Don't move and don't make a sound."

- - - - - - - - - - - - - - - < > - - - - - - - - - - - - - - - -

Sam was startled. He hadn't noticed the man coming towards him; he hadn't expected to see anyone on the island at all. He turned to see an average looking man in a bathing suit, blue tank top, floppy hat and sun glasses looking like a tourist, except he hadn't seen any other tourist holding a pistol, a pistol with a silencer on it.

"What do you want? I don't have any money on me. I got nothing you would want." Sam turned fully towards him.

"I don't want anything from you. I have some friends who want to talk to you; so you come with me and no one gets hurt." He looked back at where Mary was still asleep, "Especially the wife".

Sam didn't look back, he didn't want to take his eyes off the man. The man who had just struck a very sensitive nerve, that being 'harming his wife.'

"Now quietly get your little boat and pull it around to the next cove, and don't make any noise." He aimed the pistol not at Sam, but back towards Mary who was asleep on the sand.

Sam got the message, quietly got the anchor, and slowly pulled the boat through the shallow calm water as the man walked beside him on the beach. When they got around the cove, the man stopped Sam.

"Okay stop there and back up." Sam did as he was told and watched as the man got into the back of the boat. "Now get in." He paused and aimed his pistol at him. "And don't get any ideas on jumping me. I will shoot you, then I will go back and get her."

Sam knew this was not the time to make a move that he already suspected would be necessary and most likely fatal. He decided to take his chances on deeper water. He was a great swimmer and he figured he would make a move on this man farther out in the bay where the sea and his swimming ability would give him the advantage—he hoped.

Sam had sat down in the boat, and just as the man moved to start the little engine, an object ripped passed his arm and made a loud bang as it slammed into the side of the aluminum boat. Instantly they both looked down to see a can of Dr Pepper rolling around on the boat bottom, and then they both looked back toward where they thought it came from.

- - - - - - - - - - - - - - - - < > - - - - - - - - - - - - - - - - -

They had made love quietly and tenderly on the beach and they both fell asleep holding each other; as she drifted off to sleep under the shade of the strange umbrella-like plants on this most perfect beach, she felt wonderful, she felt content, no more so—she felt complete.

She had awakened and rolled over to see Sam, but he was already gone. Thinking he had awakened, and not wishing to wake her, he probably just went for a walk on the beach. She was thirsty; between the heat and the love making she was parched. She got up and walked straight to the cooler and picked up a can of Dr. Pepper; she smiled when she thought of how Sam was surprised when she got it from the beach bar. Taking the can in her right hand she went to open the pull tab with her left hand. In doing so she caught the sight of Sam. She almost called out but thought better when she realized he was pulling their boat ahead of another man, and that man had a gun.

Without making a sound she immediately ran after them along the surf's edge. When she came to the edge of the cove, she couldn't run any further without entering the water and alerting the other man. Realizing she still had the unopened can in her hand, she just threw it, hoping to hit the man and distract him enough for Sam to get away.

Mary heard the bang as the can struck the side of the boat; then she saw Sam, as he looked back at her. Although he was many yards away, she instinctively reached out to Sam. She never heard the sound; she only felt the sting of the bullet as it ripped through the top of her arm and she immediately went down grabbing at the wound as she went.

- - - - - - - - - - - - - - - -< > - - - - - - - - - - - - - - - -

The pistol felt wrong in his hand as he sat in the boat trying to keep the man covered while preparing to start the little engine. So far it all was going according to plan; as much of a plan that he had. Fortunately, the target's wife was asleep and not presenting any problem. He didn't want to kill her and now it looked like he was going to be able to take this guy out to the reef and kill him there. Once that was done, he was done. Done with killing, and certainly done with NECO, whoever they were.

He had gotten his target in the boat and just as he moved to start the little engine an object ripped passed his arm and made a loud bang as it slammed into the side of the aluminum boat. Instantly he looked down to see the source of the noise and was startled to see a can of Dr Pepper rolling around on the boat bottom. He looked back toward where he thought it came from.

Without even making a conscience decision to shoot, his finger squeezed the trigger and the silenced weapon made a quiet pop sound. He saw the target's wife grab at her arm and go down. He now realized that the sudden surprise attack by the woman meant he had to kill them both. He swung back to deliver the killing shot to his passenger.

-- - - - - - - - - - - - - < > - - - - - - - - - - - - - - -

He was waiting for the moment when his attacker took his eye off of him, so he could make his move. Sam had sat down in the boat and just as the man moved to start the little engine, an object ripped passed his arm and made a loud bang as it slammed into the side of the aluminum boat. Instantly Sam looked down to see a can of Dr Pepper rolling around on the boat bottom and then looked back toward where he thought it came from. It was Mary, standing there at the edge of the cove.

Sam had looked at the soda can an instant longer than the gunman, and when he did look up he saw the gunman had already turned towards Mary and he could do nothing before the man got off his first shot. Sam had delayed moving just an instant, when the noise had surprised him, but he recovered and was already in the air, having flung his body at his assailant before the man could fire a second shot.

The assailant turned the weapon towards Sam, but Sam's lunging body blocked the gun. It fired as he hit the man causing the shot to go well away from Sam as the force of his thrust knocked the gun from the killer's hand, and it went into the water followed by both men. The water was only two feet deep by the shore and both men were upright in an instant looking for each other.

With water pouring off his body, Sam swung around looking for his assailant who had instantly started a search for the dropped weapon. At that moment, Sam knew he had the advantage. If he could get to the assailant quickly he could put him in a choke hold and it would be over in a few seconds. Sam stepped quickly towards the man, but his feet slipped on the shell-covered bottom and he fell into the assailant, hitting him in the back; again they both went under the water. Again they rose, and again they reached at each other in the shallow water trying to grab each other's throat. But the water slowed their movements and they looked more like high school boys slap-fighting instead of a professional killer and highly trained soldier.

Sam finally got a firm footing and grabbed the gunman's shoulder with his left hand, then slammed him with a right to the man's chin, then another to his throat and gunman fell back into the water. But the force of hitting his assailant forced Sam backwards, and he bumped into the boat that had been floating free. He fell backwards and in pain, as his left shoulder smashed into the side of the boat. As he continued to fall the side of his head took a glancing blow off the side of the boat, and he slumped into the water where he landed face down in the water.

He was dazed, but started to get up when he felt a pressure on his back. He couldn't get up. He could feel tightness around his neck and realized two hands were forcing him down into the sandy ocean bottom. He was a good swimmer and could hold his breath for two minutes, but the slam into the boat had knocked out his wind. He could feel his strength leaving him as the sand filled his mouth and nose. Sam made another attempted to rise, but it was hopeless; the killer had a knee on his back, and Sam was stuck in the sand and he knew it was over. He felt the pressure on his neck; he felt himself blacking out.

As his face was being driven into the sandy bottom and his life's strength was leaving him, he suddenly felt the pressure on his neck lessen. He was now able to pull his face from the sand, but he could not see. There was a darkness all around him and he fought to stand. He got on his knees, which was enough to get his head out of the water, and he coughed until he threw up the sand he had swallowed. His head started to clear and he regained enough composure to look for his assailant. He moved his arms quickly in front of him as if to fight off some imaginary blows. But none came.

He looked at the water around him and it was dark, and then he saw the man floating face up and heading towards the shore. Sam then stumbled towards his assailant still not knowing how he had gotten the man off of him, but expecting to have to reengage him immediately. When Sam got to the man, he saw he was grasping his left side, which Sam now saw was bleeding profusely.

His mind began to clear, Sam suddenly looked back to where Mary went down, but she was not there. He then looked around, and there thirty feet away stood Mary holding the pistol in both her hands. She stood there in the water up to her knees in perfect shooting form, her right hand around the pistol grip and her left hand supporting her right. She apparently hadn't moved since firing the pistol.

Sam ran to her through the water as best he could, stopped in front of her, gently placed his hand on hers, and she released the pistol to Sam.

"It's okay," he told her as he looked at her and then her arm. "Come on, I need to clean this up," and he started to lead her away to the shore.

"He tried to kill us, Sam," she said in a subdued voice as she looked at the man now half on the beach and half in the water. Then she screamed, "The bastard tried to kill us." She pulled away and ran to the wounded man and stood there over him. "Why? Why?" She repeated. Sam was right there with her and held her back.

"Help me, I can't move. I'm bleeding, I need help," came a pathetic request for aid. The man lay there on the beach pushed by the surf and unable to move. He was holding the area under his left arm with his right hand, trying unsuccessfully to hold back the blood that was flowing from the wound. Sam knelt down beside him, looked at the wound and gently rolled him over slightly to check for an exit wound; there was none. When he moved the man's hand to look at the wound, blood gushed out. Sam had seen this before.

The bullet had entered through his left side. If he had been standing, the bullet would have struck his arm, but Mary must have hit him while he was bent over and his arms were extended into the water. Since there was no exit wound, Sam suspected the bullet slammed into the spine, shattering the bone and sending fragments throughout the body causing major damage and blood loss—this was a fatal wound.

Sam bent down to look at the wound. "You're not that bad, I can fix you right up. But first tell me who are you and why did you want us dead."

"Help me," was the only reply.

"I'll help after you tell me what I want to know."

"I'm bleeding, you got to help," came another cry for help.

Sam leaned closer to the wounded man until he was just inches from his face. He quietly, but sternly said to him; "Listen. You have 30 seconds to tell me what I want to know, or I'm leaving you here to get washed out to sea." The man said nothing but looked back and forth in a panic. Sam stood, took Mary's arm, then started to slowly walk away.

The surf was no longer washing the blood away and it now lay there covering the lower part of his body in a thick red ooze. He looked at his wound and then at Sam. The man was in full panic and he yelled to Sam.

"Okay, okay, but you've got to fix me up."

Sam turned back, "You got it. Now tell me, what's your name?"

"Name," the man paused just a moment then continued, "my name is Rowe, James Rowe."

"Good start," Sam replied. "And who sent you to kill us and why."

"Not both, just you," he looked at Sam. "It was going to be an accident. Drowning."

"It would have been if Mary hadn't got thirsty." Sam looked over to Mary briefly and gave a small, almost indiscernible smile. "And who sent you?"

There was no response.

Sam yelled again, "who sent you?"

"I don't know."

"Don't think me an idiot. You come all this way to kill me and you don't know who sent you?" Sam grabbed the man by his shirt.

"Russo. It was supposed to be Russo, but it wasn't." Rowe was confused. The loss of blood was making him lose his train of thought; he blinked his eyes and fought to focus. "Not Russo."

Sam pulled on Rowe's shirt again, "Who? I need to know who."

"Not Russo."

"What? Don't screw with me, or I'll leave you here for the crabs to pick at." Sam yelled as he pulled the man up by his shirt.

Rowe screamed in pain.

"I need a name! I want a name!" Sam let go of Rowe's shirt and the man fell back to the beach in pain.

"I swear to Christ, NECO is all I know," He paused and gasped. "All I know is its government."

Sam bent back down and quietly coaxed Rowe, "How do you know that?"

Rowe gasped a large breath then seemed to settle down. His breathing got easier and he looked at Sam in the eye for the first time and spoke in short choppy sentences. "They flew me in by private plane. Work alone. Got my contracts from a crime boss... but days ago... these guys told me... he gave me up for a deal." He paused and breathing became labored again. "That's all I know I swear to Christ."

Sam stood, then turned and started to lead Mary away.

Rowe turned his head toward Sam, "Wait. Help me; you gave me your word." The man reached out with one bloody hand.

"Buddy you're going to bleed out. I suspect you'll be dead before we get clear of the beach." Sam looked down at him with contempt. "And as far as my word goes, when you shot my wife—you were already dead." He paused for a moment and his voice changed from one of contempt and hatred to one of sympathy. "I would highly suggest that you make peace with whomever you call God."

Sam looked around the isolated bay and saw his boat floating out with the tide; it was almost to the coral reef. Rowe's boat was beached just twenty yards away so he immediately led Mary to the boat, climbed in, and started back to the beach site where he picked up their belongings. Without her leaving the boat, he used a bottle of water to clean her arm, and then wrap the wound with a towel. Within two minutes, they were headed back to the resort dock.

"By the way," he looked at Mary and waited for her to look up at him. "Thanks for saving my life," then added, "That was a lucky shot for me."

"Lucky shot?" Mary paused, and looked Sam straight in the eye, and without emotion said, "I am from Texas, or have you forgotten."

- - - - - - - - - - - - - - - < > - - - - - - - - - - - - - - - -

The surf had picked him up and taken him off the beach but he did not seem to feel anything. The pain had left him, and he was no longer aware of his wound or his situation. He opened his eyes but did not see a small boat moving away from him or even blink from the bright sunlight that streamed down from a cloudless sky and shown in his sightless eyes. Nor did he feel the water rushing over his body as the current started to take him out towards the reef. He did see a small shop with a glass front and inside one long counter stretched the length of the room. Behind it he saw a young woman who was looking back at him, and she was smiling. He saw her wave to him, and he raised his arm and returned the greeting.

"Sophie!" And his lifeless arm slapped down into the water.

- - - - - - - - - - - - - < > - - - - - - - - - - - - - -

It was 1500 hours when Sam pulled the boat into the little harbor, and as he did the attendant came over to assist in securing the boat.

"My wife has cut herself on some coral. Where is the nearest doctor?"

"Tortola, and you have to go by water taxi. I'll call the main office right now." The attendant left Sam and Mary, went inside the little maintenance building, and called the office. He returned just as Sam had finished getting Mary out of the boat along with their personal things.

"They're sending a cart to get you right now. It will pick you both up and take you to the main dock."

"Thank you," Sam turned to finish securing the boat.

The man took the line. "I got it."

"Thanks again," Sam touched him on the shoulder in gratitude and then walked with Mary to where they had left their bikes.

"How's the arm, Hon?" Sam looked at the towel and saw that there was no bleeding.

"Nothing really." She looked at the arm and touched it with her uninjured hand. "Just stings a little. It's more like a bad burn; not like what I thought gunshot would feel like." She looked over her shoulder back as Sam, who was now holding her gently and stroking her hair.

"Someone tried to kill us Sam. What the hell is going on?"

"I don't know Hon, but I'm going to sure find out. No one knows yet what has happened and you can bet this wasn't because we didn't pay a phone bill. They wanted me dead; whoever they are, they wanted it to look like an accident."

"Yes, but why?"

"Another equally good question." Sam looked down the trail and saw the cart coming for them. "I must assume this is a professional hit, and the accident was meant to keep it low key in the news. Sam stood in front of Mary and put his hands on her shoulders. "We aren't saying a word about the man out there. We were snorkeling and you got distracted by a fish, turned and cut yourself. I'll call David; we'll figure this out." With that the cart stopped by them and they got in.

The trip to the main office took just three minutes, and the office had already confirmed the water taxi would arrive in fifteen minutes. So Sam had the driver take them to the bungalow where they both changed and retrieved their passports, Sam's wallet, Mary's purse and other essentials which Sam put into Mary's tote bag. Ten minutes later they were in the water taxi in route to Tortola.

The water taxi trip took forty-five minutes, and it was another thirty to the hospital via a land taxi. After an initial triage by a nurse to check for the seriousness of the injury, Mary's case got in the queue to be seen behind the two men from a vehicle accident in which an open taxi (a type of faster golf cart used on the island in lieu of cars) ran into the back of a dump truck, and a ugly looking eye injury involving a tourist and a fishhook. Realizing that the water taxi did not run after dark, Sam knew he had to make arrangements to stay the night on Tortola or just take the plane home from there whenever Mary was ready.

Sam needed to make one call.

"Hello, David, this is Sam."

"Hey there, don't tell me you are bored already," David joked.

"We have a problem David; I'm not kidding. Someone tried to kill me today."

"What!"

"While Mary and I were out on another island. It's a long story; he wanted to make it look like an accident, but Mary stopped him." Sam looked back at Mary who had turned and was now looking out the sliding doors towards the ocean. "She shot him. He's dead."

"Damn, how is she?"

"Well she got wounded in the arm, it's not serious, but we are at the hospital on Tortola. As for the other part, we'll have to wait and see."

"Yes, we both know how that is my friend," David quietly responded remembering his own experiences.

"David, before the shooter died he told me he was only after me and that he had been sent by a group called NECO. He also said they flew him in and he thought it was a government agency."

There was a long pause on David's end of the call. "Real clandestine shit."

"Affirmative."

"What about the body?"

"I left it on the beach, and I haven't told anyone about it yet. I wanted to get Mary out of there to see a medic, and besides, whoever wanted to kill me would have another opportunity if we stayed."

"I agree. Is there anyway to tie it back to you other than Mary's wound?"

"I'm not sure. It's really remote out there and I didn't see another boat the whole time we were there or coming back. Mary and I did notice the man at the resort last night at dinner. He was with this very expensive looking woman that I don't think he got on his looks."

"So he was watching you, then saw you take a boat, followed you out, and tried to kill you out there where no one would find you, at least for a while anyway."

"Yes, but what about Mary? He said he wasn't going to kill her."

"Well, I suspect that if the island was that remote, then if he took your boat, she would be there until the resort searched for her or another couple came along the next day also looking for privacy. That tells me he most likely would have wanted to leave before the body was found, just avoid any kind of involvement with the local authorities."

"Sounds reasonable to me, David.

"Have you got your passport and money?"

"Yes, why?"

"I don't think you should go back to the resort. I figure if you do you will be trapped there for days, maybe weeks."

"What about the police and leaving? Don't you think the BVI police will get a little pissed?"

"They'll just have to get over it. Besides we can inform the authorities when you get back if we need to. But that's a problem for another day. Can you make flight arrangements?"

"Affirmative. I'll call the agent who set this up and have them get us out right away."

"Call me back."

"Roger." Sam hung up and immediately called his agent who provided the change in flights, and Sam returned the call to David. "If all goes well we are leaving tonight from San Juan on American Airlines 2314 at twenty-ten hours. We have to stop over in New York, so we are not getting into Atlanta until zero-seven-zero-five hours on Saturday. If we don't make the flight I'll call."

"Roger! Either Bob or I will meet you in Atlanta. You have luggage?"

"No. We changed, got the essentials for the trip here and left the suitcases at the resort. "

"I suggest you buy a cheap suitcase and fill it with souvenirs. It would be bad to raise suspicions with customs and checking through without luggage would do that."

"Thanks, David."

"I have a friend on St. John Island named Chad Mitchell. He has a small charter boat thing going. I'm going to call him and ask him to sail over there and check things out. See you when you get back. Out here." And with his military efficiency, David was off.

1515 hours, Atlanta, GA

"Bob, this is David. I want you to find out whatever you can on a group called NECO."

"What's up?"

"Sam and Mary have had some trouble. I'll brief you later on it. I'm not sure what NECO does, but they *may* be government and they *may* be out of D.C. I am picking them up at Hartsfield at zero seven hundred hours then taking them to a hotel. I'll want to meet as soon as I get them settled. You got it?"

"That's November, Echo, Charlie, Oscar, possible D.C., possible government."

"Roger."

"I'm on it."

1520 hours, St Johns Island, U.S. Virgin Islands

"Hey, Chad, it's for you. A guy named Lytle." The man called from the charter shack to the man cleaning the catch of the day off the stern of the boat. A good-looking average-size man of five feet ten inches, with a slightly receding hairline, dressed in cut off jeans, a T-shirt with Mitchell Charter embroidered on the upper left side, deck shoes, and wearing a very worn baseball cap, with LNMB embroidered in small letters on the back, strolled over to the shack. He was forty-two, looked thirty, and was strong and fit as a twenty-five year old.

Mitchell had never been married. It wasn't for a lack of women, and in fact it may have just been the opposite. Despite his experience, his age, and his living on the rougher side of life, he had the face more like a sweet young man than of a hardened former soldier and now fisherman, which he was—and the ladies couldn't resist it.

"Mitchell here." He listened to the man on the other end of the call without interruption for just under a minute.

"Roger. I'm on it." He hung up the phone, picked up the charter book, and read the schedule. He turned to the young man. "Mac, call the party for tomorrow morning and tell them there is a change in the charter. Tell them the Marlins are striking off of Virgin Gorda and we are leaving at sunrise, which is zero five fifty-two hours. Make sure you are ready to go to by zero six hundred hours. I've got business on Gorda, so you are taking them out; you can get your brother to crew for you." He took a step towards the boat and then turned back. "And tell him if he screws it up, I'll use his worthless ass for bait."

1930 hours, Biras Creek

She got back from sunning herself on the beach just after 6 PM, took a shower, and lounged around on the deck waiting for him to come back from his boating trip. When he hadn't returned by 7:30, she put on a slinky black dress that accentuated her figure, especially her cleavage, and she went to the dining room. She ate alone, but not unnoticed as just about every man in the small restaurant saw her, some more intently than others. When she was finished she went to the adjoining bar where she sat alone for less than ten minutes before two couples in their early-sixties asked if she was alone and asked her to join them—actually the two men asked.

They all drank for another hour until the wives said they were tired and were ready to go. Both men played the part of concerned gentlemen, and said they would wait with her until her companion returned. The wives, saving as much dignity as they could, then left without fanfare. An hour and two bottles of very expensive champagne later, she announced she was giving up on her companion and going to bed. The two men followed her down the sand road to her bungalow each only thinking of how they wanted to bed this incredible looking woman.

When they got to the door of her bungalow, she was now quite sober, but the two men were still very drunk; she said good night and the younger of the two asked if she wanted them to come in. Standing inside the bungalow door, she looked at them both on the porch, told them it cost a thousand dollars to come inside, pulled her dress over her head and stood there in her silk bra and panties, which matched perfectly the color of her dress—not that either man noticed that fact.

Both men came in with wallets in hand and had no problem producing cash. She took care of each man in less than ten minutes.

Chapter 13

Saturday, October 22

LNMB

"Here he is." The crewman standing next to Chad at the wheel of the boat pointed to the fat young man running down the dock to the boat.

Chad looked back at the boy as he climbed on board. He turned back to the front, and seeing that there was nothing in his path, called back to the crewman. "Cast off the stern line."

The crewman untied the line from the dock, threw it into the boat and jumped aboard. He secured the line out of the way of the passengers and then cornered his brother in the stern of the boat.

"Damn man. I can't believe you're late."

"Traffic was heavy, Mac."

"At this hour? You think I'm a fool, Greg?" He sniffed his brother. "Well, at least you don't smell of it."

The fat boy, dressed in his faded blue jeans, T-shirt, and well-used baseball cap, pretended not to understand his brother's reference to his indulgence in cheap beer.

"And you better shape up. Mr. Mitchell is still pissed from the last time you crewed for him."

"What? I didn't do anything."

He stopped his work and stared at his brother. "You mishandled the gaff, lost the customer's Marlin, and then stabbed Mr. Mitchell in the leg with the gaff before you lost it overboard."

"Oh that," The fat boy looked down at the bottom of the boat as if saying 'Ah shucks.'

"Yes. Oh that," the crewman waited for his brother to look up at him. "Mr. Mitchell has business to do on Gorda, so I am captaining the charter. You screw this up and I'll use your ass for bait."

The fat brother shook his head understanding his brother's seriousness.

"Now secure the bow lines."

And the boat with its captain, crew of two, and five would-be deep-sea fisherman were off.

0730 hours, Atlanta, GA

The aircraft carrying Sam and Mary along with some two hundred flight weary travelers arrived remarkably on time, and even more remarkably was not delayed getting to the gate. The flight was mostly business men hustling out of the plane to either get to their first client visit, or hustling to get home and escape from a trip full of hustling to clients. Sam and Mary were in the back of the plane, and they would be almost the last to exit. That suited Sam just fine, as he did not want to risk someone bumping into Mary's injured arm. They slowly and quietly left the plane and took the underground train to the baggage claim area, and when the train arrived, they took the long escalator up to baggage claim.

As soon as Sam exited the escalator, he saw David standing there in his jeans and corduroy coat, which was his 'uniform' whenever he wasn't on the job.

David walked immediately over to Mary who was wearing a baggy tourist shirt that she had purchased in Tortola to hide the bandage. He reached to her and hugged her but was careful not to touch either arm or the wound. He leaned into her and gently kissed her on the cheek and whispered to her. "Whatever you need."

Mary kissed him back and looked tenderly into his eyes and knew he meant it. Whether she needed him to run errands, just listen to her rant and rave about what happened, or kill the bastards responsible for this, she knew he would do it without question.

David and Sam shook hands and they pulled each other together and hugged while slapping each other gently on the back. David hugged a little longer, grateful for Sam's safe return. They went to the baggage claim area, retrieved the luggage, and walked to the car without a word about Biras Creek.

0740 hours, Biras Creek

The boat pulled into the dock at Biras Creek and Chad jumped off. He had already covered the route with his young crewman and reviewed the schedule. Mac had crewed for Chad for three seasons; so Chad was confident in his young assistant's abilities. They could call each other on the ship-to-shore radio, and Chad had the portable with him to contact the boat with any change in plans.

He watched from the dock as the young crewman perfectly backed the boat away from the dock and then steered into the main channel; then he set about his task of gathering data for David.

0815 hours, Atlanta, GA

David paid the toll for the short-term parking lot and guided his car into the traffic. Once he was comfortably into the flow, he turned to Sam. "So tell me everything you know about this man."

"David, I know so little about this guy I don't even know what I don't know." Sam thought for a moment. "I think he was straight about what he told me. He didn't want to die, and he would have sold his mother if it would have saved him."

Sam again thought for a moment. "He wasn't career military."

"Why?" David asked.

"He was totally unprepared for getting shot. I don't think he knew how bad he was hit, or would have had a clue what to do if he did. I think he was a professional but not a shooter."

"He was there to arrange an accident, not shoot you. Something must have caused him to change his plan." David looked in the rearview mirror and saw Mary. "Mary?"

"I agree with Sam. As I look back at him now, he seemed uncomfortable with the weapon. Not like a professional at all."

"So you think he wasn't a professional killer?"

Mary shook her head as Sam responded, "I agree with Mary that he was unfamiliar with the weapon, but I'm sure he was a professional, just not a gunman. I think he was a professional *death by accident* killer just like he said, but for some reason he was forced out of his world of comfort."

"Death by accident. Interesting work if you can get it." David thought for a moment. "Maybe you were going to have your accident in Atlanta, but your departure surprised him. That could explain why he got sloppy down there in the islands."

"Looks like the weekday supersaver fare I got was a *super save my ass* fare."

"Well, we've got enough to get started. We know he was not local. He was flown in for the job by a group, or contracted by a group called NECO, most likely out of D.C.—and he was a professional." David looked over at Sam, "Concur?"

"Affirmative. I think we can also assume the woman he was with was eye candy just to make him fit in at the resort."

David shook his head in agreement. "Probably provided to him just like the transport and maybe the weapon as well."

Sam switched subjects, "So what do you think I should do about informing the police about all this?"

"Sam, I think you need to stay under the radar. Someone wanted you dead. They missed. I'm sure they want you just as much now, maybe more. If they don't know the hitter failed by now, I should think they will soon. We have time, at least until they discover the body."

"Okay," Sam looked back at Mary. "We wait until we know more. At least until we hear from your friend in the Islands. Both Laura and Sarah are away at college, and Kate and Maggie are with Mary's mother in Texas; so they are all safely away from the public eye. We are going to need to tell them about this, so if they get a call or hear something they won't panic."

0815 hours, Biras Creek

The attendant was busy readying the ten little boats for use by the resort guests. He worked six days a week at the resort during in-season, working the beach side Tuesday through Friday, maintaining the canoes, kayaks, and small sailboats for the guests that wanted to sail. On Saturday and Sunday, he worked this facility on the bay side for those guests who wanted to snorkel. The work was easy, the pay reasonable, and switching work sites during the week made the time go faster.

This morning he arrived on time and made sure all the boats were dry, clean, had a full tank of gas, and had the necessary oars and safety equipment. He lined the boats up in order and in doing so immediately noticed boat number seven was not there. His first thought was that one of the guests had gotten an early start and had taken the boat out before he arrived. He had looked at the log and no one had signed out a boat that morning but a guest name Call had taken boat number seven out the day before. Since the only thing on the entire island that had a lock on it was the bar and everything else was open to the guests at any time, guests taking a boat out early was not uncommon; so he went about his business without any other thoughts about the missing boat.

As he finished putting the life preservers in the last boat, he heard a motor boat approach his little dock; it was a launch from the *Bitter's End,* a yacht club across the bay. It was towing a Boston Whaler just like one in his tiny fleet.

"Hello there!" The boat operator called as he approached the dock.

"Mornin'. Que Passa Amigo." The attendant, Jorge Castro, called in his own form of English. He was not uneducated; he spoke English, Spanish, Portuguese, and French all of which he learned at home living with his French father and his Portuguese mother in an English and Spanish speaking country. From that upbringing, he often heard his volatile parents fighting in their native languages. He developed a unique style of speech in which he often combined the words of all four languages. At first his combination of speech was unintentional, but as he mastered the languages he purposely continued with his mixing of the languages. It seemed to provide him with a uniqueness that he otherwise would have lacked. Again he greeted the boat operator, "Hola copain!" and he waved as he walked towards the docking boat.

The operator pointed to the stern of his boat. "I got one of your boats."

The attendant looked at the little boat that clearly displayed his Biras Creek logo on the bow. "Yes it is. Where did you get it.?"

"Found it floating north of the reef, north of Pear near Eustasia. One of our yachting guests reported it this morning, and we picked it up about thirty minutes ago. We figured one of your guests went to Prickly Pear and let it get away."

"Yes, they like to go there and screw on the beach."

"Yeah I know, I've seen them." The operator picked up a pair of binoculars and smiled.

Castro shook his head at the operator and laughed. "With all this they have to go out there to find a place to play. Go figure."

The operator had untied the little boat from the cleat in the stern of his own boat and had pulled it around to Castro. "I sailed as close as I could, just outside the reef, but I can't take this boat in too close there, too shallow. I checked out the east side cove with the binoculars where most of them go, but I didn't see anyone. Figured you guys had a handle on it, so I just brought her in." He passed the line to the Castro.

Not wishing to have a competitor think he wasn't on top of things, he acknowledged the operator's comment and that he had things well covered. "Yep, got it under control. Thanks." Then he waved to him as the operator guided his boat away from the dock and back into the main channel. He then pulled the boat along the dock and secured it in its usual position. Staring at the boat for a moment he then looked out across the bay towards Prickly Pear Island. "Damn guests!" He went inside the maintenance hut and called the office.

"This is Jorge down at the outfitter dock. Just had one of our Whalers towed in by a *Bitter's End* launch. He said he found it north of the reef, floating free."

"Really?" The young female clerk was busy working on the computer with the list the guests scheduled to depart today and those arriving. "How did it get out there?"

"Don't know. If I knew do you think I be calling you, woman? No one has signed out a boat this morning and this one was last signed out by a guest named, Call."

"Okay." The clerk, unimpressed with the urgency of the situation just wanted to get back to preparing her list of comings and goings.

"So is Call there?"

"Well, I haven't gotten any calls."

Frustrated, Castro yelled at the woman. "Femme, ce que tu peux ete bete." He paused, gained control and then continued, "I want to know if a guest named Call is there and if he's okay, or has checked out, or if he is maybe missing."

"How would I know if he is here? All the guests are paid up before they even arrive. and they leave by Water Taxi and they don't need to even check out. No keys to return, no bills to pay." She checked her list. "There is a Sam and Mary Call due to leave today."

"Have they?"

"I don't know. The first morning taxi left at eight and the next leaves at nine."

"Why don't you have housekeeping check the room?"

"Fine." She hung up and made a mental note to ask a housekeeper whenever she saw one.

0815 hours, Biras Creek

She awoke in a disheveled bed, naked and tired. She sat up and looked out the window at the beautiful red morning sky, a picture-perfect morning, which was totally wasted on her. She stood up and walked naked to the dresser, opened her purse, first counted the twenty one-hundred dollar bills, put them safely away, and then took out a travel schedule to confirm that she was leaving by helicopter that morning at 10:15 am. She called the front desk and told the clerk to have a cart pick up her luggage from the bungalow after 9:30 and to have another one pick her up at the restaurant at 10:00. The clerk cheerfully acknowledged both her requests and then she hung up the phone without any words of thanks.

She went into the bathroom looked into the mirror and grabbed her own breasts and gave a motion like she was modeling. "A thousand a pop, I'm worth it."

She showered, dressed in comfortable traveling clothes, took her purse, and left the bungalow for breakfast. She hadn't packed a thing.

0900 hours, Alpharetta, GA

David droved the car into the parking lot of the Holiday Inn. "I think its best to stay here and not go home right now, just until we figure out where we are."

Sam looked at Mary as he spoke. "I agree. We can call the kids from here, but we will need a car."

"Probably get it here through the hotel," Mary offered as she got in the door that Sam was holding for her.

Wanting to keep Sam's name out of the system, David checked in at the front desk under the reservation he had made prior to going to the airport. He then signed for a rental car that was quickly dispatched by the clerk and the three of them went to the room.

Once in, Sam put the one suitcase of souvenirs in the closet. "We'll need to buy some clothes too."

"In every dark cloud there is a silver lining." Mary joked and flopped down in the soft chair. "Ouch!"

"You okay, Hon?" Sam concerned about her, came to her quickly.

"Yes. I guess its time to pop another pill. God bless pharmaceuticals," and she motioned to Sam to get her handbag. He did and she took two pills and popped them into her mouth then drank a sip of water that David had retrieved from the bathroom in anticipation of her need. "Thanks."

Both men sat.

"We have three avenues to work." David began as he finished looking out the window in an unconscious but trained reflex to ensure they had not been followed. "First, find out more on NECO; I've already set Bob in motion on this one. Second, we need to find out everything we can on our hitter...." David looked to Sam for help.

"Rowe, James Rowe."

"Roger, James Rowe. Third, figure out what to tell the locals about the shooting, but we need to wait until we hear from Mitchell on that one." David looked to Mary and then to Sam. "We put the IdentityPoint job on hold for now."

Sam had a pen and paper and he had been half note taking and half doodling as David spoke. He wrote 'Hold on IdentityPoint' then tapped on the paper. His pencil tapped on circled IdentityPoint several times—he paused, then dragged his pencil to 'NECO' and circled it.

"Maybe we shouldn't do that?" Sam looked to David.

"Say again?" David looked to Sam for some further input.

"Maybe there's more going on than greedy executives scamming money. Perhaps I did something there that spooked them."

"And they needed to take you out for it?" David shook his head. "I've met these guys Sam; they don't have the guts to arrange a hit."

Sam shook his head. "This is bigger than just insider trading. Don't forget NECO and a possible government connection."

"Okay, I'm listening," David checked the window again.

"What if there is a connection between the two," Mary offered.

For an entire minute no one spoke. Each was thinking of what the team had been doing at IdentityPoint and about the POW case and Ream.

"I was using IdentityPoint's systems to try to find a link between Ream and anyone working with PEI during that time. I was hoping that one of those records would lead us to just one of the POWs." Now standing, Sam seemed to be pleading his case.

"Maybe you did." David had been sitting on the window ledge his arms crossed and one hand on his chin thinking. He turned to Sam, "find a link that is."

Mary looked at Sam. "If it's true; then Chicago didn't die with Ream."

"I stand corrected; we have four tasks. Task four is to determine if Sam hit a trip wire while using IdentityPoint's systems."

"We need to see the data," Sam said, "And I know someone who can help." Sam opened his wallet and took out a business card and read the name and title, *George Bailey, Seasoned Geek*. He called the number on the card marked *home*.

"Hello."

"George, this is Sam Call."

"Hey Sam, back from vacation?" came a warm and friendly reply.

"In a manner of speaking. George, I have a problem." Sam stopped for a moment and looked back at David as if looking for the go ahead to tell him. "Something happened in the islands." He paused again to be sure what to say, "A man tried to kill us. It was a professional hit, and we think it might be related to what I found at IdentityPoint."

"My God, Sam, are you alright?"

"I am, but Mary was injured. George, I need to get into the IdentityPoint systems now and re-examine the data we got from the PEI batch run. We think somehow I may have actually found the link I was looking for, but I don't know what it is or how someone could know about it."

"Hold it right there, Sam. I can't get you into the systems now. Certainly not at the level I think you need."

"I understand, George. I would appreciate if you don't tell anyone I called about this." Sam was disappointed and it was clear to David and Mary that he didn't get the answer he had wanted.

"Sam, I said I couldn't get to the level, but I didn't say I didn't know someone who could. Meet me at the Architect's house at eleven."

"Thanks, George. Sempre Fi."

"It's the least I can do for an army puke."

Sam hung up the phone. "The Architect's house at eleven hundred hours."

"Well, Bob can meet us there. We should get going Sam." David motioned to Sam as he stepped towards the door.

"Excuse me!" Mary stood and picked up her bag. "Don't you even think that the men are *off to war* and I'll be the quiet strength at home in the kitchen?" Before either man could interject, "Need I state the obvious that there is no kitchen here, and in case you have forgotten, I'm the one who got shot. So if anyone is going to get to kick some ass, it's me!" Mary walked to the door, opened it, and left without looking back.

0930 hours, Biras Creek

The bellman knocked on the bungalow door but no one answered, which he expected. He opened the door and found not only the room in a mess, but the bags were not packed. One suitcase was laying on the bed, opened with some woman's clothes in it, and the other was standing in the closet. He opened the one in the closet first and found it was already packed with a man's things. He closed it and carried it to the cart. He then packed the second suitcase with everything else that was in the bathroom and drawers. It was not completely uncommon for a guest not to pack and leave the task for him, but an envelope containing some cash was always left as a tip. He looked carefully around the room, but there was no envelope. He disgustingly took the luggage to the helipad.

0955 hours, Biras Creek

The pilot of the chopper went through his checks as the co-pilot put the two bags into the cargo compartment.

"Just two to pick up today?" the porter asked.

"Yep. Whether it's just two or a full load the price is the same," the co-pilot said as he took the first bag.

"Must be nice to travel like this. No bumpy water taxi, no lines, no airport security, no waiting," the porter commented as he handed the co-pilot the second bag.

"I wouldn't know. I can't afford to travel this way," the co-pilot joked.

As he shut the cargo door a second cart arrived with one female passenger. She carried one small hand bag, and she walked to the helicopter with an aggravated walk that caused every curve of her body to move. The co-pilot helped her into a passenger seat. "Will the gentleman be joining us shortly?"

"No. He has already left," she said. Now knowing that she was the only passenger and thoroughly enjoying the knowledge that she had the luxury of a helicopter to herself she added, "This ride is just for me."

As the co-pilot closed her door and turned to the porter. "Yep. Whether it's just *one* or a full load the price is the same." The engine roared life and the helicopter and its one passenger were on its way.

0955 hours, Biras Creek

He stood there under a tall palm tree and watched as the helicopter left the landing pad, and for a moment he had a flash back of days gone by but not forgotten. One day in a jungle that forever changed his life, a day when five of his fellow soldiers did not return with him on the chopper. He watched the chopper lift off and as it did it changed from the sleek Bell 206 Long Ranger to a Huey with open doors and wounded soldiers lying clearly visible on the deck as she lifted out of the landing zone. As it turned and headed out, the familiar wump, wump, wump sound of the Huey gave way to the smooth sound of the seven-passenger commercial helicopter and the image was gone from his mind as quickly as it had come.

He waited for the porter to come by. "That was some hot looking woman there." He pointed to the chopper as it became just a tiny blip in the sky.

"Oh yes sir, she is."

"I noticed she was alone." He wanted to get her actual name, so he pretended to know her. "Isn't she with the guy down there past the pool? I wanted to see him before they left. Is he still here?" Using the pool as a landmark was better than using an actual bungalow number, since there was no telling who was really in that bungalow, and he would seem less credible if he said bungalow 12A and there were two old ladies staying there.

"Yeah, I guess, down there in 5B. But she said he had left already, must have gone out on the water taxi last night or early this morning."

"Sorry I missed him. Well, thanks anyway." He had gotten what he needed. David told him the hitter was with a woman like that and it was unlikely there were two like her on this island, on any island he thought, especially one that was now solo. His next step was to go to the office and get a name. That would be easy enough. It was a one-person office and all he had to do was wait until the person was on the phone or left the room and he could look at the guest list, which is what he did. It took all of two minutes.

1015 hours, Biras Creek

Jorge Castro brushed past a man in a baseball cap coming out of the office as he entered, "Excuse me, sir."

"No problem," came the reply.

"So what have you got for me, Woman, it's been over an hour." He confronted the check-in clerk. He wasn't happy that he had to leave his job and walk up to the office.

She was taken back by his sudden and angry assault on her, and was going to give him a piece of her mind when she remembered that she had forgotten to get with housecleaning to check the room. She just looked at him and made a frown like he was the one in trouble, and left it at that. First she checked the guest list and found the Calls were in 7A and then called housekeeping.

"Have you cleaned 7A yet?'

"Yes, did it twenty minutes ago. Why?" came the reply.

"Are they still there or did they leave?"

"They are scheduled to leave today, but they are still here, at least I think they are."

"You think they are? You're not sure?"

"Well, their luggage is here, but the beds have not been slept in. Yesterday I made one of the dog figures out of a towel, put a pair of sun glasses on it and put it on the bed; it's still there. So I don't know."

"Okay, thanks." She hung up the phone and turned to Jorge. "Seems their luggage is here, but maybe they're not. No one has used the room since yesterday morning."

"Crap! Where is Mr. Bruce, this is something the manager of this place needs to handle."

"I think he is up in the restaurant area talking to the service manager."

He quickly exited the office, took the steps that led up to the open restaurant that overlooked the bay. "Mr. Bruce."

"Ah yes, Mr. Castro. Good Morning!" He was a proper Englishman with the elegance and style that comes from a long line of both breeding and service to customers.

"Good morning, Sir, I think we may have a problem. This morning one of our boats was towed in by a launch from *Bitter's End*. The boat was last signed out yesterday by one of our guests, a Mr. Call from 7A. Housekeeping says the room has been untouched since yesterday morning, and their luggage is still in the room."

"I see," he said with a quiet unemotional tone. "Is it possible that perhaps they left yesterday and the porter neglected to put the luggage on the water taxi? We should check with the office."

"I have, Sir, and they are not due to leave until today." He looked at the manager and the service manager waiting for their action.

"Well, this won't do at all." Then without changing his level of emotion he continued, "Where was our boat found?"

"Outside the reef off of *Pickly Pear*. I checked with the hostess and they made a picnic lunch for them yesterday. They were going to *Prickly Pear*."

"Its very shallow there; only the Whalers can cross over the shallow bottom. Would you be so kind as to get some men from the beach facility and see what you can find please, Mr. Castro?

"Yes, Sir, I can."

The manager turned back to the service manager, "Now as I recall, you had said you were considering replacing the Sea Bass with Sheared Tuna this evening."

For a moment Jorge had a problem grasping the conversation, then realized the manager had returned to his duties in the manner he always had, so he did as well.

As Jorge walked away he quietly mumbled, "Porque voce nao coloca voce para ser o jantar em vez de Sea Bass."

From a doorway Jorge had just passed, a female voice quietly asked him, "Replace the Sea Bass with Mr. Bruce?"

He turned in surprise to see one of the cleaning ladies looking at him with a smile that said, 'I caught you.' "I, I..." was all Jorge could say.

"I think we should keep the Sea Bass." She looked at Mr. Bruce and then back to Jorge, "Less fatty, don't you think?" She smiled, winked, and continued on with her duties.

1110 hours, Alpharetta

They pulled the car into the driveway and parked next to a small gold Saturn sedan in front of a two-car garage. One door of the garage was open and Sam saw George Bailey pop out of the door that led into the kitchen from the garage.

"George!" Sam cheerfully called to his friend. He had already opened the door for Mary and was giving her his hand, as he always did. George walked right over to Sam and shook Sam's hand.

"Hello, Sam." He turned to Mary.

"George, I'd like you to meet Mary."

George put out his hand to shake hers, not the rough way a man does but a soft gentle greeting. "It's a pleasure to meet you Mary."

"You can be assured the pleasure is mine," Mary said as she took her other hand and held his hand. "I cannot tell you how much this means to Sam—to both of us."

George just humbly acknowledged her with a gentle nodding of his head.

"And this is David Lytle." Sam pointed to David who was now standing beside them.

"David."

"Thanks for helping us with this, George."

"The least I can do for a fellow man of the service."

"Semper Fi," David said as he shook his head.

"Semper Fi, young man." George smiled. Not just a pleasant greeting to a new person, but rather one that greeted an old friend, a comrade. Both David and George felt an immediate bond. "Let's go in."

As soon as Sam walked into the house, he noticed that it was not the same house he had entered the week before. The kitchen was clear of empty bottles, dishes and had actually been cleaned. It looked 'lived-in' not the musty, smelly house of depression it was just a few days before.

George led them to the room by the front door that Sam thought was most likely the formal living room; he had not seen that room during his other visits, as the French doors had been closed. The doors were open now, and as they walked in, Sam stopped to visually take in the room. There was a long desk by the window with a computer; beside it, next to the far wall, was table with two more computers and a host of small blinking devices that Sam immediately recognized as routers and cable modems. Sitting at the desk was the Architect intently looking at one screen.

George stopped in the doorway and coughed to let him know he was back.

The Architect stood up, and Sam stepped into the room. Sam stared at the Architect for a moment; this was hardly the man he had visited before. Today he had shaved, his hair was cut, he was dressed well and Sam noticed he just looked better and there seemed to be a new attitude about him. The Architect even smelled of cologne. "It's very good to see you again." He shook the Architect's hand and then turned toward David. "And this is David, David Lytle."

"George filled me in on the mission." The Architect stopped for a moment almost to see if the military types would object, or worse, make fun of his use of terms. They didn't, and he continued. "We have been examining the list George brought, and we have found some interesting data if you'd care to see."

"Most definitely, please." Sam moved forward and the Architect sat back down in the chair. The rest of them huddled behind the two of them.

"As you know, the data is from residents of Milwaukee from the period 1945 through 1950. That provided a list of just under one million names. When you search for a PEI connection, there are 8,350 names that remain. Now as we understood it, this company, PEI, was in business from 1946 through 1957, and the man you were looking for, this Ream fellow, apparently arrived in 1946 and went to Chicago in 1953. We also understand there was a Dahl fellow who apparently died in 1952." The Architect turned to Sam. "Correct?"

"Affirmative."

"We sorted the remaining names numerous ways—actually George did." He moved the computer's mouse and opened another spreadsheet. "Some interesting data came forward. The data was sorted by address, years, names, last names, cars."

Sam interrupted, "Cars?"

"Oh yes, you'd be surprised what you can find about relationships from car records, joint ownership for one, sales to relatives for another, and mostly corporate relationships."

"How's that?" David asked as he strained to look at the data on the screen.

"Well, corporations lease vehicles and often give them to employees for their use. When they do, the owner of the vehicle is the company, but insurance companies list the address of the vehicle where the user resides." George pointed to some data on the screen that the Architect had called up. "This sort has given us some interesting relationships."

"You can see that these cars are corporate; they are all owned by PEI and appear on the PEI report. However, they have addresses other than the corporate address. They also appear on individual person reports."

"You can see the registration date right there." The Architect pointed to the date field. No one other than George saw the significance of the date and they all continued to look at the screen in anticipation of George, or the Architect, continuing on and providing some significant finding. He repeated the finding, "You can see the date right there, 1975, the date of registration."

"Hold on," Sam tried to get closer to the screen. "PEI shut down in 1967. Why would there be a car registration in 1975?"

"Good question," the Architect swung around in his chair. "It would seem by this data that the company continued on in some form until at least 1975."

"Do the cars link back to specific people?" David asked as if he anticipated the connection, which he had.

"Yes," George gave a big smile and looked at Sam. "We crossed referenced the addresses of the cars, and we hit twenty-three names."

"We tried to sort the lists to determine if the addresses hit on any names on the list. I was sorting on the street address fields and then re-sorting by name, but I didn't find anything. Then I was going to sort by street address again and I sorted the wrong field. I missed the column by one, and I clicked on the one to the left." He pointed to the spread sheet, "Social Security Number."

"Right down your alley," Sam looked at George.

"Yes," George opened a copy of the saved spreadsheet. "I realized quickly what I had done, but since, as Sam said, its right down my alley, I thought I'd take a look. I think I found something—no, I know I have." He pointed to the field. "You can see they are sorted by the Area Number, then the Group Number, and finally by the sequenced number."

"What is this group here?" Sam pointed to the field with the Area 387. "There seems to be a lot all with Group Number 34 and 36."

George scrolled down the spreadsheet without comment in anticipation of Sam's next discovery.

"Wait. Hold it there." Sam reached out and put his hand on top of George's to stop him. "The same is true for 399; it has Group Numbers 34 and 36 also. Holy shit."

"Would someone tell me what's this all about?" David stood up away from the computer and looked back and forth from Sam to George seeking one of them to provide the answer.

"I don't get it either," Mary added.

Sam was all excited about what George had found, but he tried to calm himself to explain it clearly. "Look, socials are composed of nine numbers. The first three are Area Numbers. They are just what the name implies - in what area the social was issued. For example, those people with 208 as their first three numbers got them in Pennsylvania, and unless I am incorrect, people with 387 and 399 are Wisconsin." Sam looked to George.

"Correct!"

"Now the next two numbers are what's called the Group numbers and they go from 01 to 99. Now the interesting part about them is they are issued in batches; a group of odd numbers, then even number, then odd, and so on." Sam took a break to let it all sink in. "Now stay with me on this. "These Area and Group number are then given sequence numbers from 0001 to 9999 and then issued. But, and here's the key, these numbers are issued in sequence and once done they are never issued again."

"I still don't have you, Sam." Mary shook her head and looked to David to see if he got the significance.

David chimed in, "Say again."

"Okay." Sam thought for a moment and then looked at Mary. "When Laura was born we got her a social right away didn't we?"

"Yes. You have to have a social security number to be claimed on taxes," Mary answered.

"And when Kate came we got her one."

"Yes."

"They were both born in Virginia, Laura during our first assignment and Kate six years later. Are their numbers the same?"

"No they're not. The first three are the same but the rest are different."

"Sam pointed to the screen and the group of numbers. "That's because the girls are six years apart and the state had issued all the sequence numbers in Laura's Group number sequence, and when Kate came along, they had used other Group numbers."

"So why are so many of these the same?" David tapped on the screen at the group of Socials that had the same first five numbers.

"Because they were all issued at the same time, in the same state, and since they are even in sequence, at the same office." Sam looked once again to George for approval.

George slapped him on the back. "You're a good student there, Sam."

"I try, Sensei." Sam bowed to George as if he were the student and George his martial arts teacher.

"If you look at this column," George pointed to the column marked 'Age', "you can see they are all different ages. I looked these up in the book, Sam, the Area Numbers 387 and 399 coupled with Group Numbers 34 and 36 were issued in 1954 and 1955."

"That means some of these people were adults when the numbers were issued," Mary said.

"After 1975 you had to have a social to be included on tax returns, so as Mary said, parents got new babies socials right away. But prior to that people got them when they got their first job." George took the computer mouse and highlighted one of the groups. "All these people got their numbers at the same time and they all have ties to PEI."

Mary put her arm on Sam's shoulder. "I would say that is more than a coincidence."

George took a printed copy of the data and spread it out on the table. "Let me show what we have."

1320 hours, Biras Creek

The three small boats had inspected the waters on the south side of the island then the east side. They had cruised the crystal clear shallow bay looking for any signs of the missing couple. They had landed at four different areas and checked each beach. If they had been there yesterday there were no signs of them today, the high tide had seen to that. Now they were headed out to the coral reef. It was not that dangerous, as long as you kept your distance and you were on the bay side of the reef. The ocean side was another matter all together. The waves smashed against them with crushing force and the spray of the waves shot up ten feet, fifteen when a particularly heavy wave struck it.

A small aluminum boat was fairly safe on the bay side. It could hit the reef and maybe only suffer a dent, and as long as the boat did not capsize the occupants would be okay. A wooden hulled boat, or fiberglass boat like the sailboats at the *Bitter's End,* would be wrecked instantly. The yacht club had a strict ban on any boats of that type coming to this area. Since ninety-nine percent of the boats in this area were from the *Bitter's End,* there would be little traffic.

The three boats approached carefully and made their first sweep of the half-mile long reef, but found nothing. On the return trip, a wave struck the reef and the man in the third boat saw something on the reef. He yelled to Jorge Castro, and pointed to the beach. The two boats circled back to the third boat where the operator again pointed to what was now clearly something on the reef. They boated twenty yards closer and saw it was a body. Jorge cautiously approached the reef until his bow hit, then he very carefully got out and stood on the reef. Knowing the dangers of the coral, and anticipating having to leave the boat and possibly having to work on the sharp coral, Jorge had worn his work boots and leather gloves.

Standing next to the face-down body, he looked at the dead man. The man was dressed in a swim suit and t-shirt, and at first glance he appeared to be asleep. He tried to lift the body, but it was just too much dead weight for him to lift alone.

When he let go, the body rolled over from a combination of his lifting and the wave action, and for the first time he saw the man's face. The coral had ripped it open and it was a mangled mess, scrapped down to the bone. His stomach area was wide open and crabs scurried out of the cavity that once was a man's stomach, and retreated to the sea. Jorge immediately threw up. He almost lost his balance, but he caught himself with his right hand on the body which oozed water from the gaping wounds, and he threw up again.

When he regained his composure, he called for another man to come onto the reef. Once the second man was out of his boat, he pushed it towards the third operator, who then captured it and held it away from the reef. With the aid of this second man, Jorge was able to carry the mangled body to his boat, which he had secured on the reef. Through a combination of their desire to get away from the disfigured body and the difficulty of working on coral, they unceremoniously dropped the body into the boat. When it hit with a sickening thud, it opened, and what fluids were left in it spewed out onto the bottom of the boat—with that, the second man threw up.

While the third man sat in his boat holding the other boat safely away from the reef, Jorge pushed the boat containing the body out into the bay away from the reef and towards the other two boats. The operator of the small recovery fleet motored his boat to the reef, pulling the second small boat with him, while the boat with the body slowly drifted. When the operator got close to Jorge, he pushed the boat towards the reef and when the bow struck the reef, Jorge grabbed it. He climbed in, and then motored out and secured the floating hearse. While Jorge secured the bowline of the boat with the body to the stern of his boat, the second man of his little recovery squad climbed into the boat with the third man. With Jorge in the lead, they headed back to the resort.

Twenty-minutes later, they arrived outside the dock area. Jorge sent the men in the other boat into dock ahead of him and had them return with a tarp in order to hide the body from the guests who were waiting dockside or sitting at the beach bar. After they had completely covered the body, they took all three boats into their tiny wooden harbor.

1400 hours, Biras Creek

He watched the sea circus of three little boats circling in and out of the harbor from his seat at the table at the beach bar. When it was done, he stood and walked to the far end of the dock away from the boats and the bar. He took the portable radio out of his pocket and pushed the talk button.

"This is Chad calling *Lowe 14*. Over." He waited fifteen seconds and repeated the call. "This is Chad calling *Lowe 14*. Over."

"This is *Lowe 14*. Over."

"What's your location? Over."

"Eight miles east of Eustacia. Over."

"Roger. Make course for my location for pick up. Over."

"Roger. ETA thirty-five minutes."

"Roger, Out." He put the radio in his pocket and slowly walked back to his seat at the table and drank the rest of his beer.

1400 hours, Washington. D.C.

"This is Garrett, Sir. The plane arrived as scheduled, but with only one passenger, the girl."

"What about the mission? Is he off the grid?"

Garrett grimaced with the sound of it, how he hated that phrase. "It would appear, Sir, but we have no confirmation. According to the girl, Wood went on a boat trip and told her before he left that he was going back on his own, and for her to take the scheduled flight back herself."

"So you think our man's gone back to Florida?"

"Since he knows his anonymity with us is gone, I would think he would try to find a new place."

"Concur. This was his last operation for us. We'll deal with him later; you know I don't like loose ends."

"Yes, Sir. There is one more thing though."

"What's that?"

"His luggage was on the chopper."

There was a long pause from Luby. "Any word from down south?"

"No sir. Nothing about the target or his wife." Garrett worried about what might come next.

"Stay on top of it, but I don't want any of our people there. There's no way to justify their presence if anything goes wrong. Have someone check their place and make sure he didn't make it back. When were they due back?

"Tonight sir, I believe around 10 PM."

Again there was a long pause, and Garrett's stomach was in knots. "Watch the house until Monday. We should hear something no later than tomorrow. It probably won't make the local news, but it should at least come through on the State Department's wire. Keep a watch for it."

Garrett responded, "Yes, Sir," and Luby ended the call.

1430 hours, Biras Creek

Chad waited at the end of the dock as his boat pulled along side and without waiting for the boat to stop Chad jumped aboard. The young acting captain turned to port and swung the boat back around towards the open bay. Chad looked around his boat. His young assistant was at the wheel, and the five patrons were below in the open cabin drinking beer. The young assistant's brother was in the stern stowing the fishing gear, and he noticed the boy was wearing Chad's baseball cap.

Chad climbed the ladder to the bridge. "How'd the day go?"

"Well, the tourists are happy. Everyone caught something and the guy in the baseball shirt landed a good size Marlin. We took plenty of pictures, then let it go."

"Good show," Chad looked back at his assistant's brother.

"Sorry about the hat. Greg lost his hat when he jumped overboard."

Chad swung back and looked at him. "Say again all after, 'lost his hat'. Over."

Chad stood beside Mac on the bridge with the wind blowing in both their faces. "All the tourists were at the stern when one of them got the first hit of the day, and the rest all ran over to see. I was at the wheel and didn't even see it, but apparently one of the men ran into another guy and knocked him overboard. Greg yelled 'Man Overboard' grabbed the life ring from the bulkhead and jumped overboard. By the time I realized what happened, it was a full minute before I was able to swing the boat around; then several minutes more before I could get the boat back to where they were. They were both hanging onto the life ring. You should have seen the guy when we got him on board. He hugged everyone; he was so excited." The boy paused for a moment then continued. "The fool can't swim."

Chad looked back at the young man. "And the hat?"

"He was working hard all day out there and the sun was baking him so I lent him your hat."

Chad looked back at his assistant. "Why didn't you give him yours, and *you* use mine?"

The young assistant looked at his brother then back at Chad, "Are you crazy, I know how you feel about someone touching that hat." He looked back to the front as he steered the boat out to sea.

Chad stepped down the ladder and back to the boy working at the stern. When the boy noticed Chad staring at his hat, he reached up, took it off, and handed it to Chad. "Sorry about the hat, my brother insisted."

Chad took the hat, looked at the embroidered letters, LNMB, and then handed it back to the young fat boy. "You keep it. You've earned it today." Chad turned, walked back to the ladder then turned back towards the boy who was facing the stern and holding the hat. The boy held the hat in both hands, then after a moment he put it on his head, adjusting the brim just right, and then stood looking at the sea. Chad noticed the boy seemed to be standing taller.

1430 hours, Alpharetta, GA

There was a knock on the front door. The Architect answered it, and then returned to the working area with Bob.

"Hey boys," Bob waved as he came into the room.

"So tell me what you got," David said as he walked over to Bob.

"Sorry to say, boss, I got nothing on either account." He took out a document from a file folder he had brought with him.

"My first effort was to determine who or what NECO is. What I found was a whole lot of nothing. I got the National Ethnic Coalition of Organizations, and according to the United Nations web site, and I quote, 'it serves as an umbrella group for more than two hundred and fifty organizations that span the spectrum of ethnic heritages, cultures, and religions'."

"I got the National Equipment Corp, which manufactures of all things, NECO quick connect/disconnect couplings—go figure. I got Neco Global Inc, which, according to Dunn & Bradstreet, was incorporated in the USA to expand Neco's horizons for providing added services to the customers in Northern and Southern America. And finally I have the D.C. based United States Navy Electronic Business Opportunities, and I be damned if I know why it's called NECO."

Bob looked away from the sheet of paper and back to David, "Sorry."

"Nothing you can do about that. So give me some good news. What have you got on James Rowe?"

"I went into the office and used the PeopleFinder on our friend from Prickly Pear." Bob pulled out the report from a file folder.

"Mr. James Rowe, current address 25 Market Avenue, apartment 1511, New York City, been there five years, before that he was in Philly on Ashdale Street, and before that New Jersey. I have his driver's license, his car registration; he owned a Ford Taurus, and before that a Honda. His parents are dead, he has no brothers or sisters, and there is nothing on the relatives' side of the report. The neighbors list is twelve pages long and impossible for us to use to verify anything. We know he rented furniture in Philly from Cort Furniture Rental on 20th Street, and subscribes to *Newsweek* and *Sports Illustrated*. His only criminal record are parking tickets; three in Philly, five in Trenton." Bob paused and looked at David. "There is nothing about where he worked or what he did. There is nothing on this guy other than that. He's vanilla. I couldn't find any connection to anything or anybody."

"He's more average than Bob," Sam joked.

"I even have his social, but there's nothing to it. I ran it against criminal records, military, even marriage and divorce." Bob looked at David, "Sorry, dead end."

"What's the number," Sam asked, "George is a wiz with socials; maybe he can do something with it."

"Two-zero-four-three-four," The Architect quietly said from his chair at the computer.

Everyone turned to the Architect who was sitting motionless after having given the first five numbers of the nine digit number. David looked at Bob who was checking the number on his report. "Well?" David asked Bob.

"He's right."

There wasn't a sound made for what seemed like minutes but was just seconds. Everyone stared at the Architect waiting for him to tell them how he knew. Finally Sam spoke. "How did you know that? I would assume you know the system as well as George and maybe you could guess the first three by his birth place. But Bob didn't say his birth place. Did you, Bob?" Sam looked to Bob as did everyone else except the Architect. Bob shook his head, signaling no.

"Pennsylvania 204. He was born in 1960 in Pennsylvania." The Architect quietly, almost solemnly spoke.

Looking at Bob, Sam asked, "Is that correct?"

Bob looked down at his notes and then back to the Architect. "Yes, born March 8, 1960."

"How do you know that?" Sam asked again as he walked over to the Architect who had still not moved from his seat.

He looked around from his chair to Sam, "Because I invented him."

There was a moment when nothing was said as all the people thought about the meaning of what had just been said.

"Perhaps you might want to elaborate on that a little." Sam put his hand on the Architect's shoulder who looked up at him and then to the others.

Without looking at anyone the Architect began, "As you know I worked for IdentityPoint for many years. I worked all the major personal data systems, but I specialized the last seven years in Identity systems. Creating systems that detected fraud is where we started; then we got real good at it. We started analyzing the history of a person, and we could tell if the history was rich enough or should I say deep enough for it to be a real person, or was it a phony. We got so good that we started flagging undercover cops and feds, and that was unacceptable. We couldn't add their undercover names to every system, so if an inquiry came in the system would report the identity was okay. We decided to build identities with real histories."

"So it would beat the systems you built to detect fraud, because they were—real," Sam added.

"Indeed. We created fifty identities, common names that appear in any major phone book, gave them address histories, cars, everything. We seeded our databases with data, and even went so far as to acquire apartments in five cities just to make them more real."

"And the cars and tickets?"

"All real. We bought cars and stored them, or rather the client did. We have offices in these cities, or I should say our client does, and periodically they would use the apartments, collect the mail, and even leave the cars on the street to get tickets just to build real histories."

"You went to a lot of trouble to make the person real," Mary was reading the report she had taken from Bob.

"Yes. I did most of the work. I had two analysts who did most of my research, but I created the person, gave them a name, birthday, and even the social security number."

"But the socials are controlled and the report Bob had didn't list anyone else using the social; so how did you get non-issued socials?"

"They aren't non-issued they're dead socials." George said.

"You're right. I created a program that ran at off-hours and did searches using a list of Area and Group codes that were issued from 1965 through 1985. The program just took the first Area Code and the first Group code, then added the first sequence number of 0001 and did a search. Then it did it with 0002, and then 0003 until it got to 9999. Then it grabbed the next Group Code and started again searching the billions and billions of records. We ran that thing for four weeks during the off-hours; we got hundreds of socials with null responses."

"Null responses?" David asked.

"When the system checked all the hundreds of database and found no record that's a null response."

"And each null response represented a dead child?" Mary asked.

"Yes, well ninety-nine percent of the time. You see if it were an adult, some record would show in the system before they died; a driver's license, criminal record, something. A dead child or a social that had never been issued would show nothing."

Sam sat down at the table and looked through Bob's report. "And you selected some of these socials and used them for building identities."

"We did a lot more research on what cities we should use and such, and then selected the socials that matched the birth city and birth date."

"So the other systems you created wouldn't find them to be fraud."

"In a manner of speaking, yes"

David had walked to a window and had been looking out as the Architect had made his explanation. He walked back to the group. "And the *client* you built these for was?"

"The FBI."

"Shit," was simultaneously said by Sam, Bob and David.

"So the FBI is after me?" Sam was bewildered by the possibility that his government wanted him dead.

"So this guy was FBI?" Bob half-asked and half-announced.

"I don't think so," Sam said as he walked around the room like a caged cat. "I never met a FBI agent who couldn't handle a weapon. This guy didn't know how to handle a gun very well; if he did, I wouldn't be here."

"I agree." David turned to the Architect, "But he must have gotten the identity from them."

Sam stood by the window and although his eyes were open he didn't see the trees that filled the Architect's back yard, nor did he hear the sounds of conversations in the room behind him. What he did see and hear was a beach and a dying man lying on a beach. He saw his battle with him in reverse, he saw his adversary dead on the beach, then fighting with him, then a gun in his hand, and the gunman surprising him on the beach. He then reached back further, further than he even consciously remembered the gunman, and saw his would-be assassin in the resort restaurant having dinner with a beautiful woman. Sam wondered how it was that he was able to see him in the restaurant now, and he wondered what else he would remember.

As his mind went deeper into the sequence of events, he saw his killer at all the steps along the way even though Sam had not actually seen him. Sam's mind was racing for a reason for this event and what he did to have this man, or the FBI, want him dead. He saw the gunman at the airport before they left, and then at his home watching Mary packing for the trip. He closed his eyes tighter and he could see the gunman at IdentityPoint, watching him work at his desk while he used the PeopleFinder application.

Sam snapped out of his daze, "George, when I did my searches using the PeopleFinder application would the FBI know I did a search?"

"If the name or address you did the search on was in any of their watch lists they would."

"How would that work? Let's say I did a search on George Bailey, how would they get notified?"

"Well first of all the search engine sends the transaction to a host of watch servers that check the name or address against their stored list. If there is a hit, the system sends an email, fax, or even a phone message to the one or many contacts."

"So, are there records of which names did cause a hit?"

"Unfortunately, in this case some of the servers are encrypted, and because the client doesn't want anyone to know even who is being watched there is no record of the hit maintained by the watch server."

"So how do they know the system even works?"

"There is a bogus name in the list that they test with. Every so often they use the PeopleFinder application, make a request for the test name, and wait to make sure their contact is notified. Other than that, there is nothing to check in the secured servers. We can check the logs of those watch servers that print logs, but I can't help you with the others.

"Yes we can," the Architect stared at the computer screen.

"How?" Sam asked.

"The server is secure and the watch list doesn't print to a log file so how would we know?" George walked over to the Architect.

"Yes, it is true that the Watch Server is secure. Everything it does is secure." The Architect stood up as he spoke to the group. "The key is *it* is secure in what *it* does."

"But it doesn't do everything," Sam stood. "It doesn't notify."

"Exactly!" The Architect pointed at Sam. "When the watch list gets a hit the secure server sends a message to one of the notification services, the fax server, the email server, or the phone server. That server receives the request, executes it, then it writes to the log, so that the billing server can count the entries and bill the client."

"Yes, but the secure watch servers I am aware of are monthly fee with no per-transaction costs, so the billing system doesn't send bills on those."

"No, they don't, but they do process them along with the others; they just don't send a bill."

"I thought that the FBI stuff was all separate—that it didn't use the same fax, email and phone servers." George looked back at his friend.

"They weren't supposed to, but the financials were down that quarter when we were going to install. Thompson insisted we make our numbers, so the CFO instructed the CIO just to use the same servers and we saved a ton of bucks."

"And we didn't tell the client?" George asked.

"Not that I knew of."

"So we just have to get the daily logs of the servers."

"Actually they are monthly logs—to match the billing cycle. But I can't get them from here. I still have some ability to use PeopleFinder and such with some hidden accounts, but the logs are behind the firewall, and I can't get there without hacking the system."

"I don't have access," George volunteered.

"I can give you an account and a password." He wrote two words on a sticky note as he spoke then gave it to George. "I wrote it into the Middleware system, so it can access all the servers at the admin level, and knowing who is managing security, my guess is they haven't found it. All you have to do is to be able to log onto the Middleware server and it can access the secure servers through that account."

George was already walking to the door. "I'll go to the office and get them."

"Just copy the logs and bring them here, we can examine them when you get back."

1645 hours, Alpharetta

David felt the vibration of the pager on his hip and looked down at the display screen and immediately recognized the number of Chad Mitchell. He tapped the Architect on his shoulder. "I need to make a call; may I use your phone?"

"Of course, there is one in the kitchen, and if you need privacy you can use the one upstairs in my bedroom."

"The kitchen will be fine." David went to the kitchen took a calling card from his wallet, dialed the card number, and then the phone number for Chad."

"Mitchell here."

"Hello, its David."

"Hello, David. I got some news for you." Chad went though his report and when he was through told David he was still waiting for him to come down and do some fishing with him.

David thanked his old friend, promised him he would get there soon, and then went back into the main room where this newly formed team was working, all except George, who had gone to IdentityPoint to steal the data logs. He walked up to Sam. "I just ;got the call from my friend on St. Thomas, apparently *your* body has been found. According to Chad, the body was found on the coral reef and was pretty torn up; identification will take awhile."

"The tide and current must have taken him off the beach and out to sea." Sam grimaced as he thought about the body and how the coral would have torn at the dead man's flesh.

"Chad also had some other interesting data for us on our Mr. Rowe, or whoever he was. Apparently, his lady friend left on schedule on a chopper. According to a resort attendant, Rowe left prior to her, either on the early water taxi or late the night before. So no one down there is looking for him."

"What do you think we should do now?" Mary stood and walked over to Sam, "I mean about the shooting and all?"

David thought for only a second, "Nothing. I think that you should stick to the accident story. If they asked why you left, you just say you were on Tortola already at the hospital, which can be verified. Then since you were leaving the next day anyway you decided to go home early and not do the long water taxi trip back to the resort only do to it again the next morning. Later on, if we get pressed about it you can say what really happened and that you were quiet about it for fear of your life."

"Well that's no lie." Mary half-heartedly joked.

"The BVI authorities should contact the American authorities and eventually they will try to determine if you arrived home," David said.

"And when there is no answer at the house?" Mary asked.

"I would guess they would start with the neighbors. Ask if they have seen you."

Sam added, "And they will tell that Kate and Maggie are at Mary's mother's ranch in Texas."

"Affirmative. Then they will contact your mother and she will tell them you are home safe and sound."

"So we don't need to do anything until they call mother or it hits the news." Sam looked at David and they nodded to each other in concurrence.

"Hit the news?" Mary was surprised about that possibility.

"It's possible. Especially since it's fairly gruesome and you're missing." David pointed to Mary, "They might be thinking right about now that you *offed* your husband."

"Oh," she sat down and thought of the possibilities. Then after a minute or so added, "What about the luggage?" Mary asked both Sam and David at the same time. "We left our luggage behind."

"Ah, well." Sam thought a moment, "I think it would be reasonable for us to say that we were going to call them and ask the resort to ship the luggage to us when we settled in back home."

"I agree." David nodded affirmatively to Sam's suggestion.

"Well, I think the news report will protect you from the FBI for a while, or whoever is behind this. But on the other hand, there is just so long you can go with pretending you haven't heard the CNN report," David added.

"I am supposed to be at work on Monday. Certainly by then I am going to have heard the report and called the police; or when I walk into the office, someone will be bound to notice I am alive."

"Astute comment, Husband," Mary joked then grabbed at her arm, which had given her a shot of pain.

1645 hours, Atlanta

George signed in with the security officer at the door to IdentityPoint.

"Must be a big emergency to bring you in on a weekend George." The security guard commented to George as he collected the sign-in log from George.

"You know this place can't run without me, Frank."

"It must be running fairly well there, George; since I haven't seen you in on a weekend in six months."

"And hopefully not for another six." George waved and went down the hallway to his office. Once inside he powered up his workstation and got a writable CD ready while the system booted. Once the system was ready it presented him a log-on screen. He used his user ID and password to gain access to the network. He then activated a UNIX shell program and attempted to access the Middleware server. The system recognized a request and presented another log-on screen; using the data his friend had provided, he entered 'oldman' into the user ID field and 'ageless' into the password.

The system seemed to hang for a moment then a new screen appeared with 'Welcome Back Creator' centered on the screen.

"It looks like someone has a sense of humor," George said out loud to the computer. "Now let's see what you have for me." He didn't have administrative rights to all the systems so he could not log onto the communications servers to get the logs from them. The Middleware system received all the requests for work and processed them to all the other servers—and this system had records of everything in an extensive database. He accessed the administrative module and entered the commands that would extract all the transactions that occurred over the last three weeks that went to the communications servers: including the fax, phone, and email servers. He was not worried about copying too much data, as each transaction would be small; he could copy tens of millions of records onto the CD. It took just a few minutes. The computer had completed its search and created a file of the data, which George then copied to the CD. George removed the CD, logged off, shut the workstation down and walked to his door. He was just leaving the office when he had a thought. He stopped, turned around, and looked at the computer, as if he was computing a solution himself; which he was. He returned to his desk and restarted the workstation.

1730 hours, Alpharetta

"I don't know about you all, but I haven't eaten in like two days." Sam was sitting at the dinner table which had been converted to a work area and now was the depository of an array of spreadsheets and printouts.

"I can eat something," Mary added quickly and both David and Bob concurred. The Architect continued working and seemed oblivious to those around him.

"What would you all like?" Sam asked.

"I could go for Chinese," David offered.

Bob added, "Some Burgers."

Without looking away from the screen the Architect chimed in, "How about Italian?"

There was some quick eye to eye contact among the team agreeing to his suggestion.

"Italian it is! And I know just the place." Sam put down what he was working on. "I'll get a selection of stuff, and we can share." All agreed and Sam started for the door.

"I'll come along." David jumped up and followed. Ten minutes later they were at Casa Nuova.

"Hello Sam!" came a warm greeting from Maria as she saw Sam enter.

"Maria, hello," Sam gave her a hug and a kiss on the cheek.

"Good to see you. Will Mary be joining you?"

"Not tonight. In fact we can't stay either. We are working and wondered if you can get a few dinners to go."

"For you, of course." Maria led them to a booth and they ordered four meals for the six of them to share, and then ordered two Moretti for themselves while they waited.

Maria left to get the beers and the two of them were alone in the booth. "So what do you think?"

"I'll tell you, Sam, we know that you have obviously pissed off someone."

"That's an understatement for sure."

"But who's doing it and why, are a bit fuzzy."

"The name from the FBI list is incriminating for sure, but why would the FBI do it? If it is them, it must be a splinter group. I really can't see the FBI doing this."

"What I can't see is them screwing it up this bad."

"If we knew what NECO is, we might have a better chance."

"Death," Maria casually added as she brought the beers and overheard their conversation.

"Death?" Sam asked, "You sure?"

"Sam, NECO is Latin, and I am a good Catholic girl, and good catholic girls were taught Latin. It means death." She put the beers on the table.

Sam looked at David, and immediately both knew what they had on their hands. "Maria, you are beautiful!" He stood up and kissed her making a loud 'smacking' sound as he did; then he sat back down. Maria was flushed from the public display and put her hands to her hair to straighten it, while looking around at the customers who were close enough to witness the event.

Before Maria started off she turned her head back to Sam, "I'll bring your dinners in a few minutes—and just to let you know, I know lots of Latin." She winked at both of them as she left.

"It's a black ops group," David said as he grabbed his beer.

"Affirmative. But I suspect they are operating outside of the normal realm of FBI."

"Roger that. I'll get with some people in D.C. and see what the word is around town. Even in the clandestine world, someone's talking."

"I would guess when you say 'around town' it's not the tourist bureau."

David took a grip on the beer and looked around almost instinctively to ensure he was not overheard. "You know the work I used to do. When I left, or should I say when I was booted, they recruited me. There is a huge market for men in my line of work—or rather my former line of work."

"Who?"

"Say again."

"Who recruited you, David?"

"The CIA and the NSA. You would be surprised how many of our guys are making a very good living at it."

"Okay, I'm curious," Sam asked as he drank his beer.

"It's a good deal for both sides. The going rate for a top flight mercenary is a hundred 'K' per mission, and if the Merc doesn't make it out, there is no connection to our government. They can disavow the entire affair."

"A hundred 'K,' not bad work if you can get it," Sam joked.

"Oh, they can get it; a lot more often than you think."

"Where?"

"Mostly South America and Africa. There is work in the Middle East, but most of my guys are not conducive to that environment."

"How's that, too hot?"

"No, we don't look the part; there are no jungles to hide in. We are too easy to spot. Most of the men are big, strong, and highly trained athletes. They kind of stand out in a world of smaller men whose usual workout includes trying to keep the sand from blowing them away."

"I see your point," Sam took another sip, "What about Europe?"

"The targets there would be high ranking officials and such, and there is way too much visibility in Europe. Nothing happens there that doesn't attract someone's attention. The targets are mostly political with large followings that would be really pissed if their guy got eliminated. In South America there is a plethora of drug dealers, kidnappers, and terrorists whose deaths would not cause a ripple of dissent."

"Plethora?"

"Means lots of, or excessive."

"I know that, David, I just never thought of you as using any word not found in a field manual, not the literate type."

"One need not have a degree to be literate, my friend."

Sam did not respond, just nodded in agreement.

"It takes a lot more finesse, as well as ground support in the Middle East. It takes longer to set it up, and it's harder to execute the mission. The targets move a lot and are religious fanatics. They don't have big houses or compounds to defend, and it's harder to take them out. There's a fundamental difference between the Middle East problem and the South American and African problems. The targets in South America and Africa are in it to acquire wealth and power, and they build compounds to protect it and themselves. The Middle East target has an entirely different objective, and it does not include wealth."

"So they have no base, no entourage, and no trail, and therefore they are tougher to find," Sam interjected.

"Affirmative," David responded.

After a minute or so, Sam leaned over towards David. "Did you?" Sam did not have to finish the question.

"A half-dozen in South America." He paused and then smiled as he took his beer and drained it. "How do you think I financed this outfit?"

With that, Maria signaled them that she had the food upfront and ready to go. David paid the bill and they departed.

1820 hours, Alpharetta

Sam and David had barely set the food out at the house when George arrived.

"Welcome back, George. I hope you like Italian." Sam motioned George to the table, which had been cleared of the papers and now had plates and tableware.

"Thanks," George walked over to the table and placed the CD on the table.

"That took you longer than I would've thought," the Architect said as he left his workstation and joined the rest at the table. "Soft drinks are in the kitchen, and there is beer in the refrig in the garage.

"Outstanding." Sam replied. "What's everyone drinking?" The group all responded with a request for beer, except the Architect who wanted a Coke.

"No Beer?" George asked him quietly.

"No, I already drank my authorized limit—for the next two years."

George gently put his hand on his shoulder and then went to join Mary and Sam in the kitchen as they got drinks.

The team shared the four dinners among themselves Chinese style—the dinners all in the center of the table and everyone taking a portion. There was lasagna, a veal shank in a mushroom sauce, shrimp and scallops on pasta with herbs and lemon, and finally a crab and shrimp ravioli in a lobster sauce that was so good they almost fought over it.

The meal was fun. They spoke of sports, the weather, movies they had liked and hated. George was nuts over *True Lies* because he loved the action and the comedy; Sam joked that the movie was good but not in the memorable category and that George's judgment was being swayed by Jamie Lee Curtis's role in the movie, whom Sam knew George adored.

"Good movie," Sam went on, "but Arnold is no Tom Hanks, but I do find myself wanting to take tango lessons."

"Especially if you're dancing with Jamie Lee," George stood and did a couple of dancing steps then dipped with his imaginary partner.

"Jamie Lee is hot—no question, but I got to tell you I just saw *Forrest Gump* and I can't tell I've seen a better movie.:

"That's a big statement from you, Sam," Mary said. "Better than *Citizen Kane* and *To Kill A Mockingbird*?"

Sam raised his hand and shook it in front of him, "Can't even consider Gump in that category yet; ask me in five years. To enter the hollowed list of best ever movies it has to have stood the test of time: *Twelve Angry Men, Casablanca, African Queen, The Searchers,* now these are great movies that are just as good today as they were the day they were made."

"Is it equally true for the bad ones there, Sam?" Bob joked.

"That's a negative Bob, a stinko can make the list on day one."

"*Serial Mom*," George grabbed his nose. "A mom as a hit woman? Poor Kathleen Turner, she must have really needed the money."

Bob grabbed one of the food containers and drug his bread through it to get the last of the sauce. "When the career goes south in the movie business it goes south fast."

"*Major League II*, instant *double* stinko."

"Double stinko?" George looked at Sam.

"*Major League* was funny, even had a story line; you really wanted the team to win just to stick it to that team owner. But *Major League II* was an embarrassment; ought to be a law that if you screw up a sequel that bad you shouldn't ever be allowed to make another movie."

For almost an hour they relaxed and enjoyed the moment.

1930 hours, Alpharetta

"I can't eat another bite, I am so full." Sam pushed his chair back acknowledging he had eaten far too much.

"Well, that's good, dear, since there is not one bite left anywhere." Mary joked as she lifted the containers slightly to show they were empty. "Unless, of course, you want to lick the sauce out?"

Sam sat forward, "Sure, send them over."

Mary shook her head and collected the containers, and then stood up to clean off the table.

"I'll help." Bob picked up the plates, and he and Mary cleared the table, rinsed the dishes off, and threw away the containers their dinner had come in, while the others returned to the computer room.

"I hate to bring us back to reality, but what did you get there, George?" Sam asked as he sat back in his chair again.

"I got the logs from the Middleware server's database." He turned to his friend, "That was slick. The transactions were tight and maximized the storage. You had a fixed named field for the common information and a blob field for the uncommon data with XML to mark the fields. Nicely done."

The Architect nodded in gratitude to the compliment.

"I don't have a clue what he just said," Bob interjected as he and Mary returned to the work area.

"Look," Sam started, "All transactions have the same basic information: Date, time, who sent it, things like that, and it is easy to store in a database when the elements are the same. But when you have a system that takes transactions from many systems with many different elements and you try to save them in one database the number of elements becomes huge if you try to name each field and save space for each field in each transaction. Plus every time you add a new system along with its new data, you need to expand the database to include the new fields."

"I still don't get it. What's the bottom line?" Bob was puzzled and looked around the room for those who shared his affliction.

"It means that bottom line is—it was slick," Sam said, and George and the Architect smiled again.

George stood up from the table and went to the Architect's workstation where he put the CD into the system, and then copied a file to the hard drive. "Here, you can search this." He took the CD out of the workstation, put it into the second system and sat down. He opened the file and as it loaded he turned back to the Architect.

"I created a file for the period we were looking at records on PeopleFinder. It's a record of every notification transaction that went from the Middleware server to any communication server." George looked to the Architect.

"Yes, I see," the Architect looked at the data as it appeared on his screen. After a brief review and without looking away from the screen, he said, "It can be sorted by sender or destination; so I can sort it on sender, then look for *AliceK*."

"AliceK?" Mary asked.

"Yes, it's the name of the project's server, and when a message goes out, it says 'Message from AliceK'," the Architect explained as he continued worked.

"Is that some secret FBI acronym?" Mary asked.

"No, it's the name of my sister in Pennsylvania. I named the server AliceK after her. She's a real sweetie. You'd never know it, but she writes really steamy romance novels."

"You don't say?"

223

"Yes. I got her stuff over there." Without turning away from the screen the Architect pointed to the bookcase where some paperbacks were neatly stored. You'll find it under her pen name *Kate Simon*."

Mary walked over and examined the books, and then took one out to skim as the others worked on the data.

Without looking back at the others, the Architect told the others, "This won't take me long."

"So what do you have, George?" Sam asked as he peered over George's shoulder at the screen.

"It's a history file from an earlier period, I wanted to check something." George looked up at Sam who had come over and was looking at the screen. "Give me a few minutes, and let me see what's here." He looked over at his friend who now was almost frozen in his thoughts.

"Okay, George," Sam and David turned their attentions to Bob.

"So what do you have for me, Bob?"

"Here's what I got, Sam. While you were away on vacation, laying about in the sun and sand, I was back here working my little hoofies to the quick, banging on the keyboard, trying to dig information out the bowels of the beast." Bob sighed and made a false pathetic look of an overworked and underappreciated man. "But don't concern yourself with me; I am just here to serve."

Sam turned to David, "Is he always like this?"

"You mean is he always this pitiful, sorrowful wretch of a man, who is constantly seeking praise for every little menial thing he does to somehow give meaning to his otherwise shallow and meaningless life?"

Sam smiled at David, "Just what I mean."

"Affirmative, that's him pretty much."

"Shame."

"Yeah. Maybe if he got a woman or something maybe he'd not have to stoop to such pathetic displays to get validation. No, that won't work; he has already tried the *or something* and that didn't work out."

"I beg your pardon," Bob said, but did not look at either of his two teasers.

"You boys are terrible," Mary walked over and hugged Bob. "I think he's cute, very cuddly. Besides what about Tammy?"

"Tammy?" David came over to Bob, "Tammy?"

"Roger that! She's the woman from the office. She takes Bob for rides on her motorcycle."

"You don't say," David was really enjoying the tease. "How come you didn't tell me you got a woman there, Bob?"

"I don't *got* a woman, David. We are just dating."

"I'm hurt Bob, you used to tell me everything. Now I'm the last to know."

David looked to Sam, "Kids, you give them everything; then they just cut you out of their lives." Sam walked over and gave David a hug who then made some whimpering sounds.

Bob looked up to Mary, "I think I like it better when people treat me like I'm not here."

"What were you saying, Bob?" David looked back and Sam and they both smiled at Bob's discomfort.

"So now that I am back from frolicking on the beach, what do you have for me?" Sam slapped Bob on the back.

Bob wisely gave up and just went on with business. He had pulled up the business reports from IdentityPoint. "We have the same info on the Investment groups that we spoke of before. Now I have used the business systems to check on the incorporation of the companies, and I have three names that come up in each company."

"So Louwaert Investments is the original company and Sunset Investment, J&D investment, and Ricky Tech Funds are all the same company."

"Correct!"

"And the names that appear in all four companies are the same."

"Yep. There's the Louwaert brothers, Jim and Dave, and then there's Robert L. Pearson and James W. Twiggs."

"That's it?"

"Yes. They appear to be clean, as far as I can see. Pearson, originally from Charlottesville, Virginia, then Petersburg, now of Richmond.

"And Twiggs?"

"James W. Twiggs originally from Austin, Texas, then Dallas, now of Houston."

There was a crash from behind them. They all swung around to the source of the sound. The Architect had dropped his glass, and it had shattered on the wood floor. He just sat there not moving; not looking at the broken glass, nor making any signs of attending to the slip. Then, as if it had not happened, he stood and left the room, walking upstairs without a word.

"What was that about?"

"Not a clue," Sam went over to the broken glass and started to pick up the pieces and place them in a trash can that Mary had brought in from the kitchen.

Mary turned to George, "You think he's alright? Should someone go see him?"

"I'll give him a minute and go see." George paced a moment and then started towards the stairs when his friend returned. He had a sheet of white typing paper in his hand and the look in his face was of a man who had just gotten some extremely bad news; like the death of a loved one. It was a sorrowful look.

"What's the matter?"

He held out the paper and gave it to George. "It's a list of the names I created for the program."

George looked at the list of fifty names, "Oh my God!" George looked up to his friend and then to Sam. "They're on the list. Pearson and Twiggs."

"The *FBI* is the one scamming the money from the acquisitions?" Bob walked over from his seat at the table and looked at the paper, which George had now given to Sam.

"It's not the FBI, Bob," Sam paused, looked at the paper and then at the Architect. "It's the boys from IdentityPoint."

"How can you be sure?" David asked as he looked at the names on the list.

"Because he's sure," he looked at the Architect, "aren't you?"

The Architect just nodded in agreement, and then sat down. "That's a list of the names of all fifty identities I made for the system. I had them here in my safe; because I worked on the project a lot from here. When they canned me, I just forgot I had the list in my safe. Never even thought about it until now."

Sam looked at the list, "Yep, both Twiggs and Pearson as well as our would-be killer James Rowe. Fifty names."

The Architect went back to his computer, "I was just about to tell what I found on the log." Everyone walked over to his computer to hear. "I have found the transactions that went from the Middleware server to AliceK, one on Monday, October 16, 0946.22 hours and the other on the same day at 1456.05 hours."

"Can you tell who they are?" Sam asked.

"I have the message and the pager it was sent to."

"What is it?"

"The first one was to 240-814-5124 for the name David R Curry and the second was to the same number for Phillip L. Brock."

George looked at the list, "But neither of these names are on this list of fifty. I thought that the list of fifty was on AliceK?"

The Architect looked to Sam, "I did too."

"So what do you think?" Sam asked the Architect.

He didn't respond, but George did. "I think that someone changed the list."

"Why do you say that?"

"Because I have the records of the system here," George pointed to his screen.

The Architect left his terminal and walked to George. He looked at the screen. "You are running Oracle. You loaded the data?"

"Yes. Take a look."

The Architect took the mouse and scrolled down the window reviewing the data. "How did you get the data? I didn't have the passwords for the communications servers."

"Correct. I logged on the network as me, then the Middleware Server as you. Since the Middleware Server has global Administration privileges, the AliceK server let it sign in; so I took the history file. The data file that holds the current data is encrypted, but the history file is not encrypted it was just restricted to System Administration level access. May I?" George reached for the mouse and then scrolled to a point in the file. "The system went on line in June of 1992, and since then there have been only a few hundred transactions."

"Which makes sense, since it was designed to support fake identities and hits on them would be limited," Sam joined the discussion.

"Exactly." He continued with his demonstration. "You can see this code here on this line." He pointed to the second column. There is an

'A' that stands for added. That means that the record was added. This one with the 'D' code means it was deleted."

"On the 17th of September in 1993, it looks like eleven were deleted and ten were added to the table." George scrolled down the screen so all the transactions were on the screen, and counted them by touching his finger to the screen one at a time.

"The added names are David R. Curry, Phillip L. Brook, Martin O. Lindquist, Ernest E. Wall, Phillip B. Richards, Arthur Bickell, Manuel Fuentes, Jr., John W. Watson, Paul P. Trujillo, and John F. Buckley."

"The names don't strike any familiar notes to me."

"What about the deleted ones?" David asked.

"William McCarter, Robert Wray, Robert L. Pearson, Benjamin F. Hopper, James Rowe, Harold Crabtree, Blake Mariano, Alvey R. Rollins, James W. Twiggs, Henry W. Nelson and " George paused and looked at his friend before continuing, "and Charles M. Robinson."

"Charles Robinson! Oh my God, what did they do?" The Architect stared in disbelief.

"Who is Charles Robinson?"

"That's the undercover name of the FBI agent whose cover was blown and was murdered," George answered.

"But his name was removed from the system. Why?" Mary asked.

"I don't know."

"That's why there weren't any notification of the inquiries. The name had been removed. There was nothing to trigger the alert." Sam looked closer at the data on the screen.

"Why?" The Architect just stared at George.

"I don't understand what's happened here. I don't remember adding any names or removing any after December of '92 when we went live. The only one with access was me. George had left the project after the testing phase was complete and before we put the actual names in."

David got the Architect's attention, "Why do you keep saying we?"

"There were two of us then who were managing the names in the system, me and Brenda Palm."

"I must have done it, I just don't remember. I don't understand" The Architect seemed on the verge of tears; he lowered himself back into his chair.

George turned from his seat at the computer and saw his friend and the miserable state in which he was in. "It wasn't you. It couldn't have been. You weren't there on the 17th of September." George turned back to the computer screen and pointed to the date field displayed on the screen. Sam stepped over to the computer to get a look, as did David, but the Architect remained in his chair.

"Don't you remember? That was my fifteenth year at the company. They gave me two tickets to the Mets Braves game; I took you. We took off the entire day." George waited for his friend to look up and at him. When he did, George repeated, "We were gone all day."

"The Braves lost 3 to 2 in the tenth inning. I remember, you love the Mets and you beat us in the tenth." A look of obvious relief came over the Architect as he realized it could not have been him. "If not me then who? Only me and Palm had access."

"Well?" Sam used his hands to urge him to continue.

"Well, what?" The Architect looked at Sam and then realized what Sam was implying. "No. I can't imagine it was her. Why would she?"

David immediately jumped in, "Why does anyone? Money."

"Face the facts old friend." It was clear by his voice that George was getting angry at the revelation. "You took the fall and she took over. She even got a promotion and a large salary increase."

"No, I can't believe it. She was not one of them."

"Why? Because she always talked bad about 'the boys' and she couldn't wait to leave, to go to North Carolina and return to academia? It was all crap. It's been over two years and she is still there, more involved than ever before. Have you seen the car she's driving? It cost more than my entire year's salary." He paused and looked around at the others in the room, then back to his friend. "She's got an office in the Executive wing, for God's sake." George was getting angry with his friend for failing to admit the truth.

He thought for a moment and took in George's passionate arguments then quietly agreed, "She was the only one with access."

"So Palm changed the list; she must have screwed up and deleted Robinson by mistake." David looked to Sam who shook his head, no.

"And the other deletions and additions?" David asked.

"Well, based on what we have seen thus far, whoever has control over the program, I presume it is the NECO group, removed the ten names for other purposes."

"And we are guessing the FBI brass didn't know," Mary said from the other room.

"In this case I don't think so. After all, it is a classified system to monitor, if anyone is looking at their secret names. Why would they take some out of a protection system? "

"But what names were added? What were they for?" George asked David, then Sam.

Sam just shrugged acknowledging he didn't know.

"Well, whoever they are, Sam accidentally found two of them."

Having said all they knew on the subject they all went back to what they had been working on. Sam sat at the table and started to write down the Essential Elements of Information, the EEI as it was called in the army, on what he knew about the three separate events: The attempt on his life, IdentityPoint, and Ream.

ATTEMPT TO KILL ME, ROBINSON, NECO, DEATH SQUAD, FBI,
IDENTITYPOINT, ADD & DELETE NAMES, FRAUD, JOHNSON, 2
ALERTS (DAVID R CURRY, PHILLIP L. BROCK)
REAM MURDER, UNKNOWN KILLER, MISSING POWS, PEI WITH
EMPLOYEES AFTER CLOSING,

Sam looked at his list. He circled the word 'alerts' then drew a line to 'NECO.' From NECO he drew another line to 'Ream', then drew another line from NECO to 'kill me.' Without getting anyone's specific attention, Sam asked the collective group. "What if everything is related? What if Ream's death and the attempt on me are related? What if all of that is related to IdentityPoint?"

David had been sitting in a comfortable chair reading PeopleFinder reports, but the long hours had caught up to him and he was nodding off. His eyes were heavy and he struggled to make sense of the words on the reports. In the ten minutes that had passed he had failed to read one complete report, and mentally captured even less. His mind heard Sam and attempted to communicate, "What was that, Sam?"

"I said, what if Ream, IdentityPoint and Biras Creek are all related? What if they are all connected by some common thread? What if some action or event I did caused the three to collide?

David was now a little more lucid, but not fully there. "That's lot of 'What ifs' there Sam."

"Yes, but what if the names are the common link," Sam picked up his notes.

"Go on." David rubbed his eyes and sat forward in the chair.

Sam could not. He couldn't make the connection from what he had. "I don't know what it is, but I am sure they are all connected somehow."

No one spoke, each was tired and the amount of data was staggering. Finally, David broke the silence. "I don't know about the rest of you, but I'm wasted. What do you say we break for the night?"

"I agree. It's late and we have a lot to do tomorrow. David, how about we try to plan for tomorrow."

David and Sam worked out the tasks for the next day while Bob and Mary helped George clean up. The Architect had left the house and was on the back porch just staring into the night. Five minutes later they had their assignments and were on their way to their respective homes. David would track down the owner of the phone number that got the alerts. Bob was to research Nichols and the FBI agent that had been killed, while Sam and Mary were to work out their cover story.

George's job was to see to his friend.

2000 hours, Alexandria, VA

The bed was a king, the sheets were silk, and the air was filled with the scent of incense. The bedroom was lit only by the light of the candles she had positioned in five different places around the room. The night was exceptionally dark and the blackness of the evening sky made the view of the city from her bedroom window look more like a backdrop painting than an actual skyline as the bright skyscrapers seemed to be cut out of the cloudless, jet-black sky and pasted onto an immense canvas. The mood in the room was sultry and a perfect spot for romance and passion.

When her date had brought her home from dinner she excused herself, went into the bedroom, started the incense, turned down the bed and changed into her pink Ben De Lisi runway dress. She called it her 'closer dress.' It was fashionable, sleek, silky, comfortable, showed her very ample figure, and most importantly, when it was time for him to take it off, it came off quickly. When she played a man, and she knew how to play one, she set him up all night and when he saw her in this dress, the deal was closed.

The man in the other room, who by now she hoped was in hot anticipation of her return to the living room, had been pursuing her for weeks. He was tall and most thought him good looking, but she found him more pretty than handsome and really preferred the more rugged, manly looking man. When he first started to court her, she was not interested; there was just something about his too-good looks for her, and she did not respond to his advances. But he didn't give up and frequently, if not purposely, bumped into her in the hallways, met her at the cafeteria, personally delivered data to her office when sending it though the distribution system would have sufficed. When he did see her, he always had a clever comment for her about her style, or some other aspect of her attire, or her good looks.

She was a sensual woman who not just liked sex, she loved it. She was not afraid to let her emotions go and was both passionate and aggressive when it came time to getting satisfied and satisfying her man. But she hadn't had a man in months and was more than ready to have an active evening of hot, steamy sex; hopefully one that would include multiple sessions.

Despite her gut feeling that this man was less than she was looking for, she finally decided to accept his offer of dinner.

The selection of the restaurant was first rate, and his wine selection was straight out of *Wine Enthusiast Magazine*. He was charming in his manners and despite his somewhat self-centered dinner conversation, she was attracted to him and decided to take him to bed. When he took her home, she asked him in and he jumped at the invitation. He made himself comfortable on the couch, and she excused herself to the bedroom. When she returned to the room in her closer dress, he took one look at her large breasts that were now free in her outfit, and he acted like a dog in heat. The façade of his gentlemanly manners and manly control fell away the instant she sat next to him on the couch. He kissed her weakly, immediately buried his face in her neck, and then nuzzled to her breasts. She was turned off by his less than romantic manner and she felt more like a mother cuddling her baby than a passionate woman ready for some sweaty sex.

He was even less than what she thought he would be, but she was horny and hoped that maybe what he lacked in style, he would make up for in substance in the bedroom. She brought him straight to the bedroom where he quickly removed his own clothes and literally jumped into bed, leaving her to undress herself. As soon as she got into the bed, he went for her breasts.

The phone rang and she rolled over slightly, saw the caller ID and took the call. "Hello"

"Hi, Colleen, it's me, David."

"Hi, Angel. Are you in town, and if you are why aren't you here?"

"No baby, I am in Atlanta."

"And you need a favor," she said sassily.

"Just a little something darlin'."

"Don't you darlin' me. The last little something almost got my ass in a sling, and it wasn't the kind of sling I like—if you know what I mean," she laughed a sultry laugh.

"I know but I made it worth your while."

"Oh, yes, you most assuredly did, several times." She cooed in the phone to her playmate on the other end, tempting him with sounds of kisses over the phone. "So what do you need, besides me naked of course?"

"I have a phone number, and I need to know who is using it?"

"That's it? Have you thought of using the Reverse Phone Directory?"

"It's one of the Bureau's numbers," David said in a serious tone.

"Well, I wouldn't think you would call me if it was the number to Wal-Mart. Standard fee sweetie."

"I'm good for it," David responded.

"You most certainly are." She opened the side table drawer and took out a pen and paper. "Okay, give it to me."

David complied.

"I'll have it for you in the morning. Okay?"

"Yes, Darlin'. Bye."

She hung up and rolled back in her bed.

"Who the hell was that?" The man who had been the focus of her attention five minutes earlier was sitting up in bed, naked, and totally pissed at her for not only taking a call and ignoring him, but for talking sex with the man while she was in the bed with him.

"Never you mind that. Just know he's all man, and there's nothing I won't do for a real man." She reached over and stroked his face, then let her hand run the full length of his chest and stomach. "Now if you want me to treat you like I treat him, its time to show me what you got." She kissed him hard and he responded by moving back to her breasts.

They rolled around the bed, not making love but having sex, for five minutes. He finished and rolled over and smiled at her as if he had provided her a great service, and she smiled back. She rolled over, looked out the window at the perfectly romantic sky, one that was wasted on the man next to her, and she mentally crossed him off her list.

2230 hours, Northern Minnesota

The Old Man lay asleep in his small, humble bunk in his austere, well-built two-room cabin, far out in the forest country of the northern mountains of Minnesota. Constructed of ponderosa pine, the cabin was built like a fortress and stood strong against the harsh winters for fifty years. The Old Man, now seventy-four, had moved to the cabin twenty years ago after his wife died. Without children or family of any kind to keep him in Milwaukee, he withdrew to the solitary life of the mountains where he could escape all the complications of the city life—especially the people.

It was freezing cold outside, brought on by an early winter storm that had blown in yesterday. The Old Man had added extra logs to the fire, made soup, ate it by the fire, and then retired to his small bedroom where he read *Der Kopf*, by Heinrich Mann, while his dog Jake slept on the floor. The Old Man was cold; he had left the bedroom door open to allow the heat of the living room fireplace to warm the bedroom. As he slept, a stream of cold night air was drawn into the cabin through the inch wide space under the weather-beaten door that separated the warmth of the cabin and the desolate cold of the night. For the last ten years the only other living creature to spend time at the cabin, other than the night creatures was Jake, a mangy, mixed bred longhaired brown dog whose lineage had too many limbs to track.

Ten years ago, while trout fishing at the stream that ran through his thirty acres of solitude, a wet, cold, and nearly dead puppy came slowly floating by clinging to a tree limb that had been swept away by the stream's current. The Old Man rescued the pathetic looking animal from what would have been his death, took him to the cabin, and nursed it back to health. After a week, the puppy was fully recovered. The Old Man fed the dog, which of course encouraged him to stay, but he fed him in the open barn and that allowed him to roam freely without restraints. Some days the dog would remain gone all day, but he always returned before dark and slept in the cabin with the Old Man. After a month, it was apparent that the dog was going to stay; so he named the dog Jake, and moved the food bowl inside.

After ten years of living totally alone, the Old Man welcomed a partner to share his solitude. Each occupant of the little cabin had his job. The Old Man secured the food; fish from the stream, and deer meat was plentiful, which he shot, dressed, and butchered himself. What little sundries they needed, the Old Man got at the local store in town once every few months. As he grew, Jake assumed his role—protector. The once frequent and destructive raccoons no longer bothered the cabin, and the bear that roamed the area by night knew the bark of the eighty-pound dog and gave the cabin a wide berth, opting for situations where they did not have to face an aggressive, barking dog.

This night the Old Man's ever vigilante friend was at work. A wet, black nose was in the second stage of detecting the stranger outside. The big dog had been awakened from his light sleep by what was the slightest of sounds. No human would have heard it much less been awakened by the sound, but somewhere out in the night, in the cold, snowy night, was an unfamiliar sound. He heard it just once, but he popped his head up immediately and stared at the door. After a few seconds he left his warm bed near the fireplace stopped a foot from the door, head turning side-to-side, staring at the space under the door, quietly searching the night with perked ears and an unbelievably sensitive nose.

He inched closer and closer then crouched down and pressed his nose tight against the bottom of the wide plank door to the outside. A deep inhale brought the smell to his nostrils, and he knew an unfamiliar predator was just outside the door.

The dog walked back to the bedroom and to a sagging bed where the Old Man was sleeping. He stopped several inches from the bearded face and stared at his friend. A minute passed, then another. The Old Man continued to snore. Jake moved closer and nudged his arm.

"Uhhh..." was followed by a snore.

The dog inched closer and then when within an inch of the weathered face, he snorted.

"What the..." said the Old Man rising up quickly, still half asleep. He was startled by the snort, but more by the dog's closeness than the noise.

The big dog let out a low, deep, growl from way down inside and then the Old Man understood. He wiped his eyes with his big leathery hands, sat up quickly, pushing the warm blanket aside and reached for his rifle, which was hanging on the wall just to the left of the open bedroom door. He levered a 30/30-caliber shell into the chamber of his Winchester and began to survey the cabin; no windows broken or open, and the door was secure.

Nothing seemed wrong or out of place. It was all as it was when he went to bed. As he became more awake he realized that no one was in the house; he knew Jake would have been eating someone's leg by now if there had been.

He looked at Jake who now was standing tall and straight as he stared at the door motionless and without fear. However, fear uncharacteristically came over the Old Man. It welled up within him and made him sweat. He remembered the last time Jake had acted this way when a bear, mad with gangrene, was trying to gain access to the cabin—and to him. Normally Jake would bark and growl and scare any animal away even through the closed cabin door, but when Jake was quiet and alert, seemingly ready to strike, the Old Man knew it was a serious situation.

Jake had been watching and waiting patiently. Finally, he barked once and turned back from the door to the Old Man.

Stretching upright the Old Man said, "I'm coming."

His body cracked and popped as the bones took to standing. He reached for a long dark cloth shirt and while switching the rifle in between hands, always ready, he pulled the shirt over his flannel underwear. Pantless and coatless he moved to a ready position next to Jake in front of the door.

As the Old Man reached for the handle he saw his own shadow on the door in front of him. He turned and looked at the source of the light. Realizing the fireplace was still burning and the bright red coals acted like a backlight exposing his big frame in the opening. He knew he would have to exit quickly in order not to expose himself to the eyes of whatever, or whoever, awaited him outside.

He returned to his ready position where Jake was now impatiently pawing at the wood floor. He paused, hand on the handle, took a breath, depressed the lever and pushed the door open. Like a flash, Jake bolted through the opening disappearing almost instantly into the dark. The Old Man followed, moving straight out, then sideways against the wall, pulling the door closed behind him. He stood in the dark shadow of the porch, back pressed tight to the wall, motionless. He scanned the area while letting his eyes adjust to the night.

The snowstorm that howled a few hours ago was now just a memory with the only evidence of its passing being the eight inches of new snow. A yellow three-quarter moon on the horizon surrounded by winter's shining stars and the brightening night sky, was causing moon shadows to appear across the snow-covered meadow in front of him. The clouds full of weather, which had brought the snow earlier that night, had moved east but still covered half of the eastern sky. The moonlight was following the weather and was creeping across the open pasture like a sunrise.

One hundred feet away and directly in front of him was the barn. It was a small one-story structure with a hayloft above and a big double door in front. He observed that the handle was pulled down tight and secured exactly as he had left it a few hours before. The window to the hayloft in the rafters above the door was also closed tight and seemingly undisturbed.

Behind the barn were fast sloping snow covered banks that lead to the stream that was only partially frozen over. It was impassable, as the quick moving water beneath the thin ice would claim any victim, man or beast without remorse.

Satisfied, he scanned to his left and across the pasture, which was several hundred yards wide and ended at the rocky edge of the mountain forest. He saw only the wind occasionally tossing the fresh snow into the air like the spray off an ocean wave.

To his right, was the field where once Timothy wheat had been planted in the fall and corn in the spring, and now only remnants of them grew wild. It, like the pasture, stretched out several hundred yards to the foot of the forest beyond.

He had visually cleared the areas he could see from the porch. He knew he would not see Jake, but he knew he was out there, in the shadows, looking. The Old Man took a small breath and eased his grip on the rifle, and prepared to move. He felt the cold air in his lungs and then again, he felt the fear.

Again, he shook off the unfamiliar feeling and tried to concentrate. He slowly moved to the edge of the porch, stepped down into the snow but remained in the cabin's moon-cast shadow. He knew that if he hadn't been seen coming out the door, and if he could get from this shadow to the woodpile near the barn, he would have a superior position and the advantage.

His first step found that the fresh snow was actually a foot deep, and it was like walking on a bed of cotton. The fresh, dry powder would help make his movements noiseless; he suddenly thought, "How did that fool dog hear anything moving in this new snow"?

With his eyes now used to the light, he had an easier time examining the distant clearings. The snow clouds had retreated even farther to the horizon, and he could even see into the forest at the edge of the clearings. He then re-examined the pasture to the west of the cabin.

The wind was pushing cold through his long underwear and his feet started to let him know that they were improperly prepared for this adventure. Not seeing any immediate danger and not hearing Jake barking, he returned to the cabin, put on his jeans, slipped on his boots and his winter coat and was back out on the porch in less that sixty seconds.

Upon his return to the porch he rescanned the edge of the hardwood forest just beyond the shadows of the wheat field to the east. About two hundred feet away, coming down what was the dirt drive to his cabin he saw a movement. It was low to the ground at first. Then it rose up; it was a man—and a dog.

The Old Man squinted in the moonlight's snowy glare. He could see the shadow was struggling to his feet. Slowly, it began to walk. The dark figure took one high step lifting his leg up and out of the snow. Then perched like a bird as he paused before putting his foot back into the cold snow. His unsure step made him stumble and he fell twisting awkwardly and face first. The Old Man watched as the stranger pushed himself to his feet again and feebly shaking the caked white crust from his body, he stumbled along for about another five steps, swayed sideways, and fell again. This time the dog nudged him.

The Old Man slowly left his safe observatory and walked towards Jake and the stranger. The fear he had felt earlier was gone, dispatched by Jake's quietness. If the stranger had been a threat Jake would be barking and growling—there was neither.

He came up to the man and stood over him with the Winchester ready. He balanced his weight on his back foot and with Jake by his side, he reached down to the man. The Old Man could clearly see he was nearly frozen.

The Old Man asked, "You alive?"

"Barely," came a muffled and shivering reply.

The Old Man looked to the dog as for reassurance that it was okay to assist this man. "Here. Let me help you." The Old Man pulled on the fallen man's arm and helped him to his feet.

It took five full minutes to help him walk the few hundred feet to the cabin. They got inside and the Old Man sat the stranger in a chair by the fire. Putting the Winchester aside, he got blankets from the bedroom and then added logs to the fire. The red-hot coals of the fireplace quickly ignited the logs and in a minute, the fire was roaring. The Old Man carefully removed the stranger's shoes and then helped to position him closer to the fire.

"So," the Old Man paused to let the stranger engage. "What where you doing out there at this time of night? And dressed like that." The Old Man pointed to the stranger's dress shoes.

"I was driving when the snow came. I got lost. I couldn't see a thing in the driving snow and I, I slid off the..." The stranger stammered from the cold and struggled to speak clearly. I worked for a long time getting the car back on the road, but in the blizzard I couldn't tell which way was which. I sat in the car for a while thinking and then I must have dozed off. When I woke up…"

"You were out of gas," the Old Man interjected. "And you got cold, so you thought you would walk."

"Yeah, I guess." The stranger paused and reached forward towards the fire and warmed his hands. Jake had accepted the stranger as a guest and was already lying by the fireplace ready to resume his most import task of sleeping. "I knew there was nothing behind me, and I thought I saw a light so I walked towards it. I must have walked for hours. It was so, so very cold."

The Old Man smiled and shook his head. "Son, looking at the way you're dressed you are a city boy through and through, and since you are completely unprepared for the weather, I suspect you were out there about twenty minutes." He pointed to the stranger's shoes and light coat. "Any longer than that and you would be dead."

The stranger nodded and rubbed his hands.

"I guess you must have seen the light coming from that window." The Old Man pointed to the window on the side of the house. "It faces the road you were walking down."

The stranger looked up at the window then back to the Old Man. "I guess I am a very lucky man."

The Old Man nodded and put the kettle on the stove for hot tea. The Old Man intended to wait until he finished the tea before they both went to bed, but half way though the second cup the stranger fell asleep. The Old Man covered the stranger up with an extra blanket, added another log to the fire and then went to bed, exhausted.

Chapter 14

Sunday, October 23

0745 hours

The next morning the Old Man awoke as the light of day broke though the window. He looked into the other room and saw the stranger was still sleeping. He dressed quickly and quietly. Jake got up with the Old Man, but seemingly knowing the stranger needed sleep, he made no noise. He and Jake took a short walk, returned, and he made breakfast. Within a few minutes, the air was filled with the scent of eggs, bacon and coffee. As he poured the coffee, the stranger awoke.

"Morning!" the Old Man said cheerfully. "You *are* alive!"

The stranger rubbed his eyes and looked about without speaking, then realized where he was and what had happened. "Yes, I think I am."

"Good, then I haven't wasted all this food. Come eat."

The stranger stood, stretched, and came to the table where they both ate like they hadn't eaten in a week.

As they ate, the stranger got more relaxed and less anxious about having almost frozen to death.

"Jake and I took a look outside before you got up. You can see your car from here. Less than a half mile I would think."

"No kidding. I thought I'd walked ten last night," The stranger replied as he stuffed the forkful of eggs in his mouth.

"When you're ready, I have a can of gas in the barn. It will be enough to get you to town."

The stranger took a drink of coffee, "You are too kind." For the first time he looked about the room. There were several fine firearms stored on a wooden rack along with a pistol than hung neatly in a leather holster on a hook next to the gun rack.

"You have a nice collection," he pointed to the weapons on the wall.

"Well, out here, you must have a firearm you can trust."

"Is that a Sauer?"

"Yes, it is. That is a 7x57JR Mauser, 24-inch barrel, 12 gauge 1944 edition."

"And the other is a Merkel?

"It is! You know your weapons, Sir. That is a Stoeger Merkel Model 303E, 12 Bore."

"Yes Sir, I guess a little." He pointed to the holstered pistol. "Is that a Peacemaker?"

The Old Man was impressed. "Wow! Now that is impressive. In the holster and you can tell."

"It does have a very distinctive look."

"Indeed it does." The Old Man got up from the table, took the pistol out of the holster and brought it back to the table. "Take a look."

The stranger took it gently, almost reverently. He held it in both hands as if he were firing it. He looked at the revolving chamber and spun the empty chamber ever so slightly. "Absolutely beautiful!"

"Thank you." The Old Man put the prized weapon back in its holster. "It's a great weapon, but it's not my favorite." He went to the bedroom and took the Winchester off the wall. Holding it out to the stranger, "This is my love; the gun that won the American west, a lever action Winchester '93. Light, durable, shoots fast and straight." The Old Man handed the weapon to the stranger, who took it with care.

"Careful, that one is loaded." The Old Man returned to the stove to get more coffee as the stranger inspected the weapon. "Yes sir, you are doubly fortunate that I found you last night, and that I didn't think you were a wolf and shoot you."

"Yes." The stranger slowly stood and put the weapon to his shoulder. "Lucky for me." He aimed the weapon at the sleeping dog. "But I am sorry to say not for you."

There was one slight clicking sound made as the lever action of the weapon chambered a round then an instant later there was a loud blast and a bullet ripped though Jake as he slept. The blast threw him a foot towards the hearth and blood splattered over the stones. One second after the first shot the stranger swung around to the Old Man, who was stunned by what had just happened. In that first instant he thought the weapon accidentally went off. Then as he saw the stranger aim, he knew he was terribly wrong. Just as he moved, the stranger fired. He felt a searing pain and he instinctively reached to his left side were the bullet had ripped through his arm. The force of the bullet knocked him down, and he crumbled to the floor. The stranger calmly walked over to the Old Man and fired again.

The stranger stood over the dead man, "If you had left rounds in the Colt, it would've been easier on you. I wouldn't have missed with the first shot."

The stranger washed the dishes he had used, careful to eliminate any evidence of his presence. He then found a bag in which he put his shoes and socks, and then he helped himself to the Old Man's winter boots and a pair of good wool socks, as well as his heavy winter coat and gloves. Opening the door, he first dragged the Old Man outside, then the dog. Next, he put the Winchester on the ground beside the Old Man and then finally he dropped the three empty shell casings he had retrieved from the cabin next to the bodies. Returning to the cabin, he made one final sweep of the area to remove any trace of his presence there, and then walked back out leaving the door open.

"Yep, not lucky for you." He looked to the nearby mountains and then to the bodies and knew that the coyotes would strip the two bodies within days.

0745 hours, Dawsonville, GA.

With no pressing engagement, David had slept almost till 0700 hours. He got up, changed into his running clothes, did a quick two miles in the already 65-degree heat, and then ran quickly back to the house. He made up for the less than normal run by doubling up on the pushups and working the heavy bag.

He was sitting in a kitchen chair, sweaty from his workout and drinking a glass of juice, when his cell phone rang. It was charging on the counter, and he grabbed it on the second ring.

"Hello," he listened for a moment.

"Got it darlin', thanks." He pushed the 'end' button and then dialed another number.

"Sam, Lytle here."

"Morning David. Miss me already?"

"I just got the call from Coleen Rowley. The phone that the alerts went to is a mobile number belonging to the FBI and assigned to Christopher Garrett, Southern Towers Apartments, 4901 Seminary Road in Alexandria, Virginia."

"That was fast. I hope she doesn't charge you double," Sam joked.

"I hope she does."

Sam laughed and then remembered what the lady looked like. "Perhaps she would prefer payment in two *separate* installments; I do have frequent flyer miles available."

"At ease, soldier. What if—Sigourney was to find out?"

"Ah, you're right as always, David. One fantasy at a time. What would I do without you, David?"

"I don't know there, Grasshopper. It is a burden being me, being the leader of this little group. Taking care of you troops, keeping you safe from the dangers of the big bad world. That's why I have to take care of Coleen alone."

"That's what I love about you David, that you are so willing to take one for the team."

"That's me, Sam, just give, give, give. I'm just that kind of guy."

"You're my hero, David."

"What can I say, Sam? It's my curse."

"So back on earth there, David, are you going to visit our friends in the city of power?"

"Affirmative. I'll leave as soon as possible." I'm going to call Bob and have him arrange the flights, but we should meet before I go. How about we meet at your hotel? It should be easier for you that way. You know, since you're dead and all that."

"Very funny, David. You know you really should cut down on the caffeine."

'Roger that. See you at, say eleven thirty hours."

"Eleven thirty hours, roger."

David then called Bob and repeated the facts of the conversation he had with Rowley, and asked him to meet him at Sam's hotel.

1138 hours, Alpharetta, Holiday Inn Hotel

Bob took out some papers from a folder he had brought along and while he was distributing them to the group, David asked, "By the way, you got my flights?"

"Yes, you are going out on Delta 1164 at thirteen fifty-nine hours, arriving fifteen forty-six hours, and returning Monday night on Delta 1173 departing at nineteen fifteen hours and arriving at twenty-one zero five hours," he said from memory, while continuing with his distribution.

"Impressive. The whole number thing, no notes," David joked.

"I liked the military time thing," Sam added.

"You boys done?" Bob looked coldly at David and Sam, like a teacher at two misbehaving schoolboys. "I have researched all the sites I could, and from what I can tell, Nichols is a Vet, Special Forces no less. Served in Vietnam from 1968 to 1969. I have also read no less than ten articles on the guy, that talk about his service and his soon to be published novel, *The Killing Zone*." Bob put copies of five articles on the table, he had printed from his Internet research.

"So that's what you read, now what do you think?" David asked.

"Something doesn't ring true."

"How?"

"It's the way he talks. I mean they quote him in the articles with words like 'Gook' and 'Charlie' and such."

"I can concur with that," Sam interjected. "How he describes his reactions is too..." Sam struggled for the right words, "I don't know, but describing Nam as 'the thrill of battle' and 'the drama of human challenge,' I just got this odd feeling about him.

"Theatrical," Mary interjected.

Bob nodded in concurrence, "I never met anyone whose been there that has spoken like that." Bob paused, and looked to David, "You've never spoken like that. And then, there's the book."

"What about it?" David questioned.

"He's been spouting about it for fifteen years and its still not published—hell even I write faster than that."

"I see your point," David said.

"I think I know someone who can help." Sam walked over to the phone and dialed a familiar number. "Hi. This is Sam Call calling, may I speak with John please."

1155 hours, Stafford, VA

John Mack sat on the couch waiting for the game while he was reading the Sunday paper. It had been a long week and all he wanted to do was to relax and watch the Redskins – Colts game. He heard the phone ring and his wife answer it in the other room.

"John, it's for you. It's Sam Call."

John popped up from the couch eager to talk with an old friend, and he half-jogged over to where he wife held the phone. "Thanks, dear," John said to her as she walked back to where her husband had been sitting and picked up the paper.

"Sam! How are you?"

"Well, let me tell you, not so good."

"What's up? Everything all right with the family?"

"Actually no. Mary was injured, but she is going to be all right, John."

"Damn Sam, what can I do?"

"I'm glad you asked old friend. I need to know about a Harvey Nichols, supposedly served in Nam in 68 or 69. He was a lieutenant at the time, retired as a lieutenant colonel."

"You need to know where he is now?"

"No, John, I know that; he's in Atlanta. What I need to know is what his real history is. I think he's not who he says he is."

"I guess I can do that, Sam. Really shouldn't, but I guess I can just confirm a few things for you unofficially as it were. I'll get on it first thing when I get to the office."

"Thanks, John. I owe you."

"No you don't, Sam. I still owe you. Talk to you Monday. Can I reach you at the same number?"

"Yes. Thanks again and give my regards to your wife."

"Will do."

John hung up the phone and went back to the couch where his wife was reading the headlines. He sat down and told his wife about what had happened to Sam, but left out what he had asked him to do. She continued to read the front section while he again picked up the Sports section.

1359 hours, Hartsfield International Airport

Delta flight 1164 lifted off the runway headed for the Washington-Dulles Airport. David Lytle looked at his watch and saw the time was exactly 1359 hours. 'That's a first,' he said to himself, 'right on time.'

1616 hours, Atlanta, CNN

Sam and Mary sat on the couch of the hotel room, executing their part of the plan, waiting, waiting for the news that they were dead. The half-hour news program was just about to get to the weather when the CNN newscaster reported a news story.

"One American is presumed dead and his wife is missing and may have drowned while vacationing at a small resort on the island of Virgin Gorda. According to the report by BVI police, retired United States Army Major Sam Call, died while snorkeling with his wife, Mary. A body was found on a reef and is presumed to be that of Major Call, but a positive identification of the remains has yet to be made. The body of Mary Call has not yet been found. You might recall that Major Call was in the center of the bizarre case in Chicago four years ago in which he claimed many of the graves that were marked as German POWs were actually American soldiers who had been murdered and thus allowed German POWs to assume the identities of the American soldiers. Mr. Michael Ream, then a prominent businessman of Chicago, was accused by Call to be one of those POWS, and during the unearthing of one of the graves, Ream shot and killed Lieutenant Colonel Dana Jackson and wounded Major Call. He was later convicted of murder, and attempted murder, and was sentence to twenty years to life. The search continues for Mary Call."

Sam reached for the phone.

1616 hours, Stafford, VA

He was reading the paper when he thought he heard something familiar from the TV, he looked up to listen. "According to the report by the British Virgin Islands, retired United States Army Major Sam Call, died while snorkeling with his wife, Mary."

"Oh my God!" He listened to the rest of the CNN broadcast. When it was done he stood up, went to the closet, and got his coat."

"I've got to go to the office; I'll be back in a couple of hours."

"Do I want to know why?"

He walked over and kissed her goodbye. "No," and shook his head, "you don't."

1616 hours, somewhere in the Washington D.C. suburbs

It had been a long day. First there was the boring drive from the cabin to O'Hare airport, the hassle he had to go through to change his scheduled flight from the Orlando back to D.C., then that flight was delayed, and then the traffic. He had picked his car up at the short-term parking lot, left the airport, and traffic on 267 was fine. All he had to do was take 495 one mile to 66, then off at the first exit, Gallows Road, and he was done. But halfway down 495, there is an accident at Leesburg Pike interchange, traffic was completely stopped, and he was trapped. Normally he'd flash the FBI badge, drive up the side of the road, and out of the traffic, but not today. Today he was transporting some property it would not be good to be caught with.

When he finally got to the apartment complex, he parked his car in the parking garage, then half drug his exhausted body into the elevator, then down the hall to his lonely, and barely used apartment. Standing in front of the door with a small suitcase in his left hand, he stared at the door as if he were begging it to open on its own, he was just too tired to do it himself. Dropping the suitcase to the floor, it hit with a quiet thud. He reached into his pocket, received the door key, then slowly opened the apartment door. Not slow like the cautious professional he was, not slow as to not alert the potential victim, or adversary inside, but slowly like a man too tired to drag himself into the apartment.

He pushed the door and watched as it opened wide. He looked inside with a blank stare, then without thinking, picked up the bag, walked inside, and then dropped the suitcase on the floor by the small kitchen table. Taking a plastic trash bag from under the counter, he put the coat, gloves and boots he was wearing into the plastic trash bag, sealed it, and placed it by the door. He would take it to a commercial dumpster in a few minutes when he went out for some food.

Returning to the table, he picked up the suitcase and placed it on the table. He opened the bag, pushed some dirty clothes out of the way and retrieved a towel that been used to protect this new prize. Laying the towel gently on the table, he carefully unwrapped the object as if it were a delicate treasure. With just the mere touch of his new prize his exhausted state had been replaced with the energy of a well-rested man, and his rough, steel-handed actions replaced with the gentle movements of a surgeon.

He pulled back one corner of the towel, then the next, and finally, with great care, almost love, picked up the vintage weapon, and admired his new possession, a Colt 45 caliber revolver, commonly known as The Peacemaker.

"What a weapon," Lee said out loud. "U.S. Army standard Calvary issue from 1873 to 1892, and..." Lee stopped and examined the weapon closer, rubbing some dirt off the serial number, then read it, 4583. He stopped and went to a book case at the other side of the room, put down the revolver and looked through the bookcase until he found it, *Pistols of the world : a comprehensive illustrated encyclopedia of the world's pistols and revolvers from 1870 to the present day* by Ian V, Hogg. He quickly found the page on the PeaceMaker and read it outloud. "The Peacemaker was used by Col. G.A. Custer's 7th Cavalry at the Little Bighorn. The number range of possible Little Bighorn Colts is 4500 - 7527."

Lee looked at his new prize, put down the book, picked up the revolver, and reread the serial number. "Four Five Eight Three. Oh my God, the fool didn't know what he had."

As he gently caressed the pistol his cell phone rang, startling him and he almost drop the revolver.

"Lee here."

"Are they off the grid?"

Lee immediately knew the familiar voice of Luby. He had hoped to have completed both missions before having to speak with him but that was now impossible. "The first one is, and I am about to depart for the second location now." There was a long pause without a response from Luby, and that made Lee even more anxious.

"Are you in Orlando?" came a stern yet concerned reply.

"No, Sir. I had to return to D.C. for," he paused, he had not planned on this conversation and he was unprepared to respond with a sufficient excuse, "for new equipment."

"I don't give a damn what you need. The commission is shut down, Ream's off the gird, and the target in Orlando is the last connection to the entire affair. Take care of it."

"Yes, Sir," Lee answered quietly and subordinately.

"Now," Luby screamed, and the call ended.

Lee held the phone in his right hand and stared at the phone as if it were the source of his anger and not Luby. He suddenly pulled his arm up to his shoulder as if he were a pitcher about to throw a baseball. His body shook a little from held-in frustration, then he completed the delivery towards the wall, but did not release the phone.

"ARGH!" Lee stood there for a moment with his eyes closed. He opened his eyes, looked at the phone, then smiled as he saw the revolver on the table. Without taking his eyes off the revolver, he put the phone on the table and picked up the Colt. Holding the weapon in his hand, he looked up and saw his reflection in the window.

"What are you looking at, Luby?" Holding the pistol in his hand, he stepped back from the table, then as if he were in a movie, he pulled the colt to his side and pretended to put it into a holster that was strapped to his hip.

"If you feel lucky?" Lee taunted his imaginary foe. He stepped back one more step and readied himself. Then, as if he were the principle player in an old west gunfight, he drew his weapon. He squeezed the trigger, and the hammer made a loud click as the firing pin struck the unloaded weapon. Lee stood motionless for a moment, then pulled the barrel to his lips and blew on the end of the barrel, as if he were blowing the smoke away from his just fired weapon.

He looked down at the ground like he were looking at his fallen victim. He smiled, one of satisfaction, then, with the reverence he had shown it while unpacking, he rewrapped the weapon and placed it in a drawer. Turning back to the 'dead gunfighter' he spoke to him, "I'll go to Orlando when I damn ready." He picked up the cell phone, pushed the 'power off' button, and then went to take a shower.

1616 hours, Washington-Dulles Airport

David looked at his watch as he exited the plane, 'Not bad' he thought, 'only twenty-five minutes late. Almost on-time.' As he walked towards the rental car counter, his cell phone ran.

"Lytle here."

"It's Sam, have you seen the news?"

"Just arrived, still at the airport. Did it hit?"

"It hit CNN."

"Damn man, you hit the big time."

"It would seem. Mary had already called all the kids and her mother, so there won't be any panic if and when they see the report. And presuming the other side has seen it too they should be relaxed."

"You can be sure they have," David said as he continued to walk to the terminal exit.

"I decided to wait until after seventeen-hundred hours before going to the police. I think it will be less likely that the local guys will think it necessary to run it up the flagpole and make it a major issue on a Sunday night."

"Good idea. Break a leg, as they say."

Sam caught the dramatic play on words. "Hopefully it won't be that painful. Out here."

1710 hours, Pentagon, VA

John Mack signed in at the security desk telling the guard he had to check something for a briefing in the morning and that he wouldn't be long. He went directly to his office, logged on to his terminal and accessed the PERSCOM personnel database. Once the system was up, he entered the name Harvey Nichols, and the screen filled with a number of entries. He scrolled down to the only officer in the list, selected the line, hit 'Return,' watched as the entire record was delivered, and then hit the 'Print' button. He read the screen as the report was being printed. He thought about using the office phone, but wisely had second thoughts. He logged off, left the building, and drove straight home.

1710 hours

David knocked at the apartment door, and a moment later, a beautiful woman opened the door, saw him, and smiled. She put her finger across her lips, moved her left hand to the top of the door, and then stood beside the open door with her right hand set upon her more than ample hips. "Well hello, darlin'. Now that's what I like, a man who is prompt on making good on what he owes."

"Now I thought you liked something else about me."

"Give me a minute, Baby," she cooed as she had him enter and then closed the door behind him. "I'll be getting to that."

"By the way, I'll need that 9mm I asked you to hold for me. You still have it?"

"Of course," she took him by the hand. "But you owe storage fee on that too, Baby."

"I don't know if I brought enough to pay all these bills."

She stopped and kissed him softly, "Baby, you always have enough."

1755 hours, Stafford, VA

John Mack walked into his home and immediately went to the phone and dialed.

"Hello, Sam."

"Hi, John," came the reply.

"I have the data you wanted."

"Already? I figured you would have waited until Monday."

"Yeah, I was going to, but I was watching TV and saw you were dead."

"Yeah, well that happens to us all. It's kind of interesting being alive and seeing it play out."

"Sam." John's tone went from friendly sarcasm to a serious one. "The guy is a fraud, he wasn't in Nam. According to the database, he was active duty for two years, then went to the reserves. Never left Indiana except for basic training, for Christ's sake."

"I thought as much. I've heard of bums like him who claim to be vets, even heroes, but I never met one."

"Until now, Sam. Until now. "

"Roger that."

"I have a copy of his Form 2. I'll email it or fax it if you like. What are you going to do?" John said as he saw his wife come into the room.

"I'm not totally sure, but I'm thinking newspapers and reporters may be involved."

"You going to say your data came from a confidential Pentagon source?"

"No, John. You know that the Army will check the log and see you made the inquiry."

"I can take the heat, Sam. I owe you."

"Thanks, Buddy, but I think the press has a way of getting data on their own once they get some helpful hints; Freedom of Information Act and all that. I know someone in Chicago I can trust to see that the story gets out."

"Okay. Good Luck, Sam."

"Roger, out here," came the reply.

John turned to his wife who had been listening.

"Was that Sam Call?"

"Yes, it was."

"Did you get what he needed?" She was concerned and looked in her husband's eyes as she asked. She could always tell the truth by looking in his eyes.

"Yep."

"Good," she kissed him on the cheek. "I owe him."

"You?" John responded curiously.

She turned back towards her husband. "He saved your life, my husband." She paused then continued. "And without him, you wouldn't have come home, and we wouldn't have our son." She took the few steps back to her husband and stood in front of him. "He saved your life, and *I* owe him. And if he asks for you to go and punch the Chief Of Staff of the United States Army right in the mouth, I better not hear you hesitated," she kissed him again and went back to her work.

1833 hours, Holiday Inn, Alpharetta, GA

Sam and Mary sat in the uncomfortable chairs at the hotel waiting. Sam was drinking coffee as always, and Mary was drinking a Dr. Pepper. He looked over at her.

"I've grown to love that stuff." Sam pointed at the soda she was drinking. "Especially in cans." They both laughed a little.

"You ready?"

"As ready as I will ever be."

Sam picked up the phone again and dialed.

"Alpharetta Police Department, may I help you."

"Yes. I'd like to report I'm alive."

There was a pause at the other end. "This line is reserved for official police business and any joking around will be dealt with, Sir."

"I understand that officer, but I need to report I am alive."

Again there was a pause, but before the officer on the other end could hang up or provide another response, Sam spoke again. "I heard a report on CNN that I have been reported dead, but I am not. My wife and I are here in Alpharetta."

"Your name sir?"

"Sam Call, Major Sam Call."

"One moment." The line went silent while the officer was away. "Where are you now, Major?"

"The Holiday Inn in Alpharetta."

"We would like you to come into the station, please."

"Certainly. We can be there in ten minutes," Sam hung up and turned to Mary. "Show time!"

- - - - - - - - - - - - - - - < > - - - - - - - - - - - - - - - -

The officer on duty had been watching them on camera since they pulled into the parking lot. He followed them as they came up the steps into the building, and when they finally reached the glass barrier, he turned away from the monitor to the person standing on the other side of the bulletproof glass.

"I'm Sam Call and this is my wife, Mary. I called about being alive."

The police officer behind the bulletproof glass looked at him very oddly.

"I phoned a few minutes ago."

The officer didn't respond but instead picked up the phone and punched in two numbers, spoke something Sam could not hear then put the phone down. "Officer William Matthews will be right with you."

Two minutes later the door to the right of them opened and another police officer greeted them.

"I'm Officer Matthews. Please come with me." Sam and Mary followed the officer through the door, then down a corridor to a small room that had a table and four chairs. Sam looked about the well-lit, very white room that was otherwise bare. He noticed a small camera in the ceiling towards the back corner of the room and thought the room looked just like an interrogation room he had seen on countless TV shows.

"Please have a seat," the officer motioned to Sam and Mary to sit in the chairs that directly faced the camera. Sam held the chair for Mary, then sat beside her.

"So Major Call, you called and said you were alive; I can see you both are." The officer was smiling, but Sam knew he was not amused.

"Yes. We saw a report on CNN that we, rather I, seem to have been found dead, and Mary was missing and presumed dead. And as you can see we are neither dead nor missing." Sam was enjoying the game.

"I see," the officer paused for a moment. "We made some inquiries after you called earlier and if I may correct you, *you*, Major, are presumed dead." The officer turned to Mary, "and *you* are presumed to have killed him."

"Oh my," Mary gasped as she had planned to do.

"May I see some identification?"

Sam pulled out his wallet and got his driver's license and Mary did the same, getting hers from her handbag. The officer looked at both of the them, thanked them, but kept the IDs.

"So why don't you tell me want happened."

Sam told the story of the trip, how great the place was, and how they enjoyed everything. After a few minutes, the officer interrupted.

"That's fine, but I am wondering why they think you are dead?"

"Oh, well, I don't really know. We were snorkeling on our last day there, and Mary cut her arm on some sharp coral. We got back in the boat and went right back to the resort. But we had to go to another island for her medical treatment and it takes a long time to get there by boat. By the time we got there and got treatment, it was late evening, and we couldn't go back to the resort at night—they don't have water taxis at night. So since we had to leave the next morning anyway, we just left that night from Tortola."

"I see," the officer looked at Mary. "And you are okay now?"

"Oh yes. I went to the doctor as soon as we got home." Mary looked at Sam as if to get concurrence from Sam, who nodded.

"It seems they found your boat adrift in the ocean. Can you explain that?" The officer looked at Sam and then to Mary.

Sam shrugged. "I don't know how. We went to Prickly Pear Island, landed our boat and had lunch. Then we went into the water and swam for like an hour along the beach looking at the fish and the coral. Mary went to grab a conch shell and cut her arm."

"It was very frightening," Mary interjected with an air of dramatic innocence.

Sam looked at her and nodded again. "We came to the surface, I looked at her arm, got right in the boat, and went back," Sam looked at Mary and then back at the officer. "That's it."

"You say you snorkeled for an hour, swimming up the beach."

"Yes, that's right."

"And then when your wife cut her arm you left the water right away and took your boat back to the resort?"

"Yes."

"Well if you swam for an hour how was the boat right there?"

Sam opened his mouth as if to speak but said nothing. Then looked at Mary and then back at the officer. "I mean the boat was right there." He looked back at Mary, then stammered as he talked. "It was there on the beach, and..."

"Oh, Sam!" Mary spoke loudly, "We stole someone's boat. Are we going to jail for stealing a boat?" She grabbed Sam and looked very nervous.

"I, I didn't think about it before. I never thought how the boat was right there. It looked like the resort boat. I mean it was a little Boston Whaler, a little red engine, Biras Creek cushions—the whole thing." Sam looked at Mary then back to the officer. "Now what?"

"Well it seems to make sense. You came back in a resort boat someone else had signed out. The report says the man on duty remembers you coming back and sending you, or someone, to the hospital. Then later on, they found the boat you had originally signed out. I suspect that person found his boat missing and then used yours."

"Oh my God!" Mary grabbed Sam again, "And the boat sank. Oh my God, Sam."

"No ma'am. The boat was fine. It wasn't the boat, he must have fallen out and drowned or tried to walk on the coral. When they found him the coral had pretty much torn all the flesh off the front of his body."

Mary looked like she was getting sick, and putting her hands to her mouth she buried her face in Sam's chest. Sam put his arms around her to comfort her.

"I think we have enough for now," The officer said as he stood up. "We will inform the proper authorities that you are both safe and sound, and this is a case of mistaken identity." He motioned to the door and Sam stood and helped Mary. The officer gave Sam their IDs and led them to the entrance.

"We will call you if we need you," the officer said as he opened the door for them. Sam thanked him, escorted Mary to the car, opened the door, and Mary got in. Sam then calmly walked to the driver's side, got in, started the car and pulled out onto the road. After a minute, he looked over at Mary who was still looking out the window.

"Are you familiar with the phase, 'Over acting'?" Sam said as he pulled onto Georgia 400.

Mary turned to Sam looking fresh and alert, not at all like the distraught woman of a few minutes ago. "Over acting? Are you kidding? I was Meryl Streep in there. I'm thinking Academy Award time."

"Meryl Streep, huh? You know who she went to high school with?" Sam looked over and smiled. "Sigourney Weaver. No, Really."

Mary's face got all scrunched up and her eyes became slits as she frowned at Sam. "You and Sigourney Weaver. You are so dead, Call. I should have left you there in the water waiting for her." Then she punched him in the shoulder.

"Ouch! That hurt"

"Serves you right," Mary smiled at Sam as they sped down the highway.

Chapter 15

Monday, October 24

0945 hours, Chicago

It was a small group of offices in a rundown building in an equally rundown section of Chicago. The area was not a bad section of town where a person wasn't safe walking the street, nor were prostitutes hanging on every corner waiting for their lonely or sometimes dangerous johns. It was just an old, tired, business district, inhabited by companies and organizations that were on the downward side of solvency or in most cases never had it. It was the home of struggling middlemen and making a buck by reselling everything from bulk chemicals to socks and never touching the product. It was the home of young entrepreneurs with real ideas, real dreams, with no money, and who were grateful for a building they could afford. It was a home for old bookstores that cleared just enough to keep the proprietor alive. It was home to "Save the Earth", "Save the Whales", "Honesty in Government", and numerous other organizations whose heart and dedication to their cause far exceeded their ability to pay.

On the third floor of one of the many buildings whose better days where now just distant memories, one such dedicated group of appointees and volunteers worked to help solve a nearly fifty-year-old series of crimes.

Four years ago, when the story rocked the populous and the local newspapers were full of editorials and Letters to the Editor all clamoring for justice, a small multi-organizational group was formed with the mission of uncovering a forty-five year old mystery of stolen identity and murder.

The commission was hindered by the lack of cooperation from the only known witness, and principle perpetrator in the plot. With a lack of any leads that weren't almost a half-century old and a general lack of cooperation between the governmental agencies assigned to the task force, there was little accomplished in four years other than producing a long report that reiterated the basic knowledge that was known, when the commission began.

While the news was smack in the public eye, every politician in ear shot of the Trib, Times, or local TV used the commission to advance their agenda, and while the news was hot, they were all to willing to provide their support. However, as the years went on and the news media's interest waned, so did that of the politicians. As the news coverage ended, the commission appointees hustled to create a final report and move on to more 'in the news' causes.

There was one bright spot in the bureaucratic mess: how the local people responded by volunteering to conduct searches, make calls, and do whatever they could to help a charming, old Italian lady finally find the truth about the death of her husband of just four days. Through local action groups, the volunteers had convinced the City government to continue to fund the operation of the commission; however, their generosity was limited to paying for the building space and limited phone service and supplies. Everything else, including all labor, would be volunteers except for one low-level bureaucrat, who would act as the city's representative.

It was the job of this single government official to oversee the operation, make sure the funding was not overspent, and to keep the District Attorney's office informed of any significant developments or findings. The DA's representative on the commission was Parnell Thomas, a twenty-eight year government employee whose contribution to his community had been in the form of two years as a clerk in the welfare office followed by twenty-six years of managerial duties that included collecting data on work performed by subordinates and forwarding reports to his managers.

Despite his totally innocuous service and his successful efforts to remain completely anonymous and accomplish nothing except getting a paycheck, he wasn't all that bad of a person. Parnell Thomas was a fifty-six year Old Man, who made no effort to hide nor shed the thirty extra pounds that hung over his belt. He was balding, and had been for ten years. What little hair he had on the top of his head, he grew long, and he jelled it to cover what he could. He was a man who never exercised, and even as a boy, he did not engage in any sports, not even with the neighborhood kids. He was soft; his skin hung loose on his frame from over eating and under working. He was so out of shape he panted just walking up a flight of stairs. His only goal in life was to complete thirty years on the city payroll and spend the rest of his life in his tiny home watching TV and drinking his cheap wine.

He was aware of the commission, but he didn't follow it in the papers—he didn't read newspapers. He knew little from the radio or TV news, as he only watched game shows, and cooking shows. When the DA's assistant asked him to take the coordinator's job on the commission, he didn't care that his job was the only city job left on the commission. He had no concern that the commission was being moved from a nice downtown building to a run down walkup in South Chicago. His only concern was that he do as little as possible until his retirement date. So when the DA's assistant asked him if he would be able to keep the DA informed of any important events within the commission, he agreed without hesitation.

Thomas was in his office, the only private office in the group's operation. He was nearly asleep from inactivity and his overweight body struggled to remain in the chair. Outside the office, volunteers made phone calls, tracked down leads, researched old courthouse and newspaper records searching for clues that would help solve the mystery. Coordinating the day-to-day operations on behalf of the FEB was Tim Walsh.

After graduating from University of Georgia, Walsh had moved to Chicago. He told everyone he needed to be 'in the hub of the financial action,' but actually he was following the love of his life, Maggie. He had met her while attending UGA and had fallen hard for her. She was beautiful, charming, educated, and focused on her career in child psychology, and that was just fine for Tim, for career for him was first and foremost. When Maggie graduated from her Masters program, Tim was in his internship in Atlanta. Tim was enthralled with business; his drive for success in the financial world had been well honed over years of study, and association with the right people.

After dating for over two years and being together every day, his internship in Atlanta gave them some time alone. When Maggie left for Chicago, they parted as friends, and Tim used the added free time to immerse himself in learning the corporate world. Three months later Tim completed his internship and accepted the position in Chicago. It was just coincidence that his best offer was in the same city as her, at least that is what he told Maggie, when he just happened to bump into her on his first day in Chicago. He never told her that it took three calls to her father to get the address of her office and eighty dollars for a taxi to sit at the curb outside her office while he waited to 'bump into her.' He took her to dinner that Friday night, and two weeks later, he spent the night at her place. Three weeks later he gave his landlord notice he would not be renewing his month-to-month lease.

Tim was a natural with people, and even those with vastly more experience were charmed and at ease with his confident and respectful style of conversing with people. Although he was the junior man, he was the natural selection to represent his company in the FEB.

He was having a lunch meeting at the Chicago Federal Executive Board (FEB) on South Dearborn Street in Chicago when he saw Major Sam Call first interviewed on TV. He immediately became captivated by the events that were being reported. When the word came down that a commission was being put together, Tim was the first volunteer.

Since he worked at the FEB, which is a most unique federal agency in that its charter was not to manage, build, disperse funds, or inspect anything. The mission of the organization was to serve as a meeting place and a communications portal for every federal agency in the country; everything from the FBI to the Peace Corps, from The Department of Agriculture to the Department of Veterans Affairs, the office of the Senators, FDIC, DOD, DOE, NRC and everyone in between. Anyone who is anyone is represented on the FEB, and when the shit hit the fan in Chicago, everyone wanted an ear inside the committee. A few calls from well-placed Department heads, and Tim was named as the FEB's representative to the committee.

Tim was there Day One when the doors opened and greeted Sam warmly when he first arrived, and he said goodbye to Sam when he left the team. Having watched the news unfold, Tim had first thought of Sam as a crusader, some sort of brave, selfless hero who had to fight for justice, and he wanted to be part of that crusade. Over the two years they worked together on the commission, they had become good friends and he learned that Sam was just an honorable man who couldn't leave another soldier behind.

Tim had been reading through one of the thousands of records the army had provided in hope that there was a clue that would shed some light on the identities of the POWs but what he had heard on CNN made it difficult to concentrate. A good friend was dead and now he was even more committed to solving the puzzle his friend had begun. He dropped one record into the pile and picked up another when the phone rang.

"POW investigation Center, Tim Walsh speaking."

"How many times do I have to tell you? Its The United States Attorney's Office, United States Army, and City of Chicago Special Joint Review Team, Investigating the Events of 1944 and 1945, Relevant to the Reported Deaths of German POWs, United States Army Sergeant Jonathan Simon and Associated Deaths of that Period."

"Sam?" came a tentative reply.

"It's me buddy."

"Sam, is it really you?"

"Yes. I take it you saw the news. I'm still alive. It wasn't me, just a case of mistaken identity."

"Holy shit, Sam. I don't know what to say."

"Say you're glad I'm not crab bait on some island coral reef."

"Oh yeah, Sam, it's so good someone else is crab bait. I mean that you are not crab bait. I mean that I am glad you're alive"

"Settle down old boy, I am glad I am alive as well," Sam paused for a moment. "Can you talk?"

"Sure, Sam."

"I want to know about Ream."

"Ream?"

"Yes."

"Why? I mean you know what I know—more. We didn't learn anything new on him since you left the team, you know that Sam."

"I want to know about why he was coming to Chicago. Why you guys called him in again?"

"We didn't call him in Sam, he called us."

"What? He called you? Why?"

"We really don't know what he wanted, just that his lawyer contacted Thomas, then Thomas called the District Attorney. I wouldn't have even heard about it at all if Cynthia Cooper hadn't called me from the DA's office."

"Ream called, not the other way around?"

"Yes. Ream's lawyer told Thomas that Ream wanted to talk to us."

"I don't get it. I talked to Curling, and he said that you guys just wanted to close the books on the case, that you called Ream in."

"I don't know why he'd say that. The whole thing is strange."

"Why's that?"

"Well for one thing, we had tried to talk to Ream for four years and when we finally get a chance to talk to him, no one did anything."

"Say again," Sam asked.

"Well, according to Cooper, Ream would have come in on Monday, but as of Friday we hadn't made any arrangements for his visit. There was no agenda prepared, no invitees, no list of questions to ask, nothing. It was almost like he wasn't coming–but he was. I don't get it."

"I don't either. Tim, I need you to call Cooper and see what you can find out. See if she knows what Ream was going to do?"

"Sure thing."

"And Tim."

"Yeah?"

"Be careful what you say. It could be dangerous if certain people think you are snooping. Okay?"

Tim said nothing for a moment while he thought of the implications. "I can do it, Sam."

"Thanks. Listen I got to go. Be sure and give my regards to everyone."

"Yeah, I'll tell them you're alive."

"That will be good. Bye." Sam hit the speaker button and ended the call.

- - - - - - - - - - - - < > - - - - - - - - - - - - - -

Sam put the phone down and turned to Mary who had heard the entire call, "What do you think?"

"I think your Mr. Curling has some explaining to do."

"I don't get it. Why would he do this?" Sam raised both his hands into the air and shrugged his shoulders.

"I suggest you make some calls about Mr. Curling."

"Yes. I think that would be advisable."

1530 hours, Washington. D.C

It hadn't been hard for him to gain access to the parking garage. He had parked across the street, got a good vantage point for the garage and waited for a likely target to appear. He was waiting for a woman, a small man, or an older couple to drive up. Not that it was essential that it be one of them, but doing so lessened the likelihood of running into some macho man who would give him trouble just for the fun of it. Within twenty minutes a Cadillac with an older couple pulled up to the gate and David quickly walked over to the car. As the driver opened the window to enter the entry code David greeted them.

"Hello there folks." He opened his wallet and showed them a fake ID. "I'm with condo security just checking to make sure you are comfortable, that you haven't seen anyone hanging around that shouldn't be here, things like that?"

"Why? Have there been?" The man asked worriedly.

"Nope. Not a one. But we keep asking just to be sure," David smiled at them to reassure him of his friendliness.

"Well, that's good to hear," the man said.

The passenger, a woman and obviously the man's wife, leaned over towards David. "We haven't seen anyone hanging around."

"Well that's good to hear too. You folks have a grand day." David gave them a casual salute and a big smile as he stood there by window.

"You too young man, and thank you."

"My pleasure," David replied as he watched the Old Man enter his pass code. The gate opened and the Cadillac slowly entered the garage as David waved. When the car was out of sight, he returned to his car. He started the engine and slowly moved his car from its illegal parking place across the street. He pulled up to the gate and entered the code he had just stolen from the Old Man. The gate opened and David drove in slowly. He drove all the floors of the garage looking for both a good spot to park and to see if there was any security in the garage. After covering the four levels, he found there were no security guards and the only cameras were facing the elevator doors on each floor. He knew he could park and wait without detection. He drove back to the first level, backed into a parking place where he could see the comings and goings at the garage entrance, and waited.

1530 hours, Chicago

Curling sat at his desk at home reviewing the case file. This one would be perfect for the media; a corrupt local bureaucrat murdering his girl friend to keep it away from his rich wife. "Damn what a beautiful case. It's a slam dunk." A couple more like this and watch out Mr. Mayor, I'm right behind you," he said aloud to himself, as the phone rang; it was his personal line.

"Curling here."

"This is Garrett."

"I've asked you not to call me at my office. I am not comfortable with a connection to the FBI for God's sake, especially now. I took a big enough chance already."

"Look, nothing's going to happen. Ream is dead and no one is going to make the connection to Ream's travel schedule and you. You're safe, it's over. Ream's dead, Call's dead, and the rest of the operation is shut down. No one cares about this anymore. You just need to make sure the Commission stays closed."

"What are you talking about, Garrett?"

"I'm talking about you settling down and putting this behind you. The commission is done and nothing has come of it. It's over."

"No, I mean Call. When did he die?"

"He drowned a couple of days ago snorkeling off some island. They found his body yesterday."

"Call's not dead. I just talked to him yesterday."

"What!"

"Yeah, he called me about Ream. He wanted to know what happened to him."

"When did he call? From where?"

"I don't know from where, like I said. he called Monday sometime around seven or so. I was at the office late."

"Jesus Christ! I've got to go. Don't say a damn thing about Call to anyone. And for God's sake if he calls again, find out where he is calling from and call me."

"What's going on?"

"Just do what your told, Curling," and Garrett hung up the phone.

1545 hours, Washington, D.C.

Christopher Garrett sat in his office staring out the window. He now knew where Wood was, and he also knew he had to call Luby. He picked up the phone and apprehensively dialed. Two rings and the all too familiar voice answered.

"Luby here."

"This is Garrett. We have a problem."

"What is it?"

Garrett whispered into the phone, "Call is alive, he phoned Curling in Chicago asking about Ream."

"I thought Call was off the grid. What happened to Wood?"

"Somehow Call must have gotten him. Obviously it's his body they recovered in Virgin Gorda."

There was a deadly silence on the other end of the call.

"Where is Call now?"

"I don't know. He didn't tell Curling or Curling didn't ask. Either way we don't know yet."

"Anyone on it?"

"Not yet."

"Why not?"

"I was thinking how to work it."

"What's to think about? He was a loose end before, and now he's more so. Take care of it; don't you use Lee, I got him busy."

267

"I am having a problem with this one." He stammered for a moment, surprised he had even spoken the words, and now he was unsure how to proceed. He hadn't been fully behind this one since the beginning, being unable to personally find any way to make the soldier a threat to society. The order to 'take Call off the grid' had pushed him to the edge, and now he was having a problem continuing with the mission. "Besides," Garrett continued, "If Call is taken out now there is no way anyone is going to believe it was an accident."

"It no longer matters. Ream is dead. The commission is done and the names are safe. AliceK is secure and there is no activity on it. Is there?"

"No Sir, not since the first two hits."

"Then you complete the mission; take Call off the grid and the problem is eliminated."

"I understand about Call and Ream, but there are still two living. What about them?"

"There is just one living and the other is scheduled."

Garrett was shocked to hear this, and now realized Luby had assigned Lee to take care of the two. "Is that necessary?"

Luby's normal voice was low and deep, and it naturally connoted command and control. When he spoke, people unconsciously found themselves feeling subordinate. When needed, Luby could exaggerate that talent to impose his will by merely speaking; those who worked for him sometimes actually felt fear when he spoke. Luby invoked his talent. "Don't you worry about that. You need to worry about Call. Find him, complete the mission, and do it now." With that, the phone went silent.

1905 hours, Washington, D.C.

Ten cars had come in and only one had exited since he had taken his position in the garage. A light silver-colored Ford Taurus stopped at the gate and a male driver entered his pass code and the gate opened for him. The car slowly drove up the ramp, passed David and proceeded up the ramp to the next floor. David started his car and slowly followed making sure he did not alert the driver ahead of him. The car went up one more floor and took the first parking spot. David went past him, parked at the far end of the parking deck near the elevators, exited the car, moving quickly towards the elevator but at the same time trying to act as every other resident would after a long day at work.

- - - - - - - - - - - - - - < > - - - - - - - - - - - - - - -

Garrett was distracted; he was an experienced FBI agent, but right now he was totally unaware of his surroundings. He was more like a rookie then the veteran he was. The normal job was a strain, but that went with the territory; he could handle that. He was prepared and trained for that. As he drove his car up the ramp, he caught sight of himself in the mirror, and he thought he looked like a man near the edge—or maybe over the edge.

He parked the car and thought, well at least he was home, alone as always; or at least as always since Carrie walked out. He locked the car and walked directly to the elevator just looking at his own feet as he drug himself to the door. As the elevator door opened, Garrett entered and pushed the button for his floor. Later, when he thought about it, he wouldn't be sure if the second man was exceptionally quiet or was he just that distracted that he didn't see him walk to the elevator or enter it until he was in his face.

"What do you want?' He stared at the man who was now facing him. He could see he had a gun in his right hand and that it was pointed directly at his mid-section.

"Just go upstairs to your condo, Mr. Garrett, and there's no problem."

Garrett was not surprised that the man knew his name, he was only surprised that he had not even noticed him until it was too late. Garrett said nothing while the elevator rose. The man had stepped to his left and got his back to the side of the elevator so he could see him, the door, and the light that indicated his floor. Garrett had pushed the button for the sixth floor, and now the elevator door was opening on his floor.

"Get out slowly and go to your apartment, please," the assailant directed him out of the elevator. As he stepped out of the elevator he added, "And for both our sakes, Mr. Garrett, let's not try some FBI counter measures. Neither of us wants to end up dead."

Garrett nodded and walked to the door and then stopped. "I need to get my key."

The man, keeping his distance, acknowledged with a simple, "By all means."

Garrett slowly reached into his pocket, got his key ring, selected the door key, and opened the door.

"Now just push it open and step back, please." The man had stepped to his left preventing any chance of Garrett being able to push him away and escape inside his apartment.

Garrett opened the door and stepped away. He knew the assailant was well trained and wasn't going to let Garrett use the heavy door as a weapon to slam on him as he entered. The would-be assailant, while watching Garret, stepped into the room first, and motioned him to follow. When Garrett had entered the room the door closed behind him.

"Now carefully take off your jacket and lay in on the floor please."

Garrett complied.

"Now put your service weapon on the jacket."

Garrett was thinking about making a move to get the weapon and take his chances, at least he would have a possibility of taking him out.

"Please don't think about making a move on me. Even if I wasn't trained, and by now you know I am, I wouldn't miss with a killing shot from here."

Garrett mentally agreed and then complied with the request.

"Now drop your pants." The man motioned with his pistol for the pants to drop.

Garrett was pissed and thought how ridiculous it would look when they find his body. *An FBI man literally caught with his pants down.* In the midst of this life threatening event, he was suddenly amazed how odd it was that this is what he was thinking about. He dropped his pants.

"Now if you will," the man pointed to the small 32-caliber pistol he had strapped to his right leg.

Garrett took it and put it in the pile with the other discarded items.

"Now put your pants back on, you look ridiculous," David said in a less threatening, almost friendly tone, more like a friend than that of a potential killer.

Garrett was grateful to get some of his dignity back and quickly complied. The man walked casually over to a soft cushioned chair that sat directly in front of a full-length window and sat down. "Please, sit down." He then pointed to a hard-back dinner table chair. "There, please."

Garrett sat in the chair ten feet from his service revolver. As he tried to examine his assailant, he had to squint as the evening sun streamed through the window behind the man and disturbed his own vision, but not the vision of his captor.

"My name is David, and I am here for information."

"Well, *David*, is this an attempt to get friendly with me, gain my confidence, and have me volunteer state secrets to you? Forget it, *David*, if that is your name."

"My name *is* David and I suspect that by tomorrow you will know it and all about me. That is inevitable." David put his weapon down on the end table beside him. "I told you, I have no intentions of harming you—unless of course you move on me."

"Okay, you have my attention."

"Before I ask you some questions let me give you a dump."

Garrett nodded.

"I know you are Christopher Garrett, FBI, now of a small group that works international crime contacts, whatever that is. I suspect that is what the FBI officially calls it. You call it NECO."

That got his attention, and as much as he tried not to show a reaction, he knew he had.

"You work for Luby, an egocentric, cold-war throwback that nothing comes between him and what he thinks is best for this country. Killing 'Commies for Christ' was his favorite pastime, and when he did his dirty work, everyone looked the other way. The powers-that-be know about his death squad but as long as it got the job done, what the hell, right? When the cold war ended the playground should have also ended—but it didn't. I'll get back to that."

David stood up and picked up his pistol, and casually carrying it in his left hand, walked to the table, picked up the two weapons he had Garrett discard, and went to the refrigerator. "You have anything to drink?" Garrett did not respond. He opened the refrig, placed both weapons inside and took out two Coronas, opened a couple of drawers, found an opener and opened both bottles, then walked to Garrett, gave him one and returned to his chair. "Thanks, I'm parched," David said as if he was a guest and his host had provided refreshment. "This has got to be the last brand without a twist-off cap. Why is that?"

Garrett watched the man in fascination. He was as casual as if he was a friend of his who he had invited in for a chat.

"So, where were we?"

"Cold War," Garrett volunteered.

"Yes, thank you. Actually, I was past that. You on the other hand are about as opposite of Luby as could be. A hero rookie agent, who saved the lives of two fellow agents, and shot a suspect through the eye at thirty feet."

"Forehead," Garrett offered without emotion.

"Through the forehead at thirty feet," David continued. "Awards and promotions and then *bam* you're with Luby." David looked at Garrett for a minute. "You know I've done my homework on this." Garrett said nothing. "You were a bright, dedicated, moral agent with a good future." David paused for a moment for effect and then continued, "And a good woman. Nights at the theater, a community player involved in Big Brother activities—I did think it was kind of ironic with you in the government and already a *Big Brother* as it were." David waited for Garrett to see the humor in that play on words, but he had no reaction.

"Well either way, now it's all gone. One would have to ask, why?"

For the first time Garrett was getting emotional, but not the emotion of fearing death; now it was of a failed life—he didn't like thinking of his lost future, and he thought 'Who was this asshole to talk to me about it anyway?' "What business is it of yours how I spend my fucken' time?"

David knew he had struck a chord, "I don't. I only care how it enables me to know who I am dealing with. Where's his head at? Is he a fanatic or is he a regular guy that maybe took an unexpected turn? I just care to get my information."

Garrett took a breath and relaxed a little, waiting for what was coming next.

"You and your NECO team, for whatever reason, decided to take out a close friend of mine, and by doing so you are taking on me." David stared at Garrett looking for his reaction and then his voice got very serious. "Why are you after Sam Call?"

The reaction was slight, but David saw it and he knew he was right. This was the right man. "You had Rowe, which I know is not his real name, try to take Sam out and he got himself killed instead. As far as I can figure, your man was a professional killer, but not with a gun. He was totally out of his element with firearms and it cost him." David took a sip of beer, then continued. "You had Ream killed in prison— that was well done I might say; they don't have a clue who did it, by the way. Call is the man who took down Ream four years ago, and I'm thinking there is a common thread that ties Ream's murder to your effort to take out Call."

"Speaking of the attempt on Call, before your man Rowe died, he told Call about Rizzo. It wasn't a problem to find out that the FBI had rolled Rizzo over and I tracked it back to you from there, it was rather simple. Apparently Rowe didn't know you guys had taken Rizzo down years ago, so I know Rowe…" David paused hoping Garrett would fill in the correct name, "…well, was freelance. How am I doing so far?"

"Continue," was all Garrett would say.

"Now you know Call's alive. You didn't get the news from the woman who was with Rowe, she didn't know. It wasn't anyone on Virgin Gorda, and it wasn't from the police because Call is there right about now giving them the story. So it had to be someone Call talked to since he got back." David paused, "So how long has Curling been on the payroll?"

Garrett was taken back by how this man had put it all together, and so quickly. "Okay, I'll bite. We talked to Curling. But that says nothing."

David leaned forward as if to counsel a small child that was having difficulty in understanding what the parent was telling him. "Listen, Garrett, from what I know, you are, or at least were, a good man. I don't know what went wrong, but it's all wrong now. Call survived and unless I miss my guess, you have been ordered to complete the mission.

You can't win; too many people already know what I know. If Call even falls down and stubs his toe, people will be looking at you – and I'll make sure of that."

Garrett was now visibly shaken; he put both his hands to his head, as if it could clear away the problems before him.

David decided it was time to drop his trump card. "We know all about AliceK."

Garrett froze. Just knowing that name meant this man, whoever he was, was into everything.

"It was all in motion before I came onboard." Garrett let it out without thinking of where it would take him. "I thought it was for the good of the country, but now…" his voice trailed off.

"But now?" David coaxed him to continue.

"But now I'm in it, and I'm fucked. I can't get out. If I try he'll find me and I'll be dead. If I stay, then more will die, and eventually I will go down for everything."

"You want to know how I know about you? About AliceK? About NECO?" David waited for the man to respond. The frightened man now seemed calm and almost casual about David's presence there. "I am ex-military with an extensive network of strong-willed, highly dedicated and resourceful comrades that live for each other and for whom honor is everything. There's not one in the group that hasn't lost someone or hasn't seen some terrible wrong. We work together and sometimes, just sometimes, we get to set a few things right—and this is one of those times."

Garrett looked like he had the weight of his world on his shoulders. "And you are offering me a chance to clear my soul before I die?"

"Listen Garrett, forty-five years ago a number of my fellow army buddies, men who died before I was born, were murdered, and now lie in graves marked with other men's names. We have looked everywhere Ream lived, worked, touched, and found nothing. The only key to the puzzle we had was Ream and now he's dead. I think the names we are seeking are on AliceK, and you have the key to unlock them."

Garrett quietly acknowledged, "I do, yes. I do."

"Tell me about it." David gently coaxed him.

"Major Call was correct. Ream *is* Rossinger. In 1945, the four Americans, three officers and one sergeant, organized a plan to steal millions from German POW labor contracts, and they were quite successful. But Rossinger got wind of it and shut the labor pool off. He had the POWs refuse to work." He looked back at David, "Imagine that, the German POWs in Illinois refusing to work. Anyway he apparently cut a deal with the Americans and in return they assisted Rossinger in finding substitutes for some of his key people."

"And they killed the American GIs, took their places, and buried them in the nine German graves." .

"Yes. But not all of them."

"The first one was a natural death," David offered.

"Yes. When they saw how no one gave a shit about the accidental death of German POW, they came up with their plan."

"Then the next eight were Americans murdered by Rossinger?"

"No, actually only six. The second one was more or less a test by Rossinger. He was having problems with one of his people; so he killed him just to see if anyone would be suspicious."

"He killed one of his own?"

"That's correct; Ream was a total sociopath. He had no sense of remorse—zero. Then the number five guy was apparently one of his also. I think the poor slob found out what Rossinger had done, and so Rossinger killed him too."

"So that leaves six Americans killed, one being the real Michael Ream."

"Yes."

"Are any still alive?"

There was a long pause. "I don't know. As of yesterday, there were two old men; one in Minnesota and one in Florida, but I think Luby had them killed. I am fairly sure one is dead, not sure about the second."

"How do you know that?"

"Luby just talked to me about it, told me not to worry about them. Just to get Call, and he would take care of the rest, or rather he would have Lee take care of the rest. Then it would be sealed forever."

"What would be sealed? The Murders?"

"More than that. When Ream, or Rossinger, made his move to the big time in Chicago, is when he was found out. While Ream lived in Milwaukee he was off the radar; when his company was acquired the

FBI did a background check on Ream because the parent company had big government contracts, and that's when they found out he was not the real Michael Ream."

"How?"

"That part's a little hazy to me, something to do with his mother I think."

"Let me take a guess here," David said. "Luby was the investigator."

"Yep, and he kept Ream's identity secret from everyone in the FBI for years, using him to enhance his career. Before the war Ream's family, or should I say Rossinger's, was very powerful in Leipzig, Potsdam, and Dresden, and after the war, what was left of his family had strong connections in East Germany and Czechoslovakia. Luby used him to make contact with people behind the iron curtain."

"People who didn't mind killing other people, I would guess."

"Yes, in a manner of speaking."

"And what did Ream get out of the deal?"

"Nothing other than staying here. The others got to bring some people here."

"That's why the socials are the same date."

"What was that?" Garrett looked to David trying to understand the significance of this new info.

Realizing that Garrett did not know about the SSNs, he quickly moved past his unintentional announcement. "Nothing, go on please."

"That's all. The Cold War ended and the team didn't need them as much anymore. Besides, three of them had already died of natural causes and that left just Ream and two others, all of which we knew weren't going anywhere. It was all done. The Cold War was over and so was the usefulness of Ream. His two remaining fellow escapees had retired and Ream wasn't about to talk. Then Major Call stumbled onto the diary and all hell broke loose."

David interjected, "But Ream never said a word about anything, even at his trial."

"True, but after a few years in solitary Ream decided he wanted out. He was going to trade information about the whole sordid mess."

"And Luby couldn't have that."

Garrett just shook his head.

David looked at the dejected agent, "And AliceK?"

"AliceK." Garrett said with a sigh then paused for a while, "Somehow I knew that was going to cause trouble. With the improvements in the Public Records Industry, it was becoming harder to have a man undercover. All the bad guys had to do was to run a background check on our guy and the report would show him using either a false or stolen identity; either way he was done."

"So they created identities for you."

"Well yes, for the bureau. "

"And you took some for yourselves?"

"Luby did."

"Because the bureau didn't know what you all were doing. Correct?"

"In a manner of speaking; it was a clandestine group but the Bureau knew what he was doing. Hell, we got jobs others couldn't do—and how many of our targets died of accidents and murder." Garrett paused for a moment to reflect. "They knew."

"So what happened to Charles Robinson?"

"Robinson? Oh, you mean Shanahan, that was his real name—Edwin Shanahan. He was working undercover in narcotics when his cover was blown."

"His name was removed from AliceK, Why?"

"It was a mistake. Luby worked a deal with that prick Thompson. Thompson was to remove ten of the new identities from the system and add back ten that Luby gave him. The ten were names associated with Ream."

"Luby and Thompson? Somehow I can't see Thompson doing anything dangerous."

"Oh you mean dealing with Luby? He didn't. I don't think they ever met. They did everything through that slug Nichols."

"So how did you get Thompson to play along? It had to be personal, otherwise there wouldn't have been this 'one for me one for you' shit with identities."

"We got Thompson on stock fraud. Seems they had a security breach; actually, it was more a process implosion than a security problem. They let anyone get data as long as they filled out a form. A group in Texas took ten thousand identities and went on a spending spree."

"And nobody knew?"

"Sure they knew. Some techie figured the Texas bunch was up to something and reported it to the fraud group of the General Counsel's office who then told Thompson. But Thompson had a big stock deal going, and if that story of how his company had given ten thousand identities away to a three-time felon hit the news, the stock price would have hit the shitter."

"And being unable to withdraw his stock from sale, he would have lost a fortune."

"Correct. But he buried it for three months and he made fourteen million on the stock sale. Then when the locals started investigating the hundreds of cases of identity fraud, someone at IdentityPoint got nervous; our Fraud group got an anonymous tip on who the kid was who actually found the breach in the first place. He rolled on the General Counsel who rolled on Thompson."

"So much for attorney client privilege," David joked.

"Have you ever met their General Counsel?"

David shook his head no.

"This guy couldn't lawyer his way out of classroom no less a court room. He's a friend of a Senior VP, which is the only reason he got the job."

"So the FBI got the hook into IdentityPoint, and you guys bled them for identities."

"Correct."

"And the fourteen million?"

"Wasn't our priority. Catching bad guys was. We needed the identities to protect our guys."

"So how could you tell?"

"Tell what?"

"Who were the bad guys?"

Garrett knew exactly what David meant, but chose not to say anything.

There was a short pause then David continued, "So how did it work? Who took the names off the system?"

"Thompson, or I should say Nichols, got the woman who worked on the system to make the changes; Thompson even got to keep two of the identities out of the deal."

"But an extra name was removed, and a man was killed. Was that part of the deal?"

Garrett instantly became angry and defensive. "No, fuck no. It was a damn mistake. That incompetent bitch deleted his name. He was one of us." Garrett took a long pause, "He was a friend."

David waited until Garrett was calm before he continued. "Are you sure? Do you know what it takes to add and delete names from a database? It wasn't just a typo."

David reached into his pocket and pulled out a single piece of paper that he had carefully folded earlier and placed in his pocket. He stepped closer to Garrett and holding the paper in his left hand and his weapon in his right, he offered it to Garrett.

Garrett looked at the paper and thought about the weapon. For just a moment he considered trying to take this man by making a grab for the gun, but the desire to take this man out now was suddenly far short of his need to know what this man was selling. He took the paper and opened it, but didn't take his eyes off of the presenter.

"I have an operative, a partner really, Bob. Bob is about as useful in the field as a white shirt in a jungle. He's useless in the field. He gets lost going to the supermarket and he's lived in the same place for six years. His girlfriend drives *him* on her Harley and he has difficulty riding a ten speed bike. He can barely drive a car, so he's no good as a driver or even a reliable delivery man; using him to make a drop off would guarantee the delivery was never made. He can't tail a suspect, interrogate a witness, or strong-arm anyone over eighty pounds...but what he can do with a computer, the info, the data he can access, and the people he has come to know. I mean this guy couldn't defend himself against a girl scout," David paused and stared intensely at the man still holding the paper, "but he can kill a man with research."

Garrett held the paper but still did not open it.

David continued, "It's a long story, and getting Bob to explain it is even longer but it goes something like this. Bob accessed public info on the Internet about the killing, examined the people involved, who he was investigating, who was on his team—found nothing. But Bob has a friend in the news business, who had an friend at the *Wall Street Journal*, who told him he knew there was a reporter by the name of Tuttle who was working on a story involving a senior FBI official, but her source died suddenly and he didn't know who the source was or who the official was."

David strolled over to the window and looked out for a moment. Garrett opened the paper and started to read.

"Well, Bob, being the resourceful guy that he is, accessed phone records for Shanahan and found a number of calls to Paris."

David looked back to Garrett who looked back at him. He wasn't as scared or panicked as he had been; now he was calm, almost deadpan as if he had been drained of all emotion and was now just there, not really feeling anything at all.

"Bob traced that number to a free lance reporter named Tuttle. She lived in Paris but wrote for a number of news outlets including *Time* magazine, *The New York Times*, and the *Wall Street Journal*. Seems Shanahan may have met her while he was on assignment in Paris. According to Bob's source, Tuttle was working on a major story concerning the FBI and an organization called NECO. The source had no idea who or what NECO was and there was nothing in her home, personal papers or notes about it, and the story died with her."

Garrett looked up to David.

"Tuttle, was killed on September 22, 1993, when the military aircraft she was riding was hit by a ground-to-air missile. The plane crashed as the pilot attempted to make an emergency landing in Sukhumi; it's a city in Abkhazia, an independent state within the country of Georgia; I'd never ever heard of it. She was 34 years old."

Garrett had slumped down in his chair having thought about the death of one his own, but sat up in his chair as he contemplated what David had just said.

"Did you give the list of names to Thompson?"

"No. Nichols got it directly from…" Garrett paused and his face went white as he considered what he was about to say. "Luby."

"Did he often get involved in that kind of thing personally?" David now knew how a simple task of adding ten and dropping ten could have gone so wrong.

Garrett shook his head and very quietly answered, "Never."

Nothing was said by either man for a very long minute.

Garrett walked around the room and drained the last of his beer. "So now you know everything. Ream, NECO, Thompson, the whole sorted, disgusting tale."

David stood up and picked his weapon up from the table. Garrett looked at him and knew this was the end. In that moment before his death, he was surprised at what he was feeling. In his business, which sometimes led men to their deaths, he had often wondered what he would feel if it were to happen to him. Would he panic? Would he stare down his killer in defiance, or would he turn coward begging for his life? Many times he thought about it. Perhaps one last grasp for life, he could throw himself at the would-be assassin and kill him in a dramatic struggle. But to his surprise he felt relief. Relief that it was over, that he would be free of the struggle and pain. He closed his eyes and waited.

Mentally he felt his body tense, but nothing happened. He opened his eyes and the man who called himself David was standing there in front of him.

"I told you I had no intention of killing you," David holstered his weapon inside his jacket. "What would you do if you had a second chance? I mean if you could walk away without looking back. Would you?"

"Would I what?"

"Would you walk away from all of this?"

"Are you serious? I'm in the FBI, I know how this stuff works. I can't steal an identity; trust me on this, they will find me. I am not the mountain man type. I can't live in a shack in the Georgia Mountains for the rest of my life."

David pointed to the table beside him and he looked over. There was a folder on the table.

"What's this?"

"You know about AliceK and the project. You know there were identities made for the FBI and your team took ten for your use. There weren't *fifty*, there were *fifty-one*."

"Fifty-one?"

"Yes, the Architect of the system made one before the system went live. It was more of a test case and when he built the others he kept it, sort of a trophy. Maybe even a means of escape. I'm not totally sure why he kept it, but I have that identity now. Name, social security number, family history, seeded data in all the credit bureaus, even a credit score. He's the perfect American citizen; he even voted."

"So what is that to me? I told you everything I know."

"You don't get it friend. This whole affair has been about identities. People stealing them, people creating them, people making a new life with them." David picked up the folder and handed it to him. "It's your out, if you want to take it."

Garrett took it and reviewed it for a full two minutes. "This is good."

"Yes it is. You can leave all this behind and start again. Maybe do it right this time. Interested?" There was a long pause with nothing said between them, then Garrett put his head down and then nodded yes. David could see there were tears on his cheeks.

David walked to the door and then stopped and turned back to Garrett. "By the way, she is in McKinney, Texas, at a ranch working with special needs children."

"Who is?"

"Carrie."

"How do you know that?"

"Public Records, *Mr. Nolan*, Public Records," and with that David was gone.

1935 hours, D.C.

Lytle immediately exited the garage and started out of the city; he didn't want to hang around just in case Garrett, or now Nolan, changed his mind. As soon as he got on the highway he called Sam on his mobile phone.

"Sam, I got a lot from our Washington friend, more than I can tell you now. He gave us everything, including the IdentityPoint connection."

"Who was it?"

"Nichols, just as you thought."

"You on your way back?"

"Affirmative. I've got to make a stop and return some borrowed equipment." Lytle tapped the pistol in the shoulder holster. "Then I will be on my way to the airport."

"Bob and I are ready to make our scheduled visit."

"You sure you're up for it? This is not exactly your forte."

"Well, we're about to find out, I should say."

"Any change in plan?"

"Negative. The plan is the same. Bob has checked on the location of Nichols; he's at home, so it looks good."

"Good Luck."

"Thanks, Out here."

Lytle watched the traffic carefully as he changed lanes, the last thing he wanted was to be stopped by a cop on a traffic violation with an unregistered weapon in his possession.

1935 hours, Chicago

"Thanks for doing this, Cynthia. It means a lot to me. Bye" Walsh pushed the button down on the phone to end the call and immediately dialed another number.

"Call here."

"Sam, its Tim Walsh."

"Hi, Buddy. I didn't expect to hear from you so soon. What's up?"

"Sam, I just got off the phone with Cynthia Cooper. She's the girl I know in the DA's office."

"I remember. Everything okay?"

"She just called me from a pay phone at a bar by her office. She's really afraid, Sam." Walsh spoke quietly like he was trying not to be overheard, and he looked about the apartment as he spoke to make sure he was alone.

"Talk to me, Tim," Sam encouraged him.

"The DA prosecutes a lot of cases each year. They all have a bunch of pretrial meetings between the DA and the defense counsel, then there's the trial, then after that appeals drag on for years, so there is a lot to keep up with. The DA has a small crew, each of which are assigned cases, and who coordinate with the opposing counsel for meetings, exchange of documents, coordinating visits, and all sorts of legal back-and-forth stuff. When the defense attorney wants to communicate with the DA they start with the coordinator." Tim paused as if considering, not continuing. "The Ream case was one of hers."

There was no response from the other end of the phone as Sam pondered the significance of the statement.

"Sam, she said that Ream's attorney called Parnell Thomas, and he called her with what Ream wanted."

"Continue," Sam said cautiously.

"Sam, Ream wanted to cut a deal about the POW names in return for a transfer to a minimum security facility."

"Oh my God!" Sam moaned a low guttural cry as he heard it.

"There's more, Sam. This afternoon she was going through her working files and her entire trip file on Ream's visit is missing. She's really scared, Sam."

"Has she spoken to anyone other than you?"

"Not that I know of," came a concerned and nervous reply.

There was a short pause and then Sam came back on the line. "Tim, I want you to contact her right now. Tell her to wait for you and not to leave with anyone else for any reason. You understand what I'm saying Tim, for *any* reason."

"Yes."

"Grab a bag, put in some clothes and leave. I want you on the road in two minutes, not one second longer. Do you understand?"

Again there was a single word concerned response. "Yes."

"Is your girlfriend there?"

"No. Maggie is on her way, she stopped at the dry cleaners or something on her way home."

"Does she have a cell phone?"

"Yes."

"Call her now, and tell her you are going to pick her up. If she drove, tell her to leave the car. Don't explain it over the phone; you can tell her while you're driving. Then I want all three of you to go somewhere for a few days. Get a hotel room - one would be best, but connecting rooms at a minimum." Sam had been speaking quickly and sternly, as if he had been giving an order to one of his army subordinates. His voice then changed to a quiet, calm tone. "Tim, this is serious. Don't hesitate and don't let either of the two girls do anything except what I have told you. Call me in three days."

"I understand Sam. What about you?"

"I know what I have to do."

2045 hours, Atlanta

Bob and Sam entered the hotel carefully, not to expose too much of themselves to the security cameras. Wearing coats and hats to obscure their identities, but not so much as to raise attention, they went straight to Suite 901. The 'Do Not Disturb' sign was still on the door and Bob put the key card in the door and pushed. The door opened, and they stepped into the semi-darkened room. A quick recon and Bob saw that it was same way he left it.

Sam looked to Bob, "Let's get rolling." While Bob took out the items he needed for the upcoming operation, Sam picked up the phone, dialed, and waited.

"Hello," came the gentle female voice at the other end.

"Okay, we are a go here. Are you ready to do this?"

"Yes. I am."

"Do you know where he is?

"Yes. I have been calling him with messages I saved for him all day. He's at home. Alone."

Sam took a moment then asked, "Are you sure you can do this?"

"Yes. I'm sure I can, I need to do this," came her quiet reply.

2048 hours, Office of Chairman of the Board IdentityPoint

She sat at her desk taking a moment to look around her. She had sat here at this desk day after day, night after night for too many years. Waiting for him to call, to do whatever he needed. She thought of the call she had received two days before, and the strange, eye-opening things the stranger had to say. 'All these years, all these lies, what have I done? What am I about to do?' she thought.

She looked at the phone for a long moment then picked it up and without hesitation dialed. When the expected voice answered she started her prepared performance. "Mr. Thompson has called for you. He needs your assistance immediately."

There was a short pause at the other end and an obviously exasperated voice at the other end replied, "What's going on? What's it this time?"

"I have no idea, Mr. Nichols. Mr. Thompson said he needed you right now."

Again there was silence, then. "Where?"

"Suite 901."

The exasperated voice was now an angry voice, "Who is it this time? The blond in Public Affairs, no that was the summer thing. Or maybe the new Norwegian girl, the one with the drug issue. No, it can't be her, she's at a clinic now, which we are paying for." Again there was a long pause, "So who is the crisis tonight?"

"I really have no idea of what you're speaking, Mr. Nichols. I only know Mr. Thompson called for you and said he needed you now in Suite 901."

She heard some brief, harsh, almost indiscernible noises from the other end of the call then the distinct sound of a phone being slammed into the cradle. She hung up the phone then reached for the hand soap on her desk. She picked it up and looked at it for a moment, then shook her head slowly back and forth and put it back down without using it. She stood up, put on her coat and left the building. And she felt good.

- - - - - - - - - - - - - < > - - - - - - - - - - - - - - - -

"Well, we'll wait and see." Sam went into the bedroom. It was just as Thompson had left it the day before. The bed was a mess and so was the bathroom. Used towels were on the floor and the room smelled like someone had been sick in it. Bob had already placed four silk scarves on the nightstand along with a bottle of lubrication oil and a box of condoms.

As Sam walked back into the sitting room of the suite his cell phone rang.

"Hello."

"It's me," said the other caller.

"What do you have, Hon?"

"He just left the house."

"Thanks, Hon. Now please go home and wait." Sam pushed the end button and put the phone in his pocket. "Nichols is on his way."

"Who was that?" Bob asked.

"Mary."

"Mary! She's watching him? Is she up for that?" Bob asked.

"Well, seeing as since she's the one who's been shot, had to lie to the police, and not to mention kill a man, all in the last week, I guess she pretty well proved she's capable of being *up for it*."

"Yes, all good points."

"Glad you agree." Sam sarcastically acknowledged him. "And how about our assistant?"

"She's in a car in the parking lot waiting for my call."

Sam motioned to Bob that it was time.

"Okay," Bob took his cell, dialed, and when the voice answered said, "Bob here. It's time," then ended the call.

A couple of minutes later there was a quiet knock at the door and Bob answered it. "Hello. Good to see you again." Bob shook the lady's hand, and when she entered, he closed the door behind her. "Barbara, I'd like you to meet Sam."

She was dressed in slacks, a matching jacket and a white lace blouse with a cameo pin at the collar. Her brown hair was spun up in a bun on the back of her head, and she looked like she had just stepped out of some fashion magazine. She carried a leather brief case, the type that had two handles, one on each side giving the user easy access to the large storage area inside. She extended her gloved hand to Sam and greeted him, "Nice to meet you, Sam." She turned back to Bob, "Where can I get ready?"

Bob pointed to the door at the end of the bar. "There's a bathroom right there and also a large one in the main bedroom if you prefer."

"This one will do fine," she said in a most business-like tone and off she went.

When she had closed the door, Sam tapped Bob on the shoulder. "Are you sure about this? She's somewhat attractive, I give you that. But she looks like she would be more comfortable in a courtroom or boardroom than here."

"Relax, Sam, she's a professional. David and I have used her several times. Two minutes went by and the bathroom door opened. Sam stared at the woman, who was now as different from the woman who came in as Sam was from Bob, wearing only a red nightgown that was so sheer little was left to the imagination. The tiny straps over her shoulders strained to hold in her very full breasts, and it was only long enough to provide minimal cover while it maximized the exposure of her previously hidden, long and shapely legs. Her hair, once tied up tightly on the top of her head in lady-like fashion, now hung down her head, over her shoulders and gently across her nightgown. Sam hadn't really noticed her auburn hair when she arrived, but he did now.

All Sam could do was stare at this chameleon of a woman who went to the coffee table next to the couch and placed her leather bag on the table. She opened it, removed two glasses, and placed them on the table in front of the leather couch. She then took a bottle of champagne from the same bag.

"There's a bar behind you if you need something," Sam said as he pointed the fully stocked bar at the far end of the room.

She looked at Sam, "I bring what I need, thank you." She paused for a second, aware of the two men who were staring at her. "But if you don't mind, could you open this before you go back to your business?"

"Sure, whatever you need." Bob opened the bottle for her then turned, and realizing the meaning of the last part of her request, went back into the bedroom, leaving Sam standing there as if he were frozen.

This woman, who had mesmerized Sam, took a packet from her briefcase and poured it into one of the glasses, then filled both from the champagne bottle Bob had just opened. She carefully placed the one glass that had the powder to the left, closest to the front door, then sat down on the right side of the couch and took a sip of the champagne from the other glass.

"Very nice," she put the glass on the table, and then looked at Sam, who still had not moved. "How soon do we expect him?"

"Who?" was all Sam could think to say in his pitiful state. She said nothing, only cocked her head and looked at Sam with a 'are you kidding?' look. "Oh yes, yes. Ah, he was called at approximately twenty-fifty hours, driving time is between fifteen and twenty minutes."

"What time is it now?"

Sam looked at his watch, "Twenty-one ten hours."

"Then he should be here anytime now I would guess."

"Yes, I would think so."

She looked at him and smiled, "Are you intending to stay in the room and assist me perhaps?"

Sam stammered, "Ah, no." He turned towards the bedroom door. "I'll just go in here."

"That would be fine." She watched Sam as he left.

Sam quietly closed the door behind him. Bob, who had been further preparing the scene and checking his camera, turned to Sam. "You handled yourself well in there, Sam."

"Yes," Sam said with a blank look.

"Yes, Sam, you handled yourself well, if you were say, twelve. I take it you have seen a near-naked woman before."

Sam looked at the closed door, as if he could see her through it then looked back to Bob. "That's more than a woman, she's, she's fantasy land, she's Aphrodite for God's sake." Sam shook his head and popped his eyes open wide like a man just waking up. "That boy doesn't stand a chance."

"That's the whole idea, Sam."

2110 hours, Atlanta

The BMW cruised down the back road into the dark, moonless night. The dashboard glowed with the soft lights, and he saw his speed was just under sixty. In other cars the speed might be too much on these back roads, but not his 1993, 2 door 325i BMW convertible. This was a car built for performance, and it showed it on the turns. His previous car, a Corvette, was hot on the straightaway. When he sat in it, it fit like a glove, and he felt like some young stud. It was a muscle car, an updated, very expensive muscle car, and definitely not for the common man. It attracted the women, mostly the under twenty-five set, but he wanted a car that would appeal to the more sophisticated woman. He had only owned the Vet' for nine months and when he traded it for the BMW, he took a beating on the trade-in value; he took more of a beating when he took it home and his wife lectured him for an hour on fiscal responsibility.

As he thought of his wife, he unconsciously pushed the accelerator, and before he was realized it, he was doing seventy.

He looked down at the speedometer, "Holy shit!" He backed off on the accelerator and the car slowed to a manageable sixty.

"Damn, that's a great ride." He thought about his wife and shook his head. "I hate that bitch; she will be the death of me."

He despised his wife, but she didn't despise him; she just had no use for him other than an arm to hold at social functions. To all those around her, she was a happily married woman. That kept the men that were looking for a distraction or an office tryst at bay, which is all she wanted.

Nichols wanted more, it was not coming from her, and divorce was not an alternative for him. She was a lawyer and in the event he started divorce proceedings, she would take him for everything he had, and everything he would ever have.

They had met in college. Both were from the 'right type of family'; both were career minded, and the pursuit of their degrees was the number one priority; so there was no time for casual dating. They saw each other once or twice a month and had sex in her apartment once a month—like clockwork.

When they graduated, he took a position in the corporate world, and she went with a trial law firm at half the salary he got. Their marriage was just like their courtship—no time for anything except the career. They no longer 'dated' each other, so there was no need for dinners out together or one-on-one activities. If they went out it was a mandatory social function, and even then, they spent little time together.

After three years, she was already known as a fierce trial lawyer having won all of her seven cases that went to trial. It was said that every one of her clients was guilty, but her cross-examination of the witnesses was so intense and clever, she discredited them at will. With her victories came increased monetary reward and by the end of her third year she was making five-times his salary—and she let him know it at every opportunity.

As for their personal relations, there were none, or almost none. When they got married, they had a three-day honeymoon on which they screwed like teenagers, but that was the honeymoon and not life. Now, it was once a month, and at her suggestion—make that demand. Later, when he thought back on it, they only had sex maybe eight times between the time they first had sex and when they were married. He had thought it was just their schedules. But what did he know? She did not believe in birth control of any kind, no IUDs, no pill, not even condoms, and she was not going to have children—ever. For her, sex was on a need only basis, and she rarely needed it.

He looked at the clock on the dashboard and saw the time. "This is bullshit." He looked in the rearview mirror and saw himself, then continued talking as if the man in the glass was someone else. "Thompson, I've had it with you. You fuck everything that walks. You do every one of your assistants, and if they give you shit I'm the one that handles the mess. Why the fuck do I do it?" He looked back at the man in the glass only this time with a smile on his face. "The money. That's why I do it. I got this car, the house, the condo on the beach, and eight million in Bermuda that no one knows about."

By the time he got to the hotel his mood was very positive. The parking lot wasn't all that full and it didn't take but a moment to find a spot that was empty on either side—he didn't want some drunk or salesman with a rental car, who didn't care about dings in the paint job, to make a mess of his new machine. Pressing the remote button, the doors locked, but the headlights remained on. "Great feature," he said to himself aloud as walked towards the hotel entrance while his headlights gave him thirty-seconds of light—he loved the spotlight.

The company used the suite for all its major big spenders, lobbyists, and board members when they were in town, but Thompson was the most frequent user. The suite came complete with a leather sofa and chairs, a stocked bar, separate bedroom with a king size bed and jet tub—big enough for two, and a large balcony with a small table and two chairs. It was a first class suite that, when needed, also came with a distraction of choice, also at no cost to the guest of the corporation.

The hotel clerk knew him by sight and waved to him as he went by. Nichols entered the elevator and pushed the button for the ninth floor, and as he did, he thought of Thompson. Here was a man worth millions, yet he never paid for a night at the hotel or anything he bought. Whenever the suite was used he would always have his secretary reserve it for one extra day. He would use it, and let the books show the official guest stayed one extra day. Coincidently, that 'extra' day seemed to run up the most expenses.

2121 hours, Atlanta

There was a quiet knock at the door and she went to the door to let him in. She pulled the door back just enough for him to see her face. "Yes?"

"Thompson called me."

"Oh. Come in," she pulled the door open while standing behind it, blocking his view of her until he was in the room. "Thompson isn't here right now." She closed the door and turned to him to make sure he got the full effect.

"He left? Ah, where is he?" he stammered.

"He said he had to take care of something and would be back in a few minutes and for you to take care of whatever you need to do." She had changed her voice and mannerisms to match the outfit and the mission; the California dumb blond bimbo had nothing on her. She walked over to the table and bent down to pick up her champagne, pausing long enough for the mark to take a good look—which he did.

She stood back up and holding her glass up to him, "I just love champagne, the bubbles tickle." She giggled and made her breasts shake. She could see the mark was obviously befuddled, and he was in that state between doing what he was supposed to do and indulging in a fantasy. This was not a new situation for her and she knew just how to handle it.

"Thompson said he would be back in thirty minutes," she sat on the couch.

"Thirty minutes? Where did he go?" The man was obviously irritated, but he still never took his eyes off her.

"I don't know," she made a pouting look and put her head down a little. "You don't like me."

"What? Oh sure I do."

She looked up at him with a pitiful look. "Will you have a drink with me? Thompson left me here all alone."

"Well, I ..."

"Please, Baby." She breathed in deeply making sure her chest rose.

"Sure."

She giggled and tapped the seat next to her, and he dutifully obeyed. She gave him the prepared champagne, and he took a sip.

"I just love champagne, it makes me…" She stroked the bare portion of her ample left breast with her left hand while she took another sip. "Makes me so playful." She smiled and looked into his eyes.

He took another sip, more of a gulp than a sip, and then finished the glass. She flirted with him for about a minute then kissed him. He didn't respond, but instead sat there with his eyes open, not speaking.

"Baby, you with me, Baby?" she kissed him again, then pulled back and looked in his eyes. Seeing what she needed, she stood and walked to the bedroom door, opened it, and looked for Bob. "He's ready."

"Okay, Sam, lets get him." They went into the main room, stood on either side of him and helped him stand, then led him to the bedroom, where they laid him on the bed that they had already made sure was in *perfect* disarray.

"Let's get to it," Bob said to Sam as he began to take the man's clothes off. They had stripped him except for his underwear. "You take his briefs off, Sam, I'll get the camera ready."

"No, no. I'll get the camera."

"Sorry, it's the penalty for acting like a teenager earlier."

"I did not," Sam said quietly, still not totally comfortable with idea of talking freely while their target was lying in the bed. Sam looked back at Bob and then the woman who was shaking her head in agreement with Bob. Seeing her response Sam just said, "Fine" and went about finishing the task.

Over the next five minutes, Bob took numerous pictures of the man and women in bed together. Sam was amazed at how orchestrated it was. She knew just how to pose herself with the target so to look as if they were actively engaged in a variety of sex acts, including him being tied to the bed. Bob was careful to ensure her face was never in any picture, always having the target's hand on her face, or having her turned away or partially covered by bed linens. When he printed the pictures Bob would edit any that showed too much of his conspirator or showed the target as not fully conscious.

'Okay, that will do it," Bob said as he closed up his camera.

The woman climbed out of the bed and left the bedroom. Sam and Bob checked the bedroom and removed anything that would lead the target or Thompson back to them. They went through their mental checklist of what they had brought with them to make sure they left nothing behind. Two minutes later, they were in the main room when she came out of the bathroom. Sam was stunned to see her dressed exactly as when she had first arrived, not a hair out of place. Carrying her briefcase, she walked to the couch picked up the glasses she and the target had used, placing both glasses in a plastic bag before putting them into her briefcase.

Intending to help her, Sam picked up the Champagne bottle and started towards the bar sink to empty the bottle.

"Excuse me," Barbara said before Sam took two steps. "I'll take that."

Sam returned the bottle and she put a rubber stopper into the bottle while Sam observed. "It's Veuve Clicquot; it would be a crime to waste it."

"Absolutely," Sam nodded his head in concurrence as if he understood.

"It's a 1985er," she added but knew Sam hadn't a clue about vintage. Then she took a white rag from her briefcase, wiped down the table, the wooden armrest on the couch, went over to the bedroom and did the same to the doorknob. When she returned to the couch, she put the rag in the briefcase, closed it and then started for the door.

"Give David my best, will you, Bob?"

"You know I will."

She opened the door, nodded to Sam and quietly left.

Sam turned to Bob, "She was amazing. Had that guy's head turned in one minute and comatose in three. She has a body like the Playboy centerfold of the decade, and when she's not teasing a man to death with boobs that could kill, she dressed like a high-powered Boston lawyer."

"She is."

"Is what?"

"A lawyer."

"You're kidding me?"

"No. She really is."

Sam paused and smiled, "She might change my mind about lawyers."

"I don't think so." Bob smiled and looked at the bedroom where the sleeping mark lay. "I thought about taking his clothes."

Sam looked at the sleeping man, "That's cold, man. The man get's up," Sam stopped, "How long before that stuff wears off?"

"Four hours."

Sam looked at his watch, "The guy wakes up at zero two hundred hours with his head ready to explode." Sam again looked to Bob for concurrence of the prognosis, who nodded affirmative. "And he thinks he got drunk, ended up in bed with a woman he didn't know, and who now is gone. And you were going to take his clothes and leave him there in the room, head exploding, feeling drunk, and nothing but a towel to go home in. Very cold, Bob, very cold. You know, Bob, there is this whole other side of you the rest of the world never sees."

They closed the door to the suite and headed for the elevator.

"Who is she anyway? And don't tell me she served with David in the army."

"Nope. Her brother did." The elevator door closed. "He was visiting her in Atlanta. One night he went to the QuickTrip for gas and interrupted a car jacking by three hoods trying to hijack some woman's Lexus while she was filling her car at the pump. She was fighting with all three of them and refused to give up her keys despite being punched and kicked, when the brother drives up."

"She should have just given them the keys, it's just a car." Sam said disgustedly, "When will people learn stuff like that just isn't worth losing your life over."

"Her baby was in a car seat in the back seat."

"Damn," Sam said as his face scrunched up in regret in what he had just said.

"Anyway her brother drives in, sees what's going down and jumps right in. He takes out two of them, then the third one shoots him in the leg with a 32 and he goes down. The kid doesn't quit though, he gets up and goes after the shooter who shoots him again, this time in the knee of the other leg and the kid goes down to stay. The other two now have scrambled to their car and are trying to leave but guy number three wasn't done. He shoots the woman in the head, then shoots the kid three more times, once in the other knee and twice in the gut. He bleeds out before the medics arrive."

"And the woman?"

295

"After three weeks she came out of the comma, but can't remember anything after starting to pump her gas."

"How about the shooters?"

"The gas station attendant was an old guy who could barely walk, with bad hearing to boot. By the time he realized what was happening all he saw was a man shooting someone on the ground. Someone else ID'd the car, which the cops used to track the three scumbags. They even found the gun, but the warrant was all wrong and the gun was thrown out."

"So they walked."

"Yep. Even had the balls to laugh in Barbara's face when they walked out of the courtroom free and clear."

"And David?"

"While going through her dead brother's things she came across some photos of David and her brother. She called David."

"And?"

Bob looked at Sam as the elevator door opened on the ground floor. "They aren't laughing at anyone anymore."

2155 hours

While Sam and Bob drove the fifteen miles to Nichols' house in relative silence Sam was thinking about their organization and how it was built around the military, those who served together, or family of those who served. In all the cases he had worked with David, either the key people had direct military connections and knew David, or they had family who knew David. Either way, an intense loyalty made everything work. It opened doors, provided support without question and enabled the men and women of this very extended team to work without fear of betrayal. After years of working with David and Bob, it dawned on him that he did not know how Bob became a member of this fraternity.

"So, Bob, how did you get into this line of work, and with David? You weren't military were you?"

"Nope."

"Worked in the military as a civilian?"

"Nope."

"Had family in the military that David helped?"

"Nope."

"There has to be something? You just didn't answer an ad in the paper, 'Wanted, man who can work with undercover, ex-military investigator, slash enforcer, slash maker of wrong things right. Must have experience in investigation, breaking and entering, and suckering sleaze bag men into compromising positions."

Bob looked over at Sam and dryly responded, "Not hardly. I was living in Philly at the time and working for an accounting firm downtown. I had a pretty lousy week at the office, and I went to this restaurant in South Philly called Ralph's. The place looks like a dive, but it has the best mussels in garlic marinara sauce the world has ever seen. The place has such atmosphere and is located right in the Italian district. Did you see Rocky?" Bob was getting excited just thinking about the place.

"Affirmative."

"You remember the scene where Rocky is running down the street and all the kids are following him though a market area?"

"Affirmative."

"Well, that's where Ralph's is. Man you can't get more authentic than that. Oh, and did I tell you that a mob guy actually got murdered there? Right there in the restaurant. It was in the early thirties—no the late thirties."

"Bob." Sam repeated the call louder. "Bob."

"Yes?" Bob paused, "Yeah, okay. Anyway, I was at Ralph's eating and David was there. He was alone at a table. I noticed him, because he and I were the only ones there alone. It's a small place, at least the downstairs, ten tables max. There is an upstairs but that is reserved, you know, for the family." Bob looked over to Sam with a 'you-know-what-I-mean look'.

"Okay, I had to go to the head, so I walked towards the men's room. I pass the stairs to the second floor, and this really big guy surprised me. As I passed the stairs, he caught my eye. I jumped back a little, and he looked at me and said, 'It's closed.' Well I didn't know what he meant. How could the men's room be closed? So I looked at him, and I could see activity up the stairs behind him. I knew he couldn't mean upstairs, because I could see people so I figured he meant the men's room, so I said, 'The men's room is closed?' And then he said…"

"Bob. Bob. Bob," Sam repeated louder and louder until Bob stopped telling his story.

"What? Oh. Yeah, okay. Anyway, David was there, he was real quiet and just staring at his half eaten food. It was real obvious he had been drinking, and drinking hard."

"David?" Sam interjected, "David doesn't drink other than beer or two."

Bob looked over at Sam with a serious look on his face, "No, not any more."

Sam acknowledged and Bob continued. "Anyway, David was just staring at his plate, never looking away, as if there was some really fascinating TV show playing in it and he couldn't look away. So we finish about the same time. I'm paying my bill and David stands up, puts some cash on the table, and stumbles out of the place."

"David? Drunk on his feet, stumbling?"

"Well, you know how you walk when you are drunk, kind of wobbly, not falling down but touching things as you go, trying to keep your balance kind of thing."

"Yes," Sam rotated his finger in a circular motion telling Bob to get on with the story.

"So David leaves and I am like two minutes behind him out the door. I come outside and hear this commotion. I go around the corner and there are a bunch of people in this wild fight. Four or five teenagers are all over this guy. I stand there for a second and realize it's the drunk guy from Ralph's and these kids, no not kids, thugs, no, punks, were whaling on him." Bob takes a breath and then focuses for a moment on the drive and makes a right turn, checking the street signs to make sure he is going the right way.

"So?" Sam said trying to get Bob back on track with the story.

"All the while the group is all around him whacking on him, but its like he doesn't feel it, he just keeps fighting and the punk kids keep falling. So as I am watching, I see the drunk guy take out one guy, and he doesn't get up; then a second, and then a third. He's facing the fourth guy who looks frozen, like he's either mesmerized by what he's seen or too afraid to move. Then, all of a sudden David goes down to the ground; the fourth kid had hit him across the back with a bar or a pole or something." Bob looked away from the road and then to Sam, "I think it was a tire iron."

"Holy crap," Sam recoiled after hearing it, like he felt the blow himself.

"So he is down on the ground and one by one the dudes get up and start kicking him." Bob paused for a moment, and then continued. "I don't know what came over me, I mean I never get into fights, or get involved, but all of a sudden I was running at them, and I threw myself right into them. You know I was like this rocket that was just lit and went screaming into a target."

"Wow, and you stopped them from beating on David."

Bob looked over to Sam with a look like 'Are you kidding.' "Yeah, I am actually a black belt in three disciplines." There was a short pause. "They kicked the shit out of me."

"Oh. So how..." Sam didn't get to finish the question as Bob stopped the car with a jolt having hit the brakes a little too hard.

Bob turned off the car, "We're here." As he started to open the door Sam grabbed his arm.

"Whoa there, big guy. So what happened?"

Bob turned back towards Sam, "When I woke up we were in Ralph's, *upstairs* in Ralph's. I never got to go upstairs in Ralph's before. You know it was family upstairs, don't you?" Bob did the quote thing with his hands when he said, family.

"I gathered that, Bob."

"Good. Just trying to be thorough. Anyway, David was there drinking coffee with an ice-filled towel over his back and neck, and that big guy who had been standing on the steps earlier was next to him. There were a bunch of others, like ten I think, sitting and standing around. They were all together though."

"So the guys from upstairs in Ralph's came to your rescue as they say," Sam said.

Bob laughed and then continued. "In a manner of speaking."

"How's that?"

Bob laughed again, "Actually they came to the rescue of the Mercedes."

"Say again."

"Apparently when I threw myself at these thugs they simply tossed me onto the hood of a car. I remember flying through the air and then slamming down on the hood. I hit the windshield then slid down the hood. My shirt got caught on the hood ornament; I hung there for a few moments, half on the car and half off, until the hood ornament broke and I slid the rest of the way down." Bob started to unbutton his shirt, "I still have a nasty scar from where the broken Mercedes emblem cut my chest. Want to see?"

Sam shook both his hands in front of him and turned away slightly, "No. I'll pass on that."

"Okay. Seems the car belonged to someone important and they didn't like the kids damaging the car."

"Damaging the car with your body?" Sam repeated in a half question half confirming fact kind of way.

"Yep. Lucky they didn't throw me onto a Pinto, I'd have been screwed for sure."

"Yes indeed. And then you and David...." Sam didn't finish as he waited for Bob to complete the sentence.

"Oh yes. Ah, the people from Ralph's brought us inside to clean us up. David drank about a gallon of coffee and sobered up. He thanked me for saving him, told me that whenever I needed something. I was to call. We got to talking, he told me about what he did for a living, and why he got drunk." Bob got a serious look on his face, almost one of reverence and looked at Sam. "It was the anniversary of the Columbia mission."

Sam knew instantly what that was and what that meant to David. "I understand."

"I told David I was a no account accountant who hated what I did, and who I was. I was a nothing and never would be anything." Bob paused from telling the story and looked straight ahead.

Sam could see Bob was feeling a little emotional; his eyes were tearing, and he had the look of a person who was having a hard time holding something inside. He didn't press but waited for Bob to continue. A long few seconds later he did.

"David grabbed my face with both his hands and looked me right in the eyes. I could see he was dead serious. He told me I wasn't nothing. He said I was the man who knew what he was about to do was total suicide, and I did it anyway. I saved his life. He said I was as brave as any soldier. I had earned his respect and he was forever in my debt. Then he told me if I wanted to, I could work with him."

"And so you did."

"Yep, we shared an order of Ralph's mussels in marinara and garlic and sealed the deal with a cup of coffee. You know I never even called in to my old job. I just walked away." With a look of confidence and pride, Bob looked into the night. "You know, even drunk off his ass, David's one hell of a fighter."

Sam smiled and replied, "Of that I have no doubt."

They both got out of the car and Sam waited for Bob to join him on his side. Bob had paused to wipe his eyes with his handkerchief, and Sam turned to pretend to look down the street making sure no one observed them arriving. When Bob joined him, Sam asked, "Are we going to have enough time before Nichols' wife gets home?"

"The wife is in New York preparing a case at least until the end of the week."

"How do you know all this stuff anyway?"

"I'm just really, really smart, Sam."

"Bob, I am going to have to hurt you." Sam smiled and as they started up the driveway to the house, he looked away into the night sky.

2230 hours, Marietta, GA

Sam and Bob carefully searched Nichols' house for evidence that would link Nichols with the purchase of the IdentityPoint companies. They started in the office; Sam went to the computer and Bob began looking through any papers and records he could find. Sam turned on the computer, and as soon as it booted, he was presented with a log in screen.

"Password protected," Sam said as he reached into his pocket.

"You did bring the disk, didn't you?" Bob asked without looking up from his research.

"Already on it," Sam answered as he put a CD into the disk reader and re-booted the system. A minute later the computer which had recognized the CD Rom and booted from it and not the computer's hard drive presented Sam an open Windows screen. "When will they learn?"

"It's not that you are that good, Sam, it's just that they are that bad."

"Are you kidding; I'm a computer genius, a hacker, a wiz!"

"Sam, not to bust your bubble but it's a Windows box and you have a 'get in free CD. It's not like it's a UNIX box or a Mac and requires talent to break in for goodness sake."

"Say what you want but I *am* the computer *man*!" Sam joked as he reviewed the files.

After twenty minutes, Sam hadn't found anything. He reached in his pocket and took out another CD and put it into the computer, selected Windows Explorer, and launched a program. The computer executed the request and a menu appeared on the screen. Sam selected the box, 'Recover Deleted Files' and pressed enter. Instantly the screen displayed names of files with a comment next to each one; Recoverable, Partially recoverable, and Not recoverable. When the system was done searching Sam selected the 'Recover and Save to CD-Rom' selection. The computer started its process.

"I got eighty-two files of which sixty-three are recoverable. I am saving them all to disk now. What do you have?"

Bob looked up at Sam. "What I got is a stiff neck, and sore back from bending over all this crap for that last hour. Besides that, I got a bunch of nothing. I'm not going to find anything in here." Bob closed the drawer of the four-drawer file cabinet.

Sam stood up and stretched and walked to the closet and opened the door. There was a small fire-proof container sitting in the back of the cabinet. "How about this?" Sam smiled a, 'I got you' grin to Bob, who turned to see the find.

"Ah, a portable fire-proof safe with convenient carrying handle. A thief's best friend." Bob reached into the closet and retrieved the little safe, "Saves him the trouble of breaking into it on the site. He can carry it out and open it at his leisure."

"Convenient."

"Quite."

"You taking it with us?" Sam asked as Bob cleared away a space on the desk and put the little safe on it.

"Nope, going to open it here. It's a number lock; four numbers one to nine. Just line them up and push the lever."

"That's 9999 possible combinations. We could be here a while."

"Well, yes, if he used random numbers." Bob looked up from the safe to Sam, "Other than four of the same number or four in a straight sequence like, one-two-three-four, give me four numbers *you* won't forget."

"Zero-six-five-two." Sam quickly responded.

"Your birthday?"

"Affirmative."

Bob took a small notebook from his pocket, "Most people either use a straight sequence, and some just use the default zero-zero-zero-zero that comes set on the safe. But most use a significant date they won't forget."

"Like anniversaries, dates in history?"

Bob stopped and looked up at Sam with a deadpan look, "Anniversaries? Sam, they're men, they're simple. They use birthdays." He turned back to the safe and tried the first set of numbers he read from the book. "Well, it's not his birthday." He tried the next. "Not his wife's. Let's try the birthday with the year first then the month, his first." He dialed the four numbers and pushed the leaver and the top sprung open and he looked at Sam. "Sometimes it's just too easy."

Sam went back to the computer as Bob quickly looked through the papers. "Bingo! Bank statements and checks for an account in the Bahamas, and they're not under Nichols' name. We'll need to copy these." Bob turned on the printer copier.

"Let me see," Sam reached out for the documents.

"Make that two accounts." Sam held out a second checkbook to Bob. "Our friends Robert Pearson and James Twiggs."

"Interesting," Bob said as he started to feed the papers into the machine.

"Affirmative," Sam responded as he examined the checkbook, then quietly removed blank checks from both accounts, then returned to review some of the recovered files. "I'm not saying we got him dead, but I have a spread sheet listing every acquisition and the share for 'P' and 'T'" along with some memos that reference Thompson and his incidents with all sorts of young ladies. Looks like our Mr. Nichols has made himself some bargaining chips with Thompson."

"And I'll bet he has those in a bank safe deposit box," Bob said as he turned off the printer and placed the papers back in the portable fire safe.

Chapter 16

Tuesday, October 25

Mission's End

0845 hours, Alpharetta, GA

David and Sam sat at the dining room table at Sam's house. David had just finished reading the stack of papers Sam and Bob had 'liberated' from Nichols's house the night before. He put the papers down and looked up at Sam, who was sipping a cup of coffee and finishing up a fresh croissant David had brought from the Atlanta Bread Company.

David put down the papers he had been reading, "We're done."

"Done?" Sam asked, "Done as in, done eating, or as in, the mission is done?"

"As in the mission is done, Sam."

"How's that?"

"David straightened the papers as he talked. "Our client hired us to find out who, if anyone, was getting rich off the acquisitions her company was making, and that we've done. With what we have from Garrett and these papers," David paused and smiled, "which Mr. Nichols was so obliging to give you. We know that the Chairman of the Board, Thompson, and the company President, Nichols, used a front company to buy shares in the companies IdentityPoint had targeted for acquisition. We also know that in order to save their asses they cooked a deal with a fraction group within the FBI, and provided them some

305

identity cover. In return they got perfect false identities for their use. We can positively track the false IDs to Thompson and Nichols and their bank account in the Bahamas. So, as far as I am concerned the mission is done. Whether or not the client is able to use this in court is up to the scumbag lawyers to decide."

Mary came into the room from the kitchen and sat down at the table. "So what do you think they will get from all this?" Mary asked David.

"If I had to say, I would guess our client will present the data to Thompson, and he will work a deal with her. He will probably quietly step down and go screw some other company."

"And Nichols?" Mary asked.

"As much as I hate what he is doing, we have a contract, and she has very specific requirements for the information. Find out if Thompson and anyone else were behind the scam, find the proof, and keep the results secret." David looked sadly at Sam, "We're bound to honor the contract."

"It's not fair, it's not right." Mary looked at Sam who had turned away and was looking out the window. She looked at David, then they both looked at Sam. "As I said, it doesn't seem fair that Nichols and Thompson get rich and then all that happens is they just walk away with the money."

Again Mary looked at Sam, and again there seemed to be no interest. "You agree, Sam?"

David smiled at Mary in acknowledgement of Sam's obvious distraction. "What's up, Sam, Sigourney's got your mind again?" David joked.

"After I got the call from John Mack, I did some more reading on Robert. According to the articles, he and his company were securing some obscure, nameless hill, when the Viet Cong attacked them in force. They fought all day, then all night; they were getting the shit kicked out of them. On the second day, they overran his flank and the unit was in danger of having the enemy in the center of their AO. Cole sees them, leaves his foxhole, runs across an open area, gets hit, the *first* time, and kills four or five with his M16 as he goes. He jumps into a foxhole and uses a dead soldiers' M60 and takes out a bunch more. When he runs out of ammo for the 60, he takes off forward to another overrun foxhole and does the same thing. He drives the enemy back and then runs forward again into the next hole. By the time he's done, he had moved forward eight times, killed at least thirty, and got himself wounded three times. Seeing what he was doing, the unit responded behind him, and as he moved forward, his men filled the holes behind him—or died trying to."

"Brave man," Mary said.

"Roger that," Sam relied quietly, almost solemnly.

"Have you tried to contact him? Maybe to confirm Nichols' role?" David asked, "Or do I know the ending already?"

Mary was confused by his last comment.

"He's dead; died in 1983."

"How?" Mary asked.

"Apparently he became one of the forgotten walking wounded. Couldn't re-assimilate, as they say. Lived on the streets and it took a toll on his health. One day his body just shut down."

"So Nichols tells the world he's a hero and the real hero is forgotten," Mary said as she hugged her husband.

"Stolen Valor," David said quietly as he looked out into the room.

"Stolen Valor," Sam quietly responded.

They were all quiet for a moment saying nothing. Each reflecting on the situation in their own way. Finally Mary spoke, "So?"

Sam looked to Mary but said nothing.

"So?" She repeated.

"So what, Hon?"

"So how are you taking Nichols down?" Mary looked to David and then back to Sam. "No way you can live with this." She looked hard at Sam then to David. "Either can you."

Sam nodded his head in agreement.

"So the case continues." Mary said.

There was a pause then David quietly spoke. "No. This case is over. Watkins hired us to do a mission and we did it. It wouldn't be right to risk the mission by getting personal. As much as I want to take Nichols down, we can't risk it."

"Don't forget Thompson. He needs some public flogging at the very least," Mary added.

Again, silence fell on the room as each person struggled with their desire to extract justice and David's correct assessment on the completed mission. Mary made herself busy by taking the empty glasses to the kitchen. David organized the papers that they had reviewed and now were spread out over the table, and Sam stared out the window.

- - - - - - - - - - - - < > - - - - - - - - - - - - -

Sam stood at the window, watching the clouds go by. The sky was the crystal bright blue; the kind you only see on a clear, perfect day when the sun is just right and the air is clean and fresh. The billowy white clouds gently floated across the sky while the sun played hide and seek, popping in and out as the clouds passed gently between the sun and Sam. He looked out into the beautiful day and saw the tree gently blowing in the breeze. He stood still and quiet watching the birds come and go from the bird feeder. A Golden Finch flew in and sat on the lowest peg of the bird feeder and helped himself to the sunflower seeds that filled the container, all the while ever watchful of the dangers that could arise at any moment.

Behind him Mary and David stood wondering what he was looking at, why he was standing motionless. Mary strained to see what had captured Sam's interest outside, but she didn't see anything that appeared out of the ordinary.

After many minutes Mary gently spoke, "Sam." There was no response.

"Sam," Again Mary spoke but this time ever so slightly louder; again nothing. She walked over to Sam and touched his shoulder.

Finally, quietly, Sam spoke. "Dana would have liked this day." He continued to look out the window. "I remember that he was fond of birds."

"Sam," Mary repeated as she put her hand on his shoulder.

He reached up with his hand, crossed his chest and placed his hand on top of hers. "It's a beautiful day, a day to savor." Sam turned back to Mary and then looked at David. "It's a beautiful day out there, and I am fortunate that I am able to see it." Sam looked back at the day through the window. "Such a quiet, gentle looking day. If I want to lie outside all day in the sun I can. If I want to spend it driving around I can. If I want to pick up and go I can. I am free to do all this."

"Cole, Collin Kelly, Lieutenant Colonel Dana Jackson and so many more died to give us all this. They didn't want to be heroes, but they are. They deserve to be here more than any of us, and they are not. They deserve to have the nation speak their names with reverence. When they speak of an American hero, they should be speaking of these brave soldiers," Sam stopped and turned to David. His voice was strained, "not that lying bastard Nichols."

"We setup Nichols with the photos in case we needed his cooperation to get the data, but we got it without him. But now, I have the beginnings of a very interesting plan."

No one said anything. Finally, Sam turned back from the window. "Why don't you call Watkins, tell her we have another client, and we are going to play a little poker with Thompson and his FBI connection. Make sure you tell her we won't use the acquisition data."

"Another client? Who?"

"I have to call him." Sam went to the phone and dialed a familiar number.

"Sam, you're the worst poker player I ever saw. The last time we played five-card stud you tried to bluff me with a five, seven and nine showing when I had three tens showing. An inside straight, talk about long shot."

"Yeah, I know," Sam dialed.

1800 hours

It was a very expensive development, with million dollar homes on acres of land. Neighbors were not next door in this neighborhood; they were way down the lane on their multi-acre lot. No sidewalks connected neighbors. One reason was, they were too far away to make them practical, and for another, the main purpose of sidewalks was to enable neighbors to walk between homes and visit with their friends. That was not necessary here; people in this neighborhood did not drop in or casually walk by. This was a neighborhood of status and social prominence; people didn't 'drop in'; they were invited, and usually along with fifty or a hundred of their closest friends—or at least their closest social and political contacts.

The quiet lonely street did not see any life on this dark night except a single sedan that was moving slowly down the curbless, tree-lined lane. It wasn't one of its normal travelers, not a BMW, Mercedes, or Jaguar, and it certainly was not the Silver Shadow Rolls Royce, which only came out on bright sunny days when it could be envied by all who saw it. The lone sedan was a stranger; a simple American car of no particular style and certainly not of the lineage of the expensive models that normally haunted this lane.

With the lack of street lighting, the only ones being the very large lamps that sat upon the top of the stone columns that guarded the gateless entrance to this exclusive and private community, the blackness of the night seemed more so here in this dark and neighborless community. The clouds had blown in and their thick bodies sucked up all the light the stars and moon could give, leaving nothing for those directly below.

The driver eased the car into a parking place next to the edge of the lane and directly in front of the house. He then turned off the lights and stopped the engine.

"Damn, it's dark out there," the driver said as he strained to see outside of the car.

"Affirmative," Sam said as he looked at the house they now sat parked in front of. "It's almost like you are out in the forest."

Bob opened the car door. There was no dome light to blind them or equally important, no light to enable peering eyes to identity the car occupants. Sam had removed the fuse to ensure just that. "Wow, big house," Bob remarked as he carefully exited the car and softly closed the door—not all the way, just enough to keep the door unlocked and easy to pull open in an emergency.

Sam exited the passenger side and walked to the front of the car where he met Bob. "Seems like we are doing a lot of this cloak and dagger stuff these days."

"Yeah. I don't mind saying I would prefer being back at the Architect's house reviewing the data, than here and preparing to go in there." Bob half-pointed to the house.

"You'll be fine. You sure you've never met him?"

"No."

"How is that possible? You've worked there for a month and he's just upstairs from you."

"I don't know, just haven't."

Sam looked at him with a blank stare, took two more steps towards the house and stopped. "I was there two days, and I had lunch with him."

Bob, frustrated, replied simply, "Okay."

"Damn, you are invisible," Sam smiled then stared back towards the door again.

"Let's not get personal. Besides I'm already freaked about this."

Sam stopped again. "With all the stuff you do, the undercover, the getting people drugged stuff, and you are freaked about a little role playing?"

"I never have to confront the people. I'm just 'standing in the shadows,' as they say. And, besides, I'm not much of an actor I can tell you."

"You'll do fine. All you have to do is act like a general."

"How's that?"

"Walk slow, don't talk, and act stupid."

"What?"

"Didn't you ever see *Dirty Dozen?*"

Bob stopped his slow walk, looked at Sam and quietly said, "Of course, and no matter how many times I see it, I still hope Jimmy Brown makes it through without getting shot."

Sam nodded in solemn agreement, and then continued. "But you have to be Donald Sutherland when he pretended to be the general; so they could fake out Robert Ryan. Nichols is Ryan, and he has to think you're the general to pull this off."

Sam rang the door bell, twice, then impatiently knocked on the door.

The door finally opened and "Yes," came a half question and half annoyed greeting.

Sorry for the intrusion Colonel Nichols, I am Major Call, we met at IdentityPoint, at lunch with George Bailey." Sam waited for Nichols to remember. When Nichols nodded Sam continued. "And this, Sir, is Brigadier General Robert Drudick."

Nichols looked at the two men suspiciously. He started to speak, but Sam cut him off.

"I already know what you're thinking, Colonel. Why are these men here, now, at this hour, not in uniform? Well, Sir, the general and I are on assignment and we need your help." Sam kept his eyes on Nichols, not staring, just watching.

Nichols looked at Sam, then the General, then back to Sam, "I…"

"Your country needs you, Colonel." Sam played to Nichols's ego and then came to attention just to add to the show. "May we enter, Sir?"

Nichols nodded, opened the door wide and then stepped back.

"Sir," Sam motioned to the General to enter and Sam followed."

Nichols was only half aware and motioned his two unexpected guests into the den and then offered them seats.

"Thank you, Colonel." Sam sat after making sure the General was seated.

"So, how may I be of service?" Nichols said as he sat back in his overstuffed chair.

"Well, Colonel, the General and I are working with the FBI, and as you may have already suspected, my presence at IdentityPoint was just a cover."

"Yes, yes, of course." Nichols shook his head and gave a look to the General that said, 'of course I knew.' "So what do you need from me?"

"I'm glad you asked, Colonel." Sam opened the small leather briefcase he had been carrying and took out a typed letter and held it in his hand. "We need you to sign this paper." Sam held it up to Nichols.

"What is it?" Nichols took it from Sam and began reviewing the document.

"It's a letter from you stating that Thompson knew all about the security problem that released tens of thousands of sets of personal data out into the criminal world, and that he was involved with a rogue group within the FBI that forced your company to create false identities, and in doing so, led to the death of one agent."

Nichols sat up straight in his chair and looked at Sam in half shock and half anger. "What are you talking about?" he stammered to find the words. "I, I have no knowledge of any such thing. No, not at all. That's totally false."

Sam sat calmly in his chair, giving Nichols a moment to be obvious in his attempt to fake innocence.

"You are talking crazy. You need to leave. My wife is expected any moment, and I do not wish to trouble her with your presence here." Nichols stood, but before he could take a step Sam interjected without moving from his seat: "Your wife's in New York, working on a case, and will not be back until Thursday." Sam looked at the startled Nichols. "I know she said she would be back on Tuesday. Things change sir, you need better G2. By the way, she's having dinner at *Steamer's Landing*."

Nichols looked about the room as if there was someone there who could support him against this onslaught for which he had no response.

"Now if we can get down to business." Sam motioned to Nichols to again focus on the paper.

Nichols was confused. He had not expected these two men to be at his home, or anyone for that matter. He had no idea why the FBI and the Army should be working together, or how, or why, they were watching his wife's movements. "This is all bullshit. You two need to leave my home immediately." Nichols pointed his finger at Sam and with a short jerking motion pointed to the door.

"Have you read the document, sir?" Sam asked. "It does not implicate you at all. As a matter of fact, it really makes you look like a true patriot." Sam looked at Nichols with a slightly bowed head, spoke calmly, and seemed to genuinely be trying to show respect to the man and the rank. "You would be a…" Sam paused for moment, "a hero I should think." Sam looked over to the stoic General who had remained silent to this point. "A hero to the people I should think, General."

The General nodded, "Yes, Major, a hero."

Nichols sat back in his chair and thought for a moment. He seemed to calm down and to be considering the very positive outcome that was now possible for him.

"So why is the Army working with the FBI? And why are you two here?"

"Colonel, Thompson was directly responsible for the death of one man and indirectly responsible for the death of the only lead in a major Army investigation. We, and by we I mean, the Army, wants him to pay for it."

Nichols laughed. "You have no idea what Thompson is capable of doing, and who his friends are. He can make calls and you both will disappear."

"Well, that remains to be seen, and that is of no consequence. What is of consequence is your signature on this document." Sam leaned forward towards Nichols. "It's the right thing to do, Colonel."

"No. No. I am not going to sign any paper, now get out."

Sam looked over to the General. "Sir, it would seem as if Colonel Nichols has made his decision. Perhaps we should execute plan B now, Sir."

The General made no discernable move or change in expression and Nichols was intensely watching the two men who had shown no emotion at all during the entire conversation and in fact had barely even moved.

Slowly, Sam leaned toward Nichols, raised his arm and gently motioned for Nichols to move closer, as if Sam were about to quietly relay a secret to him. Nichols leaned in slightly.

With a quick, sudden and unexpected motion, Sam slightly rose up from the chair, and with his right hand grabbed the hair on the back of Nichols head, and then slammed his face into the desk.

In an instant, Sam was standing, leaning over the desk, placing all his weight onto the man's head, holding it down tightly against the desk. Nichols was moaning as he helplessly tried to pull his arms up to grab his attacker, but his arms, which had been resting on the chair arms were now pinned against the desk and he could not get any leverage to bring them up. His broken nose bled profusely onto the desk and Nichols start to spit blood out of his mouth, which had flowed into it from the small pool that had formed on the desk.

"Now listen to me," Sam was no longer the quiet, respectful subordinate he had been. "You're a lying bastard, and the closest you've come to a real war is the screen of a John Wayne movie." He pushed Nichols head down harder. "General, if you please."

The General picked up Sam's briefcase and retrieved another piece of paper, then put it in the face of Nichols.

"That, Colonel, is your official Form 2, and even a bullshit faker like you knows what that means. You never served in Viet Nam, you never served in any conflict anywhere, and you are certainly no hero." Sam released his captive, who slowly drugged himself back into his seat and then held his bleeding nose.

Sam stood in front of the desk. "Now listen and listen good. This is the deal. You sign the paper and tomorrow you acknowledge it to Thompson when I see him. He walks away from the company, you get the Form 2, and we forget you're a fraud." Sam, let that sit in for just a moment, "And if asked about your war service again by any magazine or newspaper, you just tell them it was a long time ago, it's now in the past, and that's where you are going to leave it. The army doesn't want this in the public eye, so you get a freebie."

Nichols had the look of a beaten man as he searched about the room for something to put on his broken face.

"Understood?" Sam asked.

Nichols did not respond but attended to his bleeding nose.

"I asked you a question, Colonel. Do you understand?"

Nichols looked helplessly at the General then Sam, "Yes."

Sam smiled ever so slightly and picked up a pen from the desk. "Now sign the paper." He paused as he gave Nichols the pen, "And make sure you sign it properly and don't drip blood on the document.

Nichols picked up the pen and signed. Sam then quickly took the paper and put it into his small briefcase. "Now, we are going to leave. No need to walk us to the door."

Sam motioned to Nichols and the General stood to leave. "And one more thing." Sam looked back at Nichols who was now trying to stop the bleeding with a handful of Kleenex, "If I ever hear that you mentioned Sergeant Cole's name again in the same sentence with yours, I will be back."

- - - - - - - - - - - - - - -< >- - - - - - - - - - - - - - -

"Bob walked slowly to the car while waiting for Sam. When Sam arrived at the car, Bob started it, and before Sam had completely closed the passenger door, he was pulling away from the curb.

"Feel better?" Bob asked Sam without looking away from the road.

"Oh yeah, much."

"That's good."

"By the way, Bob, you played Sutherland's General better than Sutherland."

"They both laughed as Bob turned the car out onto the highway.

Chapter 17

Wednesday, October 26

Betrayal

0900 hours, Atlanta

Thompson's secretary knocked on the door. "Mr. Thompson, George Bailey from technology is here to see you along with a Mr. Sam Cohen."

"What do they want?"

"They say they have an urgent message from a Mr. Luby."

"Show them in." She left the office, returned with Sam and George and then after getting the usual signal from Thompson, she left and closed the door behind her.

"I am Sam Cohen and I think you know George Bailey."

"Yes, I do. So what is so urgent?"

"In a word, NECO."

"Who?" His comment said it was unknown to him; his expression said otherwise.

"You know, Thompson, NECO, black ops, secret identities, bad guys doing bad things. Your company let tens of thousands of personal records out into the hands of felons, and you didn't tell a soul. By doing so you made millions and the common folk got screwed." Sam stepped forward, opened the envelope he had carried with him, and

317

put the contents on Thompson's desk. "Courtesy of your partner in crime, Nichols."

Thompson picked up the papers and examined the statement by Nichols. He threw it down on the desk, then pushed the intercom button.

"Yes, Sir," came the reply from his secretary.

"Get Nichols in here."

"I'm sorry, Sir, he's not been in all day today."

"Where is he?"

"I don't know, Sir. He's missed three scheduled meetings already, and he isn't answering his phone."

Thompson angrily pushed the button on the phone and ended the conversation.

"Um, I am guessing Mr. Nichols has taken an unscheduled vacation." Sam walked over to a shelf on the wall that held a collection of figurines. He pointed to one of a mouse, "Cute." Sam looked to George then back to Thompson, "After all his recent activity, I'm betting he needed to get away for awhile. It's so important to look after yourself. Don't you agree?"

Thompson said nothing, just sat back in his chair as if he were listening to one of his staff brief him on another business venture. "I'm listening."

"Thanks to some inside help," Sam looked to George, who had remained silent and almost motionless thus far, "we know all about the alias names, the FBI connection, NECO, and how you played games with the list."

Thompson leaned back in his chair, as if the increased distance made him safer from the incoming accusations. "You and Nichols screwed with the list, and that's what caused the agent's name to be missing from the system." Sam turned to George for effect, "And it wasn't this man's friend who did it—it was Nichols, and you. You are responsible for the death of the undercover agent."

"I'm listening." Thompson repeated.

"Need more?" Sam played with Thompson.

"I've heard nothing but conjecture. If there was any truth to this, I am sure a *patriot* like yourself would have taken it to the press by now."

Sam showed he was uncomfortable with the patriot comment and press comments, but he didn't have time to think more on it. "It's all in AliceK, she knows everything." Sam smiled as he knew he had struck the deadly nerve, the evidence that would take him down.

"I see." Thompson lean back in his high back expensive leather chair and took a breath, "And you believe what Nichols told you, of course."

"He has his misgivings for sure, but he's still one of the fold, and when it came crunch time, he stood with fellow soldiers for what is right." Sam looked at Thompson with contempt. "You're going down, asshole. Between what Nichols told me, and what Mr. Bailey will be able to get out of AliceK, you're done."

Thompson leaned forward in his chair for a moment and rubbed his head with both hands, and quietly spoke, "Nichols?"

"Yes. A war hero with credibility who sorrowfully announces to the press that he has found out what you have done, how he cannot live with that, and is willing to give all up because he has to make things right."

"And in return?" Thompson asked.

"And in return some very damning photos disappear," Sam replied.

"Then what? I resign and then he takes this office." Thompson was quiet and sullen. He slumped down in his chair. "And what do you get?"

"I don't want anything. My client," Sam looked to George, "needs some assurances that he won't end up like so many others you have taken disfavor to."

"Continue."

"He gets a contract for five more years at twice the salary, and five thousand shares of unrestrictive stock options."

"Everybody wants something." Thompson pushed back in his chair and then sat forward, aggressively. "And AliceK makes sure you get it."

"I guess it does." Sam said with a tone of arrogance.

Thompson looked at Sam and his silent accomplice, and then pushed the intercom button on the phone. "Send him in." He sat back and grinned.

Both Sam and George showed a look of surprise by Thompson's call and where even more so when the man he called for walked in. George looked startled when he saw him. "What are you doing here?"

"Hey, every major company needs an architect and we have been without the services of ours for far too long." Thompson looked to the Architect, "Welcome back."

"Thank you, Sir." The Architect said as he stood there purposely not looking at his long time friend.

"What the hell is this, Thompson? Some more of your blackmail or strong-arm bullshit. Well, I can tell you it's not going to work."

"Tell me this isn't true," George said to his old friend as he stared in apparent disbelief of his presence in the room. But the Architect did not look at his friend, but instead had his eyes fixed on Thompson.

"Now, now boys, just relax. Our Senior Architect and new Vice President of Technology has just returned to the company on his own," Thompson looked to Sam with the look of a man who had just suckered a gambler into a fools bet. "In fact, he came to me last night and asked for his job back." Thompson didn't take his eyes off of Sam, who now had the look of a man who's fortune was about to be lost. "Isn't that right?" He now looked to the Architect who nodded in agreement.

"So tell me, what's your report?" Thompson looked to the Architect who still had not looked at Sam or George, but had remained purposely still as if he were unable to face the men he had apparently betrayed.

"Sir, the system in question has been," he paused for a moment as if he were a child about to admit his wrong doings to his parents, "eliminated."

Thompson smiled again at his would be accusers, "You don't mean it has just been turned off for a while or perhaps it is on some disk waiting reloading?"

"No, Sir."

"You mean this system that these two men are so concerned about is…." Thompson let his words just hang in the air.

"As far as the IdentityPoint datacenter is concerned the system known as AliceK never existed."

"Why?" George said, "Why?"

"May I leave now, sir?" The Architect asked quietly, and without waiting for a response, he turned away from Sam and George and quickly left the room.

Thompson no longer gave the appearance of a sullen, beaten fighter, trapped in a corner being beaten by the better fighter. It was like the bell sounded for a new match, and he came out swinging. "You know it must be the weather, I'm forgetting things. I asked for Nichols a bit ago and I forgot—I sent him on a vacation late last night. When he returns, I'm sure he will swear he never wrote that memo nor does he have any knowledge of any cover-up."

Thompson looked at the two would-be adversaries and opened his desk drawer and removed an envelope just like the one Sam had brought with him. He saw Sam notice the envelope had the same hotel label as the one he had brought with him. More importantly Thompson saw the look of concern in Sam's face. "By the photos did you mean these?" Thompson poured the contents of the envelope out on his desk. He picked a small package containing photos and taunting Sam with it. "Oh and look, the negatives. I hope these weren't your only copies."

Thompson gave Sam a disgusted look. "And you have the nerve to think you could take me down. You're nothing."

Thompson picked up the phone again. "Send them in now." As he hung up the phone, two security guards entered the room, Thompson nodded and they approached George. "I suggest you go with these gentlemen." George looked to Sam who only nodded to George and they left, closing the door behind them.

Sam looked to Thompson, "And what about him?"

"Well, there is some loyalty, misplaced, and certainly of no matter to me, but part of the deal our Architect struck with me when he came to me yesterday and gave you and your plan up, was that Mr. Bailey was not to be fired."

"Decent of you."

"I could give a shit about him, and even less about you. You have nothing, you are nothing."

Sam said nothing, just looked back at Thompson with contempt.

"There is no system, and no tapes, no history, nothing. And in case you are thinking back up tapes..." Thompson pointed to a box that was sitting at the back of the office. "...your Architect had every backup tape from the project returned from storage early this morning and every drive replaced."

"Thorough," Sam replied matter-of-factly.

"Yes, he is." Thompson agreed. "No system, no evidence, no testimony, nothing."

"And Nichols?" Sam asked as he looked out the window to see if the guards had taken George out of the building.

"I had dirt on him before and thanks to you," he picked up a few of the photos and waved them at Sam, "now I have more."

Thompson lifted the receiver, "Send them in." Two more security guards, larger than the two that had escorted George, now stood behind Sam. "So, Mr. Cohen, or should I say Major Call, it's time for you to leave." The two guards grabbed Sam by each arm. "You're the second so called soldier I've taken down in less than twenty-four hours. It's pretty pathetic what they call soldiers these days." Thompson looked at the security guard. "Take this loser out of my office.

Sam said nothing and offered no resistance.

Chapter 18

Thursday, October 27

Casa Nuova

Noon, Alpharetta

It was a bright and sunny day. There wasn't even a hint of a breeze coming from the clear blue sky; the seventy degree weather felt eighty degrees, and it was more like a spring day than a fall day. Wanting to suck up every warm ray of the sun, Sam, Mary and David had captured the only outside table at Casa Nuova and were having drinks: ice tea and Dr. Pepper. The team needed to get together to go over the final aspects of the case so Mary suggested Casa Nuova and made the arrangements with the team and Maria.

As they sat there relaxing, the distinctive sound of a Harley suddenly filled the air. A young woman was driving a sleek, all black, 1991 FXDB Dyna Glide Harley Davidson. The bright chrome of the headlamp and the front bars gleamed in the noon sun. It was so bright they could not look directly into it. The driver, a confident looking woman, dressed in a leather jacket and looked all of the professional driver, as she calmly glided her machine to a graceful yet powerful stop. Her experienced look was in total contrast to her passenger whose only hint of belonging on such a machine was that he was hearing a helmet. The short, non-athletic looking man in his brown jacket and black pants, clung onto the back of the motorcycle with such ill ease that it would be obvious to a blind man.

The driver stopped the motorcycle, and put her foot out to steady the machine as the passenger attempted to get off. The passenger successfully put his left foot down but got the cuff of his right leg caught on the frame, as he tried to pull his leg over the seat. He tried to catch himself, but the combination of his loss of balance and his lack of conditioning of any sort made that an impossible event and Bob crashed backwards, his back bumping into the parked car beside him. With as much dignity as he could muster, he dusted himself off and joined the others at the table,

"Hello. What a great day!" Bob cheerfully greeted the others.

"Is it?" David laughed at the sight of his friend and employee in his business attire and half helmet, which he had neglected to remove.

"What? Oh you mean that." Bob turned and pointed back towards Tammy who had removed her helmet and secured it to the roll bar. "Actually, I am getting better at it. Last week I knocked the whole damn thing down twice."

Everyone laughed and Bob sat down.

"As bad as that was, my friend, I am about to make your day worse." David's demeanor took a serious turn. "I am sorry to say that today will be your last day on the job."

The group was dumbfounded, it was unexpected and certainly seemed inappropriate to tell him in front of Sam and Mary, no matter what the reason. The look on the poor man was pathetic and he seemed more shocked than anything else.

"Yes, my friend, when you get back from lunch our sponsor is going to fire you." David looked sternly at Bob and then laughed. "Good job, Bob, good job."

Realizing that his *firing* was his planned escape and their sponsor's way of remaining outside of the investigation, Bob smiled in both relief that he wasn't really being fired and gratitude in receiving David's off-handed praise, "Thanks boss."

"It was a job well done," David said to the group.

"Indeed it was," Sam added.

"The client is happy with the results and that really is the main objective, you know."

"You're right about that, David, but I wish we could have stuck Thompson and that scummy COO of his." Bob formed a fist and made a jab in the air like he hit an imaginary foe.

"We have to face the facts, all the data we got was stolen. There isn't a court in the land that would convict him and even as much as the SEC could ruin Thompson, we would have had to take down George and his friends for helping us. Don't forget what they did were felonies."

Yes, but is just doesn't seem fair." Mary was equally disappointed.

"Besides, the Architect destroyed all the data within IdentityPoint concerning AliceK." Sam stopped in mid sentence as a car drove up. All eyes watched the driver as he opened his door and he walked toward the group. Standing directly in front of Sam was the Architect. Both Sam and the Architect stared at each other. No one spoke for a full twenty seconds.

Finally, Sam broke the silence. "You were good," and he wrapped his arms around him in a bear hug.

Sam slapped him on the back and they both grinned like ball players who had won the big game. The rest of the group joined in and greeted the Architect.

George came up to his friend and shook his hand tightly. "You were so good in there, I thought you really had betrayed us."

The slight Architect shook his head slightly and innocently, "No, never. Never could I do that to you."

David came up to him and shook his hand then slapped him on the back. "Well done, soldier, well done."

The Architect, happy for the praise, but more so for the reference to 'soldier' stood straighter and more confident.

After greeting the new arrival, Bob sat back down next to Tammy, "It's great how it turned out for our client and him." Bob looked toward the Architect, "Our client got the financial data she needed and our friend here got his job back. I just wish we could have done something about Thompson and Nichols."

Sam stood there with his arm around the Architect's shoulder like a proud father who's just announced his son winning a scholarship to a great college. "Well, you know that may just be the best part."

"How's that?" Tammy and Bob both said at the same time.

"So George, what's Data Seeding?" Sam asked.

George was caught by surprise by the request for a technical answer. "Data seeding as in database operations?"

"Yes," Sam was smiling like a Cheshire cat and still hugging his 'college-bound son'.

"Basically it is when you put data into a database that didn't exist there before."

"And then what happens?" Sam asked, already knowing the answer.

Mary took a step closer to Sam and gave him an inquisitive look. "Why are you smiling like, like –Sigourney Weaver finally said yes." Everyone laughed.

"And then what happens?," Sam repeated to George.

"The data begins to link to other data and ..." George stopped in mid-sentence, "You didn't?" George stared at his friend with a look of amazement and anticipation.

With a bigger beaming smile, Sam answered for him. "Oh yes he did."

"Did what?"

"What are you talking about?"

"Okay soldier, give." David finally put an end to the guessing game.

"As George said, when you add data to a database and let's say it has a name and address, or a name and a company, or a company and a liability, the intelligent systems will start to develop links between this new person and its history and real people or companies with the same addresses and assets."

"And?" Mary asked carefully.

"When a report is requested for a person, or let's say the IRS, who is looking for, let's say for information on a man who has millions of dollars of unreported income that was transferred from a U.S. bank to a bank in the Bahamas; that report may just have a link from that man to a company, and that company to a shared asset, let's say a 1994 S65 AMG Mercedes, and that Mercedes links to an insurance policy by a certain corporate executive."

No one spoke. They all looked to the Architect in either stunned silence or confusion.

"Thompson's going down and his own corrupt public records systems are going to do it. That's *beautiful!*" David made a fist and held it up by his head and shook it in victory.

George was sitting back in his chair having listened quietly to his friends brilliant and quiet ingenious exploits. "When do you think something might happen?"

Sam quickly answered, "Soon, very soon I should think."

The Architect, who had said nothing throughout the explanation meekly spoke up, "Actually it already has."

Sam took his arm off his shoulder and backed up to get a better view, "Say again?"

The Architect looked to George. "Ron Cash sent out a message this morning."

George's eyes got wide and he half stood, "Ron Cash?"

"Yes. It went out this morning."

"Okay, who is Ron Cash?" David asked. "And when did he become involved?"

George solemnly responded, "He's dead." There was a short pause and George continued, "Ron was a close friend of ours, a programmer, he died of a heart attack—he was just fifty-two." George looked to the Architect with sadness in his eyes, then to David, and then to Sam. "We named a server after him. It's a watch service; throughout the night it looks through billions of records and compares them to a list, a watch list so to speak, of people and companies that a group has interest in. If it finds a connection it sends a text alert."

"Who does it alert?" David asked as he looked at the Architect.

He put his head down as if he was a young child that had done something wrong and was about to get in trouble with his father, then said meekly, "The IRS."

George continued. "Its the IRS's list of delinquent tax payers." He looked to the Architect with a smile and a look of a pride, "And you added a name to that list didn't you?"

"Two. Robert L. Pearson and James W. Twiggs"

For a moment, there was stunned silence; then one by one everyone came to the Architect and shook his hand.

Mary, who had been sitting through all of this, finally stood and went to the door of the restaurant and called in, "Maria. Now please."

Mary walked over to her new friend and hugged him gently, "I know when Sam called you about doing this you thought you could never go through with it. That you didn't have the nerve nor the courage to do it, but that you gave your word you would do your best. Well, if it failed, my husband would have been royally screwed, so I needed some reassurance. I called someone and you know what that person told me? She said, you can have faith in him and his word, and I have never lost *my* faith in him."

Mary gently touched his cheek and then looked back to the restaurant door and the gentle looking lady standing there.

The Architect looked to the door, "Becky, oh God, Becky." He went to her and stood motionless in front of her, then she hugged him, and they both cried quietly in each others arms.

Mary looked to Sam and the others. "Now, can I plan a party, or can't I?"

Sam sat down in his chair and reached into a bag that he had placed there earlier. He pulled out two envelopes.

"Bob, on your way back to work, I mean on your way back to get fired, could you mail these for me?" Sam held out the envelopes.

"Sure, what are they?"

"Help yourself."

Bob opened the first envelope, then the second, looked at Sam and smiled.

"What are they, Bob?" David asked.

Bob showed the group the contents of the first envelope. "It's a check to Robert Cole Junior, for $200,000 courtesy of James W. Twiggs." Bob returned the first check to the envelope, and opened the second. "And this is check to Mrs. Edwin C. Shanahan for $500,000 from Robert L. Pearson."

"I didn't realize those two were so generous," David joked.

"Well, I guess sometimes people can just fool you," Sam smiled. "You think either of them will complain?"

As Bob finished putting away the envelopes, Maria walked up to the table, "Can I get you some more drinks?" She started with Sam and worked her way around to Mary, then David then Tammy, but before Bob could order she walked away.

"Excuse me. Excuse me!" Bob called out, but she did not respond. "This is unbelievable? Is she deaf? Do I have a sign on my back that says 'Ignore me'. " He looked at David and Sam in total frustration.

"I don't know what to say there, Bob."

Mary leaned over to Sam and whispered, "I never knew Maria was hard of hearing.

"Sam leaned back to her and whispered back, "She's not."

Mary punched him in the shoulder. "You're bad."

"Yes, ma'am, and don't you love it."

Chapter 19

Friday October 28

Going Home

0730 hours

Just as Sam turned to look back, he saw Ream take the gun from the soldier's holster causing him to fall backwards from the force of the surprise attack. Ream immediately raised the gun, Sam turned to see where he was aiming. His eyes opened wide in the bright sunlight, as he saw Ream was aiming at a tall soldier standing at the gravesite. He tried to shout, to warn the man, but nothing came out of his mouth. He was frozen, unable to speak. In those next terrible few seconds Ream fired, and as Sam stood there unable to move, time seemed to slow down to super slow motion. He saw the weapon fire—the bullet leave the barrel and streak towards its victim; he tried to move but couldn't.

Sam could see the intended victim's back; a tall, athletic-looking man in military uniform standing in front of an open grave. He could also see the man was totally unaware of what was about to happen. As the bullet neared its target, a second smaller man, also in uniform, jumped into its path. Sam saw the bullet hit this man's left shoulder, the shattered bone fragments of his arm striking the shoulder of the man he was trying to protect. The force of the bullet's impact spun the second man around.

The gunman fired a second shot, and still Sam was incapable of moving, incapable of stopping the gunman from firing again. He watched as the gunman fired, this time hitting the would-be rescuer squarely in the back. The force of that second bullet pushed both victims to the ground. As the gunman tried to get off another shot, a young MP grabbed for the gun; it went off and the MP took a round in the arm. In an instant, two police officers and four MPs were all over the gunman. He was finally subdued by a dozen hands pushing him hard into the ground.

Sam stood there at the center of this surreal spectacle. He could only watch as the gunman's intended victim rose, noticed the blood coming from his shoulder and then grimace in pain. The wounded soldier stood there for a moment like a man who had been awakened from a deep sleep by a loud noise and who was now struggling to grasp what had awakened him. Without moving or speaking, Sam observed the wounded soldier and then watched the MPs as they wrestled with the gunman. Sam then looked at the second victim on the ground. He was not moving, his eyes open, blood trickling from his mouth, left shoulder soaked in blood and there was a pool of blood forming under his back.

Police, reporters, soldiers and civilians, who had been attending whatever event had been underway at the time of the shooting, were now all rushing about either in a panic to escape the shooting or a frenzy to report what had happened. Hundreds of people moved about in all sorts of manner, all except three— Sam, who was in some frozen, unmovable state, the mortally wounded soldier, lying motionless on the ground, and finally the wounded intended victim, whose face Sam had not seen.

Sam looked to the intended target, the tall soldier who now looked up, saw Sam standing there, and knew just by the expression on Sam's confused face, that Sam had done nothing to stop what had just happened. That Sam had just stood there while the gunman fired and fired again; stood there while the deadly second shot ripped though the fallen man who now lay mortally wounded on the ground in front of him.

Sam recognized the man whose eyes were staring at him so intensely that he could feel his hatred for what Sam had failed to do. Sam could tell that this man was unbelieving of Sam's actions and he felt ashamed.

The wounded soldier who had been staring at Sam then looked down at the mortally wounded man on the ground beneath him.

"Dana!" he screamed. "Medic! Medic! Someone get a medic, now!"

Sam was watching as everyone was now looking at him, but still he was powerless to move.

"Sam." The victim cried as he attempted to raise his hand to him.

"Dana!" Sam screamed. His mind raced, trying to replay the last few seconds in his mind; Ream and the gun, shots fired. In an instant, he realized what Dana had done.

He ran towards Dana who lay bleeding on the ground as the first victim was bending over him. As Sam got there he seemed to step right into the first victim, taking his place, and the man was gone leaving just himself and the second victim, Dana.

Bending over Dana, Sam pressed both hands against the wound to stop the bleeding. Someone from the crowd attempted to help. "We need a compress."

Dana reached with his right hand and Sam took it. "Stay with me buddy," he begged.

"I was wrong, Sam. Sometimes you do get to say goodbye. "

"No goodbyes, man. Help is on its way and you'll be in the hospital in ten minutes. No sweat. Good as new in a week." Sam tried to keep his voice strong, but the tears in his eyes said otherwise.

"Sam," Dana started. "I told you when this first happened that…"

"What do you mean first happened." Sam held his friend but now the scene was different. There were no MPs, no gunman, no gravesite, no one but Dana and Sam. There was no noise, no sirens, no shouting people, and no confusion as people ran in search of safety while others ran in attempts to aide. Only Sam and Dana remained.

"Sam," Dana said. "When I took that bullet that day, I did it because I wanted to; because I needed to. For the first time in my life, I did something that was glorious. You keep thinking that I died because of you. I died because Ream shot me. I got shot because I chose to. I chose to, Sam, regardless of what event brought us to that point. At that moment, I chose to do what I did. At that moment, I was the soldier on a battlefield that in my life I was never going to see. I had that one moment in time to protect my comrade, my buddy. At that moment, Sam, I was the solider I dreamed of being."

Sam could feel his anger and pain leave and he listened quietly to his friend as he spoke.

"You loved me more than any person ever did, ever could. I would be honored to have given my life for you, but you won't give me that, Sam."

"What do you mean, Dana?"

"I can't have my honor with you taking the blame for my death. You didn't take my life Sam, I gave it. Give me my honor, Sam, don't make my death your cross to bear, make it my celebration. The celebration of one soldier for another. Can you do this for me, Sam?"

Sam could feel the tears in his eyes. But the pain in his heart seemed to be gone, and he managed a smile as he spoke to Dana. "I can do that, soldier."

Dana closed his eyes for a moment, sighed, and then said, "I love you, Sam." Dana paused then said, "I could really use a hug."

Sam pulled his friend to him and held him close; then he gently let Dana fall back knowing his friend was gone.

Sam looked around and saw that the cemetery was empty, everything was gone. Dana was gone, and he was kneeling in an open field on a bright and sunny day. He lay back on the ground and looked up at the sky and saw the beautiful blue sky and small white clouds move by as the gentle wind took them on their course. He felt a peace he had not felt in a long time. He rolled over and Mary was beside him asleep, and he looked at her with the love of a man for a woman that made him warm every day of his life. She lay on her side and he moved up to her and pulled her to him, holding her next to him. He put his left arm under her and his right over her and pulled them both together and fell asleep with her as if they were one person.

------------- < > -------------

It was 0730 hours and Mary awoke from a very sound sleep. She looked over where Sam should be, but he was not there. She got up and looked into the open door of the bathroom, but it was empty, then she heard a sound downstairs. She went to the stairs and recognized the sound as someone in the kitchen and a drawer opening. She went down the steps without speaking, anticipating Sam being in the kitchen. As she made the final step, something caught her eye; it was familiar, but yet unfamiliar all the same. She looked at the mantle above the fireplace and then knew it was different from the night before. On the floor by the fireplace was a cardboard box that now lay opened. She looked up and there on the mantle was a photograph that had been missing for a long time; a photo of Sam and Dana - two young lieutenants with arms around each other's shoulders standing on a Virginia Beach.

Mary walked into the kitchen and saw Sam, as he finished pouring his coffee, and as she did, Sam saw her. She looked back at the mantle without speaking and then looked back at Sam.

"Welcome home, Sam." Mary smiled at him knowing he had made his peace.

"It's good to be home."

Epilog

Friday, October 28

1000 hours, Atlanta, CNN

"In what can only be termed as a major scandal for the FBI, a joint team of officers of the United States Marshal Service and the Police Department of Washington D.C. arrested Mr. Tom Luby at his office in the FBI building this morning on multiple charges including, fraud, murder, and conspiracy to commit murder. This follows just one day after one of Luby's subordinates, Mr. David Lee, was arrested by the Florida State Police for attempted murder. According to the press secretary of the Florida State Police, the suspect, Mr. David Lee of Alexandria, Virginia, was apprehended after they received what the police department called an anonymous, but highly reliable tip from an unnamed FBI source. Lee claimed that he was on a sanctioned FBI mission, which has been flatly denied by the FBI."

"Just moments ago a spokesman for the United States Attorney General's office made these comments." The image switched from the news reporter to the Press Secretary of the Attorney General's office. "As you know, earlier this morning, Mr. Tom Luby, a senior officer of the Federal Bureau of Investigation was arrested on multiple counts of murder and conspiracy. His arrest is in part based on the written statement of another FBI agent Christopher Garrett, who was the subordinate of Mr. Luby. Mr. Garrett provided numerous documents detailing Mr. Luby's illegal operations over the past five years. In a written statement, Mr. Garrett revealed that he was a part of these

335

illegal operations and performed them in what he called, and I quote, 'a sense of duty to country based upon what I believed were the necessary and sanctioned actions to protect our country, which I now realize was nothing more than the perverted exercise of power by Luby.' Unquote.

In his hand-written letter, Mr. Garrett believed his life was in danger from Mr. Luby; he did not expect to live out the week. His statement, along with copies of numerous documents were addressed to the United States Attorney's Office but delivered by courier to the *Washington Post*. The *Washington Post* immediately contacted this office, and after a quick review of the contents of the letter and envelope, officers of the United States Marshals Office were dispatched to the home of Mr. Garrett. The Marshals Office reported that Mr. Garrett's service revolver, wallet, and a second smaller caliber weapon were found at the scene. His personal belongings appeared not to have been disturbed and all his clothing appears to be in place. Mr. Christopher Garrett is missing and feared dead."

The camera switched to the reporter. "This is Kate McAllister reporting for CNN."

Additional information

There were some names used in this work that were the names of real people who did extraordinary things. The use of their names is done in tribute to their work and sacrifice.

The following provides additional information concerning these real life people.

LTC Robert G. Cole

Lt. Colonel Robert G. Cole was recommended for the Congressional Medal of Honor for his actions that day. It was a medal that he would not live to receive. Three months later, on September 18, 1944 a sniper killed twenty-nine year old LTC Cole during "Operation Market Garden" while taking the bridge at Best, Holland. His mother, Mrs. Clara H. Cole, received his posthumous Medal of Honor while his wife and twenty-nine-month-old son looked on. He is buried in the American Battlefields Monuments Commission Cemetery in the Netherlands.

June 1944 found LTC Cole with the 101st Airborne in England awaiting the Invasion of France. On the night of June 5th LTC Cole parachuted into France with his unit as part of the D-Day invasion force. By the evening of June 6, LTC Cole had assembled a force of 250 men. They were initially placed in regimental reserve, but were soon called back into combat. LTC Cole and his men were ordered to attack four bridges along the highway from LaCroix Pan to Carentan. Despite a gallant effort, the entire unit became pinned down by intense enemy rifle, machine-gun, mortar, and artillery fire. After an hour of the devastating fire from well-prepared and heavily fortified German positions, which had inflicted numerous casualties they were no closer to achieving their objective.

By the dawn on 11 June, with the enemy still contesting any attempt at taking the bridges LTC Cole called in heavy artillery on the enemy strongpoint. When this did not appear to dislodge the well-entrenched Germans, LTC Cole took a desperate measure to overwhelm the enemy by ordering his men to fill their weapons with ammo and to fix bayonets. At 06:15 LTC Cole blew his whistle to launch the bayonet assault. Personally leading the assault from in front of his troops LTC Cole charged on and led the remnants of his unit across the bullet-swept ground and into the enemy position. This dramatic attack succeeded at last in overrunning the German stronghold. The attack though had not been without a price. The 3rd battalion paid dearly with only132 men remaining from the original force. One company was actually reduced to only 12 men. After the battle the causeway became known as "Purple Heart Lane".

*COLE, ROBERT G. Rank and organization: Lieutenant Colonel, U.S. Army, 101st Airborne Division. Place and date: Near Carentan, France, 11 June 1944. Entered service at: San Antonio, Tex. Birth: Fort Sam Houston, Tex. G.O. No.: 79, 4 October 1944.

CITATION:

For gallantry and intrepidity at the risk of his own life, above and beyond the call of duty on 11 June 1944, in France. Lt. Col. Cole was personally leading his battalion in forcing the last 4 bridges on the road to Carentan when his entire unit was suddenly pinned to the ground by intense and withering enemy rifle, machinegun, mortar, and artillery fire placed upon them from well-prepared and heavily fortified positions within 150 yards of the foremost elements. After the devastating and unceasing enemy fire had for over 1 hour prevented any move and inflicted numerous casualties, Lt. Col. Cole, observing this almost hopeless situation, courageously issued orders to assault the enemy positions with fixed bayonets. With utter disregard for his own safety and completely ignoring the enemy fire, he rose to his feet in front of his battalion and with drawn pistol shouted to his men to follow him in the assault. Catching up a fallen man's rifle and bayonet, he charged on and led the remnants of his battalion across the bullet-swept open ground and into the enemy position. His heroic and valiant action in so inspiring his men resulted in the complete establishment of our bridgehead across the Douve River. The cool fearlessness, personal bravery, and outstanding leadership displayed by Lt. Col. Cole reflect great credit upon himself and are worthy of the highest praise in the military service.

Special Agent Edwin Shanahan was shot and killed while attempting to arrest a car thief in Chicago, Illinois. The suspect was also wanted for the attempted murder of four Chicago police officers whom he had shot during previous arrest attempts.

Agent Shanahan and other officers received information that the suspect would be taking a stolen car to a garage. The officers setup a stakeout and observed the suspect enter the garage. As Agent Shanahan, who was alone at the time, attempted to arrest the suspect he was shot by the man with an automatic pistol.

On November 2, 1925, the suspect murdered Sergeant Harry Gray, of the Chicago Police Department, as Sergeant Gray attempted to arrest him. The suspect was apprehended and sentenced to 35 years in prison for the murders plus 15 years for the auto theft. The suspect was released from prison in 1954 and died in 1981.

Agent Shanahan had served with the Federal Bureau of Investigation for five years.

I wish to acknowledge some fine people who have also served their community in a variety of ways; I salute two of the many Teachers of the Year (please see the below listed website for more of the honored teacher)

http://www.ccsso.org/projects/National_Teacher_of_the_Year/National_Teachers/

Guy Doud, Teacher of the year 1986, Brainerd Senior High School, Brainerd Minnesota

Thomas Fleming, Teacher of the Year 1992, Washtenaw Intermediate School District, Ann Arbor Michigan

Printed in the United States
113328LV00005B/1-84/P